GRAND RAPIDS PUBLIC LIBRARY (GRM)

3 1307 02367 9170

FEB 2018

GY
Yankee Clipper Branch
2025 Leonard NE
Grand Rapids, MI 49505

LOVE STORIES
FOR TURBULENT TIMES

DISCARDED

D1445837

LOVE STORIES

LOVING THROUGH THE APOCALYPSE

FOR TURBULENT TIMES

EDITED BY
GENIE D. CHIPPS & BILL HENDERSON

GRAND RAPIDS PUBLIC LIBRARY

© 2018 Pushcart Press
All rights reserved

For information address
Pushcart Press
PO Box 380
Wainscott, NY 11975

ISBN: 978-1-888889-86-4

Grateful acknowledgment is given to
the authors and presses for permission to
reprint these stories.

Distributed by W. W.Norton Co.
New York

*This book is for
Lily and Ed*

INTRODUCTION

"What do we talk about when we talk about love?"
—RAYMOND CARVER

"That love is all there is
Is all I know of love."
—EMILY DICKINSON

Once upon a time *Esquire* published a book titled *Smiling Through The Apocalypse*, stories, essays and photographs about the Nixonian era of constant war and political uproar. We have borrowed that title for our current subtitle "Loving Through The Apocalypse." We figure that loving may be more helpful than smiling.

Our selected stories and memoirs are not about solutions for the alarms of our time, but they do offer insights into the balms (and pains) of love in all its forms: young, elderly, heterosexual, homosexual, married, casual, and various combinations of all these categories.

These tales are hilarious, tragic, joyous, ridiculous, blissful, heartbreaking, and hopeful. In short, just about every nuance of love not covered in the common run-of-the-mill TV, movie, internet, magazine or book mass market romance.

Here you will discover some of the stellar story tellers of our time: Karen Russell, Rosellen Brown, Charles Baxter, Elizabeth Tallent, Charles Johnson, Jack Driscoll, Frederic Tuten, Stacey Richter and many more.

Joining the fictions are memoirs by Donald Hall and Steve Adams. Hall recalls his love for his late wife, the brilliant poet Jane Kenyon, and Adams remembers his platonic and profound affection for his gay massage therapist.

Our fictions and memoirs are culled from the past twenty-five years of the annual *Pushcart Prize: Best of the Small Presses* anthology, a selection from premier literary journals. They are, in the judgement of the editors, not only very good tales but the best of the best.

The editors can't promise infallible wisdom about the benefits and bothers of modern love. We may raise more questions than answers— if indeed there are any answers. But we do promise a collection of extraordinary talent. These are rich, rare and unforgettable evocations.

Love Stories for Turbulent Times: Loving Through The Apocalypse is both a mirror of and an antidote for the passions of our raucous and dangerous century.

Genie D. Chipps
Bill Henderson

CONTENTS

THE THIRD THING

by DONALD HALL

Jane Kenyon and I were married for twenty-three years. For two decades we inhabited the double solitude of my family farmhouse in New Hampshire, writing poems, loving the countryside. She was forty-seven when she died. If anyone had asked us, "Which year was the best, of your lives together?" we could have agreed on an answer: "the one we remember least." There were sorrowful years—the death of her father, my cancers, her depressions—and there were also years of adventure: a trip to China and Japan, two trips to India; years when my children married; years when the grandchildren were born; years of triumph as Jane began her public life in poetry: her first book, her first poem in the *New Yorker*. The best moment of our lives was one quiet repeated day of work in our house. Not everyone understood. Visitors, especially from New York, would spend a weekend with us and say as they left: "It's really pretty here" ("in Vermont," many added) "with your house, the pond, the hills, but . . . but . . . but . . . *what do you do*?"

What we did: we got up early in the morning. I brought Jane coffee in bed. She walked the dog as I started writing, then climbed the stairs to work at her own desk on her own poems. We had lunch. We lay down together. We rose and worked at secondary things. I read aloud to Jane; we played scoreless ping-pong; we read the mail; we worked again. We ate supper, talked, read books sitting across from each other in the living room, and went to sleep. If we were lucky the phone didn't ring all day. In January Jane dreamed of flowers, planning expansion and refinement of the garden. From late March into October she spent hours digging, applying fifty-year-old Holstein manure from under the barn,

1

planting, transplanting, and weeding. Sometimes I went off for two nights to read my poems, essential to the economy, and Jane wrote a poem called "Alone for a Week." Later Jane flew away for readings and I loathed being the one left behind. (I filled out coupons from magazines and ordered useless objects.) We traveled south sometimes in cold weather: to Key West in December, a February week in Barbados, to Florida during baseball's spring training, to Bermuda. Rarely we flew to England or Italy for two weeks. Three hundred and thirty days a year we inhabited this old house and the same day's adventurous routine.

What we did: love. We did not spend our days gazing into each other's eyes. We did that gazing when we made love or when one of us was in trouble, but most of the time our gazes met and entwined as they looked at a third thing. Third things are essential to marriages, objects or practices or habits or arts or institutions or games or human beings that provide a site of joint rapture or contentment. Each member of a couple is separate; the two come together in double attention. Lovemaking is not a third thing but two-in-one. John Keats can be a third thing, or the Boston Symphony Orchestra, or Dutch interiors, or Monopoly. For many couples, children are a third thing. Jane and I had no children of our own; we had our cats and dog to fuss and exclaim over— and later my five grandchildren from an earlier marriage. We had our summer afternoons at the pond, which for ten years made a third thing. After naps we loaded up books and blankets and walked across Route 4 and the old railroad to the steep slippery bank that led down to our private beach on Eagle Pond. Soft moss underfoot sent little red flowers up. Ghost birches leaned over water with wild strawberry plants growing under them. Over our heads white pines reared high, and oaks that warned us of summer's end late in August by dropping green metallic acorns. Sometimes a mink scooted among ferns. After we acquired Gus he joined the pond ecstasy, chewing on stones. Jane dozed in the sun as I sat in the shade reading and occasionally taking a note in a blank book. From time to time we swam and dried in the heat. Then, one summer, leakage from the Danbury landfill turned the pond orange. It stank. The water was not hazardous but it was ruined. A few years later the pond came back but we seldom returned to our afternoons there. Sometimes you lose a third thing.

The South Danbury Christian Church became large in our lives. We were both deacons and Jane was treasurer for a dozen years, utter miscasting and a source of annual anxiety when the treasurer's report was due. I collected the offering; Jane counted and banked it. Once a month she prepared communion and I distributed it. For the Church Fair we both cooked and I helped with the auction. Besides the Church itself, building and community, there was Christianity, the Gospels, and the work of theologians and mystics. Typically we divided our attentions: I read Meister Eckhart while Jane studied Julian of Norwich. I read the Old Testament aloud to her, and the New. If it wasn't the Bible, I was reading aloud late Henry James or Mark Twain or Edith Wharton or Wordworth's *Prelude.* Reading aloud was a daily connection. When I first pronounced *The Ambassadors*, Jane had never read it, and I peeked at her flabbergasted face as the boat bearing Chad and Mme. de Vionnet rounded the bend toward Lambert Strether. Three years later, when I had acquired a New York Edition of Henry James, she asked me to read her *The Ambassadors* again. Late James is the best prose for reading aloud. Saying one of his interminable sentences, the voice must drop pitch every time he interrupts his syntax with periphrasis, and drop again when periphrasis interrupts periphrasis, and again, and then step the pitch up, like climbing stairs in the dark, until the original tone concludes the sentence. One's larynx could write a doctoral dissertation on James's syntax.

Literature in general was a constant. Often at the end of the day Jane would speak about what she had been reading, her latest intense and obsessive absorption in an author: Keats for two years, Chekhov, Elizabeth Bishop. In reading and in everything else, we made clear boundaries, dividing our literary territories. I did not go back to Keats until she had done with him. By and large Jane read intensively while I read extensively. Like a male, I lusted to acquire all the great books of the world and add them to my life list. One day I would realize: I've never read Darwin! Adam Smith! Gibbon! Gibbon became an obsession with me, then his sources, then all ancient history, then all narrative history. For a few years I concentrated on Henry Adams, even reading six massive volumes of letters.

But there was also ping-pong. When we added a new bedroom, we extended the rootcellar enough to set a ping-pong table into it, and for years we played every afternoon. Jane was assiduous, determined, vicious, and her reach was not so wide as mine. When she couldn't reach a shot I called her "Stubbsy," and her next slam would smash me in the groin, rage combined with harmlessness. We rallied half an hour without keeping score. Another trait we shared was hating to lose. Through bouts of ping-pong and Henry James and the church, we kept to one innovation: with rare exceptions, we remained aware of each other's feelings. It took me half my life, more than half, to discover with Jane's guidance that two people could live together and remain kind. When one of us felt grumpy we both shut up until it went away. We did not give in to sarcasm. Once every three years we had a fight—the way some couples fight three times a day—and because fights were few the aftermath of a fight was a dreadful gloom. "We have done harm," said Jane in a poem after a quarrel. What was *that* fight about? I wonder if she remembered, a month after writing the poem.

Of course: the third thing that brought us together, and shone at the center of our lives and our house, was poetry—both our love for the art and the passion and frustration of trying to write it. When we moved to the farm, away from teaching and Jane's family, we threw ourselves into the life of writing poetry as if we jumped from a bridge and swam to survive. I kept the earliest hours of the day for poetry. Jane worked on poems virtually every day; there were dry spells. In the first years of our marriage, I sometimes feared that she would find the project of poetry intimidating, and withdraw or give up or diminish the intensity of her commitment. I remember talking with her one morning early in New Hampshire, maybe in 1976, when the burden felt too heavy. She talked of her singing with the Michigan Chorale, as if music were something she might turn to. She spoke of drawing as another art she could perform, and showed me an old pencil rendering she had made, acorns I think, meticulous and well-made and nothing more. She was saying, "I don't *have* to give myself to poetry"—and I knew enough not to argue.

However, from year to year she gave more of herself to her art. When she studied Keats, she read all his poems, all his letters, the best three or four biographies; then she read and reread the poems and the letters again. No one will find in her poems clear fingerprints of John Keats, but Jane's ear became more luscious with her love for Keats; her lines became more dense, rifts loaded with ore. Coming from a family for whom ambition was dangerous, in which work was best taken lightly, it was not easy for Jane to wager her life on one number. She lived with someone who had made that choice, but also with someone nineteen years older who wrote all day and published frequently. Her first book of poems came out as I published my fifth. I could have been an inhibitor as easily as I was an encourager—if she had not been brave and stubborn. I watched in gratified pleasure as her poems became better and better. From being promising she became accomplished and professional; then—with the later poems of *The Boat of Quiet Hours,* with

4

"Twilight: After Haying," with "Briefly It Enters," with "Things," she turned into the extraordinary and permanent poet of *Otherwise*.

People asked us—people still ask me—about competition between us. We never spoke of it, but it had to be there—and it remained benign. When Jane wrote a poem that dazzled me, I wanted to write a poem that would dazzle her. Boundaries helped. We belonged to different generations. Through Jane I got to be friends with poets of her generation, as she did with my friends born in the 1920s. We avoided situations which would subject us to comparison. During the first years of our marriage, when Jane was just beginning to publish, we were asked several times to read our poems together. The people who asked us knew and respected Jane's poems, but the occasions turned ghastly. Once we were introduced by someone we had just met who was happy to welcome Joan Kenyon. Always someone, generally a male English professor, managed to let us know that it was *sweet*, that Jane wrote poems too. One head of a department asked her if she felt *dwarfed*. When Jane was condescended to she was furious, and it was only on these occasions that we felt anything unpleasant between us. Jane decided that we would no longer read together.

When places later asked us both to read, we agreed to come but stipulated that we read separately, maybe a day apart. As she published more widely we were more frequently approached. Late in the 1980s, after reading on different days at one university, we did a joint question-and-answer session with writing students. Three quarters of the questions addressed Jane, not me, and afterwards she said, "Perkins, I think we can read together now." So, in our last years together, we did many joint readings. When two poets read on the same program, the first reader is the warm-up band, the second the featured act. We read in fifteen-minute segments, ABAB, and switched A and B positions with each reading. In 1993 we read on a Friday in Trivandrum, at the southern tip of India, and three days later in Hanover, New Hampshire. Exhausted as we were, we remembered who had gone first thousands of miles away.

There were days when each of us received word from the same magazine; the same editor had taken a poem by one of us just as he/she rejected the other of us. One of us felt constrained in pleasure. The need for boundaries even extended to style. As Jane's work got better and better—and readers noticed—my language and structure departed from its old habits and veered away from the kind of lyric that Jane was writing, toward irony and an apothegmatic style. My diction became more Latinate and polysyllabic, as well as syntactically complex. I was reading Gibbon, learning to use a vocabulary and sentence structure as engines of discrimination. Unconsciously, I was choosing to be as unlike Jane as I could. Still, her poetry influenced and enhanced my own. Her stubborn and unflagging commitment turned its power upon me and exhorted me. My poems got better in this house. When my *Old and New Poems* came out in 1990, the positive reviews included something like this sentence: "Hall began publishing early . . . but it was not until he left his teaching job and returned to the family farm in New Hampshire with his second wife the poet Jane Kenyon that . . ." I published *Kicking the Leaves* in 1978 when Jane published *From Room to Room*. It was eight years before we published our next books: her *The Boat of Quiet Hours*, my *The Happy Man*. (When I told Jane my title her reaction was true Jane: "Sounds too depressed.") I had also been working on drafts of *The One Day*, maybe my best book. Then Jane wrote *Let Evening Come, Constance*, and the twenty late poems that begin *Otherwise*. Two years after her death, a review of Jane began with a sentence I had been expecting. It was uttered in respect, without a sneer, and said that for years we had known of Jane Kenyon as Donald Hall's wife but from now on we will know of Donald Hall as Jane Kenyon's husband.

We did not show each other early drafts. (It's a bad habit. The comments of another become attached to the words of a poem, steering it or preventing it from following its own way.) But when we had worked over a poem in solitude for a long time, our first reader was the other. I felt anxious about showing Jane new poems, and often invented reasons for delay. Usually, each of us saved up three or four poems before showing them to the other. One day I would say, "I left some stuff on your footstool," or Jane would tell me, "Perkins, there are some things on your desk." Waiting for a response, each of us already knew some of what the other would say. If ever I repeated a word—a habit acquired from Yeats—I knew that Jane would cross it out. Whenever she used verbal auxiliaries she knew I would simplify, and "it was raining" would become "it rained." By and large we ignored the predicted advice, which we had already heard in our heads and dismissed. Jane kept her work clear of dead metaphor, knowing my crankiness on the subject, and she would exult when she found one in my drafts: "Perkins! Here's a dead metaphor!" These encounters were important but not easy. Sometimes we turned polite with each other: "Oh, really! I thought that was the best part . . ." (False laugh.) Jane told others—people questioned us about how we worked together—that I approached her holding a sheaf of her new poems saying, "These are going to be *good!*" to which she would say, "Going to be, eh?" She told people that she would climb back to her study, carrying the poems covered with my illegible comments, thinking, "Perkins just doesn't get it. And then," she would continue, "I'd do everything he said."

Neither of us did everything the other said. Reading *Otherwise* I find words I wanted her to change, and sometimes I still think I was right. But we helped each other greatly. She saved me a thousand gaffes, cut my wordiness and straightened out my syntax. She seldom told me that anything was *good*. "This is almost done," she'd say, "but you've got to do this in two lines not three." Or, "You've brought this a long way, Perkins"—without telling me if I had brought it to a good place. Sometimes her praise expressed its own limits. "You've taken this as far as the intellect can take it." When she said, "It's finished. Don't change a word," I would ask, "But is it any *good*? Do you *like* it?" I pined for her praise, and seldom got it. I remember one evening in 1992 when we sat in the living room and she read through the manuscript of *The Museum of Clear Ideas*. Earlier she had seen only a few poems at a time, and she had not been enthusiastic. I watched her dark face as she turned the pages. Finally she looked over at me and tears started from her eyes. "Perkins, I don't *like* it!" Tears came to my eyes too, and I said, rapidly, "That's okay. That's okay." (That book was anti-Jane in its manner, or most of it was, dependent on syntax and irony, a little like Augustan poetry, more than on images.) When we looked over each other's work, it was essential that we never lie to each other. Even when Jane was depressed, I never praised a poem unless I meant it; I never withheld blame. If either of us had felt that the other was pulling punches, it would have ruined what was so essential to our house.

We were each other's readers but we could not be each other's only readers. I mostly consulted friends and editors by mail, so many helpers that I will not try to list them, poets from my generation and poets Jane's age and even younger. Jane worked regularly, the last dozen years of her life, with the poet Joyce Peseroff and the novelist Alice Mattison. The three of them worked wonderfully together, each supplying things that the other lacked. They fought, they laughed, they rewrote and cut and rearranged. Jane would return from a workshop exhausted yet unable to keep away from her desk, working with wild excitement to follow suggestions. The three women were not only being literary critics for each other. Each had grown up knowing that it was not permitted for females to be as aggressive as males, and all were ambitious in their art, and encouraged each other in their ambition. I felt close to Alice and Joyce, my friends as well as Jane's, but I did not stick my nose into their deliberations. If I had tried to, I would have lost a nose. Even when they met at our house, I was careful to stay apart. They met often at Joyce's in Massachusetts, because it was half way between Jane and Alice. They met in New Haven at Alice's. When I was recovering from an operation, and Jane and I didn't want to be separated, there were workshops at the Lord Jeffrey Inn in Amherst. We four ate together and made pilgrimages to Emily Dickinson's house and grave, but while they worked together I wrote alone in an adjacent room. This three-part friendship was essential to Jane's poetry.

Meantime we lived in the house of poetry, which was also the house of love and grief; the house of solitude and art; the house of Jane's depression and my cancers and Jane's leukemia. When someone died whom we loved, we went back to the poets of grief and outrage, as far back as *Gilgamesh;* often I read aloud Henry King's "The Exequy," written in the seventeenth century after the death of his young wife. Poetry gives the griever not release from grief but companionship in grief. Poetry embodies the complexities of feeling at their most intense and entangled, and therefore offers (over centuries, or over no time at all) the company of tears. As I sat beside Jane in her pain and weakness I wrote about pain and weakness. Once in a hospital I noticed that the leaves were turning. I realized that I had not noticed that they had come to the trees. It was a year without seasons, a year without punctuation. I began to write "Without" to embody the sensations of lives under dreary, monotonous assault. After I had drafted it many times I read it aloud to Jane. "That's it, Perkins," she said. "You've got it. That's it." Even in this poem written at her mortal bedside there was companionship.

TELREF

fiction by EDWARD McPHERSON

Sam and Kat, Kat and Sam, as unassuming as their three-letter names but, to their minds, violent with potential. In the spring of 1998, they met in St. Louis, when they both had to board a bigger bus. Two kids in zipped pullovers smoking and picking at their fingers as they watched the driver fling their bags into the belly of the coach as if they weren't their only belongings in the world. Sam stretched his legs across two seats; when Kat came down the aisle, he dropped his feet and said, "Been saving a seat." Both were eastbound, heading away from some-where they didn't talk about. Tulsa and Topeka—what was there to say? They weren't New York City. As the now dank and belchy bus crawled out of the Lincoln Tunnel and wound the ramp into Port Authority, after twenty-three hours and fifty-five minutes of ragged conversation, Kat finally got up the nerve to say, "You know, I'm a good kid from a bad home. I've got no place to crash." Sam handed her his last piece of gum and said, "Me neither." He cocked his head at a sign that read, "To all points," with an arrow pointing up. "Welcome to Xanadu," he said.

Both had a few years of college and a little cash in their bags. They knew no one (no friends, no relatives, no couches to surf), but they found a hostel in Hell's Kitchen, then a place in Bed-Stuy, where—despite two broken windows and a split lip for Sam the first week—they'd somehow stuck it out for three years. They soon discovered other people, but theirs was first love, and Kat had always been told, "Dance with the guy who brought you."

She could scrub up and immediately found work waitressing at a hip hotel where her tattoos were appreciated. The city would always have

9

room for another pretty face. She was most at home singing bar karaoke with her friends. Sam never went with her; he knew old songs were dangerous, yanking heartstrings that no longer served any purpose. For as long as he could remember, he had been moody, reserved, but deep down he just wanted things solved, boxed in, put away, dealt with—he had little patience for problems or issues that lingered.

At first Kat's outbursts startled him, like sudden summer lightning. Things would be fine, and then one day she'd be beating his chest: "You can't stay out all night without calling!" She would twist her head back at an impossible angle, as if she meant to break it. "Three years—what are we doing?" Sam's heart would race, and he'd glance around the kitchen like he'd been caught by a pop quiz. His only thought would be to get her to stop crying. He'd say, "We're happy, baby. You and me. That's all we need." One night she grew quiet and said, "I feel like an empty trash-can," and he'd tried to gather her in his arms, but she slipped away. "You're broken," she said through the closed bedroom door. "You were born a gene short, and that makes your heart two fucking degrees colder than most." Outside the kitchen window, something small and airy threw its body against the glass.

Still, he carefully cataloged the little barbs that pricked him from waking until night, the missed trains, jammed umbrellas, and hidden potholes in the street, the minor setbacks that gathered like nettles to give his unhappiness weight. He read voraciously and complained about everything. Did she know Helen Keller wore brilliant blue pros-thetic eyes after becoming a celebrity—actually had her true ones plucked out, because one was disfigured? Or had Kat seen the recent report on the Gowanus Canal, which now contained trace amounts of gonorrhea? He knew his fits were stupid and small, but still it bothered him that Kat left dishes in the sink and lost change in the bed. He was constantly surprised by how she could wound him in places he thought were shut off, inaccessible to the public, like those graffiti tags deep in the subway tunnels that always brought him up short—what ghosts left them?

In a bit of dumb luck, Sam had found the perfect job their first month in town. He'd gone down to the vintage clothing store that stuck out on their block like a fruit stand on Mars with the idea he might be able to get a few bucks for his grandfather's old buckle. The guy behind the counter had raised one pierced brow and said, "Hot dog—cowboy chic!" before paying him eighty dollars. That was Duke, and he became their first friend. Duke had a boyfriend named Mehdi whom Sam came to like, though Duke was constantly annoyed that Mehdi wouldn't sleep over more often, and—when he did—Duke said he behaved like a tourist whose luggage had gone missing, borrowing Duke's toothbrush and oversized shirts as if to prove he was game and didn't sweat the small stuff.

Duke lived in a studio off McCarren Park that his father had bought him after he graduated from NYU, one of those hastily converted warehouses filling up with slumming trustafarians like him. Duke chose to open his store in Bed-Stuy because he thought Williamsburg soon would be on the way out. Still, he had connections he could call on when he wanted, like the friend who headed the "Young Lions," the junior philanthropic group that supported the public library. They were, he told Sam, "just a bunch of obnoxious twenty-something socialite dick-farts-in-training," for whom the library threw elaborate costume balls (Hemingway's Cuba! Dante's Disco *Inferno*!), letting them fool around drunkenly behind the stacks in the hopes of one day getting big money. This friend—whom Sam thankfully never met—landed him the job at Telref.

The phone rang, and Sam picked it up. A voice said, "Memorandum, May Day 2001: for nearly seven months, I have been the victim of covert surveillance."

Sam said, "That's not a question," and hung up.

From the next desk, Martin, a large gray-haired man, said, "Another nut job?"

"That's all I get," said Sam. "These days, my line's nothing but a shit storm of crazy."

Martin gave him a funny look. He said, "Hey, doc, it's Friday. You coming to happy hour? Been a while since we've seen your face." Martin was a West African immigrant who had moved to Manhattan and gotten a library science degree before spending two decades working his way up to become head of Telref. He had memorized most of *Paradise Lost* and skated in the roller dance party that roved through Central Park on the weekends. Wandering the Mall one Saturday, Sam had spotted Martin in a spandex singlet grooving in ecstatic slow motion with a glass of water perched on his head. Sam didn't say hi.

Across the room, a girl lowered her phone and covered the receiver. "Hey, guys—what's the rat population in Manhattan?"

Martin and Sam answered in unison: "A shitload."

11

The girl said into the phone, "A shitload. No, ma'am, that's not a technical term. It's an estimate. What I'm telling you is that no one really knows."

Sam hated that question, one he got all the time. Vermin were political—like crime or bed bugs—and reports tended to ebb and flow with election cycles. Megan would learn that. She was new to Telref, having recently moved from Boston, that city with training wheels, where she'd left behind a longtime boyfriend she said used to make hateful offhand comments and then leave her to stew. She was still getting over the guy. Later that year, she would wake up one night and drive to Boston—and him—leaving Sam and Martin to joke about "disaster sex," "catastrophe couples," and "apocalyptic bootie calls." Still, she never came back.

Megan hung up the phone. "Thanks, boys," she said and blew them an air kiss. That morning, like most mornings, Megan had asked Sam, "Honey, do you need to talk?" Meanwhile Martin had taken one look and said, "Get off the cross, doc. We need the wood." Martin was a true believer.

At first they had teased Megan, the newcomer, telling her they had in their possession a secret set of encyclopedias compiled long ago just for them, an alternate history of the world that the upstairs librarians knew nothing about. She would have to prove herself worthy to see it. Sam had read Borges. Of course. He worked in a library; they all had read Borges. Megan caught on when she realized all Sam and Martin did away from their desks was play honeymoon bridge or flick around tiny paper footballs.

The Telephone Reference Service was established by the New York Public Library in 1968, back when a dedicated call center seemed cutting edge and most of the inquiries came from secretaries trying to sound out a word their boss had used in dictation. Through the years, the number remained the last-ditch resource for fact-checkers, journalists, recluses, writers, perverts, and lunatics, their own personal oracle available five days a week, nine hours a day, just dial ASK-NYPL. Lately, of course, the department had been shrinking; you no longer had to be a trained librarian, just a warm body with time on your hands and modest powers of research. The real librarians looked down on them as glorified receptionists. Still, even with the Internet, Sam fielded about a hundred calls a day. Most were lame: Who killed Kennedy? Where is Jimmy Hoffa? What's my wife's birthday? And so there had to be rules: no medical advice, crossword clues, interpretation of dreams, or helping with homework. Recently, management had instituted a "no philosophical speculation" rule, but that one was largely ignored. His first day, Sam had heard Martin laugh and say, "God's grace? Sure it exists. It's what allows me to handle people like you."

Sitting in their cramped office off the main floor, the operators had five minutes to dedicate to each question, which was meant to rein in the researchers more than the callers. Sam would have been happy to lose an afternoon tracking down a rare Bolivian mushroom, or the number of manholes in Cleveland, or where Lady Di had bought her bras. The callers wanted answers, pure and simple; Sam's job was to cut through the dross. If he couldn't settle the request, he had to pass on the name of someone who could. Five minutes and on to the next. Question, answer, question, answer—the hours passed quickly.

Every morning Sam walked up Fifth Avenue to mount the sweeping steps of the main branch, flanked by the twin marble lions, Patience and Fortitude, which he first recognized from *Ghostbusters*. He worked in a mausoleum, the collected bones of Astor, of Lenox, of Carnegie. It fit his sense of living late in his time in a city where everything eventually was plowed under to make room for everything else. In a degenerate culture, nothing could be done to fuck things up further. They were all pretty much off the hook.

Still, Sam appreciated, even felt somewhat entitled to, the library's grandeur: the illuminated ceiling in the gilded reading room (fifty-two feet up and the size of a football field—a question they got all the time), the burnished pneumatic tubes swishing call slips through the eight floors of dark, dusty stacks stretching below Bryant Park, and the men's room urinals so grand—massive marble blocks big as beds—that it was like pissing on a Cadillac.

And—against all odds—he truly loved his job. At the end of the day, he would bring facts to Kat like a rat collecting shiny spoons for the nest. Did she know that—in proportion to its body—the hummingbird had the largest brain in the animal kingdom? That the city's power lines could circle the globe four times? She would shoot back ones he thought she made up: "Or that fifty-seven percent of men change their sheets before the first date?"

Their weekends were quiet and lazy—they found thrills on the cheap—but after reading an article on human photosynthesis, Kat began insisting they leave the apartment more often. She cited stale air, poor vitamin D, and a case of the "winter blues." And so it was on a first

Saturday in June that Sam found himself at the counter of a neighborhood diner. The place was packed. They squeezed into their seats and ordered the breakfast special. They sat in silence until the food came. Sam closed his eyes and kneaded his temples; his head was splitting. Then he looked up. "You loved him," he hissed out of the blue. It was a longstanding game: whispering lines from old film noirs just loud enough for other patrons to hear.

"No, I hated him," Kat said. The words sent a crackling of urgency across plastic plates of cold eggs.

"You loved him, you hated him—and now we're stuck good." Sam took a sip of coffee. "What's done is done, baby, and it's got to be straight down the line."

"You don't trust me?" Kat waved the waiter away.

Sam buttered his last triangle of toast. "You've never had your face on straight—not one day in your life."

Kat put down her fork. "You're one to talk, mister. You waltzed home pretty late last night."

Sam looked up. She was off script. He said, "What's it to you?"

"I'll kill her," Kat said. "Clean and simple—a morgue job. If they even find the body."

"Don't talk crazy," he said and reached for the check.

"I love you, too, dummy. We're on this trolley together, remember. Next stop: the grave."

Sam plunked down a tip, and they made a wordless exit.

When they first moved into their building, the downstairs door was broken, but the inner one seemed like it would hold firm for a while. There was a rumor that two winters ago some junkie had OD'd in the vestibule. Sam and Kat weren't sure what to believe, though it was clear that someone was peeing in the recycling. Up four flights of chipped tile steps that sloped dangerously down—"drunk-proof stairs," they called them—was a brown door with a shattered peephole that led to their tiny apartment, with its noisy radiator they had no control over and a bathroom so narrow they had to brush their teeth standing in the tub. Upstairs, a fearless six-four giant—who surprisingly worked underground as a sandhog—bent the floor nightly as he earned his dishes from his TV tray to the sink. They didn't have a TV, but on summer weekends they listened to the boy across the alley announce pro-wrestling matches in his room. Down the block was a playground with a few old pieces of equipment with a vague nautical theme and a faded mural dedicating the park "to fish and children and all things that need water."

They knew the city broke people like them every day. Almost immediately Sam had his Discman jacked, and one evening, while closing up the shop, Duke was attacked by kids he had watched only years before swing on the playground, kids who called him a faggot while beating him with a board with nails driven through it. They didn't even bother to rob him. When Sam came by the hospital a few days later, the bruises ran thick and ropey beneath Duke's skin, making his face look like a watermelon. The neighborhood was appalled, the kids went to juvie, and Duke started walking the long way to work.

The first fall they arrived, they told and retold the story of the young cousin of Kat's coworker, Maureen, until it finally came back to them slightly disfigured but essentially still true months later at a bar. The girl, whose name they never remembered, was new in town and nervous to be making her first trip alone on the subway. But job interviews were hard to come by, and Maureen told her not to be silly—nothing ever happened at rush hour. And so the girl printed her resume, put on brave lipstick and heels, and boarded the train into Manhattan. All was fine until the doors opened on her stop, and she found the platform blocked by a bum's upended bare ass, which was gloriously growing an enormous shit tail. The next day the girl went back to wherever she came from.

Another weekend and Sam and Kat were sitting in a bar that had archery. The room was below street level and black with smoke; the booths smelled sweet, either from whiskey or piss. Sam and Kat's conversation was punctuated by the rhythmic *thwack* of arrows burrowing into something.

"A little dark for target practice," Kat said. "How can you hit what you can't see?"

Sam said, "It's the other way around—what you hit is what you get."

Kat put down her drink. "I'm nervous to get up and go to the bathroom. I can see the headline: 'Talented, Unwed Girl Taken Out in the Crossfire.'"

Sam laughed. "Oldest story there is."

Kat said, "You know I won't always be sitting here."

Sam said, "I know—you're going to the bathroom." He turned to the door. A low, ugly man walked in carrying a crossbow. Sam said, "There goes the neighborhood."

Kat said, "You just don't get it, do you? I'm not asking for much, just a little encouragement. It's like I'm the first woman to land on the moon—only to find a sign saying, 'Go back where you came from.'"

Sam transferred at Jay Street from the A train to the F. He was late to work, but by now the others were used to covering for him. Last week, Martin had looked up and said, "Love is like a shark. It must move forward or it dies."

Sam asked, "West Africa?"

"No. Woody Allen."

This morning, Sam had forgotten his book, so he stared at the MTA signs with their black-and-white typeface. (Helvetica, he thought, formerly Standard Medium—same as on the space shuttle.) The train's AC wasn't working; sweat ran down his neck. Next to him sat a wan couple whose kids were climbing over the seats and pressing their tongues to the glass. Unprovoked, one of them let out a bloodcurdling scream. The passengers jumped in unison; Sam smiled, lest anyone think he was judging.

Two pixieish girls got on at York.

"Oh my God, Suzy! What's new?"

"Well, I'm engaged."

"You're shitting me! That was quick. Gimme the story!"

"He's a young thirty-eight and runs a hedge fund in Connecticut. On our first date he took me to Bouley. I drank so much I ended up puking. He must have liked that because he called the next day."

"Wow."

"Yeah. We're getting married at the Botanical Garden in August."

At West Fourth, the car filled with more commuters and transfers. Sam gave up his seat to a woman who was either pregnant or fat. A man got on wearing a string of keys around his neck and a bright button on his jacket that read, "Happy Anniversary! Thirteen Years of Attitude Adjustment." The man didn't move to the middle but stood blocking the door. At the last minute, a woman jumped on and gave him a pretty good bump. They got into it. Thirteen years down the drain.

The conductor opened his cabin door to see what was up, but before he could read the situation, the train came screeching to a halt. Anyone not holding onto a pole ended up in someone's lap. The air smelled like metallic brake dust. A voice erupted from the squawk box, "Twelve nine! Twelve nine!" and the conductor, a pale, rangy guy with a slight lisp, said, "Aww, fuck-fuck-shit."

Sam asked, "What's going on?"

The conductor said, "Twelve nine. Body under train."

The pixies gasped. Mr. Attitude Adjustment looked confused, as if he'd been upstaged.

"A jumper," the conductor said. "Folks, we won't be going anywhere for a while."

A man in a tan suit said to no one, "I've lived in this city forty-one years and of all the goddamn days."

The conductor wiped his nose on his sleeve and said, "I see this four to five times a week. You just don't hear about it because we got a PR department. Don't want to give people ideas. Jumping's messy—but efficient."

Ten minutes later, the passengers filed through the front car, which was halfway into the station. People on the platform were quietly retelling what happened, either to each other or to the cops and paramedics standing idly by. Flashlights crisscrossed beneath the wheels of the train. Sam heard a little girl say, "She flung out her arms like she was doing jumping jacks."

"Explain it to me again," Kat said. It was past noon, and they were still goofing around in bed.

He looked at her and the lock of dark hair that fell over her face. He had always loved her brown eyes. He said, "There are facts, and then there are *facts*, and then there are FACTS."

"Like what?" She brushed her hair back.

"Okay. First level: unimportant facts. You might say 'trivia.'"

Kat said, "Oh, I would never."

Sam smiled. "Well, they're lightweights. Cool, but so what? So butterflies can see yellow, red, and green; so the ballpoint pen first sold for $12 in 1945; so cows can go up stairs but not down; so the most popular name for a boat is *Obsession*; so you can't kill a mouse in Cleveland without a hunting license; so the first toilet shown on TV appeared in *Leave It to Beaver*."

Kat said, "Got it, got it. Continue, professor."

Sam said, "Second level. A little weightier. The stuff of science teachers,

17

lifeguards, and all solid citizens. Might even save your life one day. When taken intravenously, nutmeg is a poison. To kill germs, you should wash your hands as long as it takes to sing 'Happy Birthday.' You can't pump your own gas in New Jersey. The termites of the world outweigh humans ten to one."

Kat said, "Hmm, most useful. Termites of the world, unite!" She made a halfhearted poke at his crotch. "Beware the uprising!"

Sam stifled a laugh. "Third level. Those that might create what they call a sense of moral obligation. In other words, the ones that go bump in the night. The exact names and numbers of the dead. The location of sailors lost at sea. The percentage of children killed by indifference or foul play in any given year. The knowledge that parents don't treasure their children in equal measure, and that even when true, 'I love you' is rarely enough."

Kat groaned. "Oh, brother. That last one came from a commercial."

Sam shook his head. "Billboard. In SoHo."

Kat propped herself up on an elbow. "What I want to know is if you laid all those facts end to end, would they be enough to reach all the way from me to you?"

In the summer, Kat caught the eye of some big shot at the bar, and he offered her a job at Windows on the World. It wasn't like that, she told Sam. More money. Better hours. Breakfast and lunch service with a chance at dinner if everything worked out. "Come on, baby," she said. "I'm headed right to the top!"

On a clear day she could make more than in a month at her old gig. When she first saw the view, she thought she could trace the curve of the globe. She had never before wanted to come to work on the Fourth of July. Cloudy days meant cancellations, but she didn't mind it when things slowed down, and she got to hang around in the back with the rest of the waitstaff, who came from thirty different countries and were already taking bets on next year's World Cup. It was a running joke after the tips were distributed to slap each other high five and say, "God bless America." One day Kat had her picture taken with Hillary Clinton. Her ears popped as she soared 107 floors to the tip of the tower. She told Sam the ride lasted a full sixty seconds. How many restaurants had a gift shop *and* a million dollars in wine?

The captain, Jesús, was supporting a wife and baby girl back in Ecuador. Because Kat reminded him of his little sister, he let her bring home leftover racks of lamb from lunch, which she would stick in the fridge until Sam walked in for dinner. One day, one of the Wall Street execs left one of the girls his number and two tickets to *The Producers*, which she scalped for more than $500 apiece and took anyone who wanted out for all-night drinks in Tribeca. Sam hadn't answered his phone, so Kat hit the town right from work in her smart tailored jacket and shiny brass pin.

At Telref, Megan told Sam, "You know, maybe the greatest compliment we can pay something or someone is to be devastated by them."

Martin looked up from his call and rolled his eyes. Sam ignored them both. The night before the three of them had gone to a poetry reading given by one of Megan's roommates in a bar where everything—ceiling to floor—was painted red after an Eggleston photograph. The reading was for a collection of breakup verse called *Fuck Cupid*. Kat had been working an extra shift and wouldn't be home until late.

It was Sam's first reading, and he'd been appalled by the audience, the way everyone made little grunts of assent from time to time to show that they were on the same special wavelength as the reader. The end brought applause and a vigorous nodding of heads. Sam gave a loud hoot.

Megan leaned over and said, "Behave yourself, mister."

Sam said, "Why? Can anyone tell me what she was talking about up there?"

Megan reached for his hand. "I think her point was that two can be miserable better than one."

Hours after the reading, drunk in a dive bar, Sam watched some fatty with a shaved head and tattooed eyelids wave his fist at the tap. "Gimme another lager," the big guy demanded.

Sam crisply informed him, "That's not a lager—that's an ale."

The skinhead barreled up to him. "Time to go home, mopey motherfucker." Then everything went black. Sam woke up on Megan's couch, rolled over, and threw up in the trashcan. He left Kat a voicemail: "Don't worry. I passed out at Martin's."

On the last day of July, Sam got off work early. The city was laying new fiber-optic cables and had severed some crucial connection to the library. When the lines all went dead, Martin said, "That's our cue," and they snuck out the back, imagining the riot going on upstairs at the public computers.

Sam got off at Utica and was walking up Malcolm X Boulevard when a boy no more than twelve or thirteen peddled by on a bike. The boy cast his eyes back and forth across the street as if he were playing a game of hide-and-seek he was determined not to lose. Sam looked at the boy's bright orange backpack and thought, Shouldn't you be in summer school? But he said nothing, which afterward would seem fortunate to him. A block later he heard a loud popping sound and thought, Firecrackers, even here the kids light firecrackers. But they weren't firecrackers, he realized, when he saw the boy in the bright orange backpack tucked behind the rim of a beat up DeVille taking potshots with a small snubbed handgun at a group of his peers across the street.

The kids sprinted up the avenue, ducking behind a van before returning fire. Afternoon crowds burst apart like startled birds. Sam hit the pavement, putting a parked cab between him and the action. He stretched flat on the ground, his mind strangely blank. The hot concrete close up. The cracks, he thought, who fills those in?

Meanwhile, tiny guerillas had appeared out of nowhere, and now two distinct gangs were scurrying behind cars, winding their way up the wide avenue. In the distance, a siren careened toward them. Sam raised his head and locked eyes with the kid in the backpack, who had not moved from his original position just two cars down from Sam. He had a slight bruise above one eye, and his little-boy lips were set in a thin grim line. Sam had only two thoughts: What I am seeing is not real. And, These kids have seen too many cop shows.

Miraculously, no one was hurt. When the police sped up, lights blaring, the boys scattered down alleys and side streets on their way, Sam imagined, to hide in the park. He got up, brushed off his chest, and calmly walked home. When he was halfway down his block, his legs started to shake.

The city was tearing itself to pieces.

When Kat got home, the apartment was already dark. She crawled into bed.

"Rough day?" she asked.

Sam held her, saying nothing, by the light of the streetlamp.

In mid-August, Kat turned twenty-four, and Sam surprised her with a party just for two. He told her to meet him after work at Martin's apartment. It was the kind of neighborhood where parents sent birthday presents by bike messenger. Kat arrived after her afternoon shift, and Sam led her to the roof. He had made dinner, a simple cold couscous that Martin had coached him on, even going as far as to cover Sam's calls while he went shopping. After inspecting the ingredients, Martin had given him the spare key and said, "Now get going, doc, and make that pretty lady proud. I won't be back before midnight."

Sam had set the teak table and lit some citronella. Money was tight, but at Kat's place sat a pair of packages wrapped in green paper. After dinner, she opened them to find two matching black hoods.

"What are we, ninjas?" she asked.

At the edge of the roof stood a six-pack and a bucket of water balloons. They spent the rest of the hot night launching them at unsuspecting passersby. Drop, watch the bomb fall, then step back into the shadows. If they were lucky, and if they felt the person deserved it, they could get the same victim twice by sneaking over to the next roof and dropping another balloon. Only one person ever saw them, and he shouted bloody murder.

As they clutched each other—sweaty, sudsy, and doubled over with laughter—Sam said, "Forget him. Did you know the average person will make and lose 363 friends in a lifetime?"

Kat smiled and said, "Or that in Iowa it's illegal to make love to a stranger?"

Sam stuck out his hand. "Hi. I'm Sam."

"Tell me something I don't know," Kat said and pulled him down to the still-warm tar of the roof.

The phone rang at Telref. Martin answered, waited for a reply, then put down the receiver. He shrugged. "Wrong number, I guess."

Megan picked up her phone. After a moment, she hung up. She turned to Martin. "Is something going on with the lines? This has happened twice to me this morning."

Martin smiled. "What—you got a heavy breather? Pass them to me. I *love* a heavy breather."

Megan said, "Nope, it's silence and then 'click.'"

Martin tilted back in his chair. "I guess no one's willing to speak up these days."

Sam's phone rang. All eyes turned to him. He picked up. "This is Telref."

A familiar voice said, "I'm looking for answers."

Sam stared down at the pencil on his desk. He tried not to look surprised, but the back of his neck was hot. He felt dumb for not seeing this coming. Their old game—as with all things, she was just taking it to the next, obvious level.

After a minute, he said, "That's what I'm here for. I'm the answer guy."

The voice said, "I've been trying to get through for some time."

Sam said, "Well, our operators are busy. We're in pretty high demand." There was a pause. Then he said, "Please, Miss, what is your question? You only have five minutes—then I have to hang up." He could almost picture her huddled in a whitewashed bathroom stall or ducking down in some dark-paneled phone booth while well-heeled patrons padded by. Did places like that still have phone booths? He didn't know.

She said, "What I want is some information on the progress of love."

"Oh," he said. "You mean the paintings? By Jean-Honoré Fragonard? I think they're hanging in the Frick. I believe the cycle goes: *The Pursuit, The Meeting, Love Letters, Reverie, The Lover Crowned, Love Pursuing a Dove . . .*"

"Yeah, okay. Sure. So how does it end?"

"No one knows the exact order. Perhaps with *Love Triumphant*."

"Or perhaps not. What about *A Fool for Love*—is that part of the story?"

"Sure—*Love the Jester*. That's in there too. Right next to *Love the Avenger*."

"How do you know what painting you're looking at?"

"It's quite clear by the context."

There was a long pause. Sam heard her sob twice. Then she said, "Listen, why are we still together?"

Sam couldn't think of what to say.

She was fighting to hold her voice steady. "What I'm asking is, are we just a habit? A product of circumstance? How do you know when it's time to end a good run?"

After a moment, Sam said, "I don't know the answer to that."

"Then who does?"

Sam looked at his watch. "I'm sorry. Your five minutes are up."

That day in September that had started out so clear, Kat woke to find Sam was gone. They'd had a fight the night before: more than three years since Port Authority, and where were they going? What had changed? Everything and nothing.

Kat had stood in the kitchen and banged a pot on the stove.

"Stop it," Sam said. "You're being silly. Don't take it out on the cookware."

Kat was crying. She said, "You didn't used to be mean."

"Are you kidding? That's what we liked about each other."

Kat looked at him. She said, "It was always us against *them*."

Sam threw back his head and regarded the ceiling. "Did you know the average person stays with their bank two years longer than with their romantic partner?"

Kat stopped crying and put down the pot. She stared at the dinner dishes, then looked at Sam sadly. "When did we become average?"

"I'm just saying—do you realize the odds of us having already lasted this long? That means something. That's nothing to sneeze at."

Kat said, "What makes you happy?"

"You, me, my job."

"Really? The way things are?"

"Yes, the way things are makes me happy."

"Is that a fact?"

Sam smiled. "Yes, that's a fact."

The pot hit the floor. "I am so fucking sick of FACTS!"

Sam said, "What do you want then? Lies?"

Kat said slowly, "I don't care about her; I don't even care about the truth." She slumped in a chair. "All I want is to see an *emotion*."

They went to bed, where they sat still and stubborn in the shadows, neither wanting to be the one who gave in to sleep. In the morning, still angry, Sam hadn't bothered to wake Kat. She had already overslept. Let her miss her shift, he thought, if she can't bother to set an alarm. Days and then years later, he would struggle with the fact that this thoughtlessness was perhaps the greatest act of his life.

Kat woke to the sound of every TV on the block tuned to the same channel and knew something was wrong. She crept upstairs and knocked on a neighbor's door. She stayed there curled up on the couch watching the news until Sam found her that afternoon, having left the library and walked across the bridge into Brooklyn. Eight or nine miles had never felt so far. No cell phones were working that day. He had never seen the streets so wide, so empty of parked cars.

Sweaty, out of breath, he rushed through the door. He said, "Sometimes 'I love you' just isn't enough."

She said, "Billboard. In SoHo."

"So what?" he said. "You know that it's true."

In the days ahead, they would read the accounts, one after another, that appeared in the papers. There was an hour and a half between the impact of the plane and the north tower's collapse. Kat pictured Jesús looking down and seeing flames licking up the side of the building. No one knew about the plane half-buried, half-vaporized seventeen floors below. His nose burned with the chemical smell seeping from the carpet that had started to bubble. Soon smoke turned the room from day into night. There was no word from the Tower Fire Command, which, as they had drilled again and again, was supposed to tell them which exit to use. At that point all four stairwells were already gone. Because of the expensive broadcasting equipment, the door to the roof was permanently sealed shut.

The staff realized first what kind of situation they were in. They rushed to the windows some of them had cleaned only hours before, carefully wiping off the smudges and prints—as they did every morning—but only after first pressing their noses against the glass. Not once had their stomachs gotten used to the sight. Now, in the distance, white boats bobbed like gulls on the Hudson. Someone soaked a thick linen napkin in a pitcher of water and put it over her mouth, inhaling for a brief instant the sharp smell of lemons. Between 8:46 and 10:28, the temperature in the restaurant reached two thousand degrees. Long before then, one of the prep cooks, Roshan, the ace reliever who wasn't even supposed to be on duty that day, heaved a heavy padded chair through one of the plate-glass windows. Everyone was surprised at how easily it broke.

As if a spell was shattered, one of the Wall Street guys leapt out headfirst. No one could bear to look down. Thinking of his baby girl, Jesús took the hand of the accountant, a small-spirited man who had often accused the staff of stealing. Together they stepped out over the abyss, and the air, for a second, caught and cradled them, because how could it not?

That night, after dinner, after news, after seeing the last of their neighbors come home covered in dust, Sam and Kat crawled into bed. They left the window open above them, as if to keep the street company. Kat sobbed, and he hugged her body to his, and they listened to emergency vehicles wail in the distance.

Sam said, "It's getting cold. Want me to close the window?"

Kat said, "I can't sleep. Tell me something, anything."

Sam said, "I can't think of anything. There's nothing to say."

Kat said, "Please."

They watched the curtain billow in the blue night. Beyond, they could make out a few stars.

Sam said, "You know the light that reaches us is already dead."

"That's not exactly comforting."

"But here I am, here you are, here we are—still breathing."

Kat looked at him.

Sam said, "It's going to be okay. You know we're going to make it."

Kat said, "Sure. Straight down the line." She kissed his forehead. Eventually she slept.

Sam thought of the black smoke still raining upon Brooklyn, how it would settle on every roof, park, and pond, collecting in dim corners and on the sills of cracked windows, small specks of dark matter that wouldn't brush off.

He pulled the covers to his chin. Kat shifted and surfaced halfway from sleep. She said into the pillow, "Do you know where we're going?"

Only his heart dared to answer back its own quiet lie.

"Sure, I do," he whispered.

And together they lay there in the dark.

SABOR A MÍ

fiction by ALEX MINDT

The song says, "So much time we have enjoyed this love." But songs aren't life. What do you do when your grown daughter, a mother of two, comes to you and says she wants to be now with women? I am old, too old for this. So I tell her to leave and I will pray. My whole life I pray and look around, what good has it done? What do I have? My son, my first son Juan, Jr., in Los Angeles, his body found in a car under the freeway. My second son Javier sent back from Vietnam in a bag, for nothing.

In Mexico, you don't lose your family, even after they die. Here, everyone is alone. Loneliness made this country. When you are lonely, you either find some way to kill yourself or you work hard and make money. People here, they either die or they become rich.

When I was fourteen, I waded across the Rio Grande at Ojinaga and saw this country from the back of a pickup truck, picking sugar beets in Minnesota, apples in Wenatchee. In Ventura there were strawberries. In Calabasas, tomatoes. Figs in Palm Springs. Cotton in Arizona and Texas. Now I live in New Mexico. Many years have passed. I saved and saved until I had my own small restaurant and raised my family. I insisted they speak perfect English. Now not one of them speaks Spanish. When I talk to them I have to think about every word.

I do not have a home, I have this facility, in Santa Fe, the second oldest city in America. My youngest boy, Mario, he pays for this place. He owns a body repair shop in Albuquerque. Every month I get a check. But does he come out? Does he take his gringa wife and their kids to see their Papí? Last year, I went down to his big house for Lori's quinceñera. But where was the pan dulce? The dancing? After a few minutes, the kids, they get in their cars and drive off. My son, he just shrugs.

Last week I received a letter in the mail. It was from my daughter. There was a picture of her and a dog and another woman. The dog had long ears. The woman had short hair. Inside was an invitation to a wedding. I had to read it several times.

My daughter, Raquel, wants now to marry this woman. Her first husband was named Charlie; her second will be named Diane. Raquel was so smart. She learned English so fast. And then in school, she learned French and could speak that too. But not Spanish. She went to Paris and became a cook like her father. Only what she makes, with those thick creams, I don't eat so much.

Rosalinda, what do you say to me now? I wait for your voice when the noise fades and the crickets sing. But you are silent. Why won't you speak to me? I live in a facility now, Rosí. For my sadness, the nurses, they give me pills. I still think of that day, climbing down the fig tree. You were at the meal truck, holding a stainless steel tray, the sun shining twice on your lovely skin. I remember your long black hair pulled back tight, and the mark of dirt on your forehead, and how all I could do was smile and look away.

Rosí, I know what you would say. But Raquel wants to love this woman, and I say no. She has a son and a daughter, you remember Stephen and Elizabeth? But who listens to me? She did not ask my permission. Am I not her father? I do not know my own children. They move around me like ghosts.

The food here is hatred on my tongue. Eggs and toast too hard to chew, not even beans have flavor. But I am leaving now. I have eaten breakfast. I have put on my good suit, and now Raquel will hear what I have to say. The gate is open in the back behind the Piñon tree, and outside the cars are rushing. A river of steel and rubber roars past. It is late morning, but the sun is rising fast in the sky. I will walk until darkness, and then I will keep walking if I have to. Outside Santa Fe, the air is dry and sweet from the lavender and poppies. The sign says Taos 78 miles. I will walk 78 miles if I have to.

I do not hold out my hand. Cars will stop. An old man, walking a highway, a slumped, old man, surely someone will stop and ask where I'm going. Gringos are not all bad. They clean up after themselves and act nice, even if they don't mean it.

I need you now, Rosalinda, for I have walked a long time and the sun is pushing down on me. The road is uphill. In a car you don't notice so much. But when the foot comes down, the ground is so much closer than when the foot came up. I have walked almost to the Indian reservation outside of town. Cars and trucks do not see me.

The dirt on the roadside is hard and dry, and the ravine beside me is full of rocks and no water. In this country, rivers and streams, they dry up: The sky takes our lives away. We become clouds. When it rains I see all the people who came before me. Mamí, Papí, and my baby boys. I see Tío Julio on a mattress under an apple tree, playing a guitar with only three strings. There are black birds and rotting apples.

But I don't see you, Rosí, and every time it rains, I ask, what is wrong? What did I do? I would like it to rain now. It is so hot. Sweat is now bubbling up under this wool suit I still have, this suit you bought for me, for Raquel's quinceñera so many years ago. Do you remember Tío Julio and his band playing "Sabor a Mí" in the darkness and how we danced? Do you remember the lovely noise of that night and the sangria, how the neighbors came over and then more and more until our yard was full of dancing?

I need a car to pull off now. My knees are burning with every step. I will stop and wait here until someone pulls over. This is a country made of rushing. Here, no one is anywhere, they are in between places. Only the dead are content.

Voices are singing from the shrubs and red stones. "Tanto tiempo disfrutamos de este amor." Even the cars sing as they rush by. "Nuestras almas se acercaron tanto asi." And I have to sit down. There is a pale rock, a large stone. Its shadow goes down the hill by the dried up river.

Behind me, the wind rises up and a car pulls off the road. It is green, covered in dust, like a fig tree. A gringo gets out and looks at me over the roof, his light hair blowing sideways in the wind. "Hey," he says. And then he says something else. But a truck passes, and I can't hear him. And then he comes around the car and opens the door. He is kind of fat in the chest, with thin, pale legs, and he wears sandals, brown shorts, and a flowered shirt that hangs open over a white t-shirt. "I came by a minute ago and saw you walking," he says.

"Thought I'd double back and see if you needed a lift. You okay?"

He wipes off the seat for me and he tells me to push some buttons under my legs to be more comfortable. But I am fine.

"My name's Peter." He holds out his hand to me.

"I am Juan."

"Juan. That's John, right? In English, I mean."

"Yes." Inside the car, cold air is blowing at me.

"This a little cold for you?" he says. "Here, let me crank this down a bit." He turns a dial. "As you can see, I like my air conditioned." He turns the steering wheel and goes onto the highway. "You want something to drink? Water, beer? You look a little thirsty."

"No, thank you."

Sunlight bounces off the car's green hood and voices come out of a small speaker on the dashboard. "What's your 10-20, Wayward Juice? Wayward Juice, you read me?"

The gringo, Peter, he frowns at the speaker. "This guy's been calling for Wayward Juice all morning. I don't know why I bought this stupid CB, thought it would keep me company, I guess."

The tops of the mountains are white in the distance ahead of us.

"So, where you heading, Juan?"

"Taos."

"No kidding? Well, serendipity-do, so am I. I hope you're not in a hurry, 'cause I was planning on taking the scenic route."

"I have to be there by seven."

"Oh, well we've got some time then." He speaks very fast, this gringo. "So, why are you walking up to Taos on a hot day like this?"

"For a funeral." I do not know why I say it. God forgive me. But how do you tell someone that your daughter is marrying a woman?

"I'm sorry to hear that," he says. "I hate it when people die. Was this person close to you?"

I turn my head and look out the window.

"Well, I'm sorry about that. I'm real sorry." He holds up his can of beer. "How 'bout a toast? To those who've come before, who've paved the way, and showed us how to live." He drinks his beer and places it between his legs.

"Horny Buzzard, we got a Kojak with a Kodak in a plain white wrapper."

Peter chuckles and shakes his head. "You hear that?" he says. "Man, they say the funniest things. 'Kojak with a Kodak.' I don't get half of it."

He turns onto the road that goes through the mountains, the high road, they call it. "I have to go the scenic route," he says. "I just can't stand those freeways. Freeways are just beginnings and endings. You know what I'm saying? You're either leaving a place, or arriving at another place. And really, there's nothing in between. I've been reading some books lately, you know, things I never read in college. Never had any use for them until now, I guess. But let me ask you, Juan, do you think it's a coincidence that the trans-continental freeways were being constructed at the precise time that existentialism had its greatest hold on the American psyche?"

I look out the window. Piñon trees are green spots on the hills around us.

"No comment, huh? I mean, don't get me wrong, America is great, right? The greatest country in the world. But there's something missing, isn't there? That's what I've found, and you know where I found it?"

"The freeways."

"Yes!" he says. "The freeways. They're like an empty stomach, you know, and they just want and want and want." He reaches under the seat and pulls out another can of beer. "You sure you don't want anything to drink? They're getting kinda' warm."

"No, thank you."

"You know what, Juan? This is my first time in the Southwest, and it's beautiful, it's flippin' unbelievable, the mountains, the sky. I know what you're thinking. I'm one of those crazy gringos, right? A car full of crap, driving all over hell? Yeah, well." He smiles and shakes his head. "I got this friend, Gary. Now Gary's a computer guy, you know, one of those coke-bottle glasses type, all hunched over half the time, jerking off three times a day to some porno website, *motherjugs.com* sort of thing. He's got a *shooowing* for old ladies with big *cowangas,* if you get my drift. But don't get me wrong, Gary's brilliant, just like wow, his brain, and he talks about systems, how things work, interconnected grids and all that, you know, overload and whatnot, and the truth of the matter, Juan, is, well, my wife left me a couple weeks ago. Took the kids with her. So I just got in the car and put my foot on the pedal. My mainframe just overloaded, as Gary would say. My firewall, or whatever, was just burning up. You're the first person I've had the chance to really talk to. Lucky you, huh? This CB, nobody wants to talk about real stuff. Just like police warnings or scary sex talk. I mean, some real unpleasant doo-doo." He smiles and blows out air. "That's what Tyler calls it. My son. He's twelve and he still calls it doo-doo."

He is quiet for a while, humming to himself, tapping the steering wheel with his fingers. "Hey" he says, "you know about this church up a ways? What's it called?" He reaches down for some papers. The car begins to swerve. "It's down here somewhere." All over the road, we are swerving. He finds the paper and grabs the steering wheel. "Whoa!" he says. "Ride 'em, cowboy!" He straightens the car out. "Anyway, like two hundred years ago," he says, "or something like that, this friar was digging and he found a crucifix, this miraculous crucifix in the dirt, and then they built a church around this pit, and over the years several miracles have been documented. I don't normally believe in that stuff. But then again, I don't normally just hop in my car and haul-ass around the country."

He keeps talking. He talks and talks, but he is fine. Strangers will say things to you your family would never say. He tells me that he is afraid of heights and the ocean. And then he says, "Have you ever felt so sad that you can't feel anything? Have you ever just done something, just anything, I mean stupid things too, well mainly stupid things really, to just maybe show yourself that you're still alive?"

I don't answer. We drive past a gringo market selling *Native Arts and Crafts,* and a restaurant with a sign that says *Savor the Flavor.* I think of Raquel, and how after coming back from France she told me there's more to flavor than chilé and salt. "Why not use all the spices available to us?" she said. Then she said I was limited, I never opened my mind. I remember all the shouting and yelling, and never knowing why she was so angry at me. "With my limited money," I told her, "I gave you everything you wanted." And now she cooks snails.

Peter talks on and on until we drive through the Nambe Indian Reservation. He goes off the road and stops at a small adobe church, brown and leaning this way and that. "Hey," he says. "You want to take a look?"

"No thank you," I say.

"Okay. I'll only be a minute." He takes a silver camera from the back seat and starts clicking photos.

Raquel is right now preparing for her wedding. The first one, so many years ago, in the church of St. Francis de Assisi, she took my arm, and my whole body shook she was so beautiful. Her wavy brown hair was all up on her head, and her white dress dragged on the ground behind her, like a queen. As I look down now, I cannot believe it, but this is the same suit I wore to her first wedding. And there is the button you sewed on, Rosí, that looks almost like the other buttons. Hush, you said, nobody will notice one silly button. And I was still angry you spent so much on fabric stitched together for me. We cannot afford this, I said. But then you said Raquel cannot afford to have her father show up in picker's clothes.

Peter gets back into the car and says, "That sucked. No one's around, and I couldn't get in." Peter puts the car back onto the highway and says, "Atheists for Jesus!" and punches the roof with his fist.

"10-11 Blutarski! 10-11!"

Peter looks down at the radio and then at me. "I wonder what 10-11 means," he says.

"I said, that's a 10-42 Apache Bob. We got a meatwagon on yard-stick 39."

He leans forward and turns off the radio. "A meatwagon. You think that's like a mealtruck, Juan? Cause I'm getting kind of hungry. Maybe they're selling sandwiches or tacos." Peter keeps talking about what he likes to eat, spaghetti, pot roast, what his mother used to make him when he and his brothers and sisters would come in from playing in the park. He talks, this gringo, like no gringo I've met, until we make it to the dusty junkyards of Chimayo, where everything has been left for dead. He stops in the dusty parking lot of the Shrine at El Santuario de Chimayo.

"This is it," he says. "The church I was telling you about, with the pit and the miracles. This is a sacred place." He opens the door. "Come on, I'll buy you something to eat."

There is a burrito stand, a restaurant and a gift shop that sells t-shirts and refrigerator magnets in the shape of the shrine. Tourists bump into each other, looking at postcards and coasters. Peter talks to people he doesn't know, people behind the counter as he pays for postcards and t-shirts. Against the wall, there is a large, stuffed dog wearing jeans and a cowboy hat sitting in a chair with a pistol in his hand. *Cowboy Dog*, the sign says.

In the sacristy of the church there is a small round pit with a mound of dirt to the side. Crutches of wood and aluminum hang on the wall along with rosary beads, pictures of the sick and lame with letters and handmade shrines and crucifixes.

Peter points down to the mound of dirt. "This soil is supposed to be magical. It has healing powers, they say." He looks at me and smiles. "I don't believe any of that crap," he whispers. "But I'm definitely feeling something in here."

I get down on my knees at the pit and close my eyes. I am not pray-ing exactly. But I want to listen, Rosí, for your voice. I spend my days talking to you, my love, but I can never hear you. Maybe your voice will come to me here. I think of those other women. Is that why you are silent? I know I was wrong, but that was so long ago, and I never speak to them, or think of them. They meant nothing, Rosí. I wasn't easy to be with, I know. But what about you? After the children left, and the house was empty, you wouldn't speak to me, and I know why. That was how you did it, Rosí. That was how you punished me. But please, mi amor, please know that I loved you as best I could.

When I open my eyes, Peter is sitting beside me with his eyes closed. He is a funny gringo. The wind has taken hold of him.

He opens his eyes and whispers, "You feeling anything, Juan?"

"Yes."

"Really? What do you think it is?"

"Pain," I say. "My knees. Will you help me up?"

Before we leave, Peter takes a picture of me at the pit and then he asks a gringa to take a picture of us in front of the wall of crutches and shrines. He puts his arm around me and smiles.

Back in the car, Peter eats a burrito while he drives. He says that there is definitely something back there. He holds up his can of beer. "A toast," he says. "To history, to all those who have come before us, to all those searching like we are, Juan."

"Salud," I say.

He drinks from the can. A piece of yellow cheese hangs off his chin.

"If you don't mind my asking," he says. "Whose funeral are you going to?"

I do not know what to say. Whose funeral? I tell him, I don't know why, that I am going to my daughter's funeral. God forgive me.

"I'm sorry to hear that," he says. "I'm sorry. You must be devastated."

"At one time, we were very close."

"What was her name?"

"Raquel," I say.

"She must have been very special."

"She was my baby. And I loved her more than the others. But everything she ever did, it seemed like she wanted to disappoint me," I don't know why I say these things.

He nods and then is silent for a while.

"There is cheese on your chin," I say.

We drive through the villages of Truchas and Las Trampas. There are fields of blue flowers. Out my window, a dirt road swerves between

Piñon trees, up a distant hill and ends at a large white cross that stands against the pale blue sky.

"You ever been to the Church of St. Francis Assisi, Juan?"

"Yes. Many years ago."

"So, is it as spectacular as the photos and paintings?"

"I don't know."

"I've seen the pictures, you know, Ansel Adams, Georgia O'Keeffe. It's something I've always wanted to see. Some atheist, huh?"

I don't tell him that yes I have made this drive before, that years ago we all drove up to the Church of St. Francis de Assissi, that my wife and sons were in the car with me, and that we were going to my daughter's first wedding.

When he stops in the square in Ranchos de Taos, he sits silently staring out the window at the giant church, at its round buttresses and bulky vigas. There are many cars parked here and many people in work clothes standing outside the church.

"Wow," Peter says. "This is incredible." He gets out of the car and stands by the white cross in front of the church and stares up at the two bell towers.

I remember the irises and columbine, the petunias and roses. It was a spring night, like this. Remember, Rosí? Remember Raquel with flowers in her hair and the church full of family and friends from Texas, California, Arizona? Remember Tío Jorgé, the Garcias, the Tofoyas, little Juan Armijo, Dale Seaver, Renata, Pilar, and their families, José and Felicia, and Charlie's gringo friends and family? Remember the lights in the square and the Mariachi band with the violins, trumpets, bassos and guitars? And the singing! Oh, those voices! How we danced that night under the candles and the string of lights?

Peter comes back to the car and says, "I forgot my camera." He reaches into the back seat. "They're mudding the damn thing. The people, they're all slapping mud on it."

He leaves the car and begins taking pictures of the golden church. I get out and walk up to the flowerbeds by the white cross and look up at the bell towers. All around, there are people, young and old, gringo and Latino, adding to the church's giant walls. It is like a woman. There are no sharp angles, only curves, and over the years she gets bigger, but only grows more beautiful.

"Hey Juan," Peter says, "turn around. Lets get you in the picture."

He snaps his camera and says, "That will be really nice, by the cross, with the bell tower in the background." He points at the people with mud on their hands. "They say they're renewing the church. Everyone gets together and does this renewal thing. They've learned how from the people who came before and will pass it on to those who will come later. Tradition," he says, holding up his can of beer. "Ritual!"

I nod at Peter and then go into the church, where it is quiet and cool. There are paintings on the walls, colorful paintings from the Bible, like I remember it. I begin down the aisle, Rosí. This time I am alone. But it is the same aisle, the same pews, the same church. I am not the same, and Raquel is not the same.

Charlie was young and nervous that night. He was tall, with light hair and blue eyes, in a white tuxedo. And he shifted from foot to foot. And I remember the argument we had, Rosí, the night Charlie came over and asked for our blessings. "Raquel loves him," you said. "And that's what matters."

"All that matters is what Raquel wants," I said. "That's all that ever matters. But what about our family? Why is that not important?"

"You left your family in Mexico, remember? This is your new family, get used to it."

Charlie read her a poem, they said their vows, Father Thomas blessed them, and I had a gringo son-in-law who called me by my first name.

Later, little Juan Armijo stepped in front of the band to sing "Sabor a Mí," and I took you in my arms and you moved with such grace, and everyone stopped to watch. Maybe we couldn't talk too much, especially then, but did that matter when the music started? Tell me, Rosí, weren't we talking then, as we danced, did you not love me then?

"Tanto tiempo disfrutamos de este amor," I sing to myself. "Nuestras almas se acercaron, tanto asi."

I stop and sit in a pew and think I should pray. I do not know why. What do I ask for? I have asked for so much. Maybe God gives only to those who ask for nothing. I get on my knees, and I ask one more time for forgiveness. Please forgive my indiscretions, dear Lord. I was young and foolish. But I always loved my Rosí. Please bring her back to me, please let me hear her voice.

Back in the car, Peter sits like a stone, staring at the church. I climb in and close the door and expect him to say something. The keys hang in the ignition, waiting for him to turn them. But his hands are in his lap, and he is staring down for a long time. Then he looks up at the church. His eyes are shiny. He sniffs and says, "There was something wrong with my son's kidneys, Juan. He had end-stage renal disease. They didn't know what it was exactly, they never found out what was wrong, just the kidneys, they weren't filtering the blood properly." He leans back and takes in a breath. "We had him on dialysis, but that wasn't working. He was getting sick all the time, and they told us that he needed a transplant. My wife, Sharon, well she's diabetic, so she says to me that I need to donate my kidney. But here's the thing, for some reason, I don't know, I hesitated. I flinched. And she saw it, my wife, she caught me. I didn't just step up to the plate."

The church bells begin chiming. The people around the church start cleaning up. Men climb down from the ladders.

Peter wipes his eyes with the back of his hand.

I clear my throat. There is so much sadness, I do not know what to tell him. The bell stops ringing and I say, "We have all done bad things."

Peter looks at me and nods. He sits up and takes in a long breath.

"Yeah," he says.

"What happened to your boy?" I ask.

"Tyler? Well, he's doing fine, actually. That's the funny thing, his little brother happened to be a much better match and it all worked out okay in the end. But Sharon and I know the truth. And that's why she left me, and that's why I'm out here. New Mexico is a long way from Cincinnati."

"It is a long way from Chihuahua too. We are both a long way from home."

Peter wipes his eyes again and looks at me. "Chihuahua? Is that where you're from? That's the place where the dog comes from, right? The little dog?"

Peter turns the key and the car starts. He pulls the car out of the parking lot onto the main road and says, "Yeah, those dogs, I don't know, they're always shivering, aren't they? They must be cold or something. Maybe they're scared."

On the road into Taos, he talks about his boys, Tyler and Evan, how Tyler was an accident and was always sick with something. "Evan has always looked out for his big brother, taking care of him and whatnot," he says. "Hell, Sharon's right, they don't need me or my lousy paycheck. Selling fire alarms doesn't get your kids into private school, I'll tell you that much. But they'll be just fine without me. Better, probably."

"You are a weak man," I tell him. "You are weak because you would rather drive a car than do what you know you should do."

"I'm sorry," he says. "I didn't catch that. What did you say?"

"Your family is more important than your pity."

"Let me think about that for a minute." He is quiet, then he says, "Damn. You're right. You're like a sage or something, Juan. See, I knew I picked up the right guy. You're right, you're totally right, pity sucks. I hate people who feel sorry for themselves."

We drive into town, past markets, restaurants, the post office.

He says, "Time has gotten away from us a little bit. I'm sorry about that. What is that address again?"

I pull out the card and show it to him. "Arroyo Seco?" he says. "I thought you said Taos?"

"It is near Taos. Just past."

Peter stops into a gas station and takes the card with him as he gets out of the car. When he comes back, he says, "Okay, no problem. There are directions on the back of this, you know. It tells you how to get there." He looks at the card and says, "Are you sure you're going to a funeral?"

As we drive through Taos, past art galleries and restaurants, Peter tells me that this is where he'll be staying for the next few days. "I'm going to look at some art, do some exploring, see the Rio Grande. Maybe I'll take off my clothes and sit in one of those hot springs I heard about down by the river."

The sun is slipping down into the canyon, and big red clouds are moving in. It is now past seven, and Peter is driving fast. He pulls off the main road and starts heading toward the mountains. We drive through a small town, Arroyo Seco, past a bar with people outside, drinking beer. The road comes to a fork and Peter stops. "This is where we go on the dirt road, I think," he says. "The road less traveled." His little car shakes and bounces. "You're wearing a ring there, Juan. Are you married?"

"Yes," I say. "I was. She is dead."

"Oh, I'm sorry to hear that."

"I have two children, Mario and Raquel. My first two boys died many years ago."

"You would have given your kidneys for them, wouldn't you?"

"Quit it," I tell him. "You are not the first man to act without courage."

Out the window, horses eat grass in the dusty red light. They stand like shadows, dark ghosts in the falling sun.

37

"It's something out here, isn't it?" he says. "I could see just escaping out here. Chucking it all and hiding out here."

"That's what you are doing," I say.

He thinks for a moment, and then says, "You know what? You're right. About everything." He turns the wheel, and we are going down a long, gravel driveway with cars parked along the sides. "I've been running away for a long time," he says.

"Listen," I tell him. "Get some sleep, then go back to your wife and tell her she married a coward. But you have found strength in your heart. Being alone is no good, Peter. In the short time, yes, it may be good, but in the long time you get lonely and for that you may as well be dead."

He pulls up to a large adobe house. "Strange place for a funeral," he says.

"There is no funeral," I say. "My daughter is getting married."

"I know, I read the invitation," he says. "Congratulations. But why did you tell me she died?"

"She is marrying a woman."

"Oh, right," he says. "She threw you a curveball, huh?"

I get out of the car. "Thank you for the ride, Peter."

"Take care, Juan. It was a pleasure." I close the door, and he sits in the car and watches me as I walk up to the house. He honks his horn and then drives away. Dust rises off the ground and floats in the air.

I knock on the door. There is music and voices from somewhere on the other side of the house. I knock again, but no one answers. The dust is now settling on the road behind me, and it is getting dark. Big purple clouds fill the sky.

I walk around the house and music gets louder. There is a stack of wood, Piñon logs and a rusty ax lying on the ground. There is a hole in the ground and a mound of dry, sandy dirt and a shovel leaning up against the house. Beside the hole, there is a bush in a clay pot, waiting to be planted.

The music gets louder with people shouting and laughter.

Through shrubs and around a shed, I move, and down below me on a patio of red tile, people are dancing and clapping their hands. The lights from the house shine down on them. They are mostly gringos trying to salsa, smiling, swiveling their hips. Raquel is dancing with the short-haired woman from the photo with the dog. Raquel's hair is pulled back. Her deep, dark eyes and those full lips and her cheekbones, sharp like a statue, remind me of you, Rosalinda.

38

The valley below fills with dark grey and pink clouds, and the wind pushes the branches of the trees. The bushes around me shake. The song ends and the gringos clap their hands. Some are on the side with drinks in their hands talking English to each other. Raquel's children, Stephen and Elizabeth, adults now, stand by their father, Charlie, Raquel's ex-husband. What is he doing here, Rosí? This is like no wedding I have been to. It is a small party with a few friends.

Raquel puts her hand up and moves away from the group, saying something to a young man at a wooden table, where the music comes from. Voices can be heard, people talking. Raquel comes back to the woman with the short hair and says something to the other people. They smile and nod and step back, leaving the dance floor for the two women. And then trumpets fill the air. Do you hear that? Those trumpets and that rhythm, that slow rhythm that you loved so much?

Raquel holds up her hand. A man's voice sings out, "Tanto tiempo disfrutamos de este amor," and the woman takes Raquel in her arms, and they begin to dance. "Si negaras mi presencia en tu vivir." She moves like soft wind, and her eyes show only happiness as she spins away from the woman. The man sings those words, those familiar words, Rosí, remember? I sing them out as the woman takes Raquel's hand and brings her back. "Tanta vida yo te di." I want to tell her what the words mean—*I gave you so much life.* If she only knew the language . . . *I do not pretend to be your owner,* the man sings. *I am not in control.* She turns away and then spins back into the woman's arms with such ease that I cannot contain myself. It is like I am dancing with you again, Rosí, the way your fingers touched my palm, with your thumb on my wrist and the wrinkle on your cheek when you smiled. I release you and spin around, with my arms out like a child, and then I pull you close to me, my hand moving from your hip to your back, my lips at the top of your ear.

But then the song ends, and Raquel steps back and says something, and then she puts her arms around the woman and they hold each other. There is clapping, and then the thick clouds above us start to send down rain.

"Did you feel that?" Raquel says. "It's raining!"

A flamenco starts up. Raquel turns and snaps her fingers at her ex-husband Charlie, who walks out and starts dancing. Stephen comes out and dances with his arms in the air. The short-haired woman turns and dances with our granddaughter, Elizabeth. Raindrops come down bigger and bigger, sending down those who have come before. More and more people come out, shouting and clapping. They crowd together, smiling as they dance in the rain, and laughing, these people I'll never know with people I've known forever.

A LOCAL'S GUIDE TO DATING IN SLOCOMB COUNTY

fiction by CHRIS DRANGLE

At half past ten the guy from the corner mart came into the shelter. Naomi had only seen him a few times, but he had a distinctive look, to say the least. He was young but rugged, with short-cropped hair and broad shoulders. It figured that the most attractive man in town her age was also a triple amputee. It was so hot out that even he was wearing shorts—red mesh ones with a faded Cola High School crest, below which were hi-tech black metal prosthetics inserted in grubby tennis shoes. He walked up to her and rested his elbows on the counter, and from that position looked normal, except for the one hand that was a carbon fiber hook.

"Morning, ma'am," he said.

"Hi," she said. "What can I help you with?"

"I'm here to pick up my dog. I talked to Dennis yesterday?"

"Okay, great. What's your name?"

"Fisher Bray."

"And what's the animal's name?"

"Barbie. She doesn't have a collar or nothing. I take it off at night cause it itches her. She got out two nights ago and somebody brought her here I guess. Dennis said you got her."

"I see. What kind of dog is she?"

"She's a busted-looking Dutch shepherd. Dark brown and orangeish. One ear missing. Big goofy smile."

To calm a fever, Naomi's mother had once forced her to take an ice bath. It sucked the air out of her lungs and made her skin burn. She felt like that now. The back of her neck prickled. She coughed.

"Okay," she said. Her hands were trembling so she put them in her lap under the desk. "Give me a minute. Let me go in back and find Dennis, okay? I'll just be a minute."

"Thank you," he said.

She walked to the staff room. Dennis and Portia were both there. Dennis was marking up a form on a clipboard and Portia was mixing tea. She saw Naomi's face.

"What's wrong?" she said.

"A man is here to get his dog," Naomi said.

"Great," Dennis said. "I haven't finished the list yet. That'll help."

"No," she said. "He wants the shepherd with the missing ear."

"With the limp?" Portia asked.

"Right," Dennis said. "Yeah, that's right, he called yesterday. What's the problem?"

Naomi looked at Portia.

"Holy shit," Portia said.

"You didn't put it down," Dennis said. "You put it down?"

Naomi left the staff room and walked to the kennel office. The lights were off to save electricity and the blinds had been drawn to keep out the heat, and the sun that got through was cut on the wall in long slivers. She opened the top drawer of the filing cabinet and found yesterday's PTS log and roster. On the log, in her handwriting, in the eighth space: *London, Shepherd mix, 92188. PTS'ed.* On the printed roster, halfway down the third page: *92188—intake—shepherd mix no ID.* Penciled in to the right of the entry, in Dennis's childish scrawl: *Update, contacted by owner, DO NOT PTS.*

But she had checked the roster against the log. Had she checked it? She always checked it, that was the system. The water cooler bubbled, a single thunk that sounded like a heavy stone dropped in a lake. It was hard to imagine that she wouldn't have checked the roster, but she didn't remember doing it yesterday, not specifically. She did remember what she did with the dog, and felt like she needed to throw up.

Back in the staff room, Portia was biting her nails and Dennis was stirring the instant tea.

"How did it happen?" Dennis said.

"I don't know."

"This is so fucked up," Portia said.

"Shut up," she said. "No, sorry. Let's just think."

There was nothing to think about. It had been ten minutes since she left the front desk, and Naomi had to go back. Fisher Bray was sitting in one of the chairs. He looked nervous, but smiled politely when she entered the room. Another woman was waiting at the counter, with a fluffy white cat in a hand carrier.

"I've been waiting here ten minutes," she said.

"Someone will be right with you," Naomi said, and turned to the man. "Will you come with me, sir?"

Portia took over at the front desk and Naomi showed him back to the kennel office where Dennis was waiting. She wanted to be anywhere else in the universe. She sat in a metal folding chair on the side of the room. He sat in the comfy chair. Dennis sat behind the desk and began by saying there was some unfortunate news. Barbie—that was her name?—had been put down. Tuesday had been a hectic day, and there had been some kind of miscommunication. With so many animals going in and out all the time, they relied on a set of lists, and somehow Barbie had been put on the wrong one. There were no words to express how sorry they were.

Naomi watched Fisher without breathing. He sat with his back straight, hand folded over hook in his lap. The sandy scruff on his cheeks softened the edge of a granite jaw line. He couldn't be older than twenty-two. Dennis talked, and Fisher had no reaction whatsoever.

The numbers went like this: Slocomb County was home to a hundred and twenty thousand people. The Slocomb County Animal Shelter was the only freestanding shelter in five hundred square miles. The shelter had room to house around twenty cats and ninety dogs, and operated at capacity every day. Although it operated at capacity, there was a constant inflow of new cases. Strays, rescues, walk-ins—some days they got two dozen animals. On the other hand, outflow was sluggish. The last time Naomi had seen national estimates, six to eight million pets entered shelters every year. Three to four million were adopted out.

In addition to numbers there were rules. Most of their funding came from the county, and that came with strings attached. Their contract required that they take every animal that came through the door, plus keep a certain amount of kennel space for humane cases, plus cruelty seizure and bite cases that needed boarding while the courts decided what to do. State law required strays to be held for forty-eight hours.

It was like musical chairs, except with two hundred rules, cages instead of chairs, and sodium pentobarbital for the losers.

The day before Fisher came in, she sat in the parking lot before work. The shelter was at the edge of town, on the side of the highway. A squat brick building with a gravel parking lot and a carved wooden sign. Behind it was a cotton field, black hickory tree line in the distance. She breathed slowly and checked the visor mirror. Usually she dressed in blouses and khakis but on Tuesdays, her day on PTS, it was t-shirt and jeans.

Inside the waiting room, Portia manned the front desk. She wore blue eye shadow and golden hoop earrings that would fit around a fire extinguisher. Her hair—jet black this month—was four inches shorter than it had been yesterday. She was removing and reattaching a pen cap with her teeth, and spit it out to talk.

"Hey girl," she said.

"Hey," Naomi said. "New do?"

Portia slapped the pen down and leaned forward gravely.

"It broke off," she said. "Broke. Off. I was like, okay, I guess it's summer outside, I guess we'll go short."

"It doesn't look bad."

"I'll make it work. Cut it into this shag thing. 'Layered,' let's call it."

Portia was in her early thirties, a Cola native who held three part-time jobs. Besides the shelter, she did hair at A Cut Above and tended bar at The De Soto. Her husband was a paralegal with an hour-long commute to Pine Bluff. She had confided in Naomi that she made enough at the bar to quit the other gigs, but the variety suited her. She liked dogs, hair, and beer; the system worked.

"Anyway." She turned her mouth down and arched her eyebrows. "Ready for your Tuesday?"

"Sure," Naomi said. "But it's too hot."

"Yeah. Dennis is in the staff room making the list. Let me know if you want to go drinking later."

"Check."

Dennis, their manager, was seated at one of the staff room's plastic card tables, drinking coffee from a mason jar and glaring at a clipboard. He was in his fifties, tall and portly, with white, Martin Van Buren-style muttonchops and an endless supply of pale blue, short-sleeved button-down shirts.

"Morning," Naomi said.

44

"Ah," he said. "Morning to you."

She put her lunch in the mini-fridge and poured a cup of coffee for herself, dumped in enough powdered hazelnut creamer to change the viscosity. She stirred and stepped behind him to read over his shoulder.

"Not too bad," he said. "Probably just a half-day's work, if you want to go at it like that."

On the clipboard was a single sheet of paper, a simple black-and-white grid.

"Let me know if you need anything," Dennis said.

She took a pencil and the clipboard to the kennel, a large, rectangular room with a smooth concrete floor and fluorescent lights. The two long walls were lined with tiled enclosures and chain-link gates. A half-wall in the room's center served as a divider, so that the cages didn't look directly into each other. Each cage had a number on a plastic card clipped to the gate.

The PTS list started as a page of blanks—Dennis's calculations produced a number, and a corresponding number of empty spaces for recording the work. The number today was thirteen. Not counting walk-ins—and there were always some—Naomi needed to pick thirteen dogs to put down. She made a casual circuit around the room, considering. The boxer puppies had been there a week, but they were cute enough that she held out hope for adoption. They could spend the day in the staff bathroom—that freed one cage. The elderly gray terrier went on the list. Two mutts, a collie-looking one and another terrier type, went on the list. The well-behaved shepherd mix that had come off the street with old injuries, a bad limp and a missing ear, went on the list. The dachshund with cataracts, who slept all day and had not barked once, was a maybe. The fat cocker spaniel went on the list.

She still thought of it as training, or tried to. That had been the original plan: stay in Cola for a year, get experience at the shelter, then apply to vet schools, where she would need professional composure. Millions of pet owners declined to get their animals spayed or neutered; people were too poor, or lazy, or didn't know better. She didn't like that part of the job, but it was part of the job. Of course it was harder now to pretend she was only training. She had been at the shelter four years.

When all the blanks were filled she went to the kennel office, a closet with a computer and a landline, and spent the morning making useless phone calls. The breed rescues in Jackson and Shreveport were sympathetic, but unable to get anyone to Cola until later in the week. The no-kill rescue groups in El Dorado and Pine Bluff were overloaded. No room in shelters at neighboring counties or their neighboring counties. At a quarter to eleven, Dennis poked his head into the office.

"A guy just dropped off two cats," he said.

"Did you tell him they won't last the day?"

"Yep."

"All right"

"Good news is, there's a young couple here, with a little kid, and they want a dog. I'm about to take them back."

"The boxer puppies are in the bathroom."

"Ah, good call. That's our first stop."

The kid liked the puppies but decided he wanted a snake. The mother refused, the father refused to have an opinion, and the family left arguing. Naomi added the cats to the list and worked out a schedule for the rest of the day. First, update her online dating profile. Second, eat lunch. Third, kill all the animals the shelter didn't have room for.

Part one didn't last long. There wasn't much to add. Naomi Connelly, twenty-six years old, native of Bossier City, graduate of Centenary College. Interested in veterinary science and waterskiing. Likes sushi and Brad Paisley. Transplant to southeast Arkansas by way of a college boyfriend who had grown up in Cola and wanted to move back. That wasn't in the profile. He had begged her to come with him, the shelter had liked her résumé, and it seemed like a decent spot for a layover while she saved money for vet school. They rented a truck, signed a lease—in her name to help build credit, which she later learned didn't work—and made the drive on a Saturday afternoon. Two months later he changed the plan. A Kappa Sig brother could get him in the door at a finance firm in Houston. It was too good to pass up. He loved her, he really did, but this was what he needed right now. They would be in touch. They never were.

And then, what? The job was pretty good, most parts of it. Rent was cheap. She could cover her student loans and still save a little, and living by herself was nice after four years of dorm life. She didn't miss Bobby. She took drives on the weekends, but never back home, though it was only three hours away. She found a good tamale place. She read in the evenings. A year passed, then another.

She had five messages on the dating site. One from a man who had sent the exact same text a month ago, asking for a full-body shot, one an invitation for "no-strings-attached fun," one from a sixty-year-old

46

widower looking for a backgammon partner, and two from bots notifying her of totally free, no-hassle, super hot porn. She hated the Internet.

At noon she got her Tupperware out of the mini-fridge and mixed a pitcher of instant iced tea. Every communal fork was dirty, so she leaned against the counter and ate her Cobb salad with a spoon. Portia came in and used the microwave to heat her own lunch—a tub of macaroni and cheese with bacon bits mixed in. The smell was overpowering. She chewed with her mouth open.

"I'd like to be senile," she said, "and get all my jobs confused. Get the animals drunk, cut barflies' hair, and euthanize people at the salon."

"There's probably a legal defense for that," Naomi said.

After lunch she stepped out for a short walk. It was seven thousand degrees outside. The cotton field behind the shelter was halfway into flowering, the dark bolls splitting around the cloudy blooms. In a month the strip picker would start lumbering down the rows, huge tires and green chassis and bright yellow teeth in front, thoughtless and methodical.

Tuesdays had never been easy and still weren't. But there were the numbers, and the rules, and the necessity. She hadn't cried about it this year, yet. Still the occasional nightmare, but they were less frequent. The way to do it was simply to do it, the quicker the better, and try not to think too much. So she stared across the cotton field until the back of her neck was burning, then she went back inside the shelter and through the waiting room and back to the kennel office.

She checked her list against the log and the roster, as she always did. Updates would have been obvious. She would have noticed any special instructions or changes to an animal's status. Nothing jumped out at her.

In the kennel she took the quiet dachshund with cataracts out of its cage and led it to the room in back. She lifted it onto the metal table and went to the refrigerator. While she put on her gloves and filled the syringe, it sniffed around the edge of the table, looking for a place to jump down, but the table was too high so it sat and waited. She took its left front leg in her left hand, pushed her thumb down on the vein, slid in the needle and pushed the plunger. The dog got sleepy and lay down and was dead in forty-five seconds. She took a heavy-duty plastic garbage bag from the supply cabinet and rolled the dog into it, then carried it to the floor-to-ceiling freezer and put it on the middle shelf.

She did it over and over for three hours. When she took a break to drink more tea in the staff room, Portia and Dennis did not talk to her.

An informal custom. After the break she put on new gloves and started again. All the cats went in one bag. The big dogs got their own bags, the smaller ones shared. Before she finished, the freezer became so crowded she had to shove to get the bags to fit, wedging the smaller animals in where she could. Twice she had to take some out and repack. Luckily, Dennis had scheduled a pickup for that evening, so however full the freezer got, it would be empty in the morning. Not that it mattered to her. On Wednesdays, she worked the desk.

The lights were on in the office but the blinds were still drawn. Naomi wanted to open them, to do anything to make this room feel bigger, but she didn't want to move. Fisher sat quietly, without responding or batting an eyelid. Dennis kept talking.

"Sometimes dogs will have a chip," he said. "But we didn't find one on her. So that would've made us hold on to her, but she didn't have one, our records show."

Fisher smiled suddenly. Naomi's stomach did a somersault.

"It was torn out," he said. "She was injured in combat. Barbie's a veteran."

"A veteran," Dennis said.

"Yes sir. First Battalion, 25th Infantry."

They sat in silence. Gravel crunched under tires in the parking lot. The ceiling fan spun above them. A cartoonish ceramic owl sat on the desk. It was painted a dark blue and its eyes were wide and bright. Dennis turned it around in a circle.

"I see," he said. "But you can imagine, we get a lot of strays. Lots of injuries you know, you see these dogs around. Without a chip, no collar, we can't know."

"But I called."

"That's true." Dennis did not look at Naomi. "It's very unfortunate. The lists are usually always cross-checked."

Fisher nodded and looked at the window. The blinds were still closed. He took a deep breath, let it out slowly, and looked up at the ceiling. Head tilted back, he laughed once through his nose. Dennis caught Naomi's eye and bit his lip, but she ignored him. Fisher rubbed his face with his good hand, the hard jaw with neat, light-colored stubble. Then he laughed loudly. They sat quietly until his laughter subsided into giggles. When the giggles had passed, he sighed again, and apologized.

"Sorry," he said. "I'm going to go outside."

"Okay," Dennis said.

Naomi wondered if she should help, but Fisher stood easily, and walked to the door. She searched for something to say and came up with nothing. When he had left the room she looked at Dennis, whose mouth was hanging open.

"Is he coming back?" he said.

She didn't answer. The water cooler burbled. Dennis left to check on Portia and Naomi walked to the window. It was unfair, of course. Was it monstrous? A mistake had been made, but the numbers all but guaranteed mistakes. The sheer numbers. Every system had its failings.

She raised the blinds and saw Fisher out in the cotton field, pacing slowly in the rows with that odd, robotic walk. The first time she'd seen him at the corner mart, she couldn't help wondering how he dealt with the items on the low shelves. Slowly, she supposed, and there was nothing wrong with that. There were no clouds in sight and he used his t-shirt to wipe his forehead. He looked, she thought, like he could use some water. She filled a paper cup.

The heat was worse than advertised. The highway rippled in a mirage and when she reached the field the dirt cracked under her flats. He was facing the distant line of black hickory, shading his eyes with his hand. When she was ten feet away he turned. She had to squint with her entire face.

"You want some water?"

He came forward and took the cup, drank and handed it back.

"Appreciate it."

"We really are sorry," she said. It was not exactly like offering comfort, but what else was there?

He nodded and looked out to the trees.

"Where's the body?" he said. "Can I see it?"

"No."

"Where is it?"

"We have so little space," she said. "And no money. We schedule pickups with freight coordinators. Reefer trucks will take the cargo for free, just stop on the way through town."

"And go where?"

She took a breath. "Wherever they were already going. Lots of hub cities have rendering plants. The plants will buy remains."

Fisher looked at her. He smiled once, broadly, then all expression left his face.

49

"Rendering plants," he said, and looked off again. "A rendering plant."

The smell of the cotton field had always reminded her of glue. Sweat dripped from under her arms and ran cold down her ribs. She put her arm up to shield her eyes and waited for words to come. When that arm grew tired she switched to the other.

"I'll tell you what," he said. "That takes the cake. And I know what I'm talking about. Not bragging or nothing. Just—I've seen bad, and this is a cherry."

She followed his line of sight into the field, trying to imagine what he saw. Nothing but acres and acres of cash crop, hunched in the light, theoretically on its way to being useful. The cup in her hand was nearly full—he hadn't taken more than a sip. She let a little water spill into the dust at her feet. The ground was so dry the water pooled instead of soaking in. It was hard to imagine anything worthwhile growing here.

"Beer?" she said.

"Oh yeah. Beer."

"I'll buy you one, I mean."

He looked at her. For some reason he didn't have to squint as much as she did.

"How's that?" he said.

"I don't know," she said. "I guess this is wildly inappropriate. I'm just saying, I'm sorry what happened to your dog. I mean, Jesus—I'll get you a beer. This isn't protocol or anything. I understand if you'd rather burn us down."

For the first time she saw despair on his face. A small change at the corners of his eyes. He looked down at his shoes. She wondered if his prosthetics absorbed the heat from the sun, if that was a concern.

"You mean The De Soto?" he said. The only bar in town.

"Sure."

"Okay," he said, and laughed. "I guess."

He walked away from her, deeper into the field. She suddenly felt rude for watching, and marched back to the shelter. Portia gnawed on a pen cap at the desk. After the heat of the field the inside air froze her shoulders. The waiting room was empty.

"How did that go?" Portia asked.

"I don't know," Naomi said. "He's not happy. Doesn't really seem angry. Sad."

"He's not going to kill us?"

"I don't think so." She hesitated. "I'm going to get him a beer."

"What, now?"

"Tonight. At the bar."

"You're kidding."

"What are we supposed to do? 'Sorry we killed your dog, bye.' That can't be it."

"No, you're right." Portia tilted her head like a cat regarding strange human behavior. She raised one eyebrow. "Sure. Why not a beer. If he says okay."

"He seemed okay."

"I'm working the bar tonight, so you know."

"I know."

"In case he chops you up, is what I'm saying."

"I know."

Late in the afternoon, the family with the snake kid came back. The father, apparently, had been forced to take a position, and decided against reptiles. Naomi directed them to Dennis, who again showed them the available animals. Again they deliberated noisily and, again, left without adopting anything. When the door closed behind them, Portia mimed a gunshot to the head.

Naomi stayed after closing to go over the PTS list and roster. She sat at the desk and stared at the documents. Not that it made any difference now, but she hoped some memory might shake loose, and she could be assured that Dennis's note hadn't been there the first time she checked. But she couldn't remember. And she hated Dennis, because although he was a goofy old man with ridiculous sideburns, between the two of them she was more likely to make a mistake.

At home she took a long shower, and afterward laid out a few tops on her bed. She tried them on and narrowed the choices to a green halter that tied at the neck, and a simple black v-neck. She considered appropriateness, comfort level, and whether or not she was going insane.

When Fisher Bray was six, his father, a roofer, moved the family to Cola to take advantage of what would turn out to be a very brief construction boom. He was sad to leave the house in Lake Village, because the dryer on its back in the side yard made an excellent racecar, when his sisters weren't using it as their bakeshop oven. Cola was hot and flat, and though the new side yard had a beech stump good for holding BB gun targets, it was a poor replacement for the dryer.

In middle school, his mother encouraged him to go out for football as a way to make friends. He played offense and defense, as there were seventeen total players on the team. In two years they won three games. He did make friends, and his house became a popular sleepover destination, at least partially because of the two high school girls who also lived there.

That lasted until his father's fourth and final back injury, the result of another, minor, twelve-foot fall. His father sold the work truck and went on disability, and became an affable but spooky presence around the house—the pain meds made him foggy, and he spent the majority of his time sitting in the recliner in the living room, watching the TV whether it was on or not. Fisher stopped inviting his friends over. His mother started work as a gas station attendant to help with the finances. She was qualified for more, but managed her income carefully—a thousand dollars too much would change the family's benefits category, and her husband's medication would cost ten thousand more a year.

In high school Fisher discovered metal and weed. He shot up to five-eleven and let his hair grow into a long ponytail that he tied with rubber bands. He was a mellow, straight-C student, not because better grades were impossible, but because Cs took basically no effort. The girls graduated when he was a sophomore and moved to the capital together, to attend culinary school. Haring two fewer dependents did restructure the family's benefits categorization, so Mr. Bray switched from a battery of prescriptions to over-the-counter cocktails. His fog dissipated somewhat and was replaced by pain and anger. He started stealing Fisher's pot, and their fights got progressively uglier until Mrs. Bray intervened, and designated Fisher as the official buyer for his father. She had recently found that four years at the One Stop had lowered her earning potential to the status quo.

His senior year, Fisher attended the Slocomb County High School career fair. He talked to a bait shop owner, a welder, a newspaper ad salesman, a pig farmer, a rice farmer, and a soybean farmer. The rice farmer in particular radiated disappointment, and Fisher, looking at the man's gnarled hands and hangdog face, felt the future closing around him like a fist. Then, in the corner of the convention hall, he was waylaid in his attempt to get a free keychain and ended up talking to an Army staff sergeant for half an hour. The sergeant had perfect teeth, a maroon beret, and a fine white scar on his temple, which he said he got rappelling. He was only six years older than Fisher, but from some other world where people wore polished shoes and knew how to break necks. He had been to thirteen countries. They looked over some forms, just to get an idea. Fisher agreed to take the ASVAB, to see what he might qualify for.

He left for Fort Benning three days after graduation. His mother cried and said she could not be more proud. His father asked where he would get his pot from. His sisters, by phone, said he was an idiot and was going to get killed. On his first plane ride, he was surprised to see how little of the earth was covered by human things.

Basic Training was a shock, mostly because of the routine. He shaved at four-forty every morning, and went to bed so tired he didn't roll over in his sleep for ten weeks. After Basic he stayed in Georgia for Advanced Individual Training—just another four weeks for infantrymen. He was fit, disciplined, and happy. In October, Private Bray crossed the Atlantic on a C-40 Clipper. It was the first time he had seen the ocean. He celebrated his nineteenth birthday a month later, at Forward Operating Base Sykes in dry, dusty, empty Tal Afar. An engineer he knew from training knew a corporal with an acoustic guitar, and someone brought Oreos into the barracks. It was his best birthday since childhood.

Two weeks passed slowly. Companies were being cycled in and out of Mosul, where the fighting was apparently heavy. Fisher's company waited for its first rotation. Part of him was afraid, of course, but he was also confident and excited. He had skills and wanted to use them. No one back home had ever done anything like this.

His two best friends in the unit were Specialist Leonard Ramos, a dog handler, and Leonard's Dutch shepherd, Barbie. Leonard was short, plump, and intensely religious. He and Fisher bonded over a mutual love for Megadeth. Barbie was sleek and lean, with giant upstanding ears, a brownish-orangey coat, and a floppy pink tongue that felt like used sandpaper. Fisher had always wanted a dog, but his father was the one man in Cola who wouldn't allow it. He and Barbie got along so well that Leonard let Fisher throw the tennis ball with her, though playtime was usually reserved for the handler. While the dog fetched, the men talked about combat. They were terrified and eager.

Their opportunity came in December. The company drove to Mosul in a convoy and initiated police operations in an outer district. Fisher's platoon was in charge of a guard post at an apparently important intersection, a square of brown dirt between four identical stone buildings. They could hear artillery in other parts of the city, but for three days the intersection itself was relatively sedate. Fisher helped man the guard station that checked passing vehicles. Leonard walked Barbie around tires and bumpers, let her sniff compartments and passengers.

One Tuesday the traffic was heavier than normal, and a line formed at the gate. The drivers—Iraqi citizens, other American soldiers, other coalition forces—were irritable and surly. It was early evening and the light was failing. The shadows in the square lengthened and grew darker. The sky glowed a soft purple. Fisher was trying to get through his checklist with a French journalist when he heard barking. He looked up, but it was difficult to see in the increasing gloom. A man was in the square, a dozen meters away. The man was running toward the guard station. Barbie was barking at him. Leonard let go of her and she ran at him. The man saw the dog coming and stopped, and then Fisher's ears blew out and everything in his vision smeared together.

When his eyesight came back, a thick cloud of dust hung in the air, and he was lying on the ground next to the journalist's car. He tried to push himself into a sitting position, but failed because his left hand was gone. He gasped and looked away. It must have been a mistake, because he could still feel the hand, still feel the fingers moving. He looked again but it remained absent. Strange—he would have to figure that out later. Right now he needed to get moving. He tried to stand using only his feet, but that proved impossible, because they were gone too. He screamed, and someone touched his shoulder. It was the French journalist, leaning down from the open car door. His face was bloody but he had all his limbs. He was saying something, probably something important, but Fisher didn't speak French, so he closed his eyes and lay back. He was confused and needed a nap.

Fisher had nine surgeries in Germany. In two months he was aware enough to ask questions and remember the answers, and he learned that Leonard had taken shrapnel through the brain stem. Barbie had survived, and was actually being treated at a veterinary clinic a few miles away. He got phone calls from his family, parents solemn and sisters hysterical. In March he underwent another round of surgery. Whenever he was lucid he made phone calls to administrators at the veterinary clinic. Barbie was getting a medical discharge. Fisher wanted her. The strings were easy to pull.

They did their rehab together at the VA in Birmingham. Barbie had lost an ear and gained a permanent limp, but Fisher's pace wasn't exactly challenging. He did pool therapy and the parallel bars to build strength, and was finally able to use the prosthetics without aid. His walk was slow and ungainly, but after eleven months without standing, it felt like a miracle to look at the world from his original height.

His sisters drove down from Little Rock to bring him back to Cola. They made a hundred chocolates stamped with a profile of George Washington, the same as his Purple Heart. They brought a three-foot novelty dog bone for Barbie. When they reached home, his father surprised Fisher by sobbing openly, then laughing and asking which of them was the gimpiest now. His mother kept a stern frown and didn't look at his legs.

He got a small apartment in the downtown area, with a tiny concrete patio and a small backyard where Barbie could drink out of the sprinkler. He went to physical therapy twice a week and the psychologist once. After a few months he got a part-time job at the corner mart, stocking shelves. He read in the evenings and barbecued on weekends, usually just him and the dog. He didn't mind the solitude. He knew he was processing, and the doctor said he was doing well.

In July his air conditioner broke, so he left the windows and back door open at night. One morning Barbie wasn't there. She had gotten out before—the latch on the backyard gate was pitiful—but he usually found her sniffing snake holes in the dirt alley just behind the property. He paced the length of the alley but didn't see her, walked a circuit around downtown and couldn't find her. He knocked on his neighbors' doors and asked, then called his parents for some reason. No one could help. He sat at his kitchen table and tried not to panic. All the walking had exhausted him. The shelter—he would call the shelter.

Someone named Dennis answered, and Fisher described Barbie, trying to keep the agitation out of his voice. Sure enough, a dog matching that description had been brought in. She was happily waiting for him to come collect her. Fisher put down the phone and choked once. He had not realized how worried he'd been. He rubbed his eyes and asked Dennis if they could keep her until the next day, when he could borrow a car from his mother. That, he was told, would be no problem.

For the second time that day, Naomi waited for the right response to occur to her. On the other side of the booth, Fisher pulled from his beer and looked up at the crossbeam that traversed the bar's interior, the crusty license plates nailed onto the black lacquer. She had chosen the green halter, and was glad—the paper streamers taped to the vent of the window a/c unit barely floated, and the condensation on her bottle was so thick that the label slipped off in her hand the second time she raised it. The three other patrons sat at the bar watching baseball on a ceiling mounted tube television. Portia cut lime wedges, as if someone might order something that required them. Naomi wrapped the sodden label around her beer again.

"Did she get a medal, too?" she asked. "Like yours?"

"No," he said. "Dogs aren't eligible for military awards."

"You were right about taking the cake. The cherry."

"Like I said, not trying to brag."

He wore a faded maroon polo with the same mesh shorts, sat with his hand on the table and his other arm in his lap. There was a wry expression on his face when he looked at the tacky crossbeam, at the door when it swung to admit another lonely sixty-year-old in overalls, at the saltshaker made from an old hot sauce bottle. But when he directed his gaze at her, it was genuine. Open and even kind. She avoided it.

"I feel like . . . like saying 'sorry' would be an insult. A joke. Like there's not really anything for me to do. Besides go to prison, or get strung up by the thumbs or something. I don't know."

He kneaded the place on his forearm where the prosthesis attached, just below the elbow joint. A strap looped around the upper part of his arm, and he undid and adjusted the Velcro before speaking again.

"You know why this place is called The De Soto?"

She shook her head, worried that now he would think she was the incurious type, who never wondered why anything was called anything. Why hadn't she wondered that?

"It's after Hernando de Soto," he said. "He's buried in the lake here. Supposedly. You know Lake Chicot, right over that way? His men sank the body so Indians wouldn't know he wasn't a god. Native Americans."

"You do what you got to do," she said. "Was he the guy looking for the Fountain of Youth?"

"Just gold, I think."

A man entered the bar, a leathery skeleton of indeterminate age in camouflage cargo shorts. He nodded at Fisher, who nodded back. He took a stool near the TV and Portia grinned and said, "Look at this old rustler, I thought you died." The air conditioner wheezed and sputtered.

"That guy used to work at the corner store," Fisher said. "He got fired for stealing porno mags."

"You do what you got to do," she said.

He laughed and cracked his neck. She was glad to make him laugh.

"Anyway," he said. "What exactly are we doing here?"

"What do you mean?"

"I mean, it's pretty weird circumstances."

"Right."

"But it feels like a date."

"Uh," she said.

"So I'm thinking, how all does this work? Am I trying to score a pity date from the cute woman who put my dog down?"

"It's not a pity date."

"Is it a date?"

"I don't know."

She wanted to look around the bar, in case there was a life preserver in reach, or a convenient method of suicide. But she was afraid to break eye contact with him. His elbows were posted on the edge of the table. He looked at her and didn't speak.

"This is just, I'm getting you a beer," she said. "Like people do when something happens. I know it's stupid and inadequate. If I was you I'd want to kill me. But you seem nice and I feel like shit. So I guess this is a pity party for me."

"Right," he said. "That's about right."

"Right," she said. Her stomach twisted into surgical knots. "And I hoped you'd like this shirt, I guess."

He sat back and finished his beer.

"Do you want another one?" he asked.

"Yeah," she said. "I'll get it"

"I'll get it."

As soon as he turned his back, she took a napkin from the dispenser and wiped her eyes. The window across from her was too dusty to provide a reflection, but the napkin came away clear of makeup. At the bar, Portia was doing a crossword, and Fisher waited patiently until she noticed him. He carried the bottles back to the table in his right hand, and behind his back Portia watched and gave Naomi a questioning eyebrow, her thumb held sideways on the bar. Naomi smiled at her.

"I asked her to leave the caps on," he said.

Still standing with both bottles gripped, he positioned the caps against each other. A quick slam downward sent the upper cap flying. He pushed the open beer toward her and sat down.

"One," he said. "I don't want to kill you. Two, my best friend was a

57

dog, sad as that is, and she died yesterday, so I'm a little down. And I don't blame you, or at least I can tell that I'm not going to, but I do have complicated feelings about it at the moment. Three, I do like that shirt. Can you open this?"

She opened the other beer for him. It foamed over and spilled.

"That's okay," he said. "Four. If you're getting a pity party, I don't want a pity date. I want to get pity laid."

He sipped. His mouth was cast iron and his eyes retained the sadness she'd seen in the cotton field. She waited for a grin, a tell that would alert her to the joke. After three beats she knew it wasn't coming.

"One," she said. "I'm glad you don't blame me. I think it's because you know that I know what a fuckup this is, and you're kind, and you know that I'll still torture myself. Two, I also picked this shirt because it's hot as hell everywhere in this damn town, but I'm glad you like it."

He raised his bottle to her.

"Three, nobody's getting 'pity laid.' Not by me. Not even if your other hand and your head got blown off in Iraq."

His face didn't change. He nodded his head minutely.

"Four. This is a date, if you want. That's basically insane considering how we got here, but you're probably the most eligible bachelor in town, God help us."

"Okay," he said. He laughed.

They talked about the boringness and pleasantness of baseball. They talked about war movies, good ones and bad ones. They tried to re-member the name of the Fountain of Youth guy but failed. The old men left one by one until they were alone with the bartender, and Portia brought over gin and tonics on the house, heavily garnished with lime wedges. Fisher recognized her from the shelter. He patted her arm and proposed a toast to Barbie, which he slurred slightly. Naomi supposed that a diminished body weight would increase the effect of alcohol. He apologized after spilling gin on his shirt. Portia laughed at him and left to get a rag. Fisher excused himself to go to the bathroom.

Naomi got up and propped the front door open with a cinder block. Full dark had fallen and she put the air temperature at a brisk eighty-two. She stood in the blinking neon of the window sign and had grand thoughts about how so few things in the world happened the way you expected. Those kinds of thoughts meant she was tipsy enough now to have a headache in the morning. She reentered the bar in time to see Fisher spit a chewed lime wedge back into his glass.

They took her car. In four minutes they reached his apartment, which was modest but clean, with tan carpet and new paint. A breakfast bar separated the living room from the kitchen, and he walked behind it and opened a cabinet. She sat on a corduroy sofa beneath a framed print of that Japanese woodcut where the huge waves are about to swamp the little boat.

"I hope you don't mind," he said. He set a bottle of bourbon on the counter. "I'm just going to make sure I'm drunk."

"Your house," she said. "Your rules."

"Want one?"

"Yes."

When they got to the bedroom she told herself that sex was always strange, between any two humans, anywhere on earth. She waited on top of the covers while he removed his prosthetics at the edge of the bed. Although it was too dark to see—he had made sure—she closed her eyes. After a moment she felt his weight settle next to her, then his fingertips on her clavicle.

"Do I," she said. She put her hands on her knees to stop them from shaking. "I mean, I've never, you know. Just tell me what to do."

"How should I know?" he said. "I don't know either. Should be basically the same, I think. More or less."

It was, more or less. She stayed on top, which seemed easiest, and after a few minutes her biggest worry was the heat.

"Sorry I'm sweating so much," she said.

"It's okay."

"I'm sorry."

"I heard you."

After he came they held each other for a spell, then he rolled away and fell asleep. She watched the digits change on the bedside clock, listened to cars going by on the street outside, and tried to ignore all the different parts of her brain that wanted to make pronouncements on her character, or lack thereof, her future, or lack thereof, and the mysteries of the world in general. The strain or the alcohol finally produced a throbbing headache, and after an hour spent lying awake she slipped from bed and inched through the dark, thinking of water.

In the living room she found the edge of the breakfast counter and circled around it onto the kitchen tile. Without any idea where a light switch might be, she opened the refrigerator, and fluorescent light washed over the cabinets. The cool air felt good on her skin, and the light reached into the far corner where a blue dog bowl sat almost empty. It occurred to her to make a gesture. Though the refrigerator was nearly desolate it did have a filtered water pitcher on the top shelf, and she took it out. The bowl was too far to reach, so she leaned across the kitchen, one hand holding the door open to keep the light on, the other straining to extend the pitcher as far as she could. Her arm shook. She tilted the spout toward the bowl. The water came out in a smooth stream that sparkled in the light, splashed off the lip, and spilled onto the floor.

ELDER JINKS

fiction by EDITH PEARLMAN

Grace and Gustave were married in August, in Gustave's home—a squat, brown-shingled house whose deep front porch darkened the downstairs rooms. The house lot had ample space for a side garden. But there were only rhododendrons and azaleas, hugging the building, and a single apple tree stranded in the middle of the lawn. Every May Gustave dragged lawn chairs from the garage to the apple tree and placed them side by side by side. When Grace first saw this array, in July, she was reminded of a nursing home, though she wouldn't say anything so hurtful to Gustave—a man easily bruised; you could tell that from the way he flushed when he took a wrong turn, say, or forgot a proper name. So she simply crossed the grass and moved one of the chaises so that it angled against another, and then adjusted the angle. "They're snuggling now." The third chair she overturned. Gustave later righted it.

They had met in June in front of a pair of foxes who made their own reluctant home at Bosky's Wild Animal Farm on Cape Cod. Gustave was visiting his sister in her rented cottage. Grace had driven in from western Massachusetts with her pal Henrietta. The two women were camping in the State Park.

"You're living in a tent?" inquired Gustave on that fateful afternoon. "You look as fresh as a flower."

"Which flower?" Grace was a passionate amateur gardener as well as a passionate amateur actress and cook and hostess. Had she ever practiced a profession? Yes, long ago; she'd been a second-grade teacher until her own children came along to claim her attention.

"Which flower? A hydrangea," answered Gustave, surprised at his own exhilaration. "Your eyes," he explained, further surprised, this time at his rising desire.

Her tilted eyes were indeed a violet-blue. Her skin was only slightly lined. Her gray hair was clasped by a hinged comb that didn't completely contain its abundance. Her figure was not firm, but what could you expect.

"I'm Grace," she said.

"I'm Gustave," he said. He took an impulsive breath. "I'd like to get to know you."

She smiled. "And I you."

Grace was employing a rhetorical locution popular in her Northampton crowd—eclipsis: the omission of words easily supplied. Gustave, after a pause, silently supplied them. Then he bowed. (His late mother was Paris-born; he honored her Gallic manners even though—except for five years teaching in a Rouen lycée—he had lived his entire life in the wedge of Boston called Godolphin.)

Grace hoped that this small man bending like a headwaiter would now brush her fingers with his mustache—but no. Instead he informed her that he was a professor. His subject was the history of science. Her eyes widened—a practiced maneuver, though also sincere. Back in Northampton her friends, there were scores of them, included weavers, therapists, advocates of holistic medicine, singers. And of course professors. But the history of science, the fact that science even had a history—somehow it had escaped her notice. Copernicus? Oh, Newton, and Einstein, yes, and Watson-and-What's-his-name. "Crick," she triumphantly produced, cocking her head in the flirtatious way . . .

"Is your neck bothering you?"

. . . that Hal Karsh had hinted was no longer becoming. She straightened her head and shook hands like a lady.

Gustave had written a biography of Michael Faraday, a famous scientist in the nineteenth century, though unknown to Grace. When he talked about this uneducated bookbinder, inspired by his own intuition, Gustave's slight pomposity melted into affection. When he mentioned his dead wife he displayed a thinner affection, but he had apparently been a widower a long time.

In Northampton Grace volunteered at a shelter, tending children who only irregularly went to school. "Neglected kids, all-but-abandoned by their mothers, mothers themselves abandoned by the kids' fathers," she said. Gustave winced. When she went on to describe the necessity of getting onto the floor with these youngsters, instructor and pupils both cross-legged on scabby linoleum, Gustave watched her playfulness deepen into sympathy. She'd constructed an indoor windowbox high up in the makeshift basement schoolroom; she taught the life cycle of the daffodil, "its biography, so to speak," including some falsities that Gustave gently pointed out. Grace nodded in gratitude. "I never actually studied botany in my university," she confessed. The University of Wichita, she specified; later she would mention the University of Wyoming; but perhaps he had misheard one or the other—he'd always been vague about the West.

A lawyer friend of Gustave's performed the wedding ceremony in the dark living room. Afterwards Grace sipped champagne under the apple tree with Gustave's sister. "Oh Grace, how peaceable you look. You'll glide above his little tantrums."

"What?" said Grace, trying to turn toward her new sister-in-law but unable to move her head on her shoulders. A Godolphin hairdresser had advised the severe French twist that pulled cruelly at her nape; Henrietta had urged the white tulle sombrero; Grace herself had selected the dress, hydrangea blue and only one size too small. Her grandchildren, who with their parents had taken the red-eye from San Francisco, marveled at the transformation of their tatterdemalion Gammy—but where had her hair gone to? "What?" said the stiffened Grace again; but Gustave's sister forbore to elaborate, just as she had failed to mention that Gustave's first wife, who had died last January in Rouen, had divorced him decades ago, influenced by a French pharmacist she'd fallen in love with.

Gustave and Grace honeymooned in Paris, indulging themselves mightily—a hotel with a courtyard, starred restaurants, a day in Givergny, another in Versailles. They even attended a lecture on the new uses of benzene—Gustave interested in the subject; Grace, with little French and less science, interested in the sombre crowd assembled at the

Pasteur Institute. They both loved the new Promenade and the new Musée, and they sat in Saint Chapelle for two hours listening to a concert performed on old instruments—two recorders and a lute and a viola-da-gamba. That was the most blissful afternoon. Gustave put the disarray of their hotel room out of his mind, and also the sometimes fatiguing jubilation with which Grace greeted each new venture. Grace dismissed her own irritation at Gustave's habit of worrying about every dish on the menu—did it matter how much cream, how much butter, we all had to die of something. Light streamed through the radiant window, turning into gold his trim mustache, her untidy chignon.

And now it was September, and classes had begun. Gustave taught Physics for Poets Mondays, Wednesdays and Fridays at nine, The Uses of Chemistry those same days at ten. He taught a graduate seminar in the Philosophy of Science on Thursday evenings. The first two weeks the seminar met in the usual drafty classroom. But then Grace suggested . . . Gustave demurred . . . she persisted . . . he surrendered. And so on the third week the seminar met in the brown-shingled house. Grace baked two apple tarts and served them with warm currant jelly. The students relived last Saturday's football game. Gustave—who, like Grace, professed a hatred of football—quietly allowed the conversation to continue until everyone had finished the treat, then turned the talk to Archimedes. Grace sat in a corner of the living room, knitting.

The next day marked their first separation since the wedding. Gustave had a conference in Chicago. He'd take a cab to the airport right after the Uses of Chemistry. Early that morning he'd packed necessary clothing in one half of his briefcase. While he was reading the newspaper she slipped in a wedge of apple tart, wrapped in tinfoil. After they kissed at the doorway his eye wandered to the corner she had occupied on the previous evening. The chair was still strewn with knitting books and balls of yarn and the garment she was working on, no doubt a sweater for him. She'd already made him a gray one. This wool was rose. His gaze returned to his smiling wife. "See you on Sunday," he said.

"Oh, I'll miss you."

She did miss him, immediately. She would have continued to miss him if she had not been invaded, half an hour later, by two old Northampton friends bearing Hal Karsh. Hal was visiting from his current perch in Barcelona. He would return to Spain on Sunday. Hal—

master of the broken villanelle, inventor of the thirteen-line sonnet; and oh, that poetic hair brushing his eyebrows, hair still mostly brown though he was only eight years younger than Grace. Those long fingers, adept at pen and piano but not at keyboard—the word processor was death to composition, he'd tell you, and tell you why, too, at length, anywhere, even in bed.

Gustave's upright piano could have used a tuning. Grace had meant to call someone, but she had been too busy putting in chrysanthemums and ordering bulbs and trying to revive her high-school French. The foursome made music anyway. Lee and Lee, the couple who brought Hal, had brought their fiddles too. Grace rummaged in a box of stuff not yet unpacked and found her recorder. Later she brewed chili. They raided Gustave's *cave*. They finally fell into bed—Lee and Lee in the spare room, Hal on the floor in Gustave's study, Grace, still dressed, on the marital bed. Then on Saturday they drove to Walden Pond, and to the North Shore; and on Saturday night Cambridge friends came across the river. This time Grace made minestrone, in a different pan— the crock encrusted with chili still rested on the counter.

Hal wondered what Grace was doing in a gloomy house in a town that allowed no overnight parking. Such a regulation indicated a punitive atmosphere. And this husband so abruptly acquired—who was he, anyway? "She picked him up in a zoo, in front of a lynx," Lee and Lee told him. He hoped they were exercising their artistic habit of distortion. Hal loved Grace, with the love of an indulged younger brother, or a ragtag colleague—years ago he and she had taught at the same experimental grade school, the one that demanded dedication from its faculty but didn't care about degrees. (Hal did have a master's, but Grace had neglected to go to college.) Hal thought Grace was looking beautiful but unsettled. Did her new spouse share her taste for illicit substances, did he know of her occasional need to decamp without warning? She always came back. . . . When Hal had mentioned that the Cambridge folks would bring grass, Grace's eyes danced. Well, nowadays it was less easy to get here. In Barcelona you could pick it up at your tobacconist, though sometimes the stuff was filthy. . . .

This batch was fine. They all talked as they smoked; and recited poetry; and after a while played Charades. It was like the old times, he thought. He wished Henrietta had come along, too. "I have no use for that fussbudget she married," Henrietta had snapped. But the fussbudget was in Chicago.

It was like the old times, Grace, too, was thinking. And how clever they all were at the game; how particularly clever in this round, Lee and Lee standing naked back to back while she, fully clothed, traversed the living room floor on her belly. Odd that no one had yet guessed "New Deal." Odd too that no one was talking, though a few moments earlier there had been such merry laughter; and Hal, that man of parts, had put two of his fingers into his mouth and whistled. At Lee? Or at Lee? In silence Grace slithered toward the hall, and saw, at eye level, a pair of polished shoes. Pressed trousers rose above the shoes. She raised her head, as an eel never could—perhaps she now resembled a worm, ruining the tableau. The belt around the trousers was Gustave's—yes, she had given it to him; it had a copper buckle resembling a sunburst within which bulged an oval turquoise. When it was hanging from his belt rack among lengths of black and brown leather with discreet matching buckles, the thing looked like a deity, Lord of the closet; now, above dark pants, below striped shirt, it looked like a sartorial error, a *mésalliance....*

Scrambling to her feet she found herself staring at Gustave's shirt. Where was his jacket? Oh, the night was warm, he must have taken it off before silently entering the house fifteen hours before he was expected. Her gaze slid sideways. Yes, he had placed—not thrown—his jacket on the hall chair; he had placed—not dropped—his briefcase next to that chair. She looked again at her husband. His exposed shirt bore a large stain in a rough triangular shape—the shape, she divined, of a wedge of tart. She touched it with a trembling forefinger.

"That tender little gift of yours—it leaked," he said.

He surveyed his living room. That naked couple had attended his wedding, had drunk his champagne. A pair of know-it-alls. Their names rhymed. The other creatures he had never seen before. A skinny fellow with graying bangs advanced toward him.

"Gustave, I want you to meet—" Grace began.

"Ask these people to leave," he said in a growl she had never before heard.

They seeped away like spilled pudding . . . Lee and Lee, first, dressed in each other's clothing, clutching their overnight cases and instruments, kissing Hal on their rush toward their car and its overnight parking tickets. They didn't kiss Grace. The Cambridge crowd didn't kiss anybody. But Hal—he stood his ground. He was a head taller than Gustave. He extended a hand. "I'm—"

"Good-bye."

"Listen here—"

"Get out!"

He got out, with his satchel in his left hand and, in the curve of his right arm, Grace. At the last minute she turned as if to look at Gustave, to plead with him, maybe—but it was only to snatch up her pocket-book from the hall table. Next to the pocketbook she saw a cone of flowers. Sweet peas, baby's breath, a single gerbera. An unimaginative bouquet; he must have picked it up ready-made at the airport stall.

Gustave climbed the stairs. The guests had apparently cavorted mostly on the first floor; except for the two unmade beds in the spare room, the only sign of their occupation were towels like puddles on the bathroom tiles. He went into his study and his eye flew to the bookcase where, in manuscript between thick bindings, stood his biography of Faraday, still in search of a publisher. No one had stolen it. On the carpet lay a book—open, face down. He leaned over and identified it as a Spanish grammar. He kicked it.

Downstairs again, he heated some minestrone—he had not eaten anything since his abrupt decision to abandon that boring conference and come home early. The soup was tasty. He looked for a joint—how sweet the house still smelled—but the crowd had apparently sucked their whole stash. He did find, in one corner, a recorder, but he couldn't smoke that. He put all the plates and glasses into the dishwasher. He tried to scrub the remains of chili from a pot, then left it to soak. He vacuumed. Then he went upstairs again, and undressed; and, leaving his clothes on the floor—these gypsy ways were catching—slipped into Grace's side of the bed. With a sigh he recognized as an old man's, he flopped onto his back. His thoughts—which were uncharitable—did not keep him from falling asleep.

But a few hours later he found himself awake. He got up and went through the house again. He threw the Spanish grammar into the trash bag he had stuffed earlier and lugged the thing out to the garage, knowing that anyone who saw him in his striped pajamas under the flood light at three o'clock in the morning would take him for a madman. So what. Their neighbors considered them a cute couple; he had overheard that demeaning epithet at the fish market. He'd rather be crazy than cute. He relocked the garage and returned to the house. And surely he had been deranged to marry a woman because of her alluring eyes. He'd mistaken a frolicsome manner for lasting charm. She was merely frivolous; and the minute she was left unsupervised. . . . He stomped into the living room. That rose-colored garment-in-progress now shared its chair with a wine bottle, good vineyard, good year . . . empty. He'd like to rip the knitting out. The yarn would remain whorled; he'd wind it loosely into a one big whorl. When she came back she'd find a replica of Faraday's induction coil, pink. Come back? She could come back to collect her clothing and her paella pan and the bulbs she kept meaning to plant. He picked up the sweater. It would fit a ten-year-old. Insulting color, insulting size . . . he went back to bed, and lay there.

Grace, too, was awake. The hotel room was dark and malodorous. Hal slept at her side without stirring, without snoring. He had always been a devoted sleeper. He was devoted to whatever brought him pleasure. Under no circumstances would she accompany him to Barcelona, as he had idly suggested last night. (He had also suggested that she buy the drinks at the hotel bar downstairs; she supposed she'd have to pay for the room, too.) Anyway, she had left her passport next to Gustave's in his top drawer. She hoped he'd send it back to her in Northampton— she had not yet sold her house there, thank goodness, thank providence, thank Whoever was in charge. She hoped he'd send all her things, without obsessive comment. She wanted no more of him. She wanted no more of Hal, either: it was enough that she had shared his toothbrush last night, and then his bed, and was now sleeping—well, failing to sleep—in one of his un-laundered shirts.

How hideous to have only yesterday's lingerie. Unshaved underarms were one thing: grotty underpants quite another. What time did stores open on Sundays? She'd slip out and shop, get a new sweater, maybe— that would pick up her spirits. She remembered the half-finished vest for her granddaughter she'd left on the chair; she hoped Gustave would send that back, too. . . .

"Amelie. . . ." muttered Hal.

"Grace," she corrected.

If only she were back in Northampton already, where everyone was needy and she was needed. She wished she had never visited that Wild Animal Farm at the Cape, had never paused to look at those foxes. She wished she had not married a man because he was learned and polite, especially since he had turned out to be pedantic and sanctimonious.

68

From time to time that Sunday Gustave thought of calling the lawyer
who'd married them—she happened to specialize in divorce. Instead
he read the papers; and watched the football game. What a sport: force
directed by intelligence. He prepared for tomorrow's class, the one in
which he and the students would reproduce one of Faraday's earliest
experiments in electrification. They'd all come carrying foil-wrapped
water-filled film canisters with a protruding nail. These were primitive
Leyden jars in which to store electricity. The electricity would be produced by a Styrofoam dinner plate nested in an aluminum pie pan—the
kids would bring these friction-makers too. He went to bed early. He
could see a low autumnal moon above the mansard across the street—
well, only the upper half of the sphere was visible, but he could supply
the rest.

Grace bought, among other things, a yellow sweater. She took her time
getting back to the hotel. She found Hal showered and smiling. During
a long walk by the river she listened to his opinions on magic realism
and antomasia—she'd forgotten what that was, she admitted. "The use
of an epithet instead of a proper name," Hal said. "'The Fussbudget,'
say. . . ." He told her of the Spanish medieval farsa, which was related
to farce. And just when she thought her aching head would explode it
was time to put him into a cab to the airport. He seemed to have enough
cash for the taxi. He thrust his head out of the open window as the
vehicle left the curb. "My apartment is near Las Ramblas, best location
in Barcelona," he called. She waved. The cab disappeared, and her
headache with it.

   She went back to their room, now hers, and read the papers, and
enjoyed a solitary supper in front of the TV, watching a replay of that
afternoon's football game. Nice intercept! Such brave boys, there on
the screen. But Gustave had been brave too, hadn't he, scorning *savoir
faire* as he cleansed his house of unwelcome revelers. How red his face
had become when Hal theatrically held out his hand . . . he'd felt
wronged, hadn't he, or perhaps *in* the wrong; maybe he thought she'd
summoned her friends, maybe he thought he'd failed her. If she ever
saw him again she'd tell him about Hal's lonely rootlessness. She'd tell
him about poor Lee and Lee's barn of unsaleable paintings, if she ever
saw him again. . . . She put on her new nightgown and went to bed. She

could see a curve of the dome of the Massachusetts State House, just enough to suggest the whole.

The lecture room was shaped like a triangle. The platform holding lectern and lab bench was at the apex, the lowest part of the room; concentric rows of slightly curved tables radiated upwards toward the back. Three students sat at each table. The professor stood at the lectern when he talked, moved to his lab bench for demonstrating. He and the students employed their identical home-made equipment. As he talked and demonstrated—creating the electric charge, storing it—the students imitated. There was expectant laughter and an occasional excited remark and a general air of satisfaction. Only a few of these poets might change course and become physicists; but not one of them would hold science in contempt. "Faraday made this experiment with equally crude apparatus," he reminded them. "And with faith that it would work. Faith—so unfashionable now—was his mainstay."

The woman in the back row, alone at a table, without pie plate or film can, wished that she, too, had the implements, that she could obey the instructions of the measured, kindly voice; but mostly she marveled again at the story that voice was telling of the humble young Faraday setting himself upon his life's journey. "He considered that God's presence was revealed in nature's design," wound up the little man. He looked radiant.

When he at last noticed the figure in the yellow sweater, he was cast back to an afternoon in Paris when the same glowing color had been produced by sun refracted through stained glass; and the lips of his companion had parted as she listened to winds and strings send music aloft. She had thrilled; she had become elevated; she had generously carried him with her. . . .

The lecture concluded to applause; the teen-agers dispersed; the professor materialized in the chair next to the visitor's.

They looked at each other for a while.

"I'm Grace," she said at last.

"I'm Gustave," and how his heart leaped. "I'd like to . . . get to know you."

Another long pause while he belatedly considered the dangers in so ambitious an enterprise; for he, too, would have to be known, and his shabby secrets revealed, and his out-of-date convictions as well. They'd

70

endure necessary disappointments, and they'd practice necessary forgiveness, careful to note which subjects left the other fraught. Grace's mind moved along the same lines. Each elected to take the risk. Gustave showed his willingness by touching the lovely face, Grace hers by disdaining eclipsis. "Me, too," was all she said.

GINA'S DEATH

fiction by CHARLES BAXTER

A squirrel squatted in the birdbath. Another squirrel was hanging by its claws onto the bird feeder. The girl, looking out her bedroom window at the back yard, cleaned her fingernails halfheartedly with the nail file and thought of the end-of-the-world that didn't happen on January 1, 2000, and the one that did happen twenty-one months later, and then she wondered why, if there was a word, "ruthless," that was often applied to enemies of the USA, then what happened to its opposite, its lost positive, "ruth," which would have to mean "kind," but didn't mean anything because no one used it? We had ruthless enemies but no ruth friends.

If some people were "unruly," then who was "ruly"? Nobody. When her room was messy, her mother said it was "unkempt," but when it was clean, it was never "kempt" because the word didn't exist—everybody had a word for the wrong thing but silence prevailed for the right. When her room was clean, it wasn't anything you would put into words. It was wordless.

Early in the morning, just after the sun was up, the squirrels looked like boys, somehow, she couldn't say why. Maybe because of the way they moved, skittering and chasing each other, twitching. Or maybe it was the fur. Something.

Her name was Gina, she was sixteen years old, and it was Sunday, Family Day. After staring at the squirrels, she remembered to feed her guinea pig his breakfast food pellets. Wilbur squeaked and squealed softly as she dropped the pellets down the cage bars into the red plastic tray. It didn't take much to make him happy.

On the other side of her room was a picture of Switzerland her mom had put up years ago. The picture had a lake in it, which was ruthlessly blue. Gina felt funny when she looked at this picture, so she didn't look at it very often. She couldn't take it down because her mom had given it to her.

Family Day. The plan was, her dad would show up and take them—her brother, her mom, herself—to the beach. Gina threw on a T-shirt and a pair of jeans. She grabbed her flute and went into the basement to practice for the school marching band, of which she was a member.

       ❖   ❖   ❖

Ten minutes later she heard the thud of the morning newspaper flung against the front screen door. Gina put her flute on top of her dad's workbench (he had never bothered to move it to his apartment after he moved out) and went upstairs to read the headlines. The news consisted of Iraq (bombs), Cuba (jails), Ireland (more bombs), and then there was something about Gordy Himmelman.

Gordy Himmelman! He had shot himself. To death. It was permanent. Why hadn't anyone called her about it?

She had been in classes with Gordy Himmelman since kindergarten, but he was in a class by himself, and she hadn't seen much of him since he had dropped out. He muttered and swore and blew his nose on notebook paper, and he talked to himself in long strings of garble and never had any friends you could show in public. You could feel sorry for him, but he would never notice how sorry you felt, and he wouldn't care. Pity was lost on him. It was a total waste of time. In third grade he had brought a penlight battery into school and, standing next to the monkey bars, he had swallowed it during recess to attract attention to himself. The battery was only a double-A, but even so. He had black-and-blue marks all over him most days. His breath smelled of dill pickles that had gone unfresh. You couldn't even talk to him about the weather because he never noticed it—it didn't make any difference to him what the sky was doing or how it was doing it. He had this human-junkyard don't-mess-with-me look on his face and would kick anyone who got in his way, though he did have one comic routine: slugging himself in the face so hard that his head jerked backward. He had bicycled to that teacher Mr. Bernstein's house, where he had blown his brains out in the yard, in front of a tree, in the morning, a matinee suicide. On the front page of the paper was a picture of the tree. It was a color picture, and you could sort of see the blood if you looked closely.

There hadn't been a suicide note. A suicide note would have been like a writing assignment. Way too hard. He would have had to get his aunt to write it for him.

Gina felt something stirring inside her. She was kind of interested in death. Gordy was the first person she'd ever known who had entered it. He had gone from being Mr. Nothing to being Mr. Something Else: a temporarily interesting person. She sat at the kitchen counter eating her strawberry Pop-Tart, wondering whether Gordy was lying on a bed surrounded by virgins, or eternal fire, or what.

It was sort of cool, him doing that. Maybe the smartest thing he'd ever done. Adventuresome and courageous.

If you didn't have a life maybe you got one by being dead.

✵   ✵   ✵

Her dad was late. Finally he showed up at eleven-thirty in his red Durango, saying, "Ha ha, I'm late." He and Gina's mom were divorced, but they were still "friends," and her dad had never really committed himself to the divorce, in Gina's opinion. He was halfhearted about it, a romantic sad sack. They had cooked up this Family Day scheme two years ago. Every weekend he'd come to pick up Gina and Bertie, her little brother, and their mom—Gina envied most divorced kids who went from their moms to their dads, without the cheesiness of Family Day—and then they'd do bowling-type activities for the sake of togetherness and friendliness, which of course was a total fraud since they weren't together or friendly at all. Usually Saturday was Family Day but sometimes Sunday was. Today they were going to the beach. Wild excitement. She had meant to bring a magazine.

✵   ✵   ✵

In the car, Gina studied her father's face. She had wanted to drive, but no one trusted her behind the wheel. For once she had been allowed to sit up front: semi-adult, now that she had filled out and like that, so they gave her front seat privileges sometimes, occasional woman-privileges. Her mom and Bertie were in the back, Bertie playing with his GameBoy, her mom with her earphones on, listening to music so she wouldn't have to hear the plinks and plunks of the GameBoy, or talk to her ex, Gina's dad, the driver, half committed to his divorce, an undecided single man, driving the car. He would fully commit to the divorce when he found a girlfriend he really liked, which he hadn't, yet. Gina had met one of the girlfriends whom he had only half liked, a woman who tried way too hard to be nice, and who looked like a minor character on a soap opera who would eventually be hit by a rampaging bus.

Gina had mentioned Gordy Himmelman to her dad, and her dad had said yeah, it was way too bad.

She was interested in her father's face. Because it was her father's, she didn't know if he was handsome or plain. You couldn't always tell when they were your parents, though with her friend Gretchen Mullen you sure could, since Gretchen's father looked like a hobgoblin. At first she thought her own father had a sort of no-brand standard-issue father face; now she wasn't so sure.

He was possibly handsome. There was no way of knowing. Her dad was a master plumber. Therefore his hands often had cuts or grease under the fingernails. Very large hands, made big by genetic fate. His hair was short and brown, cut so it bristled, and near his temples you could see a change in color, salty. On his right cheek her dad had a crease, as if his skin had been cut by a knife or a sharp piece of paper, but it was only a wrinkle, a wrinkle getting started, the first canal in a network of creases-to-come, his face turning slowly but surely into Mars, the Red Planet. His teeth were very white and even, the most Rock Star thing about him. His eyes were brown and spaced wide apart, not narrow the way teenage boys' eyes are usually narrow, and they drilled into you so that sometimes you had to turn away so you wouldn't be injured by the Father Look. Her father's beard line was so distinct and straight, it looked put in with a ruler and was so heavy that even if he shaved in the morning, he usually needed another shave around dinnertime. That was interestingly bearlike about the masculine father-type. His nose was exciting. His breath had a latent smell of cigarettes, which he smoked in private. You couldn't find the boy in him anymore. It wasn't there. He was growing a belly from the beer he drank at night and weekends, and most of the time he seemed comfortable with it, though it seemed to tire him out also. He didn't smile much and only when he had to. He had once told Gina, "Life is serious."

On winter weekends he watched football on television speechlessly.

He looked like a plumber on a TV show who comes in halfway through the program and who someone, though not the main character, falls in love with, because he's so manly and can replace faucet washers. He would be the kind of plumber who wise-cracks and makes the whole studio audience break up, but he would be charming, too, when he had to be. But then sometimes at a stoplight or when he saw a car pull in front of him, her dad's face changed out of its TV sitcom expression:

suddenly he grimaced like someone had started to do surgery on him right over his heart without anaesthetic, and he was pretending that nothing was happening to him even though his chest was being opened, bared to fresh air. And then that expression vanished like it had never been there. What was that about? His pain. His secret squirrel life, probably.

Still, there was no point in talking to him about Gordy Himmelman.

*　*　*

At the lake they settled in on their beach towels. Bertie, who was oblivious to everything, went on playing with his GameBoy. Gina's mom stretched out on her back in an effort to douse herself with lethal tanning rays. Her dad carried the picnic basket into the shade and started to read his copy of *Car and Driver*, sitting on the picnic table bench. Gina went to the concession stand to get herself an ice cream cone, which she would buy with her own money.

The stand itself had been constructed out of concrete blocks, painted white, covered overhead by a cheap corrugated roof. Under it, everything seemed to be sun-baking. Behind the counter was a popcorn machine with a high-intensity yellow heat lamp shining on the popped kernels in their little glass house, making them look radioactive. The sidewalk leading up to and away from the stand, stained with the residue of spilled pink ice cream and ketchup, felt sticky on the soles of Gina's feet. The kid who worked at the stand, selling snack food and renting canoes, was a boy she didn't recognize, about her age, maybe a year or two older, with short orange hair and an earring, and he stood behind the counter next to the candy bar display, staring with pain and boredom at the floor. He was experiencing summer job agony. He had a rock station blaring from his battery-operated radio perched on top of the freezer, and his body twitched quietly to the beat. When Gina appeared, the boy looked at her with relief, relief followed by recognition and sympathy, recognition and sympathy followed by a leer as he checked out her tits, the leer followed by a friendly smirk. It all happened very fast. He was like other boys: they shifted gears so quickly you couldn't always follow them into those back roads and dense forests where they wanted to live with the other varmints and wolves.

Raspberry, please, single scoop. She smiled at him, to tease him, to test out her power, to give him an anguished memory tonight, when he was in bed and couldn't sleep, thinking of her, in the density of his empty, stupid life.

Walking back to the sand and holding her ice cream cone, she started to think about Gordy Himmelman, and when she did, the crummy lake and the public beach with the algae floating in it a hundred feet off-shore in front of her, she felt weird and dizzy, as if: what was the point? She kept walking and taking an occasional, personal, lick at the ice cream. There weren't too many other people on the sand, but most of the men were fat, and their wives or girlfriends were fat, too, and al-ready they had started to yell at each other, even though it was just barely lunchtime.

She kept walking. It was something to do. Nobody here was beauti-ful. It all sucked.

The lake gave her a funny feeling, just the fact that it was there. The sky was sky blue, and her mother had said it was a perfect day, but if this was a perfect day, if this was the best that God could manage with the available materials, then . . . well, no wonder Gordy Himmelman had shot himself, and no wonder her mother had put up that picture of Switzerland in her bedroom. Gina saw her whole life stretched out in front of her, just like that, the fifty-two deck of cards with Family Day printed on one side, like the picture of the lake in Switzerland that she could barely stand to glance at, vacuuming her up. Why couldn't any-thing ever be perfect? It just wasn't possible. This wasn't perfect: it was its opposite, fect. A totally fect day. Just to the side, off on another beach towel, somebody's mom was yelling at and then slapping a little boy. Slapping him, wham wham wham, out in public and in front of everybody, and of course the kid was screaming now, screaming scream-ing screaming screaming.

Everybody having their own version of Family Day.

Gina carried the ice cream cone to the water's edge.

Right there, she saw herself in the algaed water, walking upside down holding a raspberry ice cream cone, and, next to her own water-image, another water-image, the sun this time. Gina walked into the water out to where the algae dispersed, staring first at her diminishing reflection and then at the sun. It'd be interesting to get blind, she thought, people and Seeing Eye dogs would take care of you and lead you through the rest of your life forever. You'd be on a leash. The dog would make all the big decisions. Then she noticed that when she walked into the water her images were sucked into it. As the water got deeper, there was less of you above it, as if you had gone on an instant diet. Okay, now that her legs had disappeared, she didn't have to look at her legs, be-cause they weren't there anymore. Well, they were underwater, but the water was so dirty she couldn't see them as well as she could see her reflection at the surface: of her waist, her head, her chest, the ice cream cone. She wished she were prettier, movie pretty, but walking into the water was a kind of solution, watching your girl-image get all swallowed up, until there was no image left, just the water.

She held the ice cream cone above the water and then after another lick let it go as she went under.

Under the surface she held her breath as long as she could, and then she thought of Gordy Himmelman, and, sort of experimentally, she tried breathing in some water, just to see what it was like, and she choked. She felt herself panicking and going up to the surface but then she fought the panic when she imagined she saw somebody like Gordy Himmelman, though better looking, more like her dad, under the water with her, holding her hand and telling her it was better down here, and all the problems were solved, so she tried to relax and breathe in a little more water. She registered little thunderbolts of panic, then some peace, then panic. Then it was all right, and Family Day was finally over, and, because she wasn't a very good swimmer anyway, she began to sink to the bottom, though there were all those annoying voices. She would miss Wilbur, the guinea pig, but not much else, not even the boys who had tried to feel her up.

She drifted down and away.

Her father and the lifeguard had seen the cone for the raspberry ice cream floating on the surface of the lake at the same time. They both rushed in, and Gina's dad reached her body first. He pulled her up, thrashed his way to the beach, where, without thinking, he gave his daughter a Heimlich maneuver. Water erupted out of her mouth. Gina's eyes opened, and her father laid her down on the sand, and she said, "Gordy?" but what she said was garbled by the water still coming out of her lungs into her mouth and out of her mouth into the sand. As she came around, her hair falling around her eyes, she seemed disarrayed somehow, but pleased by all the fuss, and then she smiled, because she had seen her father's face, smeary with love.

WHAT IT IS

fiction by JOAN CONNOR

They met at a conference. It doesn't matter what sort of conference. It was a hardware conference, say, at a Holiday Inn. They mingled among the bins of nails, keyhole saws, socket wrenches. He liked the way she hefted her hammer. She liked the way he tested the haft of his chisel against his palm. They were professionals; they knew their tools, their monkey wrenches from their vise grips, their Phillips-heads from their screwdrivers. The nuts and bolts of life. They introduced themselves. He did exteriors; she did interiors. They lived far apart. As two professional lonely people, they liked that about each other. They could build a bridge to span their solitariness but keep their trestles separate. He thought she looked competent. She thought he looked cute. He liked the cut of her nail apron. She thought his T-bar was cute. They exchanged business cards and half-hearted promises to meet somewhere sometime. She thought his promise was cute. Before he headed home, he gave her a copy of his recent manual, *How To Build A Lean-To*.

She read it on the plane. The guy really knew his stuff. His plumb line dropped straight. His corners were true. She thought, hmm.

Courtship in the computer age. A reticulating web of options, electronic avenues: e-mail, voice mail, mail, airmail, answering machines, the overnight expressways to your heart.

She e-mailed a careful compliment: I liked your book, *How To Build A Lean-To*, especially the section on slanted roofs. Your paragraph on gradients and outwitting ice build-up was profound.

He e-mailed back: Thank you.

She e-mailed back: You're welcome. I just reread the section on ice jams and the life span of the twenty-year shingle. No one else has ever before explored this topic with such sensitivity yet thoroughness.

He e-mailed back: I'm a sensitive guy. And may I say with Excruciating Politeness that I could not help but notice that you are an architectural gem?

She e-mailed him back with the compliment that he seemed structurally sound himself.

He e-mailed: Thank you. Let's stay in touch.

She e-mailed him an expurgated autobiography of her life to date.

When he received it, he didn't have time to read it thoroughly because he was en route to see his girlfriend, Marla, the computer programmer who was telling him to get with the program or delete. He didn't like ultimata. While Marla sketched out her blueprint for his future, he found himself reflecting on slanted roofs, ice jams losing their grip and sheeting to the ground in glorious January sun. It *was* a good section, he realized. It was in fact profound.

She sent him a carefully selected card, an etched Escher print that played with the architecture of perspective. The woman pins laundry. The man stares above the terraced hill at the sky. They are as alien to each other in the building they cohabit as Hopper figures in separate paintings: Sunday Morning. Gas. The man contemplates; the woman pins clothes. Marine plant life blooms impossibly in a gallery garden.

He sent her a postcard, telling her that his new book, *Building a Snow-fence, Slat by Slat* was out.

She sent him a note thanking him, a carefully selected box of small chocolate hammers, two tins of cookies, and a hand-braided belt. She ordered a copy of his new manual.

He left a message on her answering machine, thanking her.

She left a message on his, inviting him to come visit.

He e-mailed her saying that he couldn't visit just now, because he was putting a greenhouse on his garage.

She e-mailed back that she was building a hope chest and she'd send him the plans. She sent him the plans.

He called to thank her answering machine.

"Hello," she said.

"Hello," he said. "This is Conroy Cardamom."

"Oh my," she said.

"Oh yes," he said.

They started talking long into the night. They started talking around their short-term plans. They told each other stories which featured themselves as heroes. They put on their best faces and forth their best feet. They sketched the blueprints.

Hmm, he thought.

Hmm, she thought.

This guy/gal really likes me.

Hmm, she thought.

Hmm, he thought.

This gal/guy is really smart. This guy/gal has great taste in men/women.

She express-mailed him pickled doves' eggs, four-leaf clovers, falling stars, mermaid songs in pale pink conch shells, and the completed hope chest.

He sent her a signed copy of, *Your Friend the Retractable Tape Measure.*

She sent him a hand-carved trompe l'oeil tablecloth of ormolu. She sent him fudge, butter cookies, ladies fingers. *Feed him, feed him, she thought.*

He wasn't home to receive the package because he was off with Marla, arguing about their future. But when he got home and found the box, he thought: This has gone on long enough. He called her. "I'm coming," he said.

"Finally," she said. "When?"

"Soon."

Soon. Soon is a word with promise, eventuality, rhymes with swoon, spoon, June moons to croon at with a wayward loon on a dune. But that was silly. Snap out of it, her Alpha female said to her Epsilon male. But.

She dreamed of him, alone walking somewhere across a treeless plain. She woke wondering why this man was ambling across her dreams. She woke, singing, *If I were a carpenter and you were a lady,* failing to notice the double conditional. She shored up her empty hours raising high the roof beam, building a bungalow built for two, putting out malt for the rat in the house that Jack built. In between, there was life, interior decoration.

He thought of her occasionally. How *not* to. Why is this woman being so good to me, he wondered. It occurred to him that she was crazy. But, hey, she liked the lean-to, the passage on the longevity of asphalt. She caught on to things. She fed him. Still it might be a pretty trap. Why was she being so nice to him? He got back to work. He bricked the floor of the greenhouse. On Tuesday Marla called and crashed the hard drive. He stared at his monitor, his own impersonal computer. You have mail, it said, and raised the red flag.

"Drive," she said. She sent him a road map, room keys, directions.

Maybe, he thought, possibly. We'll see. He failed to note the red flag. (That is a metaphor.)

As she cut cloth, scalloped it, contemplated window treatments, she sang, "The bear went over the mountain to see what he could see." (That is a song lyric.)

He called her. They exchanged histories, building tips, niceties, anecdotes, favorite movies. She laughed at his halting stories, sly asides. *Feed him*, she thought, *feed him*.

"I think structure is what is important," he said on the phone. "Integrity of building materials. Decor is cosmetics."

Integrity, she thought, we are talking. We are talking. Aretha wailed from the CD player, "But I ain't got Jack."

"Cosmetics?" she asked. They had so much in common. Uncommon much.

He explained his theory of cosmetics: pretty is as pretty does. They rang off.

He thought, she gets my jokes. She has a heart as big as the Ritz cracker. He ate all the care-package fudge in a sitting and sank into a sugar low. She erected skyscrapers of meringue and sang into a sugar high, "The handyman can cause he mixes it with love and makes the world taste good." (That is a song lyric and a metaphor.)

She mailed him a meringue of the Empire State Building with a note: I won't scream, King Kong.

He called her. "I don't even remember what you look like."

"Like myself," she, no Fay Wray, said.

"I'm having anxiety attacks of approach avoidance," he said.

"Relax," she said. "Just have fun."

"Fun," he said. "Okay fun. I think if I plan ahead I could find a few days clear."

"I'm afraid," she said. He was scheduling his fun.

"Of what?" he asked.

"Of this." It wasn't fun. "What is this?" she asked as women are wont to do after the fact.

"What is this?" He growled in a gritty blues voice, "Why, darling, what it IS."

She laughed. WHAT it is. She stocked the house with groceries, planted peppermint petunias, aired out the attic, propped his book jacket photo on her dresser, tucked a retractable measuring tape beneath her pillow, baked cakes with flying buttresses, broke the ground, cleared the site, raised a cathedral of hope. In her dreams he was still walking across a vast treeless expanse. (She wasn't receiving the omen.)

This is a bad idea, he told himself. Structurally flawed. Collapsing keystone. Bad foundation work. He jerry-rigged a Tom Swift rocket to the moon.

She e-mailed him: Despite all my kidding around, I really do like you. And I have no expectations.

We'll see: he e-mailed.

We'll see: she e-mailed.

They saw.

He drove, stoned, the tunes cranked, eating up the road, lost his way, recovered, the trip growing longer by the second, the road stretching endless, seven hours. Damn. Lost an hour. She'd be worried sick. Why did they do that, worry? Now what? Cruising, Joan Osborn crooning about God on a bus. Like one of us. Like one of us. The first six hours urgent, then fatigue settling in, numbing his shoulders, the highway elation wearing off. How far away did this damn woman live? Impossible distances to span. What had she said on the phone? Courtship by interstices. Overseas acquaintance by satellite. Make up for lost time. Rolled on the right through the intersection. Uh-oh. Blue light special. Easy now. Pot in the car. He rolled down the window. "Yes, officer?"

She took a bath. She put fresh water in the flower vases. She curled her hair. She changed her clothes. Three times. She wanted to look nice but not too nice. Lace shirt, too obvious: Come hither. Button-down too prim: Head for the hills. She trimmed the hedges, vacuumed the floors, then paced them. This wouldn't do. This simply would not do. They were both in their forties. This was silly. She took a deep breath. She stared into the mirror. Gadzooks. She looked like Yoda's grandmother. Six o'clock. Seven o'clock. She set out the cheese. Where was he? She rewrapped the cheese. Why didn't he call? They never called. He might be dead somewhere and how would she know. They never called. Anticipation become anxiety become anger become anxiety again. A woman's assonant declension. Then irony: Great, now she'd never get laid again before menopause.

An hour on the side of the road, an hour while the cop ran the registration. Fucking cops, man. Everyone was doing it, rolling through the intersection on the right. Okay, he broke the law, but everyone was breaking the law. Why should he be singled out for breaking the law. Give a guy a uniform, a big gun, and he's the biggest cock of the walk all right. Officer Dickhead. Gonna get myself a uniform, man. Officer Dickhead

83

meet Officer Anarchy. Blow justice right back into the power-hungry Hitler's beady little eyes. Ka-poom. Ka-poom. "Thank you, Officer," he said, accepting back his license and registration. "Thanks very much."

Gonna cost a freaking fortune. All to see some chick who's a tool groupie. Got to find a phone. Ten o'clock. Cops. Give a guy a uniform and he thinks he pisses testosterone. Cops.

"Thank you officer." Where was the fucking JUSTICE?

He rolled up to a phone booth and dialed in the blue light.

"Hello," she said. "Hi. Thank God. I thought. Yes. How far? Poor thing." She unwrapped the cheese, put a bottle of wine on ice. What room should she be sitting in? Living room, a book, perhaps? No, no, the family room. His manual. Just a half hour now. Eleven o'clock.

When she paces in the hall, her reflection startles her. He's here. No, that's me. Where is he? She doesn't hear him arrive. She's in the bath-room, chobbling down antacids.

A knock. And then he was there in the full light of her hall. And she knew the instant that she hugged him that she had failed. He had built her from absence, raised a pre-mortem Taj Mahal from e-mail, letters, doves' eggs. She had failed. And the walls came a-tumbling down.

"Conroy," she tried on his name. Croy, it stuck in her throat. Offer him something, she reprimanded herself. *Feed him, feed him.*

Wo, he thought. This was not the Trojan Helen he'd erected in his imagination over one, two months, two and a half. No, this was what the horse rolled in. He looked the gift horse in the eye. "Hi."

She smiled, pretending not to see the flinch. "Hi. What can I get you? Something to drink? Wine?"

"Fine," he said. He didn't drink wine. No sandpaper would abrade those wrinkles away. No sir. No draw plane either. This girl looked every inch of her long days. Wrinkles, chicken neck. Be polite. The girl has chicken neck. Be polite. He followed her into the kitchen. Prefab mock oak. Lino tile. Trapped, he thought. Trapped like a rat in Kerouac's suburban nightmare of the dream house lit by TV light. Blue beams. Blue light. Thin blue line.

"You tired?" she asked. "You hungry?" Her questions pig-piled. "Wine?" She started heating something up on the stove before he an-swered. He hated that. Mother bullying.

"Cops," he said. "You should have seen this cop. Fucking police state, man." He looked around furtively for an escape but kept talking.

While he ranted, she stirred the soup. Let him run his course. It was a guy thing. Guys don't handle authority well. This wasn't the greeting she'd anticipated, hoped for. But still, he was here. Drove eleven hours. She'd feed him, rub his shoulders. They'd sip wine, talk, recover the easy banter from the phone.

He raved. She set the table. He waved his arms. She poured the wine. He thumped the counter. She served the dinner, smoothed his napkin.

"Here," she said. "Relax. Eat."

Ten minutes. He was here ten minutes and she was already telling him what to do. He smiled and sat down.

They thought, We'll just have to make the best of this.

"Do you want to smoke some pot?" he asked.

"Yes," she said. She didn't like pot.

They were high. She thought his eyes had gotten bluer since he'd eaten. He liked her crooked smile, he decided.

He impersonated the cop. "May I have your license and registration, urp, please. Would you, urp, while I urp this on the urp?"

She laughed. She fed him cookies, meringue. More soup? Wine? Yes, please, no, please, three bags full, please.

For a giddy moment, they became themselves. They thought that their laughter sounded genuine. They thought they were enjoying themselves, but, but.

She cleaned the kitchen. As she put things away, she was watching herself put things away. Butter in the butter cubby. Napkin in the basket. He was watching her. This was all too much. She was playing into his fear of her: That women always anticipated what men feared: Their domesticity. Which was what they wanted. *Feed me. Feed me.*

"Would you like to listen to this tape?" he asked.

"Yes," she lied. She wanted to run screaming blue murder into the blue moon of Kentucky. She wanted to slit her wrists and watch her blue blood trickle into a bottomless basin. Her nerves twanged like a bluegrass banjo. She was stoned. Neurally jangled. She wanted to talk.

He popped in the tape. Why did women always have such lousy stereos? He wanted another meringue. Maybe he could just stroll over and puff one nonchalantly into his mouth. He wanted to study her, but every time he tried a surreptitious peep, her green too wide eyes would catch him, appraising his disappointment, judging him for it. He hated that. It was going to be a long weekend. He sat in the easy chair. The arm was loose. Right arm. He listened to her laugh at the tape. She laughed in all the wrong places.

"I love Fireside Theater," she said.

"Firesign," he corrected.

It didn't register. "Remember that one—Don't Touch That Dwarf. Hand me the pliers."

He nodded and stared at her now downcast eyes. What was so interesting about her lap?

She stared at her suddenly old hands. It happened like this when she smoked. She turned twelve, but her hands turned old. Old leaves. Spatulate hands turned over an old leaf.

"Do you want to hear the other side of the tape?" he asked.

"Do you want to go for a walk?" she asked.

He wanted to be agreeable. He wasn't. "Sure."

They stumbled into the frosty air, clopped down the tarmac through the subdivision. He felt that he had squirted like a watermelon seed from his own pinched fingers. The pink pulp of Spielberg's suburbia, sweet watery nothing. Pretentious prefab structures loomed waiting for something ominous to happen, anything, wiggy skeletons to rise jigging from the ground, sentimental aliens to start guzzling Coke. Where was this woman leading him? What was she talking about?

"There's a field," she said, "at the end of the development. An old farm. Baled hay."

He squinted at the pond she indicated with her right hand, but he couldn't see a thing. She shuffled along a dirt road, the way becoming clearer as the development halogens' eerie orange vanished like Kerouac's vision. On the road, off the road, he chanted to himself as he kept pace with her.

"Here," she said. "Isn't this lovely?"

A thatchy field spread gray and rolling behind a ribby corncrib. The moon was a perfect quarter, a yellow rocker.

"Yes," he said.

And it was.

"I wanted you to see it." Then she said no more. She turned and walked back along the road. We are talking, she thought.

He followed her, slapped his forehead once. What? What am I doing?

"You must. You must be tired," she said.

"No," he contradicted, then, "actually."

The high was wearing off.

"I'll show you your room." He followed her up the stairs. Her ass was immense. Black leather. Maybe it was just the angle. "Here. Here's the guest room." She indicated the door. He set down his bag. They waited.

"You're welcome. I mean you can. If you want you can stay with me. I mean if you want. You don't have to."

He kicked his suitcase. "What do you think. I mean, I think maybe I should stay here."

"Okay, then. Let me get you some clean towels."

"Thanks." Why do I need towels to stay in the guest bedroom?

She flipped on a light. "Here's the guest bathroom."

He peeped in. "Fine, Thanks."

As she slipped into her nightgown, she heard water rushing, gurgling. She wasn't used to hearing water run. Only her own. It comforted her. The toilet seat flapped. The water shushed. Water, water everywhere. She cracked her door. He was there, Conroy. He was smiling. His face looked boyish, friendly.

He looked at her in her yellow nightgown, her face tilted up into the sifted hallway light. Her mouth looked like a forming question. She looked very small to him, her hair unpinned, her back bare. All those freckles. He could play Connect-the-Dots, maybe. He could constellate his own myths, find a quarter cradle of a moon to rock him.

He shuffled. "Thank you for dinner."

"You're welcome. A pleasure."

"You could come down to me. Later. If you want. It's okay." He walked back down the hallway.

"Be there in a jiffy," she called and laughed.

He stripped and crawled into bed, laughing, too. He pulled the bedspread to his neck, upsetting a tumble of pillows. "Doesn't this feel a little weird?" he called.

"Yeah," she called back. "I feel as if I'm in a pension."

He chuckled, letting the down nestle his head, wondering if she would come, nudge him, slip into bed, wondering if she would and if he wanted her there.

Down the hall, she stared out the window, fiercely insomniac. She pretended to read. *The Mystery of Edwin Drood.* I know what he's up to. He is making me decide. That way, he's off the hook. He can say, She started it. She wanted to whack him one with a hacksaw, tweak his button nose with a plumber's wrench. But did he really expect her to creep down the hall? He didn't want her there. He was being nice. But maybe. Still, why should she . . . And then she could picture herself not wanting to disturb the moment, the darkness, the surprise of it all, banging into the walls as she fumbled down the hall, stubbing her toe, hollering as she pitched headlong into his shins. Throbbing toe. A choked curse or two. Yeah, that'd be erotic. Nyuk, nyuk, nyuk. Curly does Dallas.

They fell asleep.

She woke first. Maybe it wasn't so bad. Maybe he didn't find her as loathsome as she thought. Maybe. The light spilled into the room, uncertain. Maybe. The morning was pink and yellow. She rose expectant. The sun shimmered between the pointed lace trimming her curtains. Maybe. As maybe as a butterfly's wings drying, as maybe as their iridescent color, their powdery charm.

So she went to him. The hall felt very long. She snuggled into bed behind his back.

"MMM, nice," he murmured.

But it wasn't. Something felt off. It was his stomach perhaps. She wasn't used to his girth.

He closed his eyes so he wouldn't see her chicken neck. He wanted her to be someone else, his old girlfriend Marla who was in her twenties. While he tried to recreate Marla with his hands, she slipped out of bed.

They were in the kitchen. He was complaining about the skim milk, only drinks two percent, he said. She said that she'd go out to get him some milk. He started eating Halloween candy from her freezer. "Please, don't do that," she said.

He glared at her and ate another peanut butter cup.

She wondered why he was doing that. He was overweight.

Chicken neck, he thought. They all want to be mothers.

She served him some popovers. He ate them.

"I usually have bacon and eggs," he said. She made them.

Why am I doing this, she asked herself. Why am I waiting on this boor? She hated herself. *Feed him. Feed him.*

They spent the day in book stores, CD stores. She knew what he was doing, avoiding her, avoiding talking. So many avenues for communication, but still men and women don't talk to each other. She was growing tired of waiting as he finicked over books and CDs.

When she asked him if he'd like to pick out a movie for that evening, he picked out three. Three. She knew what he was doing; he was finding more ways to avoid her, to keep from talking to her.

At the deli, she bought sandwiches for a picnic. He was throwing a hissy fit because he couldn't find ice. Milk, bacon and eggs, ice. She knew two-year-olds who were more adaptable than this. But she grinned. Her face felt tight.

They drove out to the park and sat by the lake. It was a beautiful day, late October Indian summer, drowsy sunshiny day. He wanted to climb a trail.

"Okay," she agreed and she followed. Men lead. Women follow. He got them lost, all the while pontificating about how to keep one's bearings in the woods. She pretended to joke along, but she'd had it. He'd apparently had it, too. She could feel his strain. She was getting on his nerves. They were lost in the woods, Hansel and Gretel, on a beautiful afternoon, and she felt like a witch. The path dwindled to nothing. He was playing scout, pretending to orient them. She was overdressed. Her sweater stuck to the small of her back.

Jack and Jill went up the hill. The quickest way out is down. "The lake is there," she pointed. "I'm going down." And she removed her shoes and skied down the steep hill of pine needles.

He followed, laughing, but he was pissed.

"Impulsive aren't you?" he asked.

"Maybe, but I ain't lost."

His eyes hated her. They were full of the dirty tricks he'd like to play on her, saw her chair leg three-quarters through, scatter nails on her garage floor. But she didn't care; she was skidding down the hill, holding her shoes to her chest and laughing. And Jill came tumbling after. Kit Carson, can go right to hell. I'm going back to the car. She put on her shoes at the base of the hill, found the lakeside trail and started walking.

He was brooding. It was in the hump of his shoulders. He was sulking. He was not having fun. His mood was her responsibility.

She offered to take him out to dinner. She hated herself for offering. She hated herself for opening herself to be humiliated, to give and give with no expectation of returning affection. But YES, he said, and she bought him dinner. The boy had an appetite. He ate his way through the menu. Afterwards, he said, "Thank you."

It was not, she realized, sufficient. She paid the bill.

They were lying on the living room floor. She was touching him. He was channel-surfing and trying to annoy her. He was successful. "Would you stop it?" she asked. "You're driving me crazy."

"No," he said. "You are driving yourself crazy."

"No, that is driving me crazy. Can't you find a program and stick with it."

He turned on Tom Hanks in "Big." He snuck to the freezer and popped a few more peanut butter cups, unglued the roof of his mouth, said, "That's what all men really want. A room full of toys, a girl to screw. No responsibility. What a hoot."

He was using the movie to tell her that he didn't want her. He squirmed under her touch, got up, returned with his vest.

"Would you mend this for me?" he asked. "I popped a button."

And she knew then that she was damned. If she refused she was all the bad girlfriends he'd ever had. If she obliged, she was his mother. She obliged, cursing. She jabbed the needle in and out of the vest with angry little stabs. Damn him, damn him. He brought me his mending. This is over the top. This is the date from hell, but still she sewed. She bit the thread off. "Here," she said. He took the vest. She couldn't bear it. She poked him in his jelly belly and said, "Say thank you."

"Thank you," he said and poked her back.

She pushed him, thinking this is it, the nadir, the pits. Courtship as low comedy. Slapstick love. Pigtails in inkwells. Pinkies in the eye. Petty is as petty does. They looked at each other hatefully, embarrassed.

"I don't know why I act the way I do sometimes," he said.

She smiled insincerely and he stuck in a video tape, Bergman's *Howl of the Wolf*. They watched it, pretending that they were not watching themselves on the screen. Shadowy castles, death masks, hunched vanities, horrors of empty laughing and longing through naked corridors of wretched men and women shattering each other infinitely in cloudy mirrors. It was not a good date movie. At last, at long last, it ended.

"I'm tired," she said. There were two more tapes. "I'm going to bed."

He didn't shift. He stared at the television.

Okey doke. She went to bed. She woke up at one. The moon was sifting into the room, shifty light. The hall light was on. She felt the emptiness of the bed. He hadn't joined her. She rose in her pajamas to turn off the light. The satin made a shoosh sound as she walked. She hurt; her heart was full of ashes and orange rinds. She wanted to cup her hands and find them full. But she came up empty. In the sudden darkness she leaned against the wall.

Pain is pain. Despair is despair. These were not tautologies.

Then she heard her name, and she entered his room, sat down next to him on the bed, brushed the hair back from his forehead. She took a deep breath to steady herself, because she knew that she must say what he would not. "It's okay," she said. "I'm just not your type. I told you that I didn't have any expectations, and that's fine."

"I didn't know," he said. "I didn't know until I came up to bed tonight and I realized that I wanted to sleep alone."

"I knew," she said. "But sometimes it's better just to say it, to get it out there."

"I didn't want to hurt you."

"Sometimes there is less hurt in truth. Chalk it up to lack of chemistry. Too little contact. Too much anticipation. It's fine."

"I feel very close to you now'," he said. "Would you hold me?"

She cradled him. Her hands and heart were full. The moon spilled into the room. Hansel and Gretel had lost their way. They were two scared children. There was a wolf in the woods and every way, they lost the path. They were hunted by their loneliness. Terror was everywhere. He. She. They, the motherless children.

She kissed his forehead. It was cool. "I'm tired now," she said. "I'm going to bed." She padded down the dark corridor to her room, slipped sleeplessly into her bed, and then he was there in her door frame.

"Are you going to sleep here?" he asked.

"That's the general idea."

"May I stay with you? I don't want to sleep alone."

Why, she wondered, why do they only come to us when we leave them. But, yes, she said, her heart was large, her bed, commodious. She suffered from a surfeit of affection for the world and all its sad and lost inhabitants. She was one of them. Come to bed then, child.

And together they lay hand in hand, staving off the night, the wolf beneath the bed, the squalor of loneliness, ulteriority of hope. He. She. We, two. Hansel and Gretel following a path of bird-pecked bread crumbs through the woods. We lose ourselves. We find ourselves again. We build cabins with small thatch. We raise homes in our hearts. We give each other places to abide. You're safe now, baby. You're home. For a while. This while.

What is this?

What it is, baby. What it is.

TOUCH

by STEVE ADAMS

When you receive bodywork what most people won't tell you and what you may not tell yourself is that the experience is personal. How could it be otherwise? Fears and issues are often bound in injuries, and some injuries are more personal than others. There you are, depending on the particular practice, lying naked under a sheet, or exposed in your underwear, or in sweatpants and a T-shirt, relinquishing your body to someone who begins as a stranger. We all have our polarities—male, female, gay, straight, bisexual and all the blends and permutations between, and one may be more comfortable working with some types over others. A straight male may avoid an attractive female practitioner because, worried over controlling his responses, he can't relax with her. A woman may find she more easily trusts another woman. There's nothing wrong with this. You're the one lying there vulnerable. Still, in my experience the individual practitioner supersedes the type. Some are just better than others, or match up better with you, regardless of everything else including how you view yourself. With some it is an art form, and you are their material. As in dance, you can come to know your partner quite well. As with a very good dance partner, you can travel to a place neither of you would arrive at alone. And you will think of them years later, wonder at what transpired between you.

Injuries break boundaries. They reshape us, emotionally and physically. Sometimes they create doorways and humble us to the point where we can step through.

This is a love story.

One morning in Austin about fifteen years ago, I woke to find my right testicle had suffered a trauma overnight and was fixed rigidly to the base of my member. When I prodded it the pain was so severe it brought sweat to my eyelids. After I recovered I stood and examined myself in the mirror. There it hung, or more accurately, didn't, torqued an inch above my left as if it bad tried to retract itself into my body for safety, and in failing clung on for dear life.

I had no idea what might have caused the reaction. I thought I must have injured it while sleeping and hoped if I gave it a few days it would recover. But I discovered, day-by-day, that the most basic things I took for granted—running, riding a bicycle, driving for more than a few minutes (my right foot extended and held to the gas pedal), walking more than fifty yards at a stretch, wearing jeans or boxer shorts—could, and usually would trigger a relentless, tidal pain to spread from that part of my body and engulf me as I tried to fall asleep at night. I'm also convinced the male body releases some sort of fear hormone when the testicles are threatened. As if the crippling pain wasn't enough to convince you to protect these oblong carriers of your bloodline, a completely separate dose of raw, undefined terror rages through your system. At night I would lie on my back in bed immobilized, unable to rest on either side or my stomach without setting off the response, looking at the ceiling fan as it spun in the dark room, and trying to convince myself that yes, I would be able to have sex again someday.

As it turned out I would, but not for several years. Along the way to recovery I visited doctors and urologists (they had no answers), a chiropractor (some relief lasting for no more than twenty-four hours), learned to drive my car relying on cruise control whenever possible, and switched from boxers to briefs for the support and from jeans to baggy pants or shorts to reduce constriction. What finally saved me was running across an old friend who'd just started teaching Pilates. A few days after I began working with him I went to a practitioner of deep tissue massage. As traditional forms of medicine had failed me, I was looking elsewhere, anywhere. Almost overnight everything changed. Though I was far from 100%, I found myself able to, among other things, drive my car normally or walk a quarter mile without suffering pain, terror, and flopsweats all night long. Soon that right testicle began to shift back toward its proper position. As near as I can tell by what helped and what didn't, my physical problem seemed to lie with knotted or strained tissue where my right gluteus maximus met my upper thigh, and how that troubled an L-3 vertebra. Nerve stuff. It expands radially. Point X affects Point D.

Whatever. I was just happy I was improving and had a means to deal with it. The means took me to and through a series of bodyworkers. It took me to Jonah.

I moved from Texas to New York City for the third time in my life in 1998 chasing dreams and memories and hopes, but really satisfied with nothing more than living under that skyline again. I had my physical therapy down rote. I owned a Pilates mat and barrel and knew a solid routine. I now could walk, run, ride a bike, and yes, have sex again, provided I attended to my Pilates twice a week and visited a good body-worker every month or two. Upon arriving, finding that bodyworker was one of my highest priorities.

Jonah was referred to me through a mutual friend. There are many terrific forms of bodywork, but Jonah's was shiatsu. He worked out of a martial arts studio on 14th Street. I followed him into a small space partitioned by a bamboo screen. He was maybe 5' 10", an inch taller than me with curly brown hair starting to recede and a dancer's body. He spoke softly, asked me what was going on, and I told him about my injury in shameless detail. He nodded, then I lay before him on the mat, one stranger to another. He lit a scentless candle. He circled a hammer around a small ancient-looking hand gong and the tone flowed out like water. He closed his eyes and went to work.

It was over a year before he dropped his first overt clue he might be gay. I'd just scored a rent-stabilized apartment in Greenpoint, Brook-lyn, and wanted to find a bicycle I could ride in my neighborhood. I asked him for recommendations. He was a runner as well as a bicyclist, and he guided me to a small shop on 10th Avenue run by a man from Puerto Rico. "I remind him of Celia Cruz," Jonah told me proudly, if somewhat shyly. "Tell him Celia Cruz sent you." Which surprised me. I didn't think Jonah looked like Celia Cruz at all.

After he moved from that first studio, I visited him in a room he rented in a chiropractor's office. For a short period afterward he took the sub-way to the Upper West Side and the apartment I was subletting. My small, green parrot adored him, trilled and puffed up and rested on one leg while Jonah worked on me on the floor of my living room. Finally he chose to use his own apartment. He told me he'd decided to cut back on his clients so he could do better, more focused work, and since we would be in his home he wanted to be picky about who he brought into it. I was glad to have made the cut but hardly thought about it. I only consider it now. Some clients exhausted him, he said, but I clearly didn't, even with whatever worries I brought in. Before we began a session, I'd sit on the mat, and he'd listen as I described where my body hurt, where it was tight, what was happening emotionally in my life since the last time he saw me. By his way of thinking, it was all connected. Then I'd lie down, he'd dim the lights, press the CD player to play ambient music (this, I think, was one of his systems for timing a session), and start. He'd lay his hands (they were always surprisingly warm) on my belly, close his eyes, and I'd begin to float away. He once explained that the belly informed him of where to go next, what part of the body he should address. I can only describe his state as a kind of trance. If moments later I realized I'd forgotten to tell him about a pain somewhere and blurted out the oversight he always looked startled at my voice, maybe at the fact that I was even in the room with him. But he'd recover, nod and say "okay" then close his eyes and we'd begin the float again.

I'm almost ashamed of how little I paid him. When once I asked him if I should pay more he told me that he wanted to keep his price down so I could afford to come often. The sessions lasted an hour and a half, and usually two. This was, I realized fairly quickly, not about the money for him. It was a spiritual practice. It was how he served. When once I asked him how else he paid the rent he told me offhandedly he did some teaching at Circle in the Square and also something called "clown therapy" for hospitalized children with the Big Apple Circus in New York, as well as for another group in Germany where he spent half the year with his partner. Jonah never gave me that much detail. I think part of that was his natural instinct to keep boundaries in place with clients, but more so I think he just didn't like to talk about himself. He was a body person and that's where he spoke first, and possibly best, through his hands and movement, while each session I'd blather to excess about politics, my writing, or a woman who'd hurt my feelings. He'd fly back and forth between Germany and the U.S. When he was gone I visited other practitioners working other disciplines.

From Jonah's perspective there wasn't anything out of the ordinary about what we did. He was a theater artist from Canada, a specialist in movement, physical acting, mime, and shiatsu, cobbling together a meaningful life and meaningful relationships in Germany and New

York City. Our friendship that developed over the eight years before he died was simply a logical and natural experience. He was a healer. It's what he did. But for me, going once every month or two to a gay man's apartment and giving over my body to him was a foray into new territory, and one I only wish I could return to.

Shiatsu is a relatively modern Japanese form of massage therapy derived from ancient Chinese principles. It's practiced through loose clothing. Its system follows the same meridians as acupuncture, but instead of needles, fingers press, and often deeply. Its intention is to unblock energy flow, release knotted musculature, stretch and loosen connective tissue, and create a harmonic relationship between internal organs. The practitioner may also stretch the body as he moves and breathes with his client. Jonah said he liked to work with me because it grounded him. He considered what we did a form of dance.

Jonah's apartment was on West 45th Street between 8th and 9th Avenues across from the Hirschfield Theater. My sessions there allowed me a personal foothold in what was not long ago called Hell's Kitchen. He'd taken the apartment in the late '70s and held onto it ever since. It was one of those old New York apartments where you felt the presence of generations who'd lived there before you. The paint on the windowsills was layered so thickly the windows didn't close right, and there you could see the different colors the apartment had been painted through the years cracking in spiderwebbed patterns. The bathroom door I shut when I changed into my sweatpants and T-shirt didn't close completely either because of the paint. Inside, a metal chain hung from the lightbulb in the middle of the ceiling as an on/off switch. The heavy, rounded porcelain sink and toilet came from eras back, and the bathtub sat off the floor on brass feet. Like many New Yorkers, Jonah kept the unscreened window cracked open in winter and summer, and through it came yells and sometimes the sound of bottles breaking from the homeless shelter across the alley. I would peer out, breathe the air drifting in as I watched the bodies shift through windows across the way, listen to them talk and laugh and argue, and think *this is a real New York apartment*.

The only time our relationship faltered was in 2004 after Bush won the election. My body was tied in knots at the loss, and I dragged it to Jonah so he could disentangle it as he always did. From the beginning of our session I could talk of nothing else. Finally I lay on the mat and he did his thing. Usually I would leave a few minutes after a session, but afterward we began talking again. He looked directly in my eyes and calmly, but clearly and with anger, pain, and no small amount of alarm described how the extreme right wing had used fear and hatred of gays to whip up the electorate against the Democrats. And he'd thought it wouldn't work, but it did. Jonah had moved to New York from Canada and become a U.S. citizen because he'd believed in this country. He'd wanted to be part of it. And now he wondered why. Why had he become an American? There seemed a trace of accusation in his voice.

It was palpable how exiled he felt. Even though my party had lost, I was still part of the straight world, while he belonged to the "disease" the extreme right so publicly wished to excise. Also I was native born. He was seeing me for the first time as "other," as "different." Or at least I thought he was, so of course he began to look "other" to me. Didn't he know I felt cast out too?

I could've told him he and I were on the same list, that if they got him they'd get around to me. I could've quoted the line, "First they came for the Communists . . ." But I hadn't any words, and any words would've come up short. I stood, ready to leave, and gestured toward the mat. I said, "Well, clearly I don't have a problem with it." He looked up at me, not responding, taking in my gesture. He turned to the mat; that bed, of sorts. I think it was at that moment he considered what a great distance a straight boy from Grand Prairie, Texas, might travel to come to a point where he could lie beneath him and trust him implicitly with his body. What happened on that mat, as well as my feelings for him, were hardly casual.

The last time I saw him was shortly after Katrina ravaged New Orleans. I'd decided to fly down to witness the disaster and spend some money, as that city so badly needed it. Jonah was about to return to Germany to be with his partner and do his clown therapy in one of their hospitals. As I got to my feet I told him I was going down that weekend to New Orleans to put flowers on Marie Laveau's grave. I felt a need to mourn, to ask forgiveness, to bring an offering, and I knew of no better place than the grave of the voodoo queen of New Orleans. I saw Jonah's eyes widen in recognition at the name.

He'd recently stitched and restitched me back together as I went through a lengthy and particularly devastating breakup with a woman. Tears had ran down my face as he'd worked on me, and he'd extended the sessions until he was satisfied I'd recovered enough to face the subway. During that time he showed me a picture of his partner, Michael, who was younger than him and stunningly beautiful. At the time I thought, *Way to go, Jonah!*

As wonderful as New York can be, you don't last there without help. I felt lucky to call him my friend. I don't know why, but as I stood at his door that night ready to leave, I had a subtle but unwavering feeling I might never see him again. An unlikely phrase popped into my head: "Don't ever die." But that is a horrible curse to lay on someone, so I substituted, "Don't ever retire."

A few months later, when it seemed time for him to be back I was overcome with concern. It was irrational, I knew, but I couldn't shake the feeling. I began to wonder how I would find out if he were to die. Would I wander by his apartment and see if his name had been taken off his mailbox? It dawned on me we shared no friends, no family who could inform me. I experienced a sense of vertigo. To calm myself I decided to send him an email casually asking how he was doing. He responded within a day telling me he'd developed a health issue and was being treated in Germany. Oddly, this made me feel relieved. I'd reestablished contact and my intuition had not been entirely off. He said he had a tumor in his pancreas but was doing well; he just hated the nausea from the chemo. He said he'd be back, recovered in New York.

I happily took him at his word. After all, he was the health professional and should know. Still, something pressed me in my response to tell him I'd been planning, should I ever run across him on the street in Times Square, to introduce him to my friends only as "my shiatsu angel." Years earlier when I'd told him I always staked out a spot at Spring Street to witness the annual Halloween parade, he'd informed me he would be participating as "Johnny Angel." Bright-eyed and excited, he'd asked me to look for him, and I did, but he was lost in the myriad bodies and costumes.

In his next email he said he was making progress and he and his partner would be flying to New York soon. He was planning on teaching classes that fall. Again, about the time I expected him back my anxiety over his health, along with my fear of his disappearing swarmed me. I decided to call his apartment, carefully removing any note of concern from my voice, and left a message saying I was wondering if he was back and how he was doing and to give me a call. I left my number.

When I listened to the phone message from his partner, Michael, the following day saying Jonah had passed, I was only surprised by the degree I'd been expecting it. Michael's voice was clear and measured, with just a trace of an accent. I called Jonah's number and Michael picked up. I told him I was sorry for his loss. He said Jonah had been improving and they actually thought he was going to recover. But after they came back he suddenly took a turn, and within a couple of weeks was gone. Before he died Jonah had told him to let me know. There was going to be a memorial service at Circle in the Square the next night in the downstairs theater where *The Spelling Bee* was then running.

They say it's only when someone dies you fully know who they are. Death is the final page of the final chapter, and like a finished novel its total shape only comes into view at that moment. There were certain things I knew about Jonah. I knew he had a beautiful, younger life-partner. I knew he'd been my friend for eight years, supporting me during my hardest times in this city. I knew his loss would affect me structurally, on a foundational level. I knew he'd loved New York, as I did, had come here from another culture, as I had. And the last time I saw him I had known on some deep level it would be the last time I would see him. What I did not know was who he was to others.

Making my way down the deep, three-tiered stairwell to the theater lobby was like slowly dropping into an ocean: ten steps down, a small landing; ten steps down, another landing; ten steps down, the floor and its blue carpet textured with tiny red dots. Three of the walls were white. The fourth, behind the stairwell, was red. Enormous, round, white pillars held up the ceiling. People swirled over the carpet greeting each other, smiled as they recognized a face, hugged a friend. I felt self-conscious. I knew no one. Unmoored as I was I searched for an anchor and spotted a small table where they'd created a shrine with a number of Jonah's personal objects. Beside it an easel displayed a photograph, a headshot of Jonah as I'd never seen him. Wearing a white doctor's smock, his makeup was minimal, like a mime's, and instead of smiling he looked serious. Too serious. Comically serious. On the end of his nose was a bright red rubber ball. He was "Dr. Know-Nothing," his clown doctor character. I pictured him scurrying mute around sick children's beds like something out of the Marx Brothers, putting his stethoscope to the television, taking the lampshade's temperature, sending up the real doctors and their bewildering, frightening behavior to the kids and giving them something to laugh at while he made a sane comment about that sterile, insane place. So this is who he was to sick children, I thought. A sign on the table said, "Take something." I wanted to rake away a bagful of the objects, but stopped myself. I spotted a tiny patterned incense plate I'd seen every time I'd visited him. I carefully tucked it away and walked toward the entrance of the theater.

At the door a small, somber looking woman wearing a red clown nose handed me a program along with my own red clown nose. Inside I chose a seat up high, far back and to the left of the stage. The seats were covered in red fabric. Silver numbers were stamped to seat bottoms. I recognized Michael up front by his blond hair. The bleachers down to the left were packed with what I correctly assumed were his students. Friends and family filled the lower center and right bleachers. The rest flowed into the risers above. I estimated over two hundred people had come. Many were wearing their noses. I rolled the soft foam ball in my fingers and tried it on.

The gay and theatrical communities have a lot of experience with memorial services. They know what they're for and how to make them work. There was a small group of friends present who had bonded with Jonah when he arrived in New York in the '70s, and one of them ran the show, was the stage manager and host. An official from a hospital stepped to the microphone and talked about what wonderful work Jonah did there and how he would be missed. A group of Jonah's fellow clown doctors spoke of him with the gravity of soldiers speaking of a fallen comrade. The head of the theater school at Circle in the Square talked of the great loss to his school, and stated that the legendary physical acting course Jonah developed and taught over the years would be renamed, "The Jonah Course." What was evident was that my Jonah, my quiet personal friend, was a dynamic figure in theater and in the world of clowns. The guy was a star, and I'd never known.

The group of students beside the stage sang, "You've Got a Friend," in harmony. A dancer presented a movement piece. People were coming and going onstage. Lost in my emotions, I found it hard to keep up with it all. One young woman wanted to thank Jonah for giving her her "clown name" when he'd seen the defining trait in her movement and emotional makeup one day during class. Another student, who apparently hadn't even taken his class, wept as she spoke because now she never would. Professors stood and talked about Jonah's sense of humor and the practical jokes he was always playing on them, which surprised me as he'd been so serious with me. When the host paused to ask if anyone else needed to say something, I had an urge to speak, but I wasn't a relative, I wasn't part of any of these extended families, and didn't know what to say except *you don't know me but I loved him too*. And of course that opening passed as quickly as it appeared; the host was now gesturing toward Michael, coaxing him onto the stage.

It took him a moment before he got to his feet, then he walked up the steps to the microphone. His first words were, "I don't want to be standing here." His last were, "Goodbye, Love." In between was everything else I can't remember. I only remember thinking that grief must give us these brief moments of strength he demonstrated, a window of time so we can say what we must say with some dignity and clarity before falling apart.

The lights went down as through the speakers Diana Krall sang Joni Mitchell's "A Case of You," and a video on a screen showed a sequence of slides—Jonah onstage with a group of actresses, Jonah dreamy-eyed in the late '70s with a full head of curly hair, Jonah and Michael on their wedding day. Afterward, we were asked to put on our clown noses. The room was suddenly filled with bright red balls stuck in the middle of hundreds of faces. It was almost funny. Then the clowns sang a song, and the memorial was over. The lights came up. People rose to their feet as if out of a dream. Some moved toward the exits, some toward the family by the stage. I knew if I left I'd take the emptiness I felt with me, so using the chance to give my condolences to Michael, I made my way down to the floor. Everyone there seemed filled with love and an odd joy. Unsure as I was whether it was proper for me to approach Michael or what I would say to him, my legs still propelled me his way. I felt smaller than everyone around me. He was very tall. I hesitated, then touched his arm. "Michael?" I said. He turned and smiled down at me as if he knew me but couldn't place me. "I'm Steve."

"*Steve*," he said with such warmth I can still hear his voice. He took me in his arms like I was a lost creature come home. He held me like he needed me. I don't know if I've ever been more grateful. Then he turned; Jonah's sister was watching, and he tried to introduce me. "This is Steve," he said, searching for words. "One of Jonah's . . ."

I looked at her. I didn't know what to say or how to say it. How could I describe it? "He was my shiatsu guy," I managed. She nodded, then Michael joined her as they made their way through other well-wishers and friends to carry on the responsibilities of burying a loved one.

I headed from the theater down Eighth Avenue toward 42nd Street where I was meeting friends for a show at B.B. King's club. I didn't want to go but I already had a ticket. I cradled the red clown nose in my hand inside my jacket pocket. At 45th Street I paused and looked down the block toward the building where Jonah had lived, then continued on.

At the club I met my friends wearing the clown nose. They didn't know how to respond to it and neither did I. Everyone in the place was intent on having a good time, and why shouldn't they? But I felt separated. I kept putting on the clown nose and taking it off. The waitress did her best to ignore it. *Is he trying to be funny?*

The next morning I laid out my Pilates mat and began my workout. I remembered Jonah telling me we were like dance partners, and I saw an image of a pair of professional ice skaters where the male is clearly gay and the female is straight. There is nothing sexual between them, but there is something physical. The bond is undeniable. They go on with their other lives before and after the dance. They meet on the ice.

I knew that what happened between myself and this man would be non-repeating. The circumstances couldn't be replicated. I was a different person now. Like a first best friend, a first kiss, a first pet, I would never feel this kind of intimacy again. I found my fingers pressing the same pressure points on my feet and along my shins that Jonah would press. It was then I began to cry. The truth was, more than anything, I would miss the way he touched me.

THE WEAVE

fiction by CHARLES JOHNSON

News item, July 12, 2012. Hair theft: Three thieves battered through a wall, crawled close to the floor to dodge motion detectors, and stole six duffel bags filled with human hair extensions from a Chicago beauty-supply store. The Chicago Tribune reported Saturday that the hair extensions were worth $230,000.

"So what feeds this hair machine?"

—Chris Rock, Good Hair

Ieesha is nervous and trying not to sneeze when she steps at four in the morning to the front door of Sassy Hair Salon and Beauty Supplies in the Central District. After all, it was a sneeze that got her fired from this salon two days ago. She has a sore throat and red eyes, but that's all you can see because a ski mask covers the rest of her face. As she twists the key in the lock, her eyes are darting in every direction, up and down the empty street, because she and I have never done anything like this before. When she worked here, the owner, Frances, gave her a key so she could open and straighten up the shop before the other hairstylists arrived. I told her to make a copy of the key in case one day she might need it. That was two days ago, on September first, the start of hay fever season and the second anniversary of the day we started dating.

Once inside the door, she has exactly forty seconds to remember and punch in the four-digit code before the alarm's security system goes off. Then, to stay clear of the motion detectors inside that never turn off, she gets down on the floor of the waiting room in her cut-knee jeans and crawls on all fours past the leather reception chairs and modules stacked with *Spin, Upscale,* and *Jet* magazines for the salon's customers to read and just perhaps find on their glossy, Photoshopped pages, the coiffure that is perfect for their mood at the moment. Within a few seconds, Ieesha is beyond the reception area and into a space, long and wide, that is a site for unexpected mystery and wonder that will test the limits of what we think we know.

Moving deeper into this room, where the elusive experience called beauty is manufactured every day from hot combs and crème relaxers, she passes workstations, four on each side of her, all of them equipped with swiveling styling chairs and carts covered with appliance holders, spray bottles, and Sulfur8 shampoo. Holding a tiny flashlight attached to her key ring, she works her way around manicure tables, dryer chairs, and a display case where sexy, silky, eiderdown-soft wigs, some as thick as a show pony's tail, hang in rows like scalps taken as trophies after a war. Every day, the customers at Sassy Hair Salon and the wigs lovingly check each other out for some time, and then after long and careful deliberation, the wigs always buy the women. Unstated, but permeating every particle in that exchange of desire, is a profound, historical pain, a hurt based on the lie that the hair one was unlucky enough to be born with can never in this culture be good enough, is never beautiful as it is, and must be scorched by scalp-scalding chemicals into temporary straightness, because if that torment is not endured often from the tender age of four months old, how can one ever satisfy the unquenchable thirst to be desired or worthy of love?

The storage room containing the unusual treasure she seeks is now just a few feet away, but Ieesha stops at the station where she worked just two days ago, her red eyes glazing over with tears caused not by ragweed pollen, but by a memory suspended in the darkness.

She sees it all again. There she is, wearing her vinyl salon vest, its pockets filled with the tools of her trade. In her chair is an older customer, a heavy, high-strung Seattle city councilwoman. The salon was packed that afternoon, steamed by peopled humidity. A ceiling fan shirred air perfumed with the odor of burnt hair. The councilwoman wanted her hair straightened, not permed, for a political fundraiser she was hosting that week. But she couldn't—or wouldn't—sit quietly. She gossiped nonstop about everybody in city government as well as the 'do Gabby Douglass wore during the Olympics, blathering away in the kind of voice that carried right through you, that went inside like your ears didn't have any choice at all and had to soak up the words the way a sponge did water. All of a sudden, Ieesha sneezed. Her fingers slipped. She burned the old lady's left earlobe. The councilwoman flew from her seat, so enraged they had to peel her off the ceiling, shouting about how Ieesha didn't know the first thing about doing hair. She demanded that Frances fire her, and even took things a step further, saying with a stroke of scorn that anyone working in a beauty salon should be looking damned good herself, and that Ieesha didn't.

Frances was not a bad person to work for, far from it, and she knew my girlfriend was a first-rate cosmetologist. Even so, the owner of Sassy Hair Salon didn't want to lose someone on the city council who was a twice-a-month, high-spending customer able to buy and sell her business twice over. As I was fixing our dinner of Top Ramen, Ieesha quietly came through the door of our apartment, still wearing her salon vest, her eyes burning with tears. She wears her hair in the neat, tight black halo she was born with, unadorned, simple, honest, uncontrived, as genuinely individual as her lips and nose. To some people she might seem as plain as characters in those old-timey plays, Clara in Paddy Chayefsky's *Marty* or Laura Wingfield in *The Glass Menagerie*. But Ieesha has the warm, dark, and rich complexion of Michelle Obama or Angela Bassett, which is, so help me, as gorgeous as gorgeous gets. Nevertheless, sometimes in the morning as she was getting ready for work, I'd catch her struggling to pull a pick through the burls and kinks of her hair with tears in her eyes as she looked in the mirror, tugging hardest at the nape of her neck, that spot called "the kitchen." I tell her she's beautiful as she is, but when she peers at television, movies, or popular magazines where generic, blue-eyed, blonde Barbie dolls with orthodontically perfect teeth, Botox, and breast implants prance, pose, and promenade, she says with a sense of fatality and resignation, "I can't look like that." She knows that whenever she steps out our door, it's guaranteed that a wound awaits her, that something will tell Ieesha that her hair and skin will never be good enough. All she has to do is walk into a store and be watched with suspicion, or have a cashier slap her change on the counter rather than place it on the palm of her outstretched hand. Or maybe read about the rodeo clown named Mike Hayhurst at the Creston Classic Rodeo in California who joked that "*Playboy* is offering Ann Romney $250,000 to pose in that magazine and the White House is upset about it because *National Geographic* only offered Michelle Obama $50 to pose for them."

Between bouts of blowing her nose loudly into a Kleenex in our tiny studio apartment, she cried the whole day she got fired, saying with a hopeless, plaintive hitch in her voice, "What's wrong with me?" Rightly or wrongly, she was convinced that she would never find another job during the Great Recession. That put everything we wanted to do on hold. Both of us were broke, with bills piling up on the kitchen counter after I got laid off from my part-time job as a substitute English teacher at Garfield High School. We were on food stamps and got our clothes from Goodwill. I tried to console her, first with kisses, then caresses, and before the night was over we had roof-raising sex. Afterward, and for the thousandth time, I came close to proposing that we get married. But I had a failure of nerve, afraid she'd temporize or say no, or that because we were so poor we needed to wait. To be honest, I was never sure if she saw me as Mr. Right or just as Mr. Right Now.

So what I said to her that night, as we lay awake in each other's arms, our fingers intertwined, was that getting fired might just be the change of luck we'd been looking for. Frances was so busy with customers she didn't have time to change the locks. Or the code for the ADT alarm system. Naturally, Ieesha, who'd never stolen anything in her life, was reluctant, but I kept after her until she agreed.

Finally, after a few minutes, Ieesha enters the density of the storeroom's sooty darkness, feeling her way cat-footed, her arms outstretched. Among cardboard boxes of skin creams, conditioners, balms, and oils, she locates the holy grail of hair in three pea-green duffel bags stacked against the wall, like rugs rolled up for storage. She drags a chair beneath the storeroom window, then starts tossing the bags into the alley. As planned, I'm waiting outside, her old Toyota Corolla dappled with rust idling behind me. I catch each bag as it comes through the window and throw it onto the backseat. The bags, I discover, weigh next to nothing. Yet for some reason, these sacks of something as common and plentiful as old hair are worth a lot of bank—why, I don't know. Or why women struggling to pay their rent, poor women forced to choose between food and their winter fuel bill, go into debt shelling out between $1,000 and $3,000 and sometimes as much as $5,000 for a weave with real human hair. It baffled me until I read how some people feel that used things possess special properties. For example, someone on eBay bought Britney Spears's chewed gum for $14,000, someone else paid $115,000 for a handful of hair from Elvis Presley's pompadour, and his soiled, jockey-style shorts went on sale for $16,000 at an auction in England. (No one, by the way, bought his unwashed skivvies.) Another person spent $3,000 for Justin Timberlake's half-eaten French toast. I guess some of those eBay buyers feel closer to the person they admire, maybe even that something of that person's essence is magically clinging to the part they purchased.

As soon as Ieesha slides into the passenger seat, pulling off her ski mask and drawing short, hard breaths as if she's been running up stairs, my foot lightly applies pressure to the gas pedal and I head for the freeway, my elbow out the window, my fingers curled on the roof of the car. Within fifteen minutes, we're back at our place. I park the car, and we sling the bags over our shoulders, carry them inside to our first-floor unit, and stack them on the floor between the kitchenette and the sofa bed we sleep on. Ieesha sits down on a bedsheet still twisted from the night before, when we were joined at the groin. She knocks off her shoes run down at the heel and rubs her ankles. She pulls a couple of wigs and a handful of hair extensions from one of the bags. She spreads them on our coffee table, frowning, then sits with her shoulders pulled in, as if waiting for the ceiling to cave in.

"We're gonna be okay," I say.

"I don't know." Her voice is soft, sinus-clogged. "Tyrone, I don't feel good about this. I can't stop shaking. We're *not* burglars."

"We are now." I open a bottle of Bordeaux we've been saving to celebrate, filling up our only wineglass for her and a large jam jar for myself. I sit down beside her and pick up one of the wigs. Its texture between my fingertips is fluffy. I say, "You can blame Frances. She should have stood up for you. She *owes* you. What we need to do now is think about our next step. Where we can sell this stuff." Ieesha's head jerks backward when I reach for one of the wigs and put it on her head, just out of curiosity. Reluctantly, she lets me place it there, and I ask, "What's that feel like? A stocking cap? Is it hot?"

"I don't know. It feels . . ."

She never tells me how it feels.

So I ask another question. "What makes this hair so special? Where does it come from?"

Hands folded in her lap, she sits quietly, and, for an instant, the wig, whose obsidian tresses pool around her face, makes her look like someone I don't know. All of a sudden, I'm not sure what she might do next, but what she *does* do, after clearing her throat, is give me the hair-raising history and odyssey behind the property we've stolen. The bags, she says, come from a Buddhist temple near New Delhi, where young women shave their heads in an ancient ceremony of sacrifice called Pabbajja. They give up their hair to renounce all vanity, and this letting go of things cosmetic and the chimera called the ego is their first step as nuns on the path to realizing that the essence of everything is emptiness. The hair ceremony is one of the 84,000 "dharma gates." On the day their heads were shaved, the women had kneeled in their plain saris, there in the temple *naos*, and took two hundred forty vows, the first five of which were *no killing, no lying, no stealing, no sexual misconduct,*

107

and *no drinking of alcohol.* They didn't care what happened to their hair after the ceremony. Didn't know it would be sewn, stitched, and stapled onto the scalps of other people. But Korean merchants were there. They paid the temple's abbot ten dollars for each head of fibrous protein. After that, the merchants, who controlled this commerce as tightly as the mafia did gambling, washed the hair clean of lice. From India, where these women cultivated an outward life of simplicity and an inward life free from illusion, the merchants transported the discarded, dead hair halfway around the planet, where, ironically, it was cannibalized as commerce in a nine-billion-dollar hair-extension industry devoted precisely to keeping women forever enslaved to the eyes of others.

As she explains all this, Ieesha leaves her wine untasted, and I don't say anything because my brain is stuttering, stalling on the unsyllabled thought that if you tug on a single, thin strand of hair, which has a life span of five-and-a-half years, you find it raddled to the rest of the world. I didn't see any of that coming until it arrived. I lift the jar of wine straight to my lips, empty it, and set it down with a click on the coffee table. When I look back at Ieesha, I realize she's smiling into one cheek, as if remembering a delicious secret she can't share with me. That makes me down a second jar of Bordeaux. Then a third. I wonder, does the wig she's wearing itch or tingle? Does it feel like touching Justin Timberlake's unfinished French toast? Now the wine bottle is empty. We've got nothing on the empty racks of the refrigerator but a six-pack of beer, so I rise from the sofa to get that, a little woozy on my feet, careening sideways toward the kitchenette, but my full bladder redirects me toward the cubicle that houses our shower and toilet. I click on the light, close the door, and brace myself with one hand pressed against the wall. Standing there for a few minutes, my eyes closed, I feel rather than hear a police siren, and our smoke alarm. My stomach clenches.

Coming out of the bathroom, I find the wig she was wearing and the weaves that were on the coffee table burning in a wastebasket. Ieesha stands in the middle of the room, her cell phone pressed against her ear.

"What are you doing?" Smoke is stinging my eyes. "Who are you talking to?"

Her eyes are quiet. Everything about her seems quiet when she says, "911."

"Why?"

"Because it's the right thing to do."

I stare at her in wonder. She's offered us up, the way the women did

108

their hair at the temple in New Delhi. I rush to draw water from the kitchen sink to put out the fire. I start throwing open the windows as there comes a loud knock, then pounding at the door behind me, but I can't take my eyes off her. She looks vulnerable but not weak, free, and more than enough for herself. I hear the wood of the door breaking, but as if from a great distance, because suddenly I know, and she knows, that I understand. She's letting go of all of it—the inheritance of hurt, the artificial and the inauthentic, the absurdities of color and caste stained at their roots by vanity and bondage to the body—and in this evanescent moment, when even I feel as if a weight has been lifted off my shoulders, she has never looked more beautiful and spiritually centered. There's shouting in the room now. Rough hands throw me face-down on the floor. My wrists are cuffed behind my back. Someone is reciting my Miranda rights. Then I feel myself being lifted to my feet. But I stop midway, resting on my right knee, my voice shaky as I look up at Ieesha, and say:

"Will you marry me?"

Two policemen lead her toward the shattered door, our first steps toward that American monastery called prison. She half turns, smiling, looking back at me, and her head nods: *yes, yes, yes.*

THE CAVEMEN IN THE HEDGES

fiction by STACEY RICHTER

There are cavemen in the hedges again. I take the pellet gun from the rack beside the door and go out back and try to run them off. These cavemen are tough sons of bitches who are impervious to pain, but they love anything shiny, so I load the gun up with golden Mardi Gras beads my girlfriend, Kim, keeps in a bowl on the dresser and aim toward their ankles. There are two of them, hairy and squat, grunting around inside a privet hedge I have harassed with great labor into a series of rectilinear shapes. It takes the cavemen a while to register the beads. It's said that they have poor eyesight, and of all the bullshit printed in the papers about the cavemen in the past few months, this at least seems to be true. They crash through the branches, doing something distasteful. Maybe they're eating garbage. After a while they notice the beads and crawl out, covered in leaves, and start loping after them. They chase them down the alley, occasionally scooping up a few and whining to each other in that high-pitched way they have when they get excited, like little kids complaining.

I take a few steps off the edge of the patio and aim toward the Anderson's lot. The cavemen scramble after the beads, their matted backs receding into the distance.

"What is it?" Kim stands behind me and touches my arm. She's been staying indoors a lot lately, working on the house, keeping to herself. She hasn't said so, but it's pretty obvious the cavemen scare her.

"A couple of furry motherfuckers."

"I think they are," she says.

"What?"

"Mother fuckers. Without taboos. It's disgusting." She shivers and heads back inside.

After scanning the treetops, I follow. There haven't been any climbers reported so far, but they are nothing if not unpredictable. Inside, I find Kim sitting on the kitchen floor, arranging our spices alphabetically. She's transferring them out of their grocery-store bottles and into nicer ones, plain glass, neatly labeled. Kim has been tirelessly arranging things for the last four years—first the contents of our apartment on Pine Avenue, then, as her interior decorating business took off, other people's places, and lately our own house, since we took the plunge and bought it together last September. She finishes with fenugreek and picks up the galanga.

I go to the living room and put on some music. It's a nice, warm Saturday and if it weren't for the cavemen, we'd probably be spending it outdoors.

"Did you lock it?"

I tell her yes. I get a beer from the fridge and watch her. She's up to Greek seasonings. Her slim back is tense under her stretchy black top. The music kicks in and we don't say much for a few minutes. The band is D.I., and they're singing: "Johnny's got a problem and it's out of control!" We used to be punk rockers, Kim and I, back in the day. Now we are homeowners. When the kids down the street throw loud parties, we immediately dial 911.

"The thing that gets me," I say, "is how puny they are."

"What do they want?" asks Kim. Her hair is springing out of its plastic clamp, and she looks like she's going to cry. "What the fuck do they want with us?"

When the cavemen first appeared, they were assumed to be homeless examples of modern man. But it soon became obvious that even the most broken-down and mentally ill homeless guy wasn't *this* hairy. Or naked, hammer-browed, and short. And they didn't rummage through garbage cans and trash piles with an insatiable desire for spherical, shiny objects, empty shampoo bottles, and foam packing peanuts.

A reporter from KUTA had a hunch and sent a paleontologist from the university out to do a little fieldwork. For some reason I was watching the local news that night, and I remember this guy—typical academic, bad haircut, bad teeth—holding something in a take-out box. He said it was *scat*. Just when you think the news can't get any more

111

absurd, there's a guy on TV, holding a turd in his hands, telling you the hairy people scurrying around the bike paths and Dumpsters of our fair burg are probably Neanderthal, from the Middle Paleolithic period, and that they have been surviving on a diet of pizza crusts, unchewed insects, and pigeon eggs.

People started calling them cavemen, though they were both male and female and tended to live in culverts, heavy brush, and freeway underpasses, rather than caves. Or they lived wherever—they turned up in weird places. The security guard at the Ice-O-Plex heard an eerie yipping one night. He flipped on the lights and found a half dozen of them sliding around the rink like otters. At least we knew another thing about them. They loved ice.

Facts about the cavemen have been difficult to establish. It is unclear if they're protected by the law. It is unclear if they are responsible for their actions. It *has* been determined that they're a nuisance to property and a threat to themselves. They will break into cars and climb fences to gain access to swimming pools, where they drop to all fours to drink. They will snatch food out of trucks or bins and eat out of trash cans. They avoid modern man as a general rule but are becoming bolder by the hour. The university students attempting to study them have had difficulties, though they've managed to discover that the cavemen cannot be taught or tamed and are extremely difficult to contain. They're strong for their size. It's hard to hurt them but they're simple to distract. They love pink plastic figurines and all things little-girl pretty. They love products perfumed with synthetic woodsy or herbal scents. You can shoot at them with rubber bullets all day and they'll just stand there, scratching their asses, but if you wave a little bottle of Barbie bubble bath in front of them they'll follow you around like a dog. They do not understand deterrence. They understand desire.

Fathers, lock up your daughters.

Kim sits across from me at the table, fingering the stem of her wineglass and giving me The Look. She gets The Look whenever I confess that I'm not ready to get married yet. The Look is a peculiar expression, pained and brave, like Kim has swallowed a bee but she isn't going to let on.

"It's fine," she says. "It's not like I'm all goddamn *ready* either." I drain my glass and sigh. Tonight she's made a fennel-basil lasagna, lit candles, and scratched the price tag off the wine. Kim and I have been together for ten years, since we were twenty-three, and she's still a real firecracker, brainy, blonde, and bitchy. What I have in Kim is one of those cute little women with a swishy ponytail who cuts people off in traffic while swearing like a Marine. She's a fierce one, grinding her teeth all night long, grimly determined, though the object of her determination is usually vague or unclear. I've never wanted anyone else. And I've followed her instructions. I've nested. I mean, we bought a house together. We're co-borrowers on a thirty-year mortgage. Isn't that commitment enough?

Oh no, I can see it is not. She shoots me The Look a couple more times and begins grabbing dishes off the table and piling them in the sink. Kim wants the whole ordeal: a white dress, bridesmaids stuffed into taffeta, a soft rain of cherry blossoms. I want none of it. The whole idea of marriage makes me want to pull a dry cleaning bag over my head. I miss our punk rock days, Kim and me and our loser friends playing in bands, hawking spit at guys in BMWs, shooting drugs and living in basements with anarchy tattoos poking through the rips in our clothing. Those times are gone and we've since established real credit ratings, I had the circled-A tattoo lasered off my neck, but . . . But. I feel like marriage would exterminate the last shred of the rebel in me. For some reason, I think of marriage as a living death.

Or, I don't know, maybe I'm just a typical guy, don't want to pay for the cow if I can get the milk for free.

Kim is leaning in the open doorway, gazing out at the street, sucking on a cigarette. She doesn't smoke much anymore, but every time I tell her I'm not ready she rips through a pack in a day and a half. "They'd probably ruin it anyway," she says, watching a trio of cavemen out on the street, loping along, sniffing the sidewalk. They fan out and then move back together to briefly touch one another's ragged, dirty brown fur with their noses. The one on the end, lighter-boned with small, pale breasts poking out of her chest hair, stops dead in her tracks and begins making a cooing sound at the sky. It must be a full moon. Then she squats and pees a silver puddle onto the road.

Kim stares at her. She forgets to take a drag and ash builds on the end of her cigarette. I know her; I know what she's thinking. She's picturing hordes of cavemen crashing the reception, grabbing canapés with their fists, rubbing their crotches against the floral arrangements. That would never do. She's too much of a perfectionist to ever allow that.

When I first saw the cavemen scurrying around town, I have to admit

I was horrified. It was like when kids started to wear those huge pants—
I couldn't get used to it, I couldn't get over the shock. But now I have
hopes Kim will let the marriage idea slide for a while. For this reason
I am somewhat grateful to the cavemen.

It rains for three days and the railroad underpasses flood. The washes
are all running and on the news there are shots of SUVs bobbing in the
current because some idiot ignored the DO NOT ENTER WHEN
FLOODED sign and tried to gun it through four feet of rushing water.
A lot of cavemen have been driven out of their nests and the incident
level is way up. They roam around the city hungry and disoriented. We
keep the doors locked at all times. Kim has a few stashes of sample-
sized shampoo bottles around the house. She says she'll toss them out
like trick-or-treat candy if any cavemen come around hassling her. So
far, we haven't had any trouble.

Our neighbors, the Schaefers, haven't been so lucky. Kim invites
them over for dinner one night, even though she knows I can't stand
them. The Schaefers are these lonely, New Age hippies who are always
staggering toward us with eager, too-friendly looks on their faces, arms
outstretched, like they're going to grab our necks and start sucking. I
beg Kim not to invite them, but at this stage in the game she seems to
relish annoying me. They arrive dressed in gauzy robes. It turns out
Winsome has made us a hammock out of hemp in a grasping attempt
to secure our friendship. I tell her it's terrific and take it into the spare
room where I stuff it in a closet, fully aware that by morning all of our
coats are going to smell like bongwater.

When I return, everyone is sipping wine in the living room while the
storm wets down the windows. Winsome is describing how she found
a dead cavebaby in their backyard.

"It must not have been there for long," she says, her huge, oil-on-velvet
eyes willing up with tears, "because it just looked like it was sleeping,
and it wasn't very stiff. Its mother had wrapped it in tinsel, like for
Christmas."

"Ick," says Kim. "How can you cry for those things?"

"It looked so vulnerable." Winsome leans forward and touches Kim's
knee. "I sensed it had a spirit. I mean, they're human or proto-human
or whatever."

"I don't care," says Kim, "I think they're disgusting."

"Isn't that kind of judgmental?"

"I think we should try to understand them," chimes in Evan, smoothing down his smock—every inch the soulful, sandal-wearing, sensitive man. "In a sense, they're *us*. If we understood why that female caveman wrapped her baby in tinsel, perhaps we'd know a little more about ourselves."

"I don't see why people can't just say 'cavewoman,'" snaps Kim. "'Female caveman' is weird, like 'male nurse.' Besides, they are *not* us. We're supposed to have won. You know, survival of the fittest."

"It might be that it's time we expanded our definition of 'humanity,'" intones Evan. "It might be that it's time we welcome all creatures on planet Earth."

I'm so incredibly annoyed by Evan that I have to go into the bathroom and splash cold water on my face. When I get back, Kim has herded the Schaefers into the dining room, where she proceeds to serve us a deluxe vegetarian feast: little kabobs of tofu skewered along with baby turnips, green beans, rice, and steamed leaf of something or other. Everything is lovely, symmetrical, and delicious, as always. The house looks great. Kim has cleaned and polished and organized the contents of each room until it's like living in a furniture store. The Schaefers praise everything and Kim grumbles her thanks. The thing about Kim is she's a wonderful cook, a great creator of ambiance, but she has a habit of getting annoyed with her guests, as if no one could ever be grateful enough for her efforts. We drain a couple more bottles of wine and after a while I notice that Kim has become fed up with the Schaefers too. She starts giving them The Look.

"Seriously," she begins, "do you two even like being married?"

They exchange a glance.

"No, c'mon, really. It's overrated, right?" Kim pulls the hair off her face and I can see how flushed she is, how infuriated. "I think all that crap about biological clocks and baby lust, it's all sexist propaganda meant to keep women in line."

"Well, I haven't noticed any conspiracy," offers Winsome, checking everyone's face to make sure she's not somehow being disagreeable. "I think marriage is just part of the journey."

"Ha," says Kim. "Ha ha ha." She leans across the table, swaying slightly. "I know," she pronounces, "that you don't believe that hippie shit. I can tell," she whispers, "how fucking lost you really are."

Then she stands, picks up her glass, and weaves toward the back door. "I have to go check the basement."

We stare at the space where Kim was for a while. Winsome is blinking

rapidly and Evan keeps clearing his throat. I explain we have an unfinished basement that's been known to fill with water when it rains, and
that the only entrance to it is outside in the yard, and that Kim probably
wants to make sure that everything's okay down there. They nod vigor-
ously. I can tell they're itching to purify our home with sticks of burning sage.

While Kim is gone I take them into the living room and show them
my collection of LPs. I pull out my rare purple vinyl X-Ray Spex record,
and after considering this for a while, Winsome informs me that purple
is a healing color. We hear a couple of bangs under the house. I toy with
the idea of checking on Kim, but then I recall the early days of our
courtship, before all this house-beautiful crap, when Kim used to hang
out the window of my 1956 hearse, which was also purple, and scream
"Anarchy now!" and "Destroy!" while lobbing rocks through smoked
glass windows into corporate lobbies. It's difficult to worry about a girl
like that.

It doesn't take long for the Schaefers and me to run out of small talk.
I have no idea how to get them to go home; social transitions are Kim's
jurisdiction. We sit there nodding at each other like idiots until Kim
finally straggles back inside. She's muddy, soaked to the bone, and
strangely jolly. She says there's about a foot of water in the basement
and that she was walking around in there and it's like a big honking
wading pool. She giggles. The Schaefers stare with horror at the puddle
spreading around her feet onto our nice oak floors. I put my arm around
her and kiss her hair. She smells like wet dog.

I come home from work a few days later and find Kim unloading a Toys
R Us bag. I notice a diamond tiara/necklace set with huge, divorcée-
sized fake jewels stuck to a panel of pink cardboard. Again, she seems
happy, which is odd for Kim. In fact, she's taken to singing around the
house in this new style where she doesn't sing actual words, she goes
"nar nar nar" like some demented little kid. It drives me crazy, in particular when the game is on, so I tell her to fucking please cut it out.
She glares at me and storms off into the backyard. I let her pout for a
while, but I'm in the mood to make an effort, so I eventually go out and
find her standing on a chair, hanging over the hedge, gazing at the alley.
I lean in beside her and see a caveman shambling off with a red bandana tied around his neck, like a puppy.

"That's weird."

"Look at his butt."

I look. There's a big blob of pink bubble gum stuck in his fur.

"God," says Kim, "isn't that pitiful?"

I ask her what we're having for dinner. She looks at me blankly and says I don't know, what are we having for dinner. I tell her I'll cook, and when I get back from picking up the pizza she's nowhere to be found. I walk from one empty room to another while the hairs on my arms start to tingle. I have to say, there's a peculiar feeling building in the household. Things are in a state of slight disarray. There's a candy bar wrapper on the coffee table, and the bag from the toy store is on the kitchen floor. I yell Kim's name. When she doesn't appear I turn on the TV and eat a few slices straight from the box. For some reason that starts to bother me, so I get up and get a plate, silverware, and a paper napkin. Kim walks in a little while later. She's wet from the waist down and all flushed, as if she's been doing calisthenics.

"I was bailing out the basement!" she says, with great verve, like basement bailing is a terrific new sport. Her hair is tangled around her head and she's sucking on a strand of it. She is smiling away. She says: "I'm worried about letting all that water just stand down there!"

But she doesn't look worried.

On the news one night, a psychic with a flashlight shining up under his chin explains there's a time portal in the condemned Pizza Hut by the freeway. Though the mayor whines he wasn't elected to buckle to the whim of every nutbar with an opinion, there are televised protests featuring people shaking placards proclaiming the Pizza Hut ground zero of unnatural evil, and finally they just bulldoze it to shut everyone up. A while after that, the incident levels start to drop. It seems that the cavemen are thinning out. They are not brainy enough for our world, and they can't stop extinguishing themselves. They tumble into swimming pools and drown. They walk through plate glass windows and sever their arteries. They fall asleep under eighteen-wheelers and wander onto runways and get mauled by pit bulls.

It looks like we're the dominant species after all; rock smashes scissors, *Homo sapiens sapiens* kicks *Homo sapiens neanderthalensis*'s ass.

As the caveman population drops, the ominous feeling around town begins to lift. You can feel it in the air: women jog by themselves instead of in pairs. People barbecue large cuts of meat at dusk. The cavemen, it seems, are thinning out everywhere except around our house. I come home from work and walk through the living room and peek out the back window just in time to see a tough, furry leg disappear through a hole in the hedge. The hole is new. When I go outside and kick around in the landscaping, I find neat little stashes of rhinestones and fake pearls, Barbie shoes, and folded squares of foil wrapping paper. They can't see that well, but have the ears of a dog and flee as soon as I rustle the window shaders. One time, though, I peel back the shade silently and catch a pair skipping in circles around the clothesline. One of them is gripping something purple and hairy, and when I go out there later I find a soiled My Little Pony doll on the ground. They are not living up to their reputation as club-swinging brutes. More than anything, they resemble feral little girls.

Also, our house has become an unbelievable mess. Kim walks through the door and drops the mail on the coffee table, where it remains for days until I remove it. There are panties on the bathroom floor and water glasses on top of the television and scraps of food on the kitchen counter. I ask Kim what's going on and she just says she's sick of that anal constant-housekeeping-bullshit, and if I want it clean, I can clean it myself. She looks straight at me and says this, without flinching, without any signs of deference or anger or subtle backing away that had always let me know, in nonverbal but gratifying ways, that I had the upper hand in the relationship. She tosses an orange peel on the table before marching outside and descending into the basement.

I stand there in the kitchen, which smells like sour milk, shaking my head and trying to face up to the increasingly obvious fact that my girl-friend of ten years is having an affair, and that her lover is a Neanderthal man from the Pleistocene epoch. They rendezvous in our moldy, water-stained basement where he takes her on the cement floor beneath a canopy of spiderwebs, grunting over her with his animal-like body, or perhaps behind her, so that when she comes back inside there are thick, dark hairs stuck all over her shirt and she smells like a cross between some musky, woodland animal gland and Herbal Essences shampoo. Furthermore, she's stopped shaving her legs.

The next day, I duck out of the office claiming I have a doctor's appoint-ment and zip back home around noon. I open the door with my key and creep inside. I don't know what I'm looking for. I think I half expect to find Kim in bed with one of those things, and that he'll pop up and start "trying to reason" with me in a British accent. What I find instead is an empty house. Kim's car is gone. I poke around, stepping over mounds of dirty clothes, then head out back and take the stairs to the basement. When I pull the door open, the first thing to hit me is the smell of mold and earth. I pace from one side to the other and shine my flashlight around, but I don't see anything suspicious, just an old metal weight-lifting bench with a plastic bucket sitting on top. Maybe, I think, I'm making this whole thing up in my head. Maybe Kim just goes down there because she needs some time to herself.

But then on my way out, I spot something. On the concrete wall beside the door, several feet up, my flashlight picks out a pattern of crude lines. They appear to have been made with charcoal or maybe some type of crayon. When I take a few steps back, I can see it's a drawing, a cave painting of some sort. It's red and black with the occasional pom-pom of dripping orange that looks like it was made by someone who doesn't understand spray paint.

I stand there for two or three minutes trying to figure out what the painting is about, then spend another fifteen trying to convince myself my interpretation is wrong. The picture shows half a dozen cars in a V-shaped formation bearing down on a group of cavemen. The cavemen's flailing limbs suggest flight or panic; obviously, they're in danger of being flattened by the cars. Above them, sketched in a swift, forceful manner, floats a huge, God-like figure with very long arms. One arm cradles the fleeing cavemen while the other blocks the cars. This figure is flowing and graceful and has a big ponytail sprouting from the top of her head. Of course, it's meant to be Kim. Who else?

I go upstairs and sit at the kitchen table, elbowing away half a moldy cantaloupe, and hold my head in my hands. I was hoping it was nothing—a casual flirtation at most—but a guy who makes a cave painting for a girl is probably in love with the girl. And girls love to be loved, even high-strung ones like Kim. I admit I'm hurt, but my hurt switches to anger and my anger to resolve. I can fight this thing. I can win her back. I know her; I know what to do.

I put on rubber gloves and start cleaning everything, thoroughly and with strong-smelling products, the way Kim likes things cleaned. I do the laundry and iron our shirts and line everything up neatly in the closet. I get down on my knees and wipe the baseboards, then up on a chair to dust the lightbulbs. I pull a long clot of hair out of the drain. There's a picture of us in Mexico in a silver frame on top of the medicine cabinet. I pick it up and think: that is my woman! It's civilization versus base instinct, and I vow to deploy the strongest weapon at my disposal: my evolutionarily superior traits. I will use my patience, my facility with machinery and tools, my complex problem-solving skills. I will bathe often and floss my teeth. I will cook with gas.

A little after five Kim walks in and drops the mail on the coffee table. She looks around the house, at the gleaming neatness, smiling slightly and going "nar nar nar" to the tune of "Nobody Does It Better." I stand there in my cleanest suit with my arms hanging at my sides and gaze at her, in her little professional outfit, pretty and sexy in an I-don't-know-it-but-I-do way, clutching her black purse, her hair pulled back with one of those fabric hair things.

"God, I can't believe you cleaned," she says, and walks through the kitchen and out of the house into the yard and slams the basement door behind her.

Kim is so happy. The worst part is she's so disgustingly happy and I could never make her happy all by myself and I don't particularly like her this way. For a couple of weeks she walks around in a delirious haze. She spins around on the porch with her head thrown back and comments on the shape of the clouds. She asks why haven't I bothered to take in the pretty, pretty sunset, all blue and gold. Like I fucking care, I say, forgetting my pledge to be civil. It's as though someone has dumped a bottle of pancake syrup over her head—she has no nastiness left, no edge, no resentment. Her hair is hanging loose and she has dirty feet and bad breath. She smiles all the time. This is not the girl I originally took up with.

Of course, I'm heartstick; I'm torn up inside. Even so, I do my best to act all patient and evolutionarily superior. I keep the house clean enough to lick. I start to cook elaborate meals the minute I get home from work. I groom myself until I'm sleek as a goddamn seal. I aim for a Fred Astaire/James Bond hybrid: smooth, sophisticated, oozing suaveness around the collar and cuffs—the kind of guy who would never fart in front of a woman, at least not audibly. She has a big, inarticulate lug already. I want to provide her with an option.

Kim takes it all for granted, coming and going as she pleases, wandering away from the house without explanation, hanging out in the basement with the door locked and brushing off my questions about what the hell she's doing down there, and with whom. She doesn't listen when I talk to her and eats standing in front of the refrigerator with the door open, yelling between bites that it's time for me to go to the store and get more milk. One evening I watch her polish off a plate of appetizers I have made for her, melon balls wrapped in prosciutto, downing them one after another like airline peanuts. When she's finished, she unbuttons the top button of her pants and ambles out the door and lets it slam without so much as a glance back at me. Without so much as a thank you.

I trot out after her, figuring it's about time I give her a suave, patient lecture, but I'm not fast enough and she slams the basement door in my face. I pound and scream for a while before giving up and going up into the yard to wait. The night is very still. There's a full moon and the hedges glow silver on the top and then fade to blue at the bottom. I get a glass of iced tea and pull a chair off the patio, thinking to myself that she can't stay down there forever. I think about how maybe I'll catch the caveguy when he comes out too. Maybe I can tie on an apron and offer them both baby wieners on a toothpick.

After a while I hear a rustling in the hedges. At that moment I'm too miserable to be aware of the specifics of what's going on around me, so I'm startled as hell when a cavegirl pops out of the hedge, backlit in the moonlight, and begins walking toward me with a slow, hesitant gait. I sit there, taking shallow breaths, not sure whether or not I should be afraid. She has a low brow and a tucked, abbreviated chin, like Don Knotts', but her limbs are long and sinewy. When she gets closer I see that she looks a lot stronger than a human woman does, and of course she's naked. Her breasts are like perfect human pinup breasts with bunny fur growing all over them. I can't unstick my eyes from them as they bob toward me, moving closer, until they come to a stop less than an arm's length from my chin. They are simultaneously furry and plump and I really want to bite them. But not hard.

She leans in closer. I hold very still as she reaches out with a leathery hand and begins to stroke my lapel. She lowers her head to my neck and sniffs. On the exhale I discover that cavegirl breath smells just like moss. She prods me a few times with her fingertips; after she's had enough of that she just rubs the fabric of my suit and sniffs my neck while sort of kneading me rhythmically, like a purring cat. It's pretty obvious she likes my suit—a shiny sharkskin number I've hauled out of the back of the closet in the interest of wooing Kim—and I guess she likes my cologne too. For a minute I feel special and chosen, but then it occurs to me that there's something sleazy and impersonal about her attention. I'm probably just a giant, shiny, sandalwood-scented object to her. The moon is behind her so I can't see her that clearly, but then she shifts and I get a better view of her face and I realize she's young. Really young. I feel like a creep for wanting to feel her up, more because she's about fourteen than because she's a Neanderthal.

She swings a leg over and settles her rump onto my thigh, lap-dance-style.

I say: "Whoa there, Jailbait."

The cavegirl leaps up like she's spring-loaded. She stops a few feet away and stares at me. I stare back. She tilts her head from side to side in puzzlement. The moon shines down. I reach into my glass and draw out a crescent-shaped piece of ice, moving with aching slowness, and offer it to her on a flat palm. She considers this ice cube for a good long time. I hold my arm as still as possible while freezing water trickles off my elbow and my muscles start to seize. Then, after a few false lunges, she snatches it from my hand.

"Nar," she says. Just that. Then she darts back into the hedge with her prize.

I remain in the moonlight for a while, shaking with excitement. I feel almost high. It's like I've touched a wild animal; I've communicated with it—an animal that's somehow human, somehow like me. I'm totally giddy.

This is probably how it was with Kim and her guy when they first met.

I guess I'm a complete failure with every category of female because the cavegirl does not come back. Even worse, Kim continues to treat me like I'm invisible. It's painfully clear that my strategy of suaveness isn't working. So I say screw evolution. What's it ever done for me? I go out drinking with the guys and allow the house to return to a state of nature. The plates in the sink turn brown. I shower every other day, every third. Kim and I go days without speaking to each other. By this time there are hardly any cavemen left around town; the count is running at one or two dozen. I go to the bars and everyone is lounging with their drinks, all relaxed and relieved that the cavemen aren't really an issue anymore, while I continue to stew in my own miserable interspecies soap opera. I don't even want to talk to anyone about it. What could I say? Hey buddy, did I mention my girlfriend has thrown me over for the Missing Link? It's humiliating.

One hungover afternoon I decide to skip the bars and come straight home from the office. Kim, naturally, is not around, though this barely registers. I've lost interest in tracking her whereabouts. But when I go into the kitchen, I catch sight of her through the window, standing outside, leaning against the chinaberry tree. It looks like she's sick or something. She's trying to hold herself up but keeps doubling over anyway. I go outside and find her braced against the tree, sobbing from deep in her belly while a string of snot swings from her nose. She's pale and spongy and smudged with dirt and I get the feeling she's been standing there crying all afternoon. She's clutching something. A red bandana. So it was him. The one with gum on his butt.

"Where is he?"

"He's gone," she whispers, and gives me a sad, dramatic, miniseries smile. "They're all gone."

Her sobs begin anew. I pat her on the back.

So she's curled over crying and I'm patting her thinking well, well; now that the other boyfriend is gone she's all mine again. Immediately I'm looking forward to putting the whole caveman ordeal behind us and having a regular life like we had before. I see all sorts of normal activities looming in the distance like a mirage, including things we always made fun of, like procreating and playing golf. She blows her nose in the bandana. I put my arm around her. She doesn't shake it off.

I should wait I know, I should go slow; but I can see the opening, the niche all vacant and waiting for me. I feel absolutely compelled to exploit it right away, before some other guy does. I turn to Kim and say: "Babe, let's just forget about this whole caveman thing and go back to the way it was before. I'm willing to forgive you. Let's have a normal life without any weird creatures in it, okay?"

She's still hiccuping and wiping her nose but I observe a knot of tension building in her shoulders, the little wrinkles of a glare starting around the edge of her eyes. I realize I'm in grave danger of eliciting The Look. It dawns on me that my strategy is a failure and I'd better think fast. So I bow to the inevitable. I've always known I couldn't put it off forever.

I take a deep breath and drop to one knee and tell her I love her and I can't live without her and beg her to marry me while kissing her hand. She's hiccuping and trying to pull her hand away, but in the back of my mind I'm convinced that this is going to work and of course she'll say yes. I've never made an effort like this before; I've only told her I love

123

her two or three times total, in my life. It's inconceivable that this effort won't be rewarded. Plus, I know her. She lives for this. This is exactly what she wants.

I look up at her from my kneeling position. Her hair is greasy and her face is smeared with dirt and snot, but she's stopped crying. I see that she has created a new Look. It involves a shaking of the head while simultaneously pushing the lips outward, like she's crushed a wasp between her teeth and is about to spit it out. It's a look of pity, pity mixed with superiority; pity mixed with superiority and blended with dislike.

"I don't want a normal life without any creatures in it," Kim says, her voice ragged from crying, but contemptuous nonetheless. "I want an extraordinary life, with everything in it."

The Look fades. She brings her dirty, snotty face to mine and kisses me on the forehead and turns and walks away, leaving me on my knees. I stumble into the house after her. I can smell a trail of scent where she's passed by, cinnamon and sweat and fabric softener, but though I run through the house after her, and out into the street, I don't see her anywhere, not all night. Not the night after that. Never again.

Some psychic with a towel on his head says the cavemen passed through his drive-through palm-reading joint on their way back to the Pleistocene epoch, and I finally go over and ask him if he saw Kim with them. He has me write him a check and then says, Oh *yeah*, I did see her! She was at the front of this line of female cavemen and she was all festooned with beads and tinsel, like she was some sort of goddess! He says it in this bullshit way, but after some reflection I decide even charlatans may see strange and wondrous things, as we all had during the time the cavemen were with us, and then report them so that they sound like a totally improbable lie.

It's bizarre, the way time changes things. Now that the cavemen are gone, it seems obvious that their arrival was the kind of astonishing event people measure their entire lives by; and now that Kim is gone it seems clear that she was astonishing too, regal and proud, like she's represented in the cave painting. I once thought of her as sort of a burden, a pain-in-the-ass responsibility, but now I think of her as the one good thing I had in my life, an intense woman with great reserves of strength, forever vanished.

Or, I don't know; maybe I'm just a typical guy, don't know what I have until it walks out on me.

I've been trying to get over her, but I can't stop wallowing in it. One night we hold a drum circle on the site of the old Pizza Hut, and I swear that after this night, I'll force myself to stop thinking about her. This drum circle is the largest yet, maybe a couple of hundred people milling around, having the kind of conversations people have these days—you know, they were annoyed and frightened by the cavemen when they were here, but now that they're gone they just want them back, they want the weird, vivid feeling, the newness of the primitive world, et cetera. My job is to tend the fire. There's a six-foot pyramid of split pine in the middle of the circle, ready to go. At the signal I throw on a match. The wood is soaked in lighter fluid and goes up with a whoosh. Everyone starts to bang on their drums, or garbage can lids, or whatever percussive dingus they've dragged along, while I stand there poking the flames, periodically squirting in plumes of lighter fluid, as the participants wail and drum and cry and dance.

We are supposedly honoring the cavemen with this activity, but in truth no one ever saw the cavemen making fires or dancing or playing any sort of musical instrument. Apparently the original Neanderthal did these things; they also ate one another's brains and worshipped the skulls of bears, though no one seems anxious to resurrect these particular hobbies. Still, I admit I get kind of into it. Standing there in the middle, sweating, with the sound of the drumming surrounding me while the fire crackles and pops, it's easy to zone out. For a moment I imagine what it might be like to live in an uncivilized haze of sweat and hunger and fear and desire, to never plan, to never speak or think in words—but then the smell of lighter fluid snaps me back to how artificial this whole drum circle is, how prearranged and ignited with gas.

Later, when the fire has burned out, some New Age hardcores roll around in the ashes and pray for the cavemen to come back, our savage brothers, our hairy predecessors, et cetera, but of course they don't come back. Those guys look stupid, covered in ash. When the sun comes up, everyone straggles away. I get into my hatchback and listen to bad news on the radio as I drive home.

THE HIGH ROAD

fiction by JOAN SILBER

My whole life, it always made me crazy when people weren't sensible. Dancers, for instance, have the worst eating habits. I can't begin to say how many anorexic little girls I used to have to hold up onstage, afraid they were going to faint on me any minute.

I myself was lean and tight and healthy in those days. I went out with different women, and I married one of them. I don't know why she married me, I was never kind to her, but women did not expect much then. She was probably a better dancer than I was, too. I left her, after a lot of nasty fights and spite on both sides, and I went and had my life with men. It was a dirty, furtive, sexy life then—this was before Stonewall—but it had its elations. Infatuation, when it happened, could be visionary, a lust from another zone. From the true zone, the molten center of the earth. I was in my twenties, listening to a lot of jazz, and I thought in phrases like that.

Andre, my lover, was in fact a musician, a trumpeter with a tender, earnest sound, sweet like Chet Baker, although he would have liked to have been as intense as Miles. Well, who wouldn't? I had been with men before him, but only one-night pickups, those flickering hallucinations that were anything but personal. When I met Andre, we were not in a bar but at a mixed party, and we had to signal each other cautiously and make a lot of conversation first. Andre was no cinch to talk to, either. Other white people thought he was gruff or scornful, but actually he was really quite shy.

When we went home together, after the party, we got along fine. For a shy person, he was confident and happy in bed (I was the rough and

126

bumbling one). I could still recount, if I had to, the sequence of things we did that night. I have done them many times since—there isn't that much variety in the world—but the drama was particular and stunning just then. In the morning I made him a very nice breakfast (my wife had been a terrible cook), and he ate two helpings of my spinach omelet, as if he could not believe his good luck. He had a dry sense of humor, and he was quite witty about my makeshift housekeeping and my attempts at décor, the white fake-fur rug and the one wall painted black. We put on music, and we hung around, smoking cigarettes and reading the paper all afternoon. Just passing the time.

I was working in a show on Broadway, skip-skipping across the stage in cowboy chaps and swinging my silver lariat, and he came to see me perform. I suppose the other dancers knew who he was to me. Backstage everybody shook his hand and asked him if it wasn't the dumbest musical he'd ever seen. The girls told me later how nice he was. And sometimes I was in his world, when we went to hear music in the Village or once up to a club in Harlem. Anyone who saw us probably thought I was just some white theater guy wanting to be hip. Had we been a man and a woman, we would have had a much harder time walking together on the street.

Andre stayed with me more nights than not, even if he didn't live with me. But he had to go home to practice. A trumpet is not an instrument that can be played casually in someone's apartment. His own place, up in Morningside Heights, was in the basement (a great cheap find), and he had rigged up a booth lined with acoustic ceiling tile and squares of carpeting for his hours of practice. His chicken coop, I called it, his burrow. I never stayed over with him, and I only visited him there once, but I liked to imagine him hunched over his horn, blowing his heart out in that jerry-built closet.

He wasn't getting gigs yet, but sometimes he sat in with musicians he'd met. To this day, I couldn't say whether he was a great player or not. When he was playing with anyone, I worried like a parent—I looked around to see what people thought. He was okay, I think, but so modest and unflashy that he could be taken for a competent dullard. But he had a rare kind of attention, and sometimes, the way he worked his way in and the way he twisted around what they'd been playing made the other players smile. He was just learning.

In the daytime, he worked as a salesman in a men's clothing store in Midtown. Once I walked in the door and pretended to be a grouchy rich man who needed an ugly suit to wear to divorce court. Something

127

hideous, please, something you wouldn't wear to a dogfight. This cracked Andre up. He laughed through his teeth, hissing softly. That's how bored he was there. He introduced me to the manager as his crazy friend Duncan, this lunatic he knew.

He was quite a careful dresser, from working in that place. A little too careful, I thought, with his richly simple tie and his little handkerchief folded in his pocket. I used to tell people he ironed his underwear, which he stoutly denied. For Christmas he bought me a silk shirt that probably looked silly on me but felt great. We had dinner that day with two of Andre's friends, Reg and Maxmilian. I made a goose, a bird none of us had ever had before. We kept goosing each other all night, a joke that wouldn't die. Reg got particularly carried away, I thought. Andre teased me about the ornateness of my meal—the glazed parsnips, the broccoli *polonaise*—wasn't there a hog jowl in anything? He wanted the others to be impressed with me, and they sort of were. Andre asked me to put on the record of *Aida* he liked, the one with Roberta Tebaldi.

"Renata Tebaldi," I said.

"Rigatoni Manicotti," he said. "What do I care what her name is?"

But I took to calling him Roberta after that. Just now and then, to needle him. Pass the peas, Roberta. Like that.

We were at the Village Vanguard with a couple he knew when I said, "Roberta, you want another drink?" He turned his beautiful, soft eyes on me in a long stare and said, "Cool it."

I did cool it then, but not for long. He was sleepy in the club, since he had been working at the store all day, and at one point he slumped back in his chair and dozed. Anyone who noticed probably thought he was on drugs. I sang into his ear in a loud, breathy falsetto, "Wake up, Roberta."

The week after this, he refused to take me with him when he went out with his friends. He announced it at breakfast on Saturday. "You don't know respect," he said. "Stay home and study your manners."

He wouldn't say any more. He never got loudly upset as my wife had. I couldn't even get a good fight going.

"Go," I said. "Get away from me, then."

But that night, when the show let out, I took off my satin chaps and rubbed away the greasepaint, and I went walking up and down Bleecker Street, checking out all the clubs that Andre might be in. I just wanted him to be sweet to me again. I wanted to make up. I walked through dark, crowded cellars, peering at tables of strangers who were trying to listen to some moody trio. I must have looked like a stalking animal.

What if he never came back to me? He wasn't in four places I tried, and at the fifth, I sat at the bar and drank a Scotch, but I couldn't stay still. I walked all the way to the river, close to tears. I had never seen myself like this, wretched and pathetic. I could hardly breathe, from misery. I just wanted Andre to be sweet to me again. I couldn't stand it this way.

On the pier I picked up a guy, an acne-scarred blond in a baseball jacket. I didn't have to say more than hi, and I brought him home in a cab to my place in the West Forties. He was just a teenager—the luxury of a cab ride impressed him. I could see he was less excited when we got to my neighborhood with its hulking tenements. My block looked gloomy and unsafe, which it was.

And there on my stoop was Andre, waiting. I was still in the cab paying the driver when I saw him. The boy had already gotten out.

Andre's face was worn and tired—perhaps he had been sitting there a long time—and the sight of us seemed to make him wearier still. He sighed, and he shook his head. I put my arm around the boy, and I walked him past Andre to my front door, where I fished for my key without turning around.

I could hear Andre's footsteps as he walked away—east down the street, toward the subway. I did not turn my head at all. What control I had, all of a sudden. I who had been at the mercy of such desperate longing, such raging torment.

When I got the boy inside, I made him some pancakes—he looked hungry—and then we fooled around a little, but I wasn't good for much. He fell asleep, and I got him up at dawn and gave him some money. He didn't argue about the amount, and he understood that he had to leave.

And what did I do as soon as he was gone? I called Andre on the phone. How sleepy and startled his voice sounded. I loved his voice. When I said hello, he hung up.

And then I really was in hell, in the weeks after that. I woke up every morning freshly astonished that Andre was still gone and that my suffering was still there, the dead weight in my chest. When I phoned Andre again, I got him to talk, and he was rational enough, but he wasn't, he said, "very interested anymore." His language was tepid and somewhat formal. "Not about to embark on another disaster" was a phrase he used in a later conversation. That time I told him he sounded like a foreign exchange student.

So we stopped talking. Even I could see it was no use. But he was never out of my thoughts, he was always with me. I would be on the subway and realize I had shut my eyes in dreamy remembrance of a particular scene of us together, Andre on his knees to me in the shower. How languorous and smug my expression must have looked to riders on the A train. How disappointed I felt when I saw where I was.

I might have gone to find him at work, but I knew how he would be with me. If he was frosty over the phone, he would be a parody of polite disgust in the store, trying to flick me away with noble disdain. I hated the thought of actually seeing him like that, and I didn't want to hear what I might say back.

I didn't really have many friends to talk to. I was late getting to the show a few times, from not really caring and from sleeping too much, and I was fined and given a warning. I was very angry at Andre when this happened. He didn't care what he had done to me. I went down to City Hall, to the Buildings Department, and I looked up the deed to Andre's building to see who the owner was. I phoned the realty company to complain that someone was playing a trumpet very loudly at all hours of day and night. I phoned again and gave them another name, as a different angry neighbor. I phoned again.

On the last of these phone calls a secretary told me that the tenant had been advised he could remain in the apartment only if he ceased to be a noise nuisance, and he had chosen to leave, without paying his last month's rent. I was quite satisfied when I heard this—how often does anything we do in this life attain its goal? And then I remembered that I didn't know now where to find Andre. I didn't have his home phone number anymore.

I wanted to howl at the irony of this, like an anguished avenger in an opera. How had I not known better? Well, I hadn't. There was no new listing for him in any of the boroughs. And he was not at his job, either. Another salesman in the store thought maybe Andre had gone back to Chicago, where his family was. I didn't see him anymore, not on the street, not in clubs, not in bars. Not then, not later. Perhaps he became famous under another name. Who knows how his playing got to sound? Not me.

All these years later, I don't know if he is still alive. A lot of people aren't, as it has happened. But it may well be that he settled down—he was like that—and a long and sedate monogamy would have kept him safe, if he found someone early, and he probably did. I wasn't with any one person, after him. I didn't even look for such a thing. I went to bars and took home the occasional hot stranger, and I kept to myself a good part of the time.

For a decade or so I got work pretty steadily on Broadway. Those weren't bad years for musicals, although there was a lot of junk, too. I was hired to slink around as a thirties gangster, to be jaunty with a rake in my hand as a country yokel, and to do a leaping waltz as a Russian general, clicking the heels of my gleaming boots. Only a few male dancers got to be real stars, like Geoffrey Holder or Tommy Tune, and I suppose for a while I thought I could be one of them. I had a strong, clean style, and I was a great leaper. Nothing else anywhere did for me what that sensation of flying did. But my career never made its crucial turn, and then I got older than anyone wanted for the chorus line.

Which was not even that old. I was surrounded, however, by lithe and perfect young boys. Quite vapid, most of them, but decently trained. I was not even attracted to these children, as a rule. Probably I looked like some evil old elf to them, a skinny, brooding character with upswept eyebrows.

For a while I tried teaching in a dance studio, but I didn't get along with the director. She gave me the beginners' classes, and the students really didn't want any grounding in technique, they only wanted someone assuring them they could be professionals overnight. "Ladies," I would say to them, "get those glutes tucked in before you practice your autographs."

I didn't last that long at the school. In the end I gave up the whole idea of teaching, and I got a job in an agency booking dancers for clubs. Go-go girls, in spangled underwear and little white boots. I was the man the girls talked to after they read the classified and came into the office, nervous and flushed or tough and scowling. I sent them to clubs in the outer boroughs, airless caves in the Bronx with speakers blaring disco and red lights on the catwalk. My temper was so bad that people did what I told them, which was the agency's idea of sterling job performance. I was a snarling jerk in these years. Contempt filled my every cell; I was fat as a tick on contempt.

These were not good years, and my drinking got out of hand. One night in a bar, a man threw a chair at me and split open my head. When I missed two weeks' work, the agency hired someone else while I was gone, and there wasn't much I could do about it. It was not a clean or soft business. With my head still shaved and bandaged, I went back to the bar, itching for more trouble, but instead I ran into a dancer I used to know in my Broadway days. We were too old to want to pick each other up, but when I complained of being broke, he told me about a job at the union, answering phones and filing, if I didn't think that was beneath me.

I did, but I took the job, anyway. I used to say the work was bearable because of all those pert young boys who came into the building, but in fact I was in the back offices, hovering over ledgers and, in later years, facing a computer screen. It was a painless job, a reasonable thing to do until I found something else, and then it became what I did.

I didn't go to bars after a while. We knew at the union how many people were dying, even before the epidemic unfurled its worst. Cruising had not been full of glory for me, anyway, so I stayed home and counted myself one of the lucky ones. Staying home suited me. I read more books, and I had a few regular outings. I had brunch once a month with a few theater people I still knew. Through the union I got tickets to plays and sometimes operas. And I helped out backstage at some of the AIDS benefits we sponsored.

In the early years a lot of big names pitched in at these benefits, but later, too, there were people who were impressive in rehearsals. I stayed extra hours one night to listen to a tenor with a clear, mellow voice—he was singing a cycle of songs written by a composer who had just died of AIDS. The accompanist was an idiot, and they had to keep repeating the first song over and over. The singer was a puny, delicate boy, with pale eyebrows and colorless hair in a crewcut. He closed his eyes as he sang—not good form onstage, but affecting nonetheless.

During the break I told him to keep his eyes open, and he said, "Yes, yes. You're right."

"Your Italian sounds good, though," I said.

"I lived in Rome for a year," he said. "It was my idea for Jonathan to set these poems."

The composer had been his lover—I knew this, someone had told me—and the tenor sang with a mournful longing that was quite beautiful. *Amor m'ha fatto tal ch'io vivo in foco*, he sang. Love has made me live in ceaseless fire. I myself had Xeroxed the text for the programs.

His name was Carl, and he was young, still in his twenties. Recent grief had crumpled his face and left a faint look of outrage around his eyes. I began to bring him glasses of water during his break and to keep advising him. *Look at the audience. Watch your diction.* He was quite professional about the whole thing, and he only nodded, even when I praised him.

He let me take him out for a drink after the next rehearsal. We were in an overpriced bar in the theater district, full of tourists. He ordered a Campari and soda. "Isn't that a summer drink?" I said. It was the middle of February.

"It makes me happy to drink it," he said. "It makes me think of Italy."

As I might have guessed, he had gone there to study voice, and he had met his lover Jonathan there. "The light in Rome is quite amazing," he said. "Toasty and golden. Too bad it's so hard to describe light."

He was a boy romantic. Every day he and Jonathan had taken a walk through a park with a beautiful name, the Dora Pamphilj or the Villa Sciarra or the Borghese Gardens, and they had poked around in churches to gaze at Caravaggios or had sat eating gelato in front of some ravishing Bernini fountain. I knew only vaguely what all this was. He glistened and pulsed liked a glowworm, remembering it. I did not think any place could be that perfect, and said so.

"It's not," Carl said. "It can be a nightmare city. Noisy, full of ridiculous rules and only one way of doing things, and those jolly natives can be quite heartless. But because Jonathan is dead, I get to keep it as my little paradise."

"*Il paradiso*," I said, dumbly, in my opera Italian.

He asked me if I had ever toured when I was a dancer. "Only to Ohio and Kentucky," I said. "Nothing exotic. I just remember how tiring that road travel was."

"What keeps me going," he said, "is poetry. I make sure to have a book with me at all times."

I pictured him reading a beat-up paperback of Whitman while everyone else slept on the tour bus. But his favorite poet, he said, was Gaspara Stampa, the Italian whose sonnets I had heard him sing. "She's sort of a 1500's version of the blues," he said. "Love has done her wrong, but she's hanging in there. She thinks all women should envy her because she loves so hard."

I was an undereducated slob, compared to him, but one thing about being a dancer is you know how to pick things up. "I like that line you sing," I said, "about how I'll only grieve if I should lose the burdens that I bear."

"Yes," he said. "Exactly."

I went to more rehearsals. I didn't scold or correct, and I said "*Bravo*" or "*Stupendo*" when he was done. I patted him on the arm, and once I hugged him. We talked about Verdi, which I at least did not sound like a fool about, and about the history of New York office buildings, and about what he had to do to keep his voice in health. I did not ask, really, about his health.

"I am all fire, and you all ice," he sang. I told him they were torch songs. "Gender reversals of the traditional Petrarchan sonnet," Carl said. "A woman bragging about her unquenched longing. Very modern." What a swooner he was, how in love with pure feeling. And he was a huge hit at rehearsals. He had a theory about this, too. "No good words are said anymore," he said, "on behalf of torturing yourself for love. Everybody's told to *get over it*. But a little bleeding is good."

I had noticed that hopeless passion was still in high style in certain corners of the gay world, but I kept this observation to myself. "The pianist needs to practice," I said. "You know that, right?"

I wanted to cook for him, this flimsy little Carl, and I got him to come for dinner on a Sunday night. "Whoa," he said, when he saw my tenement apartment, which had been carved out of the wilderness almost thirty years before. "You've got everything packed in, like a ship." For supper I fed him beautiful food that was good for his vocal cords, no dairy or meat, only bright and cooling flavors. Blue Point oysters, cold sorrel soup, prawns with pea shoots and fresh ginger, purslane and mint salad. Everything vibrant and clarifying. Golden raspberries and bittersweet chocolate for dessert. I had knocked myself out, as he could not fail to notice.

The food made him happy. He said that when he first came to New York, he had been so poor he had eaten nothing but tofu and Minute Rice. Even now I had to show him how to eat a raw oyster. I felt like his uncle. That was not who I wanted to be.

"This is as good as food in Italy," he said. "In my Surviving Partners Group there's a guy who's a chef. I'm sure his food isn't better than this."

"Surely not," I said.

His Surviving Partners Group met every week. It was a great group, he said. But for him personally what was most helpful was meditation.

"Eating is good, too," I said.

"Yes," he said. "I forgot how good it was."

A beautiful suspense hovered around the table when he left for a minute to go off to the bathroom. When he came back into the room, I stood up, and I put my arms around him. He was so wispy and slight, much shorter than I was. He ducked his head, like someone sneaking under a gate, and he slipped right out of my arms.

134

He did not mean to mock me, he had only been embarrassed. Neither of us moved. I felt old. A vain old queen, a self-deluded old fruit.

I asked if he wanted coffee, and we sat down and drank it. He praised my espresso so lavishly that I couldn't tell if he only felt sorry for me or if he was trying to be friends nonetheless, if such a thing were possible with a grotesque old lech like myself.

At the next rehearsal Carl waved when he saw me. He came over and told me about how much better he sang ever since he'd eaten my dinner. "When I do my vocal exercises now," he said, "my voice is so good I move myself to tears." I thought he did like me. And perhaps I had not allowed him the time that someone like him needed. Perhaps the situation was not entirely hopeless.

When I went home after rehearsal, I lay in bed musing about what might happen between us after all. If I were patient. He had not been with anyone since his lover died, and I had not been with anyone in years. I had underestimated the depth of the enterprise, the large and moving drama involved. He would probably have to make the first move. He would surprise me, and we would laugh at my surprise.

In the middle of the night I got up and looked at the condoms in my night table drawer to see if the dates printed on the packets showed they were past safe use. I threw out the one that was expired. I sat on the edge of the bed in my underwear, hunched over, with my head buried in my hands. I had never asked Carl what his HIV status was. I was ready to go to bed with him without any protection at all, if that was what he wanted. All those years of being so careful I wouldn't risk going out of my own living room, and now I would have bargained away anything to have Carl. I was beyond all reason.

At work the next day the phone rang, and it was Carl inviting me over for brunch on Saturday. He was ashamed to cook for me, he said, but he could buy bagels as well as the next person.

He lived in a remote and dull section of Queens, on a street full of what had once been private houses. He had a nice little back apartment, with a view of the yard. "Welcome to my monkish cell," he said.

It was not cell-like—it was quite cozy and bright—but I was spooked by the shrines in it. On a small table, spread with a white linen cloth, was a collection of photos of his dead lover, who was a pleasant-looking young man, dark-haired and stocky. Jonathan waved from a deck chair on a beach, he stood in front of a Roman ruin and a bright blue sky, he laughed against Carl's shoulder at someone's birthday party. In another corner was an altar to the Buddha, with a stone statue of a thin, pigeon-chested Buddha facing into the room, and a fatter, calmer Buddha embroidered into a square of fringed brocade hanging on the wall. A single deep-blue iris, pure and wilting, stood in a vase. I did not like any of it.

But Carl had clearly wanted me to see it. He gave me a tour of all the photos, naming every guest at the birthday party. He gestured to the Buddhas and said, "Those are my buddies there." He told me that he did Vipassana meditation, adapted from what they did in Burma and Thailand, but that was a Tibetan tangka on the wall. "Very nice," I said. "It's the medicine Buddha," he said. "That's his healing unguent in the bowl in his hand." I chewed my bagel and nodded.

I gossiped about the rehearsals, just to get us somewhere else. "Did you see," I said, "how Brice is ogling that first violinist in the quartet? I expect him to drool all over the man's bow any minute. It's not subtle." Brice was the show's organizer.

"I missed it," he said. "I'm bad at noticing who's after who."

"Brice is so obvious."

"What can I tell you?" he said. "I'm away from all that. It's not in my world."

What world was he in?

"People don't think enough about celibacy," he said. "It hasn't been thought about very well in our era. It has a long history as a respected behavior. It has its beauty."

I knew then that he'd brought me here to say this, with the fittings of his cell as backdrop. "The Buddha never had sex?" I said. "I thought he had a family."

"That was before he was the Buddha."

"Don't get too carried away. You know you'll want someone sometime."

"I don't think so."

"It's *unnatural* at your age."

"I'm not unhappy."

Oh, honey, I thought, I didn't tempt you for a second, did I?

"A sexless life will ruin your voice," I said. "I'm not kidding. You'll sound like some wan little old lady. You already have to worry about that."

"Oh," he said. "We'll see."

"You already have some problems in the lower register."

"Oh," he said.

"You'll sound like a squawking hen in a few years."

"No more," he said. "That's enough."

I was depressed after this visit, but lack of hope didn't cure me, either. I didn't stop wanting Carl, and what I wanted kept playing itself out in my mind over and over. At home I would sometimes be slumped in an armchair, reading a book or watching TV, and not even know that I was lost in reverie, until I heard myself say out loud, "Oh, honey." It was terrible to hear my own voice like that, whimpering with phantom love. I was afraid I was going to cry out like this at my desk at work, with other people in earshot, but I never did.

We were civil with each other at the last rehearsal. Actually, Carl was more than civil. He made a decent effort to converse, while the string quartet was busy going through its number. "I read," he said to me, "that Rome is all different now because they've banned cars from parts of it."

"You know what I read?" I said. "I read that there was a man who was very high up in a Buddhist organization who went around sleeping with people and giving them AIDS. Lots of young men. He knew he had it, and he didn't tell anyone he slept with. He thought he could control his karma."

"Oh," Carl said. "That happened years ago. When did you read it?"

"A while ago."

"Why are you telling me now?"

"Those are the guys you want to emulate," I said. "Those are your shining models."

"No," he said. "That was one guy."

"Lust crops up," I said. "Can't keep it down."

"That's not what that story means," he said. "It's about arrogance and delusion, not lust. He could have used condoms."

"Right," I said. "Sure. You'll be like him. You'll see."

He reddened then. I'd forgotten that his HIV status might be positive, for all I knew, which did deepen the insult. He shook his head at me. "Oh, Duncan," he said, sourly.

On the night of the concert, I dressed very nicely. I wore a slate-blue shirt, a beautiful celadon tie that Andre had once given me, a stone-gray sports jacket. I hadn't looked that good in years. I sat with some other people from work in a chilly section of the orchestra seats. The string quartet was first, playing a stodgy piece badly. I really did not hear anything until Carl walked onstage to sing Jonathan's songs. He looked pale as marble, an angel with a shimmering crewcut.

He had a few intonation problems at first but sounded lovely and sure once he got going. Jonathan had written him easy music, except for a few jagged rhythm changes. "*Viver ardendo e non sentire il male,*" he sang. "To live burning and not to feel the pain." Wasn't it enough that I suffered at home? Did I have to come here and hear my beloved wail about the trials of the rejected? I wanted to shout in protest. I should not have come, I saw. Who would have cared if I hadn't come?

Then my protest and exasperation fused with the plaint of the songs, with their familiar trouble, and I had a bluesy ache in my chest that was oddly close to solace. I felt the honor of my longing. This idea did quite a lot for me. My situation, ludicrous as it was, at least lost the taint of humiliation.

When the songs were over, I was surprised when the applause did not go on for hours, although people seemed to have liked the pieces well enough. I was still in a faint trance when the concert broke for intermission. I stayed alone in my seat while the others milled around. The second half was a woodwind quintet I had never liked, and they did three numbers. When they were finally done, I moved through the crowd and found Carl in the lobby, surrounded by people clasping him in congratulation. "*Bravissimo,*" I said to him. "Really." He gave me a sudden, broad smile—praise from me probably did mean something to him—but he was busy thanking people.

I stayed around long enough to get pulled along with a group that went out for drinks afterward. I did not ask if I could come, and perhaps I wasn't welcome, but no one said so. We sat at a big round table in a bar with peach-tinted walls. The accompanist, whose playing hadn't been as bad as I'd feared, kept leaning toward Carl with an excited attention that looked like a crush to me.

Carl himself was busy introducing everyone to a slick young giant of a man who turned out to be the chef from his Surviving Partners Group. "My very good friend," Carl called him. "Duncan, you should talk to

Larry about his food. You're the one who'll really appreciate what he does."

"Oh, I will?" I said.

"*I* like food," someone else at the table said. "I like it all the time."

I was about to say, "Cooks who are fans of themselves tend to show it," but then I didn't. I decided to shut up, for a change. There was no point to my baiting anyone at the table just for fun, in front of Carl. No point at all now.

But it was hard for me. I stayed sullenly quiet for a while, sulking and leaning back in my chair. When Chef Larry told a funny story about his poultry supplier, I didn't laugh. When Carl talked about a production of *Wozzeck* that he was about to go on tour with, all through Canada, from Quebec to Vancouver, I didn't ask when he was leaving or when he was coming back. I didn't say a word. But then when the pianist said he had been practicing too much in a cold room, and he complained of stiffness in his elbow, I gave him a very good exercise he could do at home. I explained it without sarcasm or snottiness or condescension. I was at my all-time nicest, for Carl's sake, for Carl's benefit. I don't know that he, or anyone, noticed.

Carl went on tour for six months, as I discovered from his phone machine when I called him later. It didn't surprise me that he hadn't said goodbye—I was probably someone that he wanted out of his life. Still, I dreamed of his return. How could I not? When he came back, I would tell him how I had begun to think of myself as a celibate, too, that I had moved toward a different respect for that as a way to be, and perhaps we could be friends now on a new basis. It made me happy to think of our new comradeship, his easy and constant company, his profile next to me at operas and plays. But I knew, even as I imagined our lively and natural conversations on topics of real interest to both of us, that my reasoning was insincere, only a ruse to win Carl to me in whatever way I could.

But since I could not talk to Carl, who was off singing to the Canadians, I was left with my own recitation of why I treasured austerity running in a loop through my mind. I was the captive audience for what was meant to disarm Carl. This was not the worst speech to be trapped with. It made the tasks I did in solitude—my exercises, my errands—seem finer.

The exercises were a particular annoyance to me. I had done exercises all my life (except for some goofing off during the booking-agency years), but now I had arthritis, plague of old athletes and dancers, in my knees and just starting in my hips. All that hopping and turning and high-kicking had been hard on the cartilage. I had to go through a full range of motion every day to keep the joints flexible, which they did not want to be anymore. Some of this hurt, and I hated being a sloppy mover. But now, swinging my leg to the side, I felt less disgraced by it. My routine, performed alone in my bare bedroom, had its merit and order. An hour in the morning and stretches at night. I had my privacy and my discipline.

Every Tuesday evening I went to a guy named Fernando for bodywork. I lay on my stomach while he bent my knees and hooked his thumbs into my muscles. The word ouch did not impress him. He had been a dancer once, too. "Stay skinny, that's important," he said. "Good for arthritis, good for your sex life."

"Good for what? I can't remember what that is."

"You can remember, Dunc. You're not that old." Free flirting came with his massages.

"I don't know," I said. "I like my quiet. A life of abstaining isn't as bad as people think."

"So they tell me," Fernando said. "I do hear that."

"See?" I said. "There's a lot of it going around. It's an idea whose time has come."

"For some. Maybe."

"I think I'm happier. Do you believe that?"

"Yes," he said. "That I believe."

I had never been able to throw away the program from Carl's concert, and it lay on a small table near the door, where I saw it whenever I came in or went out. I would read over his name with a ripple of intimate recognition. A ripple or a pang, depending on my mood. The very casualness of its placement on the table pleased me.

I knew from the message on Carl's phone machine that he was returning from Canada at the end of September. Once he was home, I would call him, and at the very least there would be friendliness between us. The wait seemed very long. Thirty days hath September, and in the last week I went to movies every night to keep busy. I saw too many bad, raucous comedies and bloody cop movies. The only thing I liked was a biopic about neurotic artists in the twenties.

When I came out of it into the lobby, there was a crush getting to the doors, and a man in front of me said, "No one pushes like this in Toronto." I took it as a good omen to hear some word in the air about Canada. The man who spoke was not bad-looking, either, nicely muscled in his T-shirt, and he held another man by the elbow to keep from getting dragged away by the crowd. It took me a second before I saw that the other man was Carl. His neck was sunburned, and he had let his hair grow longer.

And Carl saw me. "Hey! Hello!" he said.

He acted perfectly happy to see me. Once we were all out on the street, he introduced me to his companion. Josh, the man's name was, and they had met backstage in Windsor, Ontario.

"And then what could I do? I just packed up and went with him on the rest of the tour," Josh said. "I have heard *Wozzeck* performed more times than any other human being on the planet. Berg is not that easy on the ears, either."

"I like him," I said.

"It was great to have company on the road," Carl said. "You know how the road gets. You and I talked about that."

"Yes," I said.

"I had fun hanging out with the tour," Josh said.

"Are you back here for good?" I said.

"We're looking for a bigger apartment," Josh said. "I like Queens, though. It's not how I thought it would be."

"Some people like Queens," I said. "Certain timid types like Queens."

"Don't mind Duncan," Carl said.

"We'll invite you over when we get settled in," Josh said.

"Whenever that is," I said.

On the subway ride home I was too angry to sit still. All those sweet-faced declarations, and look how long Carl had lasted as a holy soldier of celibacy. I felt that he had tricked me and that he'd had the last laugh in a way that made me writhe. *A respected behavior*, my foot. And I had been ready to tread the same path. I who had never taken the high road in my life.

When I got back to my apartment, I went to the phone and dialed his number. I wanted to ask him: Don't you feel like a fucking hypocrite? Do you know what a pretentious little jerk you are? The two of them weren't back yet, of course. They were probably at the subway station still waiting for the N train to Queens. The phone machine said: Carl and Josh aren't home right now.

I breathed heavily on the message tape for a minute, just to leave something spooky for them to listen to. And what would Carl have said to me, anyway, if I had been able to hammer away at him with hostile questions? *I took my chance when it was offered. Anyone would do the same.* There was nothing else to say.

I had a shot of bourbon, which did not calm me down. It made me want to kick something, but I wasn't ready to throw out my knee from an action that stupid. I had more bourbon, but I might as well have been drinking water. I sat there with my hand pressed against my chest, the way a dog paws its snout if it has a toothache.

I understood, after a while, that there was nothing to do but go to bed. I got out of my clothes, and I went through the set of stretches I always did before sleeping. I felt confused, because for so many months these had been like a secret proof that I was worthy of Carl. I had been consoled and uplifted by the flavor of his ideas mixed in with them.

Stress was bad for my bones, and I woke up very stiff. My knee locked when I tried to get out of bed. *Look what love has done to me.* I felt like a ham actor playing an old man. I had a hangover, too, and it was still very early in the morning. I wanted to phone Carl, but in disguise as something menacing, a growling wolf or a hissing reptile. I was good at making different sounds. Let him be terrified, just for a second. But then he would know who it was. He would say my name, and I would keep growling or hissing. Duncan, he would say, is that you? Stop, please. Sssssss, I would say. Sssssss.

I was too old to do that, too old for that shit. Instead I ate my simple breakfast and had my simple bath and went out to do my simple errands. A plain and forthright man. I was so calm at the supermarket (who ever heard of someone with a hangover being calm while waiting in line?) that I wondered if the attitude I had developed in Carl's absence was now going to stay with me and be my support.

Perhaps I was going to beat him at his own game (or what had been his game) and become so self-contained that I never spoke to anyone.

I could work at my job without much more than nods and signals. I could move through the streets and be perfectly silent, quiet as any monk with a vow. Then Carl would know just who understood the beauty of a principled life.

Oh, in the Middle Ages someone like me might have been a monk, one of the harsh and wily ones, but dutiful. I could be a monk now, old as I was. (I had been raised a Catholic, although not raised well.) I could take orders the way forsaken young women used to, when they were jilted by lying men and wanted only to take themselves out of the world.

I don't know why these thoughts were such a great comfort to me while I waited at the supermarket with my cart of bachelor supplies. But I got through the day, and the rest of the weekend, without doing anything rash. At work on Monday I went about my business in my usual curmudgeonly way. I was in pain, but I wasn't a roiling cauldron. I thought that once the worst of getting over Carl was done, his influence would linger in this elevated feeling about aloneness, just as Andre had left me with a taste for certain music, for Bill Evans and early Coltrane. I was doing well at the moment, better than I would have thought.

A month later I knew differently. I was tormented by longings for Carl night and day. I hardly saw anything around me—sunlight hitting the windows of a building, a man sitting on a park bench, a kid walking in time to his boom box—without superimposing on it the remembrance of Carl and things he had said to me, the most ordinary things. In Sunday school when I was a boy, one of the sisters had told us that the Benedictine rule said to "pray always." I had a good understanding now of how such a thing was possible.

This can't go on, I would say to myself (how many billions of people have said that?), but it went on for a long time, for months and months. Sometimes I called Carl's apartment, to see if the machine still announced he was living with that twinkie from Canada, but it always did. Fernando the masseur told me that the only way to get over him was to find someone new. I picked up a man in a bar who wanted money to be with me, and that made me feel much worse.

Since I had not really known Carl that well, after a year his face did begin to lose its vividness in my mind—I had only a few shreds of encounters to hold on to. But it would not be true to say I forgot him. He was like a hum that was always in my ears. He was something that was not going to go away.

I never thought I would end up the sort of person who hoarded some cruddy Xeroxed program as if it were an artifact from Tut's tomb. As if it were my job to keep the faith. I had become a fool for love, after all. You could say this served me right, but it wasn't the worst thing that might have happened to me. Not by a long shot. No, I was better for it. I understood a number of things I hadn't had a clue about before. Why Madame Butterfly believed Pinkerton was coming back. Why Catherine's grave was dug up by Heathcliff. The devotion of these years improved me, and it burnt off some of the dross. I was less quarrelsome with other people and clearer with myself. My longing stayed with me, no matter what. Who could have known I was going to be so constant? It wasn't at all what I expected, and I had some work getting used to it.

MAN AND WIFE

fiction by KATIE CHASE

They say every girl remembers that special day when everything starts to change.

I was lying under the tree in my parents' backyard, an oak old enough to give shade but too young to be climbed, when Dad's car pulled into the garage. All afternoon I'd been riding bikes with Stacie, but we had a fight when she proposed we play in my basement—it *was* getting too hot out, but I was convinced she was only using me for my Barbies. This was eight years ago. I was nine and a half years old.

Dad came out and stood in the driveway, briefcase in hand, watching me pull up grass. "Mary Ellen!"

I yanked one final clump, root and dirt dangling from my hands, and sat up.

"Come inside. I have wonderful news."

In the kitchen Dad was embracing my mother, his arms around her small, apron-knotted waist. "I can't believe it went through," she was saying. She turned to me with shiny eyes, cleared her throat, and said in her sharp voice, "Mary, go get down the good glasses."

I pushed a chair to the cupboards and climbed onto the countertop. Two glass flutes for my parents, and for myself a plastic version I'd salvaged from last New Year's, the first time I'd been allowed, and encouraged, to stay up past midnight and seen how close the early hours of the next day were to night.

Dad took down the last leftover bottle of champagne and popped it open, showering the kitchen floor. My mother laughed and wiped her hands on her polka-dotted apron, as if she'd gotten wet.

"Hold up your glass, Mary Ell," said Dad. He filled it halfway, and theirs to the rim. When in the past I'd been curious about alcohol, my parents had frowned, taken a drink, and feigned expressions of disgust. On New Year's, for instance, my cup had held plain orange juice, and the next morning, while my parents still slept, I'd had orange juice in it again.

"A toast." My mother held up her glass and waited.

I waited, too. The champagne fizzed, bubbles rising.

"To Mary," said Dad, and then he stopped, choked up.

"Our own little girl, to be a woman," my mother said. "Bottoms up."

They clinked their glasses together, and mine met theirs dully, with a tap that brought an end to the pleasant ringing they'd created. I brought the champagne to my lips. I found that, if ingested in small sips, it was quite drinkable, no worse than my mother's Diet Coke, and it had the welcome effect of making me feel I was floating away.

"Don't you want to hear what the big news is?" said Dad. My mother turned her back on us to the cutting board, where she was chopping a fresh salad.

In a small voice I said, "Yes." I tried to smile, but that feeling was in my stomach, made more fluttery by drink. I recognize the feeling now as a kind of knowledge.

"Well, do you remember Mr. Middleton? From Mommy and Daddy's New Year's party?"

At the party I'd been positioned, in scratchy lace tights and a crinoline-skirted dress, at the punch bowl to ladle mimosas for their guests. Many of their friends introduced themselves to me that night: Mr. Baker, Mr. Silverstein, Mr. Weir. Some bent to my height and shook my hand. Mr. Woodward scolded me for insufficiently filling his cup, and his young wife, Esmerelda, my former babysitter, led him away.

"Mr. Middleton—that nice man with the moustache? You talked together for quite some time."

Then I remembered. As I served other guests, he'd lingered with a glass of sweating ice water, talking about his business. He directed his words to the entire room, looking out over it rather than at me, but he spoke quietly, so only I could hear. He offered figures: annual revenue, percentages, the number of loyal clients. And then: "My business is everything. It is my whole life." I looked up at him curiously, and his face reddened; his moustache twitched. When he finally left, patting my shoulder and thanking me for indulging him, I was relieved. I'd had little to say in return—no adult had ever spoken to me that way—and I'd felt the whole time, on the tip of my tongue, the remark that might have satisfied and gotten rid of him sooner.

"That's the good news," Dad said. "He's gone ahead and asked for your hand. And we've agreed to it."

My mother put down the knife and finished off her champagne. I wanted no more of mine.

"Well, don't be so excited," said Dad. "Do you understand what I'm saying? You're going to be a wife. You're going to live with Mr. Middleton, and he's going to take care of you, for the rest of your life. And, one day, when we're very old, he'll help out your mother and me, too."

"Yep." He smiled. "It's all settled. Just signed the contract this afternoon. You'll really like him, I think. Nice man. You seemed to like him at the party, anyhow."

"He was okay," I managed. It was as I'd feared, somewhere, all along: the toast, the party, everything. But now he had a face, and a name. Now it was real: my future was just the same as any other girl's. Yet none of my friends had become wives yet, and it didn't seem fair that I should be the first taken. For one thing, I was too skinny. They say men first look for strength in a wife. Next they look for beauty, and even with braces and glasses yet to come, I was a homely little girl. It's last that men look for brains. You may notice that I skipped over wealth. While rumors of sex spread freely at school, it wasn't clear to me then just how money fit in. It was discussed only in negotiations, when lawyers were present and we were not. It was best that way for our parents, who tried to keep such things separate.

At dinner I pushed the food around on my plate, clearing a forkwide path and uncovering the blue-and-white pattern of little people kneeling in rice fields and pushing carts. My mother was on her third glass of champagne—she wouldn't last through *Jeopardy!*—and she was laughing at everything Dad said about his anxious day at the office.

A timer buzzed, and my mother rose from the table to pull out her raspberry pie. She approached me with the dish clasped in her oven mitts.

"Take a good look at that pie, Mary."

The crust was golden brown, its edges pressed with the evenly spaced marks of a fork prong. Sweet red berries seeped through the three slits of a knife.

"It's perfect," she said, with her usual ferocity.

147

The next morning Stacie acted like our fight hadn't happened, and I wanted to play along. We went to ride bikes while my mother showered. Dad's car had left already for work, and he'd dragged the garbage out to the curb. The champagne bottle poked from the recycling bin, ready to be taken away. It was another summer day.

"We had a celebration last night," I told Stacie. "Dad let me have booze."

"Oh, yeah? What for?" She pedaled ahead and moved onto the street, which her parents, and mine, forbade.

I had to shout, she was so far ahead. "Someone named Mr. Middleton wants to take me."

Stacie slammed on her brakes and turned her bike to face me. Once caught up, I kept going.

"When?" she demanded, appearing alongside. "You know he can't take you yet."

"Why not?" I said, but I assumed, as did Stacie, that there'd be a long period of engagement. In the fall we were to start the fifth grade, and it was rare for a girl still in elementary to be taken.

"He must really like you," Stacie said, in awe. We pedaled slowly, pensively. "But you're so skinny."

Mrs. Calderón, in her silken robe, was out watering her rose bushes. She waved.

"We'd better get on the sidewalk," I said.

When we reached Maple Court, we laid our bikes on the island and sprawled in the warm grass, making daisy chains from the flowering weeds. Stacie put her hand on my arm. It was rare for us to touch.

"Whatever happens," she said, "don't dump me."

"What do you mean?"

"I mean, ever since my sister went to live with Mr. Gordon, she never plays with me anymore. When she comes over she just sits in the kitchen with my mom drinking tea." She rolled her eyes. "They talk about recipes, and my mom gives her a frozen casserole that she pretends to Mr. Gordon she made by herself."

"Okay," I said. "I promise."

She held up her pinkie, and I joined it with mine.

"I promise, when I live with Mr. Middleton, you can still come over and play Barbies."

"Not just Barbies," she said. "We'll still play everything. We'll still be best friends."

I hadn't even been sure we were best friends, since during school she spent her time with ratty-haired Cassandra and I, in protest, with the studious Chan twins. But I remained solemn. Maybe she wasn't using me. Besides, although I couldn't really imagine what it would be like to be a wife, I knew I wouldn't want to be stuck with Mr. Middleton all the time. I began to laugh.

"What?"

"He has the stupidest moustache!" I drew a thin line above my mouth with my finger, sweeping up at the edges, to indicate the way it curled.

"Probably, you can make him shave it off. My sister makes Mr. Gordon wear socks all the time, so she doesn't have to see his feet."

Stacie picked apart her chain and let the flowered weeds fall—she had a theory they could again take root. I wore mine around my wrist but lost it during the ride back. My mother was still in the bathroom, the mingled scent of her products floating out beneath the door.

After serving us tuna-and-pickle sandwiches, my mother sent Stacie home.

"But why?"

"Shhh," she said. "I need to talk to you."

I folded my arms across my chest and glared at her.

"Don't," she said. "Just don't. Come here with me."

In the living room, she sat and patted the couch beside her. The television wasn't on, which made the room feel too still and too quiet, like nothing happened in it when we weren't around.

"Now, I know Daddy explained that you're going to be a wife. But do you know what that means?"

I refused to look at her, though I could feel her eyes on my face. "Yeah. I'll go live with Mr. Middleton. I'll have to make him dinner."

"Yes," she said. "But you'll have to do more than that."

"Can I still play Barbies with Stacie? I promised her."

"You did, did you."

I nodded. I told my mother everything that Stacie had said. It made me proud that she was jealous, and I thought it would make my mother proud, too.

"I'm sorry to say, it's really up to Mr. Middleton when, and if, you can play with your friends. And he may not appreciate you, still just a little girl, telling him to shave off his moustache. He's had that thing for years." She halted a creeping smile. "What I'm trying to say is, you'll belong to him. You'll have to be very obedient—not that you haven't always been a good girl. Your father and I are very proud of you. You get such good grades and stay out of trouble."

She paused, frowning. "I don't think you realize just how lucky you are that Mr. Middleton has offered to take you. He's a very successful man, and he's made quite a generous offer, for little in return." She patted my leg. "I don't mean you, of course. Any man would be lucky to have you. But to be honest, I'm not sure why he's so eager to settle it."

I stared at the black television screen. "Can I go to Stacie's now?"

"Wait. We're not through." She stood and approached the bookshelf. On days when I stayed home sick, I'd lie on the couch and stare at that bookshelf. Each book's spine, its title and design, suggested something of its story, and their order and arrangement seemed fixed, like the sequencing of photographs along the hallway wall: from my parents' wedding—my mother thirteen and Dad twenty-seven—to the day of my birth to my fourth-grade class picture. But as my mother took out the Bible and a few romance paperbacks, I saw that behind them were more books, a whole hidden row; the shelf was deeper than I'd realized. She removed from hiding a slim volume called *Your Womanly Body*, its cover decorated in butterflies and soft-colored cut flowers blooming in vases.

"This will tell you *some* of what you need to know about being a wife. I imagine Mr. Middleton won't expect much from you at first. After all, you're still very young,"

I began to turn the pages: there were cartoons of short and tall and skinny and fat women, their breasts different sizes and weights, with varying colors and masses of hair between their legs. The pictures weren't a shock to me. I'd seen my mother naked before, and Stacie had confirmed that her own looked much the same. Once I'd even seen Dad, when I surprised him by waiting outside the bathroom door for a Dixie cup of water late one night.

"You'll have a child someday, of course. But most people like to wait until they're older and know each other better. I, for instance, had you when I was eighteen. By today's standards, that's still a little young."

"It can be scary, at first." My mother's voice had turned soft, and she was staring out the window at the tree. "The important thing to remember is, even though he's in charge, you can have some control. Pay close attention: what he wants the most may be very small, and you can wait out the rest."

I already knew there were ways to put off sex: some girls "sucked" their husbands "off," others cried until left alone. And if a girl did become pregnant too soon, if it would be unseemly for her to keep the baby, I knew there were ways to get rid of it. But still, I'd rather not think about all that before I had to face it.

My mother was saying, "A man's life is spent waiting and preparing for the right girl. It can be very lonely. In a way, girls have it easy—"

"Mommy, when will I go live with Mr. Middleton?"

"I was getting to that, Mary. You can be so impatient." She lifted the book from my hands and turned to put it away. "You'll be going to him in the fall."

"Oh." I stared down at my bare summer feet, callused, tan and dirty. "After school starts?"

"Mary. There'll be no school for you this fall. You'll have a house to take over."

The feeling was back in my stomach, more of an ache now, and all I wanted was to curl up on the couch while my mother brought Jell-O and chicken-noodle soup. On sick days you could escape the movement of the world. It was always difficult to get back into it, to catch up on schoolwork and eat real food again, but this time I wasn't sure I ever wanted to rejoin the world.

Yet the books were different now. I wouldn't be able to not think about that.

"Of course, he'll probably let you go back soon. He'll want you to. That's what Mr. Middleton told us—that he admired your mind. He said he could tell you're a very bright girl."

"I should be so lucky," she added darkly. "Your father only saw my strength."

It became routine for Mr. Middleton to spend Sunday afternoons with us. At dawn my mother yanked open all the blinds, and the acrid smells of house-cleaning began to fill the rooms. Even Dad was kept from sleeping in and given chores to do. I was ushered straight into the kitchen: "Do me one little favor," she said.

"Knead this dough. No, like this. Punch it, like you're pissed off."

"Check the stove. Has it reached the preheated temperature? Well, is it hot?"

"Okay, now we'll let that marinate. You know what's in this marinade? Just smell it—what does it smell like?"

Once I had completed my mother's "favor" ("Umm, it smells sweet." "Good! That's the honey."), I snuck out while her back was turned.

I was to be scrubbed "my pinkest" in the shower. She showed me how to use Q-tips to clean out my ears, to rub lotion over my skin, and to pluck the little hairs I hadn't noticed before from between my eyebrows. She swore under her breath when she nicked me with the pink disposable razor—my legs slathered in a thick gel that smelled like baby powder. "Here," she said. "You finish."

I slid the blade along my leg, pressing as lightly as possible.

I was to wear "one of my prettiest dresses," which meant that I rotated between the three in my closet. Their straps dug into my shoulders, their crinoline scratched my bare legs. The first Sunday my mother threw onto my bed a package from Sears. Inside were three training bras. I didn't have anything resembling breasts, and when I finally did, years into my marriage, they were so small that I continued to wear the trainers for some time. My husband didn't seem to care or know the difference.

Every Sunday had the feel of a holiday—the boredom of waiting for the guest to arrive and the impatience of waiting for him to leave. Mr. Middleton always brought a bouquet of flowers, at the sight of which I was to feign surprise and gratitude. Every week, the same grocery-store assortment of wildflowers that smelled rank and bitter, like weeds. Mr. Middleton sat with my father in the living room while I trimmed and arranged the flowers in my mother's crystal vase. She had me stir something or taste it for salt before nudging me back out to join them.

Mr. Middleton would wear a full suit and tie, despite the fact that our house had no air conditioning. As the afternoon wore on, he would take off the suit jacket, loosen and remove the tie, roll up the sleeves of the dress shirt and, lastly, undo the shirt's top button, revealing a tuft of dark, curly hair. The hair on his head was straight, and he'd run a hand through it, slicking it back with his sweat. Dad, in a short-sleeved polo shirt and khaki shorts, would watch, smiling to himself. My shaven skin felt cool and smooth. I had to stop myself from running my hands along my legs as I sat listening to them talk "business." Their tone was cordial, but they seemed to eye each other warily. I didn't consider it then, but Dad was likely sensitive to the fact that while he had to report to a boss, Mr. Middleton was his own.

"How's business?"

"Business is good. You?"

"Business is good. Clients?"

"Clients are good. Got to treat them right, keep them happy," Dad said.

"Of course."

In and out of the room bustled my mother. She refilled the pitcher of lemonade, replenished the dish of melting ice cubes, brought out bowls of mixed nuts and pretzels and onion dip. Before long, this became my job. I'd stand before Mr. Middleton with a tray of pickles and olives.

"Hmm, let's see." He'd mull over the choices, select a pimento-stuffed green olive. I'd turn to offer the tray to Dad, who had a penchant for sweet pickles, but then: "Please, wait just a moment—perhaps another. Hmm, let's see." And he'd choose a kalamata. The metal tray was heavy, but my arms grew stronger, and I learned to balance it on my shoulder.

Mr. Middleton rarely addressed me directly. Which is not to say he wasn't speaking to me. "Profit margins" and "quarterly analyses" were discussed with glances and smiles in my direction. But he never asked what I thought, how I was doing, how I had spent my week. Adults, I knew, just liked to humor children, and ordinarily those questions tired me, causing me to clam up on the pretense of feeling shy. But in this situation it was disconcerting. After all, wasn't Mr. Middleton supposed to like me? What were we going to say to each other when we were, one day, inevitably, alone? I knew I would be expected to say something; wives, especially as they grew up, didn't have to be invited to speak. They scolded their husbands for things they were doing wrong, or weren't doing at all. They had stories to tell, of what had happened that day at the market, of the rude cashier and the unmarked price of the fresh loaf of bread.

For then, I followed my mother's advice the best I could. I wouldn't speak unless spoken to. I sat up straight in the chair, didn't complain if the food at dinner was strange, didn't ask to turn on the television. I paid close attention to Mr. Middleton; I focused on his moustache, the way it moved with his mouth, studied the shine of his gold watch, viewed the gradual stripping of clothing, the sweat gathering on his forehead and alongside his nose, where his glasses slid. I suppose I may have already been following my mother's advice, but I don't remember thinking so. I never liked to admit I was doing as she suggested. I preferred to credit my own volition.

Mr. Middleton seemed to me older than my father, though he was almost a decade younger. Dad was strict, but he could be silly, wasn't afraid to be lazy, and had been known to watch cartoons that even I found stupid. Mr. Middleton was too polite and too proper. He was boring in the way a robot would be: never leaving to go to the bathroom, never saying anything Dad disagreed with or found ridiculous. They would have had much to argue about—they do now—their strategies in business so different: Dad doting on his clients, trying to keep them pleased each step of the way, Mr. Middleton acting with cool aggression against their wishes, with the long run in mind, the biggest possible profit. I suppose we were all on our best behavior.

By dinnertime the business talk had faltered, and the men punctuated their silence with compliments for the meal—something Dad never did when it was just the three of us. This was when my mother took over. "Thank you," she might say. "Mary Ellen helped prepare that."

"Did she? It's quite good," said Mr. Middleton.

"Oh, she's learning. Believe it or not, just a month ago even something this simple would have been beyond her."

Mr. Middleton smiled politely and chewed, his moustache moving up and down, a piece of couscous caught in the right-side curl.

"There is still so much for her to learn, I'm afraid. You mustn't—you mustn't expect too much, from the start."

"But of course Donna will get her up to speed," said Dad. "Won't you, honey?"

"Of course," my mother said. "All I meant was, Mary is such a fast learner. Why, just the other day the sauce was starting to stick, and instead of letting it burn or calling me, she just turned down the burner and gave it a stir. How about that?"

The heat from the kitchen was creeping into the dining room, and a bead of sweat slipped down Mr. Middleton's forehead. His top button, at that point, remained done. He offered nothing but another polite smile. Maliciously, I wanted, in front of everyone, to call attention to the couscous still in his moustache. "Right there," I'd interrupt, pointing to a spot above my own lip. This was something a wife could do, scold or embarrass her husband for his own good. But I knew I hadn't earned it yet, and it would take years of waiting, quietly noting.

Mr. Middleton seemed oblivious to my parents' fears and cover-ups, but I've come to see that he was not, nor was he too polite to lead the conversation elsewhere. I can look back now with some sympathy. I can see myself in him: he was determined to behave in the way that was expected, in the belief, often false but sometimes accurate, that this gave him some autonomy. And after all, he was getting what he wanted.

One Saturday afternoon Mr. Middleton showed up while my parents were out. They were leaving me home alone more often in preparation for the days when I'd be keeping house, with Mr. Middleton off at work. Usually I found myself frozen, unable to act as I would if my parents were around. I had a great fear of doing something wrong, either accidentally (opening the door to a dangerous stranger or coming upon some matches, which would inadvertently scratch against something and become lit, igniting a raging fire) or purposely, overcome by the thrill of risk. The only way to ensure this wouldn't happen was to remain on the couch until they came back.

At the sound of a knock at the door, I lifted a slat of blind and peered out at Mr. Middleton: no flowers in hand, no suit and tie. He wore blue jeans and sports sandals, a polo shirt like those Dad owned. His arms were covered in those dark, curly hairs. Through the peephole his nose was made long by the curved glass, and his moustache twitched nervously. It gave me a small thrill, making him wait. Just as he began to back away, I did as I should and opened the door.

"Mary Ellen. What a pleasant surprise."

"Hello," I said politely. "Would you like to come in?"

He looked down the block, both ways. It was quiet for a Saturday. Only Mrs. Calderón was out, pruning her blooming roses. She'd recently explained to me that she had to cut them back so they could grow. Mr. Middleton smiled in her direction and entered the house.

"I'm home alone," I said. It seemed best if I made that clear right away.

"I won't stay long. You see, I was just in the neighborhood and thought I'd drop by."

That was reasonable to me, but it seemed out of character for Mr. Middleton, who operated purely, I thought, on formality and routine. "Would you like a glass of iced tea with lemon?" I asked.

"No, thank you."

He wasn't sitting, so I didn't sit, unaware that I might have offered him a seat. The expression on his face was, as always, neutral, and he didn't return my stare. I felt I was doing something grossly wrong—I was still unfit to be a wife, unable to handle company on my own. My mother would scold me if she knew I'd received him in a T-shirt from last year's spelling bee and purple shorts stained with Kool-Aid.

I tried again. "How's business?"

He smiled and lowered himself to my height, his hands coming to rest on his knees. "Very well, thank you," he said. "But today, you see, I was thinking of you. I thought you might like to show me your Barbies."

No adult had ever asked to see them, and, to my knowledge, they'd never been mentioned in his presence. My mother allowed no visitors, other than my friends, into the basement. She had warned me that the Barbies would have to go when I went to Mr. Middleton. To head off my tears, Dad had added quietly that perhaps, for a while, they could leave them set up in the basement for when I came to visit.

I watched for some sign in Mr. Middleton that he was joking or only humoring me, but he reached out a hairy arm and took my hand. His wasn't sweaty, though the day was muggy and humid, and his skin was surprisingly soft. On the narrow stairway he didn't let go; my arm strained and pulled behind me as I led him into the basement. His knees cracked as he took the stairs.

The basement was unfinished, just hard tiles, exposed beams and many-legged insects. Stacie complained about the centipedes, but they appeared less often than the spiders. Strips of sunlight came in through the windows along the driveway, where you could see feet pass on their way to the side door.

Mr. Middleton dropped my hand and approached the Barbies' houses slowly, as if in awe. The toys sprawled from one corner of the room to the other, threatening to take over even the laundry area; the foldout couch, which I maintained took up valuable space, sometimes served as a mountain to which the Barbies took the camper. There was one real Barbie house, pink and plastic; it had come with an elevator that would stick in the shaft, so I had converted the elevator to a bed. The other Barbie home was made of boxes and old bathroom rugs meant to designate rooms and divisions; this was the one Stacie used for her family. The objects in the houses were a mixture of real Barbie toys and other adapted items: small beads served as food, my mother's discarded tampon applicators were the legs of a cardboard table. On a Kleenex box my Barbie slept sideways, facing Ken's back; both were shirtless, her plastic breasts against him.

Mr. Middleton asked about the construction and decoration of the rooms. He said he admired my reuse of materials. "A creative way to cut costs," he noted.

I shrugged. "Mom and Dad won't buy me anything else."

He nodded thoughtfully. "You work well within limits."

"I guess," I said, but I was pleased. He was admiring my mind.

"Well, you have quite a talent for design—I've seen professional blueprints more flawed." He suggested that in the future we might have a home built, one I could help plan.

Then he leaned down and stroked Barbie's back with his index finger. "Do they always sleep this way?" he asked.

I blushed and only shook my head. Sometimes they lay entirely naked, as my parents slept. Sometimes Barbie slept on top of Ken, or vice versa.

"Can you show me another way they might sleep?" he asked.

I hesitated, then picked up the dolls and put their arms around each other's bodies in a rigid hug. I tilted Barbie's head and pressed her face against Ken's, as if they were kissing, and laid them back atop the Kleenex box. Mr. Middleton watched with his detached interest.

"Your Barbies must love each other very much," he observed.

I'd never really thought about it that way. They were just doing what my parents and people on television did because they were married. But sometimes, when I was alone, it gave me that fluttery, almost sick feeling deep in my stomach, and I took the dolls apart.

Mr. Middleton stood and turned away. He held up his wrist to the sun strip, examining his watch, for what seemed a long time. "Well, thank you for sharing them with me. But I should be on my way."

I nodded, then recovered my manners. "Can I walk you to the door?"

"No, thank you, Mary Ellen. I'll show myself out."

On Sundays he'd shake my parents' hands before he left, and now I wondered if I should offer mine. But instead he reached out and patted me on the head, once, twice, then the last time just smoothing my hair, as my mother would to fix a stray strand, but much gentler.

When I heard the front door close, I knelt in front of the Barbie house. It was difficult, as my Ken's arms were straight, not bent like some, but I moved his arm so that it stroked Barbie's back. I startled when my mother called from the top of the stairs. I hadn't seen feet in the windows or heard a key in the door.

I didn't tell them that Mr. Middleton had been over, and the next day when he came for Sunday dinner he didn't mention it either. It didn't occur to me until years later that the whole thing might have been prearranged. I could find out now; Mr. Middleton tells me anything I ask. He may tease, but he knows when to stop. It's quite possible he's even learned to fear me. For all his skill in the world of business, I think he understands less about the world without than I do.

* * *

That September, with Stacie back at school, my days were spent alone with my mother. She was nervous about the upcoming ceremony and would sit with me at the kitchen table for hours with catalogues of flowers and dresses.

"Do you like these roses? Or something more unique—orchids? But so expensive."

I would shrug. "It doesn't matter."

Depending on her mood, she would either become angry ("If it doesn't matter to you, who does it matter to? Pick out some flowers!") or take my reticence as deference to what she thought was best ("The orchids are lovely, but we'd best be practical, hmm?").

Once, paging together through pictures of dresses, she became so frustrated with me that she disappeared into the bathroom for almost an hour. Finally I knocked on the door. "Mommy? I left it open to the one I like." I heard water running, and when she came out she caught me around the shoulders and held me against her, my face nuzzling her stomach. "That's my good girl," she whispered above my head.

One afternoon was spent sewing, another polishing silver. The cooking lessons took on new vigor, and she had me reducing wine-based sauces, braising meats, and chopping fresh herbs for most of the day. Dad would come home, see everything that had been set out on the table and everything that still simmered on the stove and roasted in the oven, throw his hands up in the air and say, "I don't know how you expect us to consume all this, Donna. Maybe you could lay off her a bit." But then he'd sit down and attack the food with an appetite that had the air of duty, sighing and unbuttoning his pants for dessert.

Stacie came over after school a couple of times a week, but she brought Cassandra; the Chan twins had forsaken me, believing my imminent wifehood to have changed me already. With only two Barbie houses, Stacie, Cassandra, and I couldn't play together fairly. Besides, I didn't want Cassandra and her ratty hair anywhere near them. Instead we sat on the porch eating gingersnaps—just talking and not playing anything. Other girls who'd been promised spent their time in this way.

Cassandra wanted to hear about Mr. Middleton. She believed her parents to be sealing up a deal with a Mr. Crowley from the neighboring town. I recounted Mr. Middleton's afternoon visit to sate her interest and swore them to secrecy. They didn't seem particularly impressed or unnerved. I yearned for either response, to anchor my own.

"Well, is he cute?" Cassandra asked, twirling a dishwater-blond lock.

I didn't know how to answer her. Unlike Stacie and me, Cassandra had always liked boys—but husbands were not like boys. I didn't know how to make her understand what it was really like, but I also had the feeling that Cassandra would handle things much differently when it was her turn. I was thankful when Stacie changed the subject to school, with stories of pencils stolen from the teacher's desk and guest story-readers, even though they made me both wistful and angry, and Stacie knew it.

The night before the ceremony, my parents entertained their friends with chilled rosé wine and a CD of lulling, smooth jazz on repeat. My mother dusted my cheekbones with her dark blush and checked my back to make sure I wore a trainer. I was to greet guests at the door until everyone had arrived, and then Stacie and I could retreat to the basement to play Barbies together one last time. According to tradition, Mr. Middleton was not invited; it was to be his last bachelor night alone. But Mr. Woodward and Esmerelda came, and Mr. Silverstein, and Stacie's and Cassandra's parents, eager to know how it had all been pulled off. Mr. Baker said, as if surprised, "You look very pretty tonight, Mary Ellen," and then he and Mr. Weir stood together in the corner, shaking their heads. The Calderóns arrived last. Mr. Calderón was so old his eyes constantly watered, and he could barely speak or hear anything. Mrs. Calderón was a young grandmother, her braided hair still long and black. She bent to me and whispered, "You're not getting cold feet now, are you dear?"

"Cold feet?" I asked. I peered down at my slipper socks, embarrassed I'd removed the Mary Janes.

"I tried to run away from this one." She winked at her husband, but his expression didn't change. "But then, I always misbehaved."

Mr. Calderón held tight to her arm, and she guided him patiently toward the drinks. She kissed his shaking hand, then placed a glass of water in it.

In the basement, adult feet shifting above us, I understood that Mrs. Calderón had been saying that she knew me and that she understood. From tomorrow on, that would be me upstairs, like Esmerelda and even my mother, laughing a stupid laugh and making frequent trips to the bathroom, with an eye on my husband and his eye on me. Mrs. Calderón had issued me a playful dare and made no promises; but if it was the last childlike thing I did, I would take her up on it.

"Stacie, I need your help."

159

She stopped pushing her Barbie car, a convertible she'd acquired from me in a trade, and said with suspicion, "You do?"

As I explained what I wanted to do, Stacie's eyes began to gleam. At one point she took my hand. I felt close to her, until she said, "You won't be married first after all!" But still she was my confidante, my partner with her own stake.

What we came up with wasn't much of a plan, but we did identify the basic elements required in running away: a note, a lightly packed suit-case, and utter secrecy. My mother had already packed most of my clothes into a luggage set embroidered with my new initials, M. M. I removed the lightest bag from the pile by the side door and had Stacie sneak it back home with her. After slipping away, having deposited the note in a spot both clandestine and sure to be eventually discovered, I would call Stacie from a pay phone and have her meet me with the suitcase. For this purpose, I used my new skills to sew a quarter into the hem of my dress, which hung, long and white, like a ghost, outside my closet door.

Beneath the covers with a flashlight that night, I composed the note to Mr. Middleton. I could not tell him, as they did in fantasy romance movies, that I had met someone else. What I wrote was this:

Dear Mr. Middleton,

I am sorry to leave you at the alter. You seem very nice but I can not be a wife. Please do not try to find me and please try to go on with your life.

Mary Ellen

I thought it sounded quite grown-up and made running away on cold feet seem a serious and viable act I wasn't worried that we hadn't de-cided where I would go. I didn't consider then that I knew of no woman who was not a wife, that anyone I might turn to would turn me in, that breach of contract was serious business and punishable by law. I be-lieved two things: that getting away would be the hardest part of the game, and that you could only plan as far as you could see. I don't know if I believed that I would make it, but I believed that I would try.

I might have left that very night, cutting Stacie's ties to my venture, but I had a romantic notion of wearing that dress. I pictured kicking off the white patent-leather shoes to run faster, and the small train flailing behind me. I pictured that the dress would dirty as I ran; it would rip and tear, and then I would know I was free.

When we arrived at the chapel, I spied Mr. Middleton's car in the parking lot. During a covert trip to the "potty," I slipped the note beneath its windshield wipers. It had always made me laugh that my parents never noticed an advertisement attached in this way until they were driving.

In the bride's room, Dad, his eyes shiny and red-rimmed, was smoothing out the fold from the contract, to which my signature was to be added. "Why don't you go sit down, Frank?" my mother suggested, but she stayed with me, adjusting my dress and hairspraying my hot-roller curls, until the final moments. She hovered in the doorway. "You are wearing, aren't you, all the things we talked about? You remember how it goes? Something old, something new, something borrowed, something blue, and a silver sixpence for your shoe?"

"I remembered," I said, thinking of the sewn quarter. If I wasn't careful to keep my skirt held as I walked, the coin hit the floor with the barest knock. "Mommy, can I have a few minutes alone? This is a very big day for me."

She looked surprised, but her face softened. "Boy, kid, you really have grown up." She kissed my cheek, then rubbed it furiously to remove any trace of lipstick. I felt sad, at that moment, to think that I would never see her again, and wondered if she would privately count me lucky or only be disappointed.

The air outside smelled like a fall barbecue, charring corn and sausages. In the bright blue sky flew a V of birds. Just as I took a breath to run, I spotted Mr. Middleton across the lot next to his car. The collar of his tuxedo was misaligned; he had skipped a buttonhole and set the whole thing off. Facing the sun, he held one hand to his face—to shield his eyes?—and in the other was my note. His shoulders seemed to be shaking with laughter. Had he been about to run away himself when he came upon my note? This possibility, however remote, might have been what led me to walk straight toward him, slowly, steadily, wholly of my own volition. I hate to believe, especially now, that it was as simple as holding to my nature; that I was just a good girl who did always as she was told, without hope and without design.

"Mary Ellen?" he said. "You're still here." I saw as I came closer that he'd actually been crying, not laughing; a tear dropped from the left-side curl of his moustache. I thought of something Dad often said, when, much younger, I'd get caught up in venturesome play with inevitable consequence: "It's all fun and games, isn't it, until someone gets hurt."

"I'm still here," I said. I raised my arms to indicate I should be lifted and let Mr. Middleton cradle me against his chest. I felt his wildly beating heart, and he began to stroke my hair as if I needed calming down. But my stomach felt only the faintest rumble of hunger, an emptiness. I knew that I had done the right thing, the only thing I could, but still, I felt foolish. If I were really as smart as everyone believed, I would never have found myself in this situation, with a ridiculous man I was obligated to care for. My escape would have been better planned and better executed. He would never have taken an interest in the first place.

"Mary," he said, "you do know that I—"

"What?" I struggled to sit up in his arms, impatient suddenly, and restless. I wanted to go inside, where everyone was waiting, and get it over with.

He set me down on the hood of his car and began again. "I think you'll be very pleased with the life I want to give you."

I stared through his windshield at the tan leather seats, sculpted to hug a body as the vehicle took the curves. I saw where the top would fold down. This car would take me to my new home.

"You do understand, don't you, that the deal is irrevocable? If you were to run off, your parents would owe me a great deal of money. They could never hope to come out of debt."

I knew that was a threat, and thought less of him for it. But then he said something I look back on now as the beginning of my new understanding of my life. "I'm yours, Mary Ellen, and if you stay, all that is mine will be yours, too."

In answer, I rebuttoned his shirt.

As I signed the contract, my eyes slid down the page, its tiny print in a formal, inscrutable language. The sum my parents had provided to Mr. Middleton seemed enormous, though I know it now to be less than the cost of my childhood home and much less than the worth of Mr. Middleton's company. Men who'd planned poorly would seek a much larger dowry and might suffer for it in their choice of wives. But it was our parents, always looking toward the future, who put money first. The dowry, like a child that would grow, was ultimately an investment.

I handed over the paper for the minister to stamp, and he pronounced us man and wife.

Mr. Middleton has kept my note folded in his sock drawer, and for years he has teased me for having misspelled "altar." Putting away his clean laundry, I look at it sometimes, not with wistfulness or shame, but because I want to remember. The contract itself is in a safety-deposit box; I'll receive a key for my eighteenth birthday, a day now close in sight. The Barbies, of course, are long gone. Dad succeeded in overriding my mother, and the toys stayed in the basement a year into my marriage. But I rarely played with them—they seemed to have lost their allure, and I never knew what they wanted to do or say or wear. Stacie still hadn't been promised, and I offered them to her, but she pretended not to be interested. She and Cassandra were thick as thieves then. "Save them for your kids," she said, and we couldn't help but dissolve into panicked laughter. By the time she was taken, at age fourteen, she was serious about having children. It is her husband who insists they wait. If we see each other now at the market, grocery baskets in hand, we merely nod in greeting. We have so little in common.

Mr. Middleton has made me apprentice to his business, which he says one day when he is dead, I will take over. Even if—and the decision to have children is entirely up to me, he says—one day we have a son. This is highly unusual and very progressive, Dad has told me. He patted my head and told me he was proud. I looked for something like greed or jealousy in his eyes, but found only love. My mother admitted, over afternoon tea, that she wishes Dad had done something similar for her. As far as I can see, he long ago reached his height on the ladder. What could he have done for her?

"I have good business sense, a ruthless mind," she insisted, and gestured to the piles of butterscotch-chip scones she'd baked for a block sale. "But I suppose I'm lucky, in that we fell in love."

I nodded in agreement, though I knew what would provoke her: *But isn't it easier if we don't think of love?*

Visiting is difficult because, although they think they act differently, my parents still treat me like a child, a newlywed bride. They don't recognize what I've become, but they won't argue when the time comes to face it, when Dad retires and I, with Mr. Middleton's money, am in charge of them. Their investment in me will have its rewards. I want the best for them, as they've managed for me.

After a morning spent at home with my private tutor, Ms. Dundee—whose husband succumbed when she was much younger and much prettier (she says) to a condition she won't speak of—I change into a navy skirt and Peter Pan-collared blouse, hop on my bike and head to the office. Mr. Middleton has given me a fine car, of course, but I normally prefer the exercise. So far I just prepare after-lunch coffee and bring it in on a tray, each cup made to the preference of each board member. Mr. Middleton sits at the head of the table. His moustache, after all these years, remains; he would shave it if I asked, but I suspect that issuing that demand would expose me somehow. Once situated beside him, I'm encouraged to listen in and, if so inclined, take notes. But it's the quiet power struggle that interests me, the way his inferiors look at him and how they cover their desires with neutral jargon, loyal reports. He takes for granted, I think, the way things are now.

"You've learned a lot so far from just watching and listening," he says to me, winking, as I take out my pad of paper. I turn away and roll my eyes: he believes we're always in on some joke. This one is meant to be in reference to the nights I join him in his bedroom, on the floor above mine. Mostly I just lie there while he touches my hair or my back, as he once demonstrated with the doll. He has mentioned in those moments love, and a feeling of fulfillment. For him they may be the same thing. Yet even with me around, taking care of things, I sense he's still a lonely man. I feel guilty sometimes, offering so little reimbursement for his attentions, though he receives more pleasure from them than I do, and I've made attempts to do for him what other girls and young wives have described. Now I believe that the hardest part of the game is staying in it, holding on to your stake. And that you can't plan too far into the future. I've taken this down in my notes: *The benefits mature with time.* I've begun to appreciate just how much work parents invest in their children, and wives in their husbands; it's only fair for the investor to become a beneficiary.

DEATH DEFIANT BOMBA OR WHAT TO WEAR WHEN YOUR BOO GETS CANCER

fiction by LILLIAM RIVERA

Paseo Basico/Basic Step

His snoring will wake you. You'll be pissed off at first but then you'll welcome the snoring over the clock set to go off in an hour. It's still dark outside and although it's warm next to him, you'll get up, your bare feet searching for your slippers. You'll say a short prayer and move the bed a bit to get him back into regular breathing. It won't work.

If the doctor's appointment is early, at 9 a.m., pull out the red sheath dress, the one that you bought on sale at Nordstrom with the famous but unpronounceable designer label. The red will wake the reception-ist up like a motherfucker and cause her to send you hate for daring to outshine her that morning. The receptionist will think you're tacky, loud, too much. In the bloodshot color, the doctor will notice that you wore the equivalent of a flag and think you're stately and in charge. You'll wear red, definitely red.

If the doctor's appointment is later, say at 3 p.m., then the only color you should wear is . . . red. Late in the afternoon the receptionist has not had time to eat the Snickers bar hidden in the drawer right next to some Orbit chewing gum, flavor piña colada, and the small box of "just-in-case" feminine napkins. The receptionist will be hungry and crabby from arguing with the old man with Alzheimer's who keeps forgetting that his appointment is not today but was last week. She can't curse at the old man but she's on the verge. When she sees the red dress, she'll think how presumptuous you are for wearing it like a drag queen, like a *telenovela* star, like a *Nuestra Belleza Latina* of the Month. But she'll remember you and that's all that matters.

You'll wear five-inch black pumps because they make that annoying noise that alerts everyone everywhere in the whole wide world that you're arriving. What you really want to wear are your red high-top Nikes, the ones that makes you feel like you're rolling back in the day with your crew of girls. You want to wear them with your baggy track jacket and a sports bra, tummy baring, all defiant. With your hair pulled up in a tight-ass ponytail and large gold hoop earrings dangling from your ears. This is what you wore when you first saw him, when he was playing handball, smacking that spaldeen like he owned it, like it was his bitch. *Toma.* If only you could reach for that outfit in your closet like an old friend, but no, you can't go back. You will wear your red, expensive-looking sheath dress and black pumps. You'll tuck in your nameplate necklace underneath the dress so that you can have some sort of protection.

Your makeup will be subtle because you're not going to El Coyote with your girlfriends to toast someone's bullshit promotion, engagement, divorce, wedding. No, your makeup will be almost drab except for the lips. The lips are going to be making a lot of moves and there's no question they have to be painted. At first, you'll make the rookie mistake of going for lip gloss like some fourteen-year-old Lolita trying to lure some *papi* in the corner. No. That won't do for today. Instead, you'll grab the orange-red lipstick. So what if it clashes with your red dress. You don't care. This is war. You're going to double up on the red.

As for your man, your boo, *tu negrito*, he's going to wear baggy jeans that are falling off his ever-thinning hips. He'll wear the dingy white T-shirt at first, but you'll force him out of that and beg him to wear a suit. When he yells at you to stop nagging, you'll give in and let him wear the Mets shirt and matching Mets baseball hat that will cover the unruly hair that you held tight last night when you guys were tearing into each other like tomorrow would never come, like the appointment would never happen, hungry for each other. Last night, when you ignored how his hips are now bones and how they're pushing up against you, hurting you. Not like before when you wanted his bulging stomach to squash you. I like my man with meat, that's what you used to say. But you don't say that anymore. You'll let him wear what he's wearing, although he's rooting for a losing team. You'll convince yourself that at least you both match. Red on red. Blue on red. Red.

You'll take your car and do the driving even though he hates that more than anything. He doesn't like to feel like a weakling. This is what he'll say but he'll give in to your driving. You'll drive to the city and curse at all the cars getting in your way. The drive will be quiet, minus your cursing. No salsa. No smooth jazz. No NPR. Nothing to distract and take away from your bleeding dress. You'll pay to park your car in the hospital's overpriced parking lot and shove your mid-sized car into a compact space. Because you are nice, you'll drop him off in the front of the building so that he won't have to walk all through the parking lot. You won't expect a thank you for this generous move. There's too much pride in him. You'll convince yourself that this is what you like about him. Two strong people doing their own thing, no questions asked, anchoring each other.

You'll surprise yourself and take his hand while walking towards the elevator. His hand is cold although it's hot outside. You will squeeze his cold hand but only slightly, only enough to let him know.

Saludo/Greeting

Your stomping heels will arrive first at the doctor's office. You'll immediately go up to the glass window, the one that resembles the *bodegas* back in the day when you would pay a dollar for a loosey in the middle of the night. The receptionist will smile and say good morning. You will not smile. You will say good morning and let her know why you are there. Why you are both there. You'll say it all angry because that's how you feel. Like everyone is at fault all the time, even the person that held the elevator door for you seconds ago. You'll say thank you but the thank you will sound more like a fuck you.

You'll fill out papers while your boo grabs the *Sports Illustrated* magazine. You'll fill out the medical history. You have it memorized but you'll pull out your iPhone and pretend to look up the information like an executive assistant. You'll have insurance. If you don't have insurance, you're not wearing red; you're not waiting for an appointment. You and your man are fucked. But you'll have insurance and when you get to that part where they'll ask you who is the emergency contact person, you will feel good knowing that your name goes in that slot. Your number goes in there. And you'll feel secure because this is your weapon of choice. You are the one for emergencies.

There is the waiting game and you hate playing that game but you know the rules already. You give them a few minutes, maybe more, but usually less. Then you'll get up and ask them when they're going to call you. It doesn't matter that there are others waiting. It doesn't matter that the old man with Alzheimer's is still at the window trying to figure out how to get back home. It doesn't matter. You will approach the window and demand to know a specific time, right down to the second. And your man will shift his bony ass uncomfortably in the sunken leather brown sofa but he won't tell you to stop.

And then they'll call his name. You'll grab everything and rush out to the door because you don't want them to change their mind and call the Alzheimer guy. No, *viejo*, you want to tell him, this is mine. You will walk so closely to the nurse who is leading you to the office that you will almost trip her. You are doing this on purpose. You want to watch her fall, to create a distraction, an obstacle you can use to climb over and show your man that whatever comes your way, you know what to do. But he is only looking at the nurse's tight ass. You will make a mental note to start working out again. You'll squeeze your butt and keep it squeezed.

When you are led to the doctor's office, you'll glare at all of the diplomas. If he got his degree from some city college, you will look at him like he's your cousin who got his degree at DeVry Institute. If the doctor got his degree at any of the Ivy League schools, you will still look at him like he's your cousin but you will do so only for a second. If the doctor is older than your own father, you will listen to him respectfully, taking down notes while he speaks, nodding when the moment is right. If he is younger than you, you will listen to him but know that you will get a second opinion because no first-year-at-my-damn-job doctor is going to know what he's doing. Hell no.

The doctor will have graduated from Columbia University. You will shake the doctor's hand firmly and will look carefully at your man to make sure he does the same. When you feel that your man's handshake was too weak, ended too quickly, you will be embarrassed by him and wish he had worn the suit. The suit would have given him the allure of power but now he looks like a punk. You'll notice that his baseball hat is almost covering his eyes and you'll fight the urge to slap it off of his face.

Piquetes/The Exchange
You will bring out your file first and lay it on your lap. One folder in it is composed of all the photocopies you insisted on making after each appointment with your man. There are annotations and articles you've torn out. Another folder has pages of your notes and a notepad. The file is marked with his name. It's your very own dossier, the type

of file given to Jim Phelps of *Mission: Impossible* on the TV show, not the movie with Tom Cruise. There are images of doctors and specialists attached to the copies. It took you hours to organize this file and you're already eager to update it tonight with new notes, new revelations, new whatever.

The doctor will follow your lead and spread out his files on his large mahogany desk. He will ask for your man's name and medical history and this will piss you off because he should know this already. You will let your man speak, for once, but will interject to clear dates, episodes, dramas. You know more than he does and he's tired of repeating it over and over. But you enjoy this part. You know more than the doctor. For now.

You will look out the window and notice that the hospital is building another facility and you will ask the doctor what the building will focus on. And you will laugh when the doctor mentions the price tag like money is some funny punch line.

You will pull out an expensive pen, not a cheap Bic and not a Number 2 pencil. A pen with black ink that you will use to highlight, jot down, and mark up your file after every word the doctor utters.

The doctor will not use a pen but his ring finger will display a rather large wedding band that you will find hard not to stare at. And you will wonder how many diamonds are in that band and how much it costs. You will absentmindedly search for your nonexistent wedding band, the one your man promised to give you but instead you both ended up in city hall with his stupid friend Manny as the only witness and no ring. An idiot is what your Mami called you when you told her what you did. And you didn't argue with her.

You will lead by asking a question first because you are in control, because you are wearing red, because you're burning up. The question will be a timid question, a starter question, just something to test the waters. You don't want to start off the bat with the big question, no, that can wait. Start slow, then build up from there.

The doctor will answer your question quickly. His lips are dry and you wish he would use Blistex. His breath stinks of coffee and not the good kind. You will sit back and make a note into your file.

The doctor will change the subject and you'll hold your breath because the moment of truth is coming and there's nothing more to do but wait for the doctor to speak.

You will notice that you have accidentally placed a pen mark on the right-hand corner of your dress. This will cause you to have a mini-panic attack. No one in the room will notice. The mark will grow larger with every passing minute until you feel as if the pen mark is now standing over you, reprimanding you for not being more careful. The pen mark is breathing down your neck and you feel your head being pressed down to your lap. And you look at your man but your man is nodding at you like nothing is happening.

When the doctor dares to say the words, when he finally utters them, birthing exactly what you and your boo were afraid to even utter, when he finally says that word, you will not cry. Not even when it hurts your throat, when your eyes feel like burning. You will not cry. Not even when he says words like, 'we will try all we can, it's growing at a rapid speed, it's an aggressive disease.' You will not cry. You will be stone cold, just like the doctor who is spurting out statistics like he's trying to impress some dumb bitch at a bar. You are impressed but he will never know that. Those same statistics you will find on Web MD and utter them to your friends later when you will all meet for tea or something stronger. No, definitely something stronger.

You will insist on asking about the trial clinics. And you will not accept the doctor's answer that he is not qualified. You'll believe it has something to do with his last name or the fact that you didn't donate money for that new building.

The doctor will start to close the file.

You must not let that happen. The file must stay open.

The doctor will close the file and will start to stand.

You will not stand and you will place a hand to stop your man from leaving. You are not done yet.

Your voice will crack.

The doctor will look nervously at your man. He won't meet your eyes. He'll excuse himself, something about having to pull up another chart. He is running away.

The desk has expanded somehow, taking over the whole room, pressing your body up against the wall. You can't breathe. There's no air. You can't move.

Despedida/Goodbye

Your man will call you by his secret nickname, the name he christened you that night at the handball court. He will call you this name, the same name he whispered in your ear last night. And you will learn

170

how to breathe again. You will breathe and lock eyes with him. And for a moment, that's all you'll do.

Then you will take the lead again.

When the doctor returns, you will alert him of his next steps, not the other way around. The doctor will agree with you. You will firmly shake the doctor's hand goodbye. You will take his card.

When the receptionist tells you that she likes your dress, you will thank her.

Tomorrow, you will take the dress and give it your cousin. Better yet, you will donate it. You will never wear that red dress again.

SAY

fiction by JOE WILKINS

Let's say we have a man and a woman.

Let's say they're riding in some old Chevy pickup, windows down, prairie earth wheeling past. Let's call it Nebraska. No harm to say some old Chevy. No harm to say Nebraska.

Though, to be honest, judging by the cheatgrass spiking the ditches, those four cow skulls nailed down a fence post's crooked length, and the great bluescape of sky, it might be Wyoming, or Montana, or a Dakota—any of those dun-colored, too-wide-open, go-crazy-you're-so-lonesome places in the middle of America.

But we'll say Nebraska. We'll say the Chevy's a faded green and has a beat-up topper on the back. We'll say the plates are nearly mudded over, the engine cranked up to a high whine. We'll say some things fell through back home, and they've heard there's work in Fort Collins. We'll say they've been on the road a long few days. We'll say that in the cramped cab of the Chevy they're close enough to touch, but they're not touching.

He drapes one hand over the wheel, reaches the other out to her, palm up, like he's trying to make a point, like he's trying to come to the point—but she's not listening. We don't even have to say that. You can see it in the way her gaze has gone as flat and vacant as these plains. See the sunburnt angle of her jaw? That quick tremble of her lip? For her sake let's say that, finally, he shuts up.

He smokes cigarette after cigarette, each one burning down faster than the last, and as the miles streak by, she has retreated to some dark place behind her eyes. It's probably fair to say they've had it hard. Not

172

only the four hundred flat, aching miles they've come since sunup in Sugar City, but his drunk father, her drunk father, the job he walked out on and wishes he had back, the two semesters she tried at state college and will pay for until she's thirty-seven, that thing he did so long ago in the night, that man who grabbed her wrist, the friend who loved him and whom he treated cruelly, the sister she let make her own mistakes. Yes, it must be said, like you or me or anyone—like everyone— they've had it hard. You can see it in the sharp wing his elbow makes, the way she shuts her eyes for miles and leans her head against the shuddering window glass. And, just to top it off, let's say the cassette deck is broken. So for hours it's been either silence or silence. Nebraska and silence. Yes, it's been a hard goddamn day.

But let's say—and it could happen, I promise you—she opens her mouth and begins to sing: *Ain't it just like the night to play tricks when you're trying to be so quiet?* Say, down the next dry hill, he can't help but offer up: *Freedom's just another word for nothing left to lose, /And nothing ain't worth nothing, but it's free.* Yes, let's say that, despite it all, they begin to sing. It's not so hard to imagine, is it? Not so hard to see them barreling down the road, the sun-washed wind in their faces, these getting-by tunes on their lips? *Out with the truckers and the kickers and the cowboy angels, /And a good saloon in every single town.*

Oh, I know, it most likely goes the other way. But, listen, I'm simply telling you that the ending's not yet written. Maybe she won't get out at that gutted Gas-N-Go in Osceola. Maybe she won't wait until he's gone to take a piss and then cross the street and turn the corner by the dollar store and simply walk away. Maybe two days later he won't meet that hatchet-faced man in a roadside bar. Maybe he won't strain bad whiskey between his teeth and clench his fist. Maybe the economies of entropy and regret won't have their way. Not today.

I'm holding on here with foolish hope. I'm telling you they sing their way through Osceola, then turn south to miss that storm boiling up over the Sandhills. I'm telling you they stop on the grassy banks of Little Dry Creek and splash a bit of water on their necks. Telling you they make McCook by nightfall and stop at that cut-rate motel he knows and split a quart of beer while they watch moths arc and spin around streetlights like kinfolk of the stars.

I'm saying that this night they undress and pull the comforter from the bed and sweat against one another and roll away to sleep as naked and tired as stones.

I'm saying, in the frog-loud Nebraska night, in the pure dark of the Middle West of America, they dream.

And his dream is of sunburn and off-brand cigarettes and a black, watery silence she dives into and through and pulls him from, and with his tired arms he greets again the light. And her dream is of all the things she has ever forgotten lined up on a country porch, and only after she has touched and blessed each one can she race down the steps and slide into the front seat beside him for the ride to the river.

I'm telling you—just trust me for a moment, won't you?—that she wakes and hears him already in the shower, and she rises and drapes one of his shirts over her small shoulders and begins again to sing. *And I remember something you once told me / And I'll be damned if it did not come true.*

I'm telling you they sing. Listen. Hear their cracked voices whirl and ring.

THE BAD SEED: A GUIDE

fiction by NICOLA MASON

MANY SEEDS DO NOT GERMINATE WHEN PLACED UNDER CONDITIONS
WHICH ARE NORMALLY REGARDED AS FAVORABLE.
—The Germination of Seeds

Recognition is all-important. None of us is safe. You could be at the corner grocery, on a lonely bus to Tucson, in the emergency room with a bleeding gash. You could be tossing Mini-Wheats to birds in the park (because most people feed them crap) or sprinting for Gate B *(Gate B, where the hell is Gate B?)*. You could be jazzercizing (if you are *wont* to jazzercize). You could be pumping fuel at a local Shell or finger-ing your tresses in a Paris café. Anywhere, at any time, *you could encounter a Bad Seed.* You could *miss the warning signs.* And if you do, you could sink like a stone into a life of untold misery. Of redoubtable doubt. Of lies that mask truths and truths that mask lies that mask truths. Of throbbing migraines. Of hope that blinks in and out, a distant galaxy. You could sink like a stone, like a waterlogged corpse, like a sack full of hammers—and you will. Because the Bad Seed is always someone you could love. And you always do.

SEED PRODUCTION NORMALLY RESULTS IN AN OPPORTUNITY FOR THE
SEGREGATION AND RECOMBINATION OF GENES SO THAT THE SEED
POPULATION CONTAINS SOME NEW GENETIC COMBINATIONS.
—Seed Dormancy and Germination

* * *

Bad Seeds come in all shapes and sizes, from all walks of life. They look just like you and me, and this makes them hard to spot. Do not be lulled by their appearance of viability. Bad Seeds like to imagine they are good seeds, and if they think you are fooled—if you laugh too long at their limericks or let your bra strap slip into view—you will become their target *may God help you*. Your only chances of repelling a Bad Seed are (1) to become frowzy (but not *too* frowzy or he will see you as a challenge); (2) to become invisible (yet not so much so that you can't grasp objects and dial phones); (3) to become a robot. TIP: *Do not act like a cast-iron, stone-cold bitch, as this only attracts the Bad Seed.* Usually none of these tactics work, and you are approached anyway.

The initial encounter is a time of extreme danger, because the Bad Seed excels at first impressions and has an endearing persona for every situation. If you are waiting in a block-long line, bored out of your skull, he is the Stand-Up Comic. If you are frantically late, he becomes Kind Soul Who Shares His Cab. At the Suds 'n' Spin, he is the deceptively helpless Guy Who Mixes Whites and Darks. In a crisis, he is Man Who Knows CPR, Man Who Can Land Plane, Man Who Can Cauterize Wound If Necessary, Man Who Can Shimmy Through Small Opening at Great Peril and Not Die. But perhaps his most insidious identity is the Bumbler. EXAMPLE: You are at a party, content with your third tequila and lime, enjoying the taste of your tooth enamel, and the Bad Seed bumbles into you and spills juice (yes, juice, that's the genius of it) on your dress. "Oh, jeeze," he may say, "I'm such a dork. Do you want to use my Stain Stick? I live across the hall." He may say, "God, I feel terrible. I'll never forgive myself if I've ruined your bodice." (Bad Seeds like to say "bodice.") He may say, "Figures I'd spill on the most beautiful woman here. Now you'll never go out with me." He may say, "I know this sounds nuts, but you look great with juice on you." If you show vulnerability, if you are flustered and flattered and sputter words of comfort—"Oh, honestly, this dress is as old as Yoda" (your MasterCard is blood-warm from the purchase); "I was conflicted about it anyway. I mean, who wears eyelet anymore?" (you adore the lace-exercising-restraint look); "Where did you say that Stain Stick was?" (his apartment, i.e., TRAP)—then he will employ the Bad Seed refrain: "Please say you don't hate me." If you allow these words to pass his lips, you are doomed to a date.

When going out with a seed of unknown viability, play it safe: bury your heart in the backyard (deep, as dogs and Bad Seeds have formed an unholy alliance). Remember that you are your own worst enemy— because you believe that most convicts just got confused; because you want Chicken Little to have a forum though he's wrong; because "trust" has become a four-letter word even for people good at math; because you are lonely and your cat's opinion matters to you ("Do you think I have a pear body? Be honest, Cumin").

The Bad Seed may take you to the ballet or the bowling alley. To the gallery opening or the Tastee Freeze. But no matter where you go or what you say (whether you use *chiaroscuro* improperly or insist the lane gutter has a magnet in it), sometime during the date the Bad Seed will reveal a Tortured Past That Has Damaged Him Irrevocably. Instead of alarming you, instead of causing your brain to fire off the following internal memorandum: MAN MAY BE THE DEVIL, this will intrigue and draw you to him. As he reveals the Shocking Facts, you will listen raptly and feel your spleen go limp with compassion. You will nod, nod, nod and maybe cry some when he says, "The musky smell of horses still haunts me," or, "Most people don't consider that animals can rape. It's a largely unaddressed issue in our society," or, "If only I'd used the spurs . . . but I was just a boy."

After his confession, you will feel shy and secretly honored that he has entrusted you with his shame. You will offer him a sip of your Sprite to show him that you don't think he's befouled, and when he accepts and sucks on your straw you will think, *This is how the ravaged suck straws.* Later, at your door, his mouth will press yours chastely, and when you try to deepen the kiss he will pull away, duck his head, and whisper, "I'm sorry . . . the horse, the horse." You will be understanding and give him a big hug (you always overestimate the allure of the big hug). You will tell him he can call you if he wants, and he fervently says he wants, so you imagine he will phone the next day, or maybe even in the middle of the night to say, "I just had this incredible dream, and you were in it," or to entrust you with the name of the horse: "It was Pierce. *Pierce.* I don't know why I called. I just wanted you to know."

Despite your expectation, he doesn't phone in the middle of the night, but you decide this means nothing, and though it is *far too soon* to dig up the heart, there you are at 3:00 a.m. in your Mighty Mouse nightshirt, carving a crater the size of a minivan out of your flower bed, the neighbors schnauzer looking on all the while, grinning its soggy, doggy grin. When you finally unearth the heart and go inside to rinse it, the Bad Seed is experiencing REM sleep across town, dreaming he is a jockey riding a mare with straining neck muscles and foaming withers. The mare's face is your face.

SEEDS . . . OF PARASITIC OR SEMI-PARASITIC PLANTS HAVE BEEN
SAID TO DEPEND UPON SECRETIONS FROM THE ROOTS OF
THE HOST PLANTS FOR GERMINATION.
—*Physiology of Seeds*

On the second date you will go somewhere alone, just the two of you, maybe to the levee to watch the river grow luminous with contaminants, or the park so he can swing you too high and hear you shriek. You stroll arm in arm, like in old movies but with far more flying insects, and as you pretend the mosquitoes aren't draining your lifeblood, he will say he knows it's way too soon, and please don't freak out, but he thinks he's falling in love with you. You freak out and protest that you've only just met, and he clutches your wrists (so you can't slap; it's a habit) and breathes, "God, don't you think I know that? It's crazy . . . but there's something about you. I've got chills, Rachel. I'm losing control. You have this power . . . it's electrifying."

You start to lean into him, then pull back and say, "Wait a minute. That's from *Grease.*"

He is unfazed at being caught and responds, "I know, I know. But Zuko sings what I *feel.*"

Because you, too, struggle to form original thoughts in a derivative world, you believe him, and suddenly you are deeply concerned because (1) you haven't polled your friends yet, and (2) his heart is in your hands—his tender, scarred, pulsating Bad Seed heart. You should crush it, of course. You should hurl it to the ground and stomp it into lasagna and *laugh, laugh, laugh* until a panel truck comes for you. Instead, you stroke his palms and say, "I don't want to hurt you." You plumb his earnest, hopeful, Bad Seed gaze and say, "I think you're an amazing person. But I have violation issues, too, and some psoriasis I'm trying to deal with. What I'm saying is, *I need more time.*"

The Bad Seed turns away to battle emotion. "Of course you do," he says thickly. "You'd think I'd know better than to blurt it out like that. You'd think I could get something right for once in my life. I fucking hate myself!"

He bolts and streaks away, past the curly slide and the bouncing ducks. After a startled moment, you realize his demons are chasing him, and because this is the most cinematic thing that's ever happened to you, you follow them.

You are more a skipper than a runner. More a hopper than a skipper. More an ankle twister than any of these. When you finally reach him, you feel you have traveled years into the future instead of fifty yards dragging your left leg. You find you have a flair for drama, and you clutch the Bad Seed, claw at him to communicate something primal, and make an embarrassing statement that involves the phrase "the cold eye of the cosmos."

Then you go home and sleep with him.

IN VERY MANY SPECIES OF PLANTS THE SEEDS, WHEN SHED FROM THE
PARENT, WILL NOT GERMINATE. . . . THESE SEEDS ARE SAID TO
REQUIRE A PERIOD OF AFTER-RIPENING.
—*The Germination of Seeds*

Transcript of a phone call:

You: "Hi, Mom. It's Rachel."

Your mother: "I hope you're not taking those metabolic grapefruit pills. I feel sorry for the women in the commercials. They lose weight, but there's no adjustment period. The fat girl is still there inside them. You can see it in their eyes—the hunger."

You: "Actually, I'm calling because I'm extremely happy. I've met someone, and he makes me extremely happy."

Your mother: "You said that."

You: "What?"

Your mother: "'Extremely happy.' You said it twice. You sound like you're trying to convince yourself."

You: "I'm not trying to convince myself. I am myself. I mean, I *am* extremely happy."

Your mother: "Your father is picking the raisins out of the raisin bread. Stop it, Linus. You know I hate it when you do that. He knows I hate it when he does that."

You: "You said that."

Your mother: "Of course I did. Rachel, what's wrong, dear? Is your young man giving you trouble?"

You: "Mother, please. I'm trying to tell you something wondrous about my life. I'm in love with Brett."

Your mother: "Isn't that the name of a hair spray?"

You: "No, that's Breck. But I'm not sure they make it anymore."

Your mother: "Well, he sounds like a snake in the grass to me." After you hang up, you wander around the house touching your possessions to make sure they aren't concealing blades. "You are mine," you tell your candlesticks firmly. To your lamps and curtains you say, "Mine." In the kitchen, you slide open a drawer and palm your bottle of grapefruit pills. You stare at it; it stares at you. "My decision," you say. You throttle the bottle and enjoy its loose-teeth sound. You declare, "I am your master!" Then you twist the cap and pour the pills down the sink and sit on the floor and cry—because your mother is always right. Even when she's not.

UNFAVORABLE GERMINATION CONDITIONS OFTEN
THROW SEEDS INTO DORMANCY SO THEY WILL NOT GERMINATE
WHEN SHIFTED TO A FAVORABLE CONDITION.
—*Physiology of Seeds*

But your mother is wrong about the Bad Seed. You know a snake in the grass when you see one, and the Bad Seed is far from snaky (he blinks, for one thing). To prove this, you dedicate yourself to making him giddy with joy at having you in his life. You know relationships don't come easy (because that's the theme of many popular songs), but this one will work because you will crush any threats to your ecstasy.

In front of a mirror, you practice making your expression of blissful transport look less like a death rictus. You employ this expression in private and in public, even at the risk of being mistaken for Julie Andrews. You build up a repertoire of stock moods and responses and alternate them. There is Rowdy You: "I am having such a rockin' time"; Rhapsodic You: "Wow. I mean, wow, wow, *wow!*"; Reverent You: "It's like we're in church. My soul is as quiet as a sleeping child."

For a while you imagine that the relationship is a perfect match instead of a tenuous connection between two people who like carob, that it is full of quixotic emotion instead of a strain on your acting ability. You expect your life will become a whirlwind, that you'll get outdoors more, pack picnics, play Frisbee, catch some fish (if you can bring yourself to kill the crickets). You are sure you'll need new clothes to wear to unexpected events, so you buy some, forgetting you aren't a contessa and don't need that much tulle. Actually, the two of you spend a lot of time watching TV at your place (which you did before). You order takeout (ditto). You read your cookie fortune to the Bad Seed instead of the cat and marvel aloud that your fortunes always seem guarded and noncommittal. ("Hard work makes strong back." "You will climb many mountains." "Luck smiles on the few, not the many.")

"Weird, huh?" you say.

And he says, "Weird," but not enthusiastically—so you worry that he is bored with the relationship, and to spice things up you model your new gowns for him, floating diaphanous and barefoot (free spirits fear not tetanus) across the room. You smile a closed-lip, mysterious smile and say, liltingly, "It feels like I have *nothing* on. Not a *stitch*." But he's watching a *Baretta* rerun, and you keep floating in front of the screen, so instead of leaping up and whirling you from wall to wall like a tulle tornado, the Bad Seed gets cranky and barks, "Can't you see he's talking to the bird!"

Your smile wobbles. Your hair (which you have worked into a spun-sugar cloud) feels sticky on your back. Your feet are cold. "I just wanted to be magical, that's all," you quaver, and stump away to throw yourself on the bed.

A little later he comes in to tell you he's a jerk. You say nothing and concentrate on breathing through your snot. He says, "I swear I amaze myself. Here I am with this incredible girl . . . this gorgeous creature from beyond . . . and I screw it up. I wouldn't blame you if you dropped me like a sack of wet garbage. I mean it. Go, Rachel. Fly." Here, he pins your ankle to the mattress. "But know this: You're my Every Woman."

You are aware that (1) he waited until the commercial to come in and console you; (2) these are probably song lyrics. Moreover, the Bad Seed has failed you in a number of respects (no fish, no Frisbee, etc.). But by now you have invested a lot of time you could have spent speculating

181

about supermodels (will Shalom go short for spring?), reorganizing your pantry, watching your married friends jam chapped red nipples into the chapped red mouths of screaming infants (God, its so beautiful. How you envy them!). Also, he has seen you naked and hasn't criticized anything.

Then the Bad Seed pulls out the stops: "Please say you don't hate me."

LITTLE . . . IS KNOWN ABOUT PHYSICAL AND
CHEMICAL CHANGES OCCURRING IN CERTAIN SEEDS.
—*Physiology of Seeds*

You love him. You do. But as the months pass, certain aspects of the Bad Seed begin to bother you: his dead incisor (is it getting grayer?); how he drinks in stereo *(agunk, agunk, agunk)*; his nail-polish fetish ("Shouldn't you fix that chip before we eat? I can wait"); how he always wants you on all fours and pretends it isn't significant ("Can I help it if you're really sexy back there?"). You tell yourself these things make the Bad Seed unique. That you are always too critical. That you have flaws yourself and he overlooks them. Still, thoughts come at you like trucks, carrying the Names of Boyfriends Past with the labels you affixed to them. Larry the Limpet. New Age Nonny (who moved smooth black stones around in a little tabletop sandbox with a tiny rake). You-Gonna-Eat-That?-Matt. Travis Trivia ("Did you know armadillos can be house trained? Quick! List the biblical plagues. EEERP. Time's up!"). The trucks hurtle toward you at unsafe speeds. There are many, many trucks. It's a convoy, Rubber Duck. And here comes another one—appropriately bringing up the rear. What's your handle, good buddy? Brett from Behind.

You resist these thoughts. All thoughts. You decide to live each moment as pure sensory experience, with acceptance and appreciation and a generous, loving spirit. This would work if each moment weren't full of unbearable irritants. Instead of saying, "My stomach hurts," he says, "I have a rumbly in my tumbly." As quickly as you can buy ChapStick, he steals it; then, when your lips crack and bleed, he offers to let you use his tube. His nose whistles like a mad piper, yet he can't hear it. Then you begin to hear it when he's not around—at the office, out shopping, until you are discovered in a Dillard's dressing room clawing your cheeks and rambling, "He's here, he's here, he's here, I know he's here!"

182

You decide you need space, but resolve to be mature about it, gentle, because he is fragile and you don't want his blood on your hands. A week passes while you wait for the right moment to break the news. Another week. (You are a physiological wonder: completely gutless, yet you can still digest foods.) Another week. Finally, as you are driving to the movies one night, he keeps punching the car lighter, though he doesn't smoke. He just pulls the knob when it pops and stares at the glowing coils, then holds it up so you can see. "These things are great," he says with fresh discovery in his voice.

"Yes," you say slowly, as to a child. "Fire." Then, because you feel your brain swelling like a blowfish, you blurt, "I think we should see other people."

Your statement is greeted with silence, and you hit the automatic door locks (in case he's a leaper) and wedge your elbow against the window (for leverage should he insanely grab the wheel).

But all he says is, "Oops"—and for an instant you think he has dropped the lighter and the car will be engulfed in flames and he'll hold you tenderly as your skin chars and your liver melts, saying, "If this is goodbye, let us burn together, Rachel." But you realize almost immediately that it's not that sort of an "oops." It's a snake-in-the-grass "oops."

So you demand, "Whadda ya mean, 'Oops'?"

And the Bad Seed shrugs sheepishly and confesses, "I didn't know we were supposed to be exclusive. You never said anything."

You are sure you did not hear correctly, hence your reply: "Come again, Zuko?"

And he says, "I didn't mean to lead you on, if that's what you're implying. It just never came up."

Though you feel a nightmare approaching, you inquire, "*Who* never came up?"

The Bad Seed is pained. "Well . . . if you must know, Gina."

"Gina? *My* Gina? My *best friend* Gina?"

He confirms: "She called a while back, when you were in the shower, and we had a really good talk."

You respond through great cotton wads of stupefaction: "You talked to my best friend? You're not allowed to talk to my best friend. That's a rule. It's a very big rule. It's *giganto*." (You have always hated romantic comedies, and now you know it's because they flout the giganto rules intolerably!) You make a new rule: "You will never talk to my best friend again."

The Bad Seed reproaches, "That's a little selfish, don't you think? Gina's going through a transitional phase, and she needs a lot of support."

You have just turned into the theater parking lot, but instead of slowing down and steering so as to miss immovable objects, you press the accelerator and aim for a dumpster at the end of the row of cars. "See that? That's a transitional dumpster," you remark with eerie calm. "When we hit it, we will change." (You are now courting death; this may signal a loss of perspective on your part.)

"Hey, whoa!" the Bad Seed exclaims. "I didn't know you felt so strongly about it. We're exclusive, okay?"

You ease your foot off the gas pedal and coast to a stop, your bumper giving the dumpster a brushing kiss. "Damn right," you say. Then you begin to tremble because you have no idea who you are.

THE QUESTION UNDER CONSIDERATION AT THIS POINT
IS WHETHER THIS RESTRICTION OF OXYGEN SUPPLY HAS
ANY RELATION TO DORMANCY IN THE SEED.
—*Physiology of Seeds*

You quickly learn to despise who you have become. Outwardly, you are cheerful and affectionate (so as not to give him an excuse)—but within, you are a cricket cage, acrawl with suspicions and needling chitinous legs that rub together to make sounds, phrases, mean little commentaries on your (appalling) life. You bury your heart again to punish it for misleading you, but the heart has been working out and paddles up through your tulips using its little aortic stubs. It scales your beech tree and howls like a bone-snapping gale. The neighbors are frightened and because they threaten to involve the police, you are forced to take the heart back, though it knows you are bitter and revenges itself by mass-producing unreasoning psycho-bitch rage.

You throw yourself into sex, performing many astonishing acts with your mind's eye blindfolded. You whinny without being asked. When it's over, you press, "Did *she* do that for you? Huh? Did she?"

The Bad Seed, basking in man-melt, replies lazily, "Who? Oh. I could never love Gina. She has inverted nipples."

This does not mollify you (you are beyond the satisfaction of minor disfigurements, *far* beyond), and when you determine he is deep in dreamland ("Breck?" you whisper to the darkness near his ear. "Breck?"), you go downstairs and pick up the phone and have a pizza delivered to Gina's house—pepperoni, so she'll know you know about the nipples.

You insist he spend all his time with you, and though he seems happy to do this, you notice certain tricks of evasion (for instance, the men's room). At the movies, he leaves his seat during the tank chase, and when you search him out a half-hour later, he is craning over the candy counter, chatting it up with the girl who earlier dispensed your Snow Caps (you swear it) icily. The Bad Seed waves when he sees you. "Hey," he says. "I want you to meet Brittany. She's having a hell of a time with geometry."

"Poor thing," you say, linking your arm with the Bad Seed's and pulling him away. "Good luck with it," you cry gaily over your shoulder. To him, you hiss, "What is she? Fifteen?"

His eyebrows gang up on you, two disapproving parabolas: "I didn't know you were such an ageist."

In the car, you smack your palm on your forehead. "Well, heck darn doo. I forgot something. Be back in a sec, lover." In a twinkling you are at the counter, clutching at the glass, darkening the Milk Duds like a poisonous atmosphere. Brittany is alone, mopping orange pools of popcorn butter. Her nose is cutely awrinkle. Her ponytail, pert. She is your enemy and always has been, and you are about to make the sort of menacing claim that results in restraining orders, when she turns to you with a look of urgency on her flushed little freckledy face. "Listen, you don't know me from Dorcas," she says, "but totally trust me when I tell you your date is a complete creepoid. Like slime central."

Instantly you crumble. Even the Junior Mints (so refreshing!) cannot console you. "Oh, Brittany," you wail. "What should I do?"

She ponders a moment, her brow adorably furrowed. "I think," she says, "you should get away from him."

THERE ARE MANY SEEDS . . . WHICH DETERIORATE
RAPIDLY WHEN EXPOSED TO OPEN AIR.
    —*Physiology of Seeds*

You try. You let days drag out of fetal dawn and form restless, questing limbs and finally stoop, broken, into the folding dark—all without touching the phone. You do not wonder what he's doing. You do not wonder what he's doing. You do not wonder what he's doing.

You make a gourmet dinner for one, wearing nothing but an apron, and comment to the cat, "I feel so free and joyous right now. I celebrate my independence and individuality. I affirm myself." Then you catch the reflection of your rear in the oven window glass, and you see you are not affirm at all but rather afflaccid. You reverse the apron, but the view does not improve.

After dinner you catch up on the things you always said you'd do but never really meant to. Like reading operation manuals on appliances you've had for years (this involves some ugly realizations about filters), checking under the house for missing children, changing all the light bulbs because you fear they'll go out at once. At midnight you decide you must have a gentler, more nourishing shampoo immediately, so you get in the car and drive straight to his apartment and stare at his empty parking place for the time it takes you to realize how pathetic you are (about an hour). Then you drive home. At 2:00 a.m. you remember you forgot the shampoo, and you are back at his apartment. This time his car is there, so you stare at his darkened windows and smoke a cigarette shakily and do not wonder if he is alone.

By 3:00 you are at an after-hours bar throwing back shots of ouzo, talking to a guy wearing a clip tie (he demonstrates) who thinks your name is Beth. You say, "My name is Rachel."

He responds, "Oh, right, Beth. Like I believe that. You must think I'm some kind of yutz. Okay, I'm a yutz." He winks and says with poke-in-the-ribs levity, "Hello, *Rachel.*" (Run fast, run far, dear Rachel. Flee with your dignity whilst you can.)

You respond with your own poke-in-the-ribs levity, "Hello, *Brian.*" His face crumples like the squeezed half of a grapefruit.

"Beth," he sobs, his fingers scrabbling at his sternum. "It's me, Stewart. Don't you recognize me?"

The ouzo is making the bar seem like an environment, and you are cozy there with the pitiful people. You are all single cells making up a pitiful animal, one that crawls on its belly as a means of locomotion. Stewart is crawling onto your bar stool. "You *know* me, you *know* me," he is saying.

You nod (slowly, because you're not sure he can detect movement) and speak with the wisdom of the ages: "What you say is true . . . but vast."

Then you take Stewart home and sleep with him.

You are now the most degraded you have ever been. Your soap shudders when you reach for it. The shower spits in your face. Even your collars reject you, straining away from your clavicles no matter how you beat them. You realize there is no one but yourself to blame—so you blame the Bad Seed. This works well. By using your hate as a stepping-stone, you emerge from the slough of self-mortification covered with scum, but with no ghoulish tattoos or uncomfortable piercings. When the Bad Seed calls, finally, to see "how things are going," your defiance leaps to the fore, so you do not say, "Like a train wreck with mangled bodies marring the countryside," or, "Okay if you discount the herpes scare," but rather, "Great! This is a very exciting time for me," and to show him you're being both productive and whimsical in his absence, you add, "I'm learning to hula hoop."

He says, "Wow, that's really something," and you say, "Yep." And he laughs a little (a trial balloon), but you don't laugh back, so he tries another tack, saying meltingly, "My life is a weeping sore without you. Rachel, you're my sexy salve."

You feel the heart staging a coup (it's now in league with your lungs, bullying your breath to catch), and you know you must be merciless or forever dwell in the land of song-lyric abominations, so you ask, "Do you know Stewart?"

A pause follows while the Bad Seed reassesses. "I don't think so," he ventures, guarded now. "Should I break his legs?"

For reasons you can't fathom, you are filled with absurd disappointment. "I guess not," you say.

And he says suddenly, "Holy smoke, I just remembered I left something in the oven." And though it's nothing like you imagined it, you grasp immediately that *this is the end,* and to let him know you grasp it, you exclaim with dismay, "And here my sock drawer just exploded. Now I'll never get them matched!"

After he hangs up, you sit quietly to await the heart's rib-kicking conniption, but the heart surprises you by ushering blood cells from room to room like a proper tour guide. You take this to mean grace is possible. Of course, there are rough days ahead. You will wallow and snuffle and chew the buds from your tongue. You will deny yourself cookie dough, and this will backfire monstrously. You will pack your sheets in a box and mail them to the Bad Seed, remembering his comment on your "sleep smell," then smash some darling collectibles when he doesn't acknowledge their receipt.

But some days will not be fresh hells. Some days will be ordinary, and you will accomplish things (like breathing, walking unaided, etc.). You will be a bit kinder to yourself. Maybe you will start a support group, write a pamphlet, stand on street corners shouting, "You, too, can like you! It's a guilt-free gift! No agony attached!" And one morning in the not-so-distant future, you will awaken with the idea that you can be happy. The sky will be a study of softness—blue on blue on blue. There will be sunlight you fail to cringe from. You will turn on the shower full force, and when you step into its mist, you'll practically be bursting your skin.

PROWLERS

fiction by JACK DRISCOLL

There's a ladder that leans against the back of the house, a sort of stairway to the roof where Marley-Anne and I sometimes sit after another donnybrook. You know the kind, that *whump* of words that leaves you dumbstruck and hurt and in the silent nightlong aftermath startled almost dead. Things that should never be spoken to a spouse you're crazy in love with—no matter what.

Yeah, that's us, Mr. and Mrs. Reilly Jack. It's not that the air is thin or pure up here, not in mid-August with all that heat locked in the shingles. It's just that we can't be inside after we've clarified in no uncertain terms the often fragile arrangement of our marriage. And right there's the irony, given that we fill up on each other morning, noon, and night—excepting during these glitches, of course, when we reassert our separateness, and all the more since we've started breaking into houses.

B&E artists, as Marley-Anne calls us, and that's fine with me, though never before in our history had we made off with somebody's horse. Tonight, though, a large mammal is grazing ten feet below us in our small, fenced-in backyard. This kind of incident quick-voids a lease, and we signed ours ten months ago with a sweet-deal option to buy. A simple three-bedroom starter ranch with a carport, situated on an irregular quarter acre where in the light of day we present ourselves as your ordinary small-town underachievers. And that pretty much identifies the demographic hereabouts: white, blue-collar, Pet Planet employed. I'd feed their C-grade canned to my rescue mutt any day of the week if I could only sweet-talk Marley-Anne into someday getting one.

189

I drive a forklift, which may or may not be a lifelong job but, if so, I'm fine with that future, my ambitions being somewhat less than insistent. Marley-Anne, on the other hand, is a woman of magnum potential, tall and funny and smart as the dickens, and I buy her things so as not to leave her wanting. Last week, a blue moonstone commemorating our ten-year anniversary, paid for up front in full by yours truly.

Anything her maverick heart desires, and I'll gladly work as much swing-shift or graveyard overtime as need be, though what excites Marley-Anne . . . well, let me put it this way: there's a river nearby and a bunch of fancy waterfront homes back in there, and those are the ones we stake out and prowl.

The first time was not by design. The declining late winter afternoon was almost gone, and Marley-Anne riding shotgun said, "Stop." She said, "Back up," and when I did she pointed at a Real Estate One sign advertising an open house, all angles and stone chimneys and windows that reflected the gray sky. "That's tomorrow," I said. "Sunday," and without another word she was outside, breaking trail up the unshoveled walkway, the snow lighter but still falling, and her ponytail swaying from side to side.

She's like that, impulsive and unpredictable, and I swear I looked away—a couple of seconds max—and next thing I know she's holding a key between her index finger and thumb, and waving for me to come on, hurry up, Reilly Jack. Hurry up, like she'd been authorized to provide me a private showing of this mansion listed at a million-two or -three—easy—and for sure not targeting the likes of us. I left the pickup running, heater on full blast, and when I reached Marley-Anne I said, "Where'd you find that?" Meaning the key, and she pointed to the fancy brass lock, and I said, "Whoever forgot it there is coming back. Count on it."

"We'll be long gone by then. A spot inspection and besides I have to pee," she said, her knees squeezed together. "You might as well come in out of the cold, don't you think?"

"Here's fine," I said. "This is as far as I go, Marley-Anne. No kidding, so how about you just pee and flush and let's get the fuck off Dream Street, okay?"

What's clear to me is that my mind's always at its worst in the waiting. Always, no matter what, and a full elapsing ten minutes is a long while to imagine your wife alone in somebody else's domicile. I didn't knock or ring the doorbell. I stepped inside and walked through the maze of more empty living space than I had ever seen or imagined. Rooms entirely absent of furniture and mirrors, and the walls and ceilings so white I squinted, the edges of my vision blurring like I was searching for someone lost in a storm or squall.

"Marley-Anne," I said, her name echoing down hallways and up staircases and around the crazy asymmetries of custom-built corners jutting out everywhere like a labyrinth. Then more firmly asserted until I was shouting, hands cupped around my mouth, "Marley-Anne, Marley-Anne, answer me. Please. It's me, Reilly Jack."

I found her in the farthest far reaches of the second floor, staring out a window at the sweep of snow across the river. She was shivering, and I picked up her jacket and scarf off the floor. "What are you doing?" I asked, and all she said back was, "Wow. Is that something or what?" and I thought, Oh fuck. I thought, Here we go, sweet Jesus, wondering how long this time before she'd plummet again.

We're more careful now, and whenever we suit up it's all in black, though on nights like this with the sky so bright, we should always detour to the dump with a six-pack of cold ones and watch for the bears that never arrive. Maybe listen to Mickey Gilley or Johnny Cash and make out like when we first started dating back in high school, me a senior and Marley-Anne a junior, and each minute spent together defining everything I ever wanted in my life. Against the long-term odds we stuck. We're twenty-nine and twenty-eight, respectively, proving that young love isn't all about dick and daydreams and growing up unrenowned and lonesome. Just last month, in the adrenalin rush of being alone in some strangers' lavish master bedroom, we found ourselves going at it in full layout on their vibrating king-size. Satin sheets the color of new aluminum and a mirror on the ceiling, and I swear to God we left panting and breathless. You talk about making a score . . . that was it, our greatest sex ever. In and out like pros, and the empty bed still gyrating like a seizure.

Mostly we don't loot anything. We do it—ask Marley-Anne—for the sudden rush and flutter. Sure, the occasional bottle of sweet port to celebrate, and once—just the one time—I cribbed a padded-shoulder, double-breasted seersucker suit exactly my size. But I ended up wearing instead the deep shame of my action, so the second time we broke in there I hung the suit back up where I'd originally swiped it, like it was freshly back from the dry cleaners and hanging again in that huge walk-in closet. We're talking smack-dab on the same naked white plastic hanger.

191

Now and again Marley-Anne will cop a hardcover book if the title sounds intriguing. *The Lives of the Saints*, that's one that I remember held her full attention from beginning to end. Unlike me she's an avid reader; her degree of retention you would not believe. She literally burns through books, speed-reading sometimes two per night, so why *not* cut down on the cost? As she points out, these are filthy-rich people completely unaware of our immanence, and what's it to them anyway, these gobble-jobs with all their New World bucks?

I'd rather not, I sometimes tell her, that's all. It just feels wrong.

Then I throw in the towel because the bottom line is whatever makes her happy. But grand theft? Jesus H., that sure never crossed my mind, not once in all the break-ins. (I'd say twenty by now, in case anyone's counting.) I'm the lightweight half in the mix, more an accessory along for the ride, though of my own free will I grant you, and without heavy pressure anymore, and so no less guilty. No gloves, either, and if anyone has ever dusted for fingerprints they've no doubt found ours everywhere.

Foolhardy, I know, and in a show of hands at this late juncture I'd still vote for probing our imaginations in more conventional, stay-at-home married ways. Like curling up together on the couch for Tigers baseball or possibly resuming that conversation about someday having kids. She says two would be satisfactory. I'd say that'd be great. I'd be riding high on numbers like that. But all I have to do is observe how Marley-Anne licks the salt rim of a margarita glass, and I comprehend all over again her arrested maternal development and why I've continued against my better judgment to follow her anywhere, body and soul, pregnant or not.

That doesn't mean I don't get pissed, but I do so infrequently and always in proportion to the moment or event that just might get us nailed or possibly even gut-shot. And how could I ever—a husband whose idealized version of the perfect wife is the woman he married and adores—live with that? I figure a successful crime life is all about minimizing the risks so nobody puts a price on your head or even looks at you crosswise. That's it in simple English, though try explaining "simple" to a mind with transmitters and beta waves like Marley-Anne's.

Not that she planned on heisting someone's goddamn paint, because forward-thinking she'll never be, and accusations to that effect only serve to aggravate an already tenuous situation. All I'm saying is that a bridle was hanging on the paddock post, and next thing I knew she was cantering bareback out the fucking gate and down the driveway like

Hiawatha minus the headband and beaded moccasins. Those are the facts. Clop-clop-clack on the blacktop, and in no way is the heightened romance inherent in that image lost on me.

But within seconds she was no more than a vague outline and then altogether out of sight, and me just standing there, shifting from foot to foot, and the constellations strangely spaced and tilted in the dark immensity of so much sky. Good Christ, I thought. Get back here, Marley-Anne, before you get all turned around, which maybe she already had. Or maybe she got thrown or had simply panicked and ditched the horse and stuck to our standing strategy to always rendez-vous at the pickup if anything ever fouled.

But she wasn't at the truck when I got back to it. I slow-drove the roads and two-tracks between the fields where the arms of oil wells pumped and wheezed, and where I stopped and climbed into the truck bed and called and called out to her. Nothing. No sign of her at all, at least not until after I'd been home for almost two hours, half-crazed and within minutes of calling 911.

And suddenly there she was, her hair blue-black and shiny as a raven's under that evanescent early-morning halo of the street lamp as she rode up to 127 Athens, the gold-plated numerals canted vertically just right of the mail slot. Two hours I'd been waiting, dead nuts out of my gourd with worry. I mean I could hardly even breathe, and all she says is, "Whoa," and smiles over at me like, Hey, where's the Instamatic, Reilly Jack? The house was pitch dark behind me, but not the sky afloat with millions of shimmering stars. I could see the sweating brown and white rump of the pinto go flat slick as Marley-Anne slid straight off backward and then tied the reins to the porch railing as if it were a hitching post. The mount just stood there swishing its long noisy tail back and forth, its neck outstretched on its oversized head and its oval eyes staring at me full on. And that thick corkscrew tangle of white mane, as if it had been in braids, and nostrils flared big and pink like two identical side-by-side conch shells.

I'd downed a couple of beers and didn't get up from the swing when she came and straddled my lap. Facing me she smelled like welcome to Dodge City in time warp. Oats and hay and horse sweat, a real turn-off and, as usual, zero awareness of what she'd done. Nonetheless, I lifted Marley-Anne's loose hair off her face so I could kiss her cheek in the waning moonlight, that gesture first and foremost to herald her safe arrival home no matter what else I was feeling, which was complex and

193

considerable. Her black jeans on my thighs were not merely damp but soaking wet, and the slow burn I felt up and down my spinal cord was electric.

But that's a moot point if there's a horse matter to broker, and there was, of course: Marley-Anne's fantasy of actually keeping it. Don't ask me where, because that's not how she thinks—never in a real-world context, never ever in black and white. She's all neurons and impulse. Factor in our ritual fast-snap and zipper disrobing of each other during or shortly after a successful caper, and you begin to understand my quandary. She does not cope well with incongruity, most particularly when I'm holding her wrists like I do sometimes, forcing her to concentrate and listen to me up close face-to-face as I attempt to argue reason.

Which is why I'd retreated to the roof, and when she followed maybe a half hour later, a glass of lemonade in hand, I said, "Please, just listen, okay? Don't flip out, just concentrate on what I'm saying and talk to me for a minute." Then I paused and said, "I'm dead serious, this is bad, Marley-Anne, you have no comprehension *how* bad but maybe it's solvable if we keep our heads." As in, Knock-knock, is anybody fucking home?

She'd heard it all before, a version at least, and fired back just above a whisper, "I can take care of myself, thank you very much."

"No," I said, "you can't, and that's the point. You don't get it. We're in big trouble this time. Serious deep shit and our only ticket out—are you even listening to me?—is to get this horse back to the fucking Ponderosa, and you just might want to stop and think about that."

She said nothing, and the raised vein on my left temple started throbbing as Paint thudded his first engorged turd onto the lawn, which I'd only yesterday mowed and fertilized, and then on hands and knees had spread dark red lava stones under the azaleas and around the bougainvillea. All the while, Marley-Anne had stood hypnotized at the kitchen window, re-constellating what she sometimes refers to as this down-in-the-heels place where the two of us exist together on a next-to-nothing collateral line.

It's not the Pierce-Arrow of homes, I agree. Hollow-core doors and a bath and a half, but we're not yet even thirty, and for better or worse most days seem substantial enough and a vast improvement over my growing up in a six-kid household without our dad, who gambled and drank and abandoned us when I was five. I was the youngest, the son named after him, and trust me when I say that Marley-Anne's story—

like mine—is pages and pages removed from a fully stocked in-home library and a polished black baby grand, and to tell it otherwise is pure unadulterated fiction. "Maybe in the next lifetime," I said once, and she reminded me how just two weeks prior we'd made love on top of a Steinway in a mansion off Riverview, murder on the knees and shoulder blades but the performance virtuoso. And Marley-Anne seventh-heaven euphoric in hyperflight back to where we'd hidden the pickup behind a dense red thicket of sumac.

Nothing in measured doses for Marley-Anne, whose penchant for drama is nearly cosmic. Because she's restless her mind goes zooming, then dead-ends double whammy with her job and the sameness of the days. Done in by week's end—that's why we do what we do, operating on the basis that there is no wresting from her the impulsive whirl of human desire and the possibility to dazzle time. Take that away, she's already in thermonuclear meltdown—and believe me, the aftereffects aren't pretty.

She works for Addiction Treatment Services as a nine-to-five receptionist filing forms and changing the stylus on the polygraph. Lazy-ass drunks and dopers, jerk-jobs, and diehard scammers—you know the kind—looking to lighten their sentences, and compared to them Marley-Anne in my book can do no wrong. Her code is to outlive the day terrors hellbent on killing her with boredom, and because I've so far come up with no other way to rescue her spirit I stand guard while she jimmies back doors and ground-level windows. Or sometimes I'll boost her barefoot from my shoulders onto a second-floor deck where the sliders are rarely locked. In a minute or two she comes downstairs and deactivates the state-of-the-art security system, inviting me in through the front door as though she lives there and residing in such splendor is her right God-given.

"Good evening," she'll say. "Welcome. What desserts do you suppose await us on this night, Reilly Jack?"—as if each unimagined delight has a cherry on top and is all ours for the eating. Then she'll motion me across the threshold and into the dark foyer where we'll stand locking elbows or holding hands like kids until our eyes adjust.

At first I felt grubby and little else, and that next hit was always the place where I didn't want to fall victim to her latest, greatest, heat-seeking version of our happiness. I didn't get it, and I told her so in mid-May after we'd tripped an alarm and the manicured estate grounds lit up like a ballpark or prison yard. I'd never taken flight through such lush bottomland underbrush before, crawling for long stretches, me breathing hard but Marley-Anne merely breath-*taken* by the kick of it all, and the two of us muddy and salty with perspiration there in the river mist. No fear or doubts or any remorse, no second thoughts on her part for what we'd gotten ourselves into. It's like we were out-waltzing Matilda on the riverbank, and screw you, there's this legal trespass law called riparian rights, and we're well within ours—the attitude that nothing can touch brazen enough, and without another word she was bolt upright and laughing in full retreat. And what I saw there in front of me in each graceful stride was the likelihood of our marriage coming apart right before my eyes.

"That's it," I said to her on the drive home. "No more. Getting fixed like this and unable to stop, we're no better than those addicts, no different at all, and I don't care if it *is* why Eve ate the goddamn apple, Marley-Anne"—an explanation she'd foisted on me one time, to which I'd simply replied, "Baloney to that. I don't care. We'll launch some bottle rockets out the rear window of the pickup if that's what it takes." I meant it, too, as if I could bring the Dead Sea of the sky alive with particles of fiery light that would also get us busted, but at worst on a charge of reckless endangerment, which in these parts we'd survive just fine and possibly be immortalized by in story at the local bars.

"We're going to end up twelve-stepping our way out of rehab," I said. "Plus fines and court costs. It's just a matter of time until somebody closes the distance." All she said back was, "Lowercase, Reilly Jack. Entirely lowercase."

She's tried everything over the years, from Valium to yoga, but gave up each thing for the relish of what it robbed from her. Not to her face, but in caps to my own way of thinking, I'd call our prowling CRAZY.

So far we'd been blessed with dumb luck the likes of which I wouldn't have believed and couldn't have imagined if I hadn't been kneeling next to Marley-Anne in the green aquatic light of a certain living room, our noses a literal inch away from a recessed wall tank of angelfish. Great big ones, or maybe it was just the way they were magnified, some of them yellow-striped around the gills, and the two of us mesmerized by the hum of the filter as if *we* were suspended underwater and none the wiser to the woman watching us—for how long I haven't the foggiest. But in my mind I sometimes hear that first note eerie and helium-high, though I could barely make out, beyond the banister, who was descending that curved staircase. Not until she'd come ghostlike all the way down and floated toward us, a pistol pointed into her mouth.

196

Jesus, I thought, shuddering, oh merciful Christ no, but when she squeezed the trigger and wheezed deeply it was only an inhaler, her other hand holding a bathrobe closed at the throat.

"Sylvia?" she said. "Is that you?" and Marley-Anne, without pause or panic, stood up slowly and assented to being whoever this white-haired woman wanted her to be. "Yes," she said. "Uh-huh, it's me," as if she'd just flown in from Bangor or Moscow or somewhere else so distant it might take a few days to get readjusted. "I didn't mean to wake you," Marley-Anne said, soft-sounding and genuinely apologetic. "I'm sorry." As cool and calm as cobalt while I'm squeezing handful by handful the humid air until my palms dripped rivulets onto the shiny, lacquered hardwood floor. The woman had to be ninety, no kidding, and had she wept in fear of us or even appeared startled I swear to God the lasting effects would have voided forever my enabling anymore the convolution of such madness.

"There's leftover eggplant parmesan in the fridge—you can heat that up," the woman said. "And beets. Oh, yes, there's beets there too," as if suddenly placing something that had gotten lost somewhere, not unlike Marley-Anne and me, whoever I was standing now beside her all part and parcel of the collective amnesia.

"And you are . . . who again?" the woman asked, and wheezed a second time, and when I shrugged as if I hadn't under these circumstances the slightest clue, she slowly nodded. "I understand," she said. "Really, I do," and she took another step closer and peered at me even harder, as if the proper angle of concentration might supply some vaguest recollection of this mute and disoriented young man attired in burglar black and suddenly present before her.

"Heaven-sent then?" she said, as if perhaps I was some angel, and then she pointed up at a skylight I hadn't noticed. No moon in sight, but the stars—I swear—aglitter like the flecks of mica I used to find and hold up to the sun when I was a kid, maybe six or seven. I remembered then how my mom sometimes cried my dad's name at night outside by the road for all her children's sakes, and for how certain people we love go missing, and how their eventual return is anything but certain. I remembered lying awake on the top bunk, waiting and waiting for that unmistakable sound of the spring hinge snapping and the screen door slapping shut. I never really knew whether to stay put or go to her. And I remembered this, too: how on the full moon, like clockwork, the midnight light through the window transformed that tiny bedroom into a diorama.

"Emphysema," the woman said. "And to think I never smoked. Not one day in my entire life."

"No, that's true," Marley-Anne said, "you never did. And look at you, all the more radiant because of it."

"But not getting any younger," the woman said, and wheezed again, her voice flutelike this time, her eyes suddenly adrift and staring at nothing. "And Lou, how can that be so soon? Gone ten years, isn't it ten years tomorrow? Oh, it seems like yesterday, just yesterday . . . ," but she couldn't quite recollect even that far, and Marley-Anne smiled and palm-cupped the woman's left elbow and escorted her back upstairs to bed. Recalling the run-down two-story of my boyhood, I noticed how not a single stair in this house moaned or creaked underfoot.

Standing all alone in the present tense with that school of blank-eyed fish staring out at me, I whispered, "Un-fucking-believable." That's all I could think. As absurd as it sounds, these were the interludes and images Marley-Anne coveted, and in the stolen beauty of certain moments I had to admit that I did, too.

That's what frightens me now more than anything, even more than somebody's giant, high-ticket pinto in our illegal possession. But first things first, and because Marley-Anne's one-quarter Cheyenne she's naturally gifted, or so she claimed when I asked her where she learned to bridle a horse and ride bareback like that. In profile silhouette, hugging her knees here next to me on the roof, she shows off the slight rise in her nose and those high-chiseled cheekbones. She's long-limbed and lean and goes one-fifteen fully clothed, and I've already calculated that the two of us together underweigh John Wayne, who somehow always managed to boot-find the stirrup and haul his wide, white, and baggy Hollywood cowboy ass into the saddle. Every single film I felt bad for the horse, the "He-yuh," and spurs to the ribs, and my intolerance was inflamed with each galloping frame.

Perhaps another quarter hour of silence has passed when Marley-Anne takes my hand. Already the faintest predawn trace of the darkness lifting leaves us no choice other than to mount up and vacate the premises before our neighbors the Bromwiches wake and catch us red-handed. They're friendly and easy enough to like but are also the type who'd sit heavy on the bell rope for something like this. I can almost make out the outline of their refurbished 1975 midnight blue Chevy Malibu parked in the driveway, a green glow-in-the-dark Saint Christopher poised on the dash and the whitewalls shining like haloes.

Not wanting to spew any epithet too terrible to retract, neither of us utters a word as we climb down in tandem, the horse whinnying for the very first time when my feet touch the ground. "Easy," I say, right out of some *High Noon*—type western. "Easy, Paint," but Marley-Anne's the one who nuzzles up and palm strokes its spotted throat and sweet-talks its nervousness away. I've ridden a merry-go-round, but that's about it, and I wouldn't mind a chrome pole or a pommel to hold on to. But Marley-Anne's in front on the reins, and with my arms snug around her waist I feel safe and strangely relaxed, Paint's back and flanks as soft as crushed velour. Except for our dangling legs and how high up we are, it's not unlike sitting on a love seat in some stranger's country estate. Marley-Anne heels us into a trot around the far side of the house and across the cracked concrete sidewalk slabs into the empty street. Paint's shod hooves don't spark, but they do reverberate even louder, the morning having cooled, and there's no traffic, this being Sunday and the whole town still asleep.

Marley-Anne's black jeans are not a fashion statement. They're slat-ted mid-thigh for ventilation, and I consider sliding my hands in there where her muscles are taut, and just the thought ignites my vapors on a grand scale, everything alive and buzzing—including the static crackle in the power lines we've just crossed under, and that must be Casey Banhammer's hound dream-jolted awake and suddenly howling at who knows what, maybe its own flea-bitten hind end, from two blocks over on Cathedral.

We're slow cantering in the opposite direction, toward the eastern horizon of those postcard-perfect houses and away from the land of the Pignatallis and Burchers and Bellavitas, whose double-wides we've never been inside without an invitation to stop by for a couple of Busch Lights and an evening of small talk and cards and pizza. Guys I work with, all plenty decent enough and not a whole lot of tiny print— meaning little or nothing to hide. Marley-Anne negotiates their back-yards this way and that. A zigzag through the two or three feet of semidarkness ahead of us, and the perfect placement of Paint's hoof-pounds thudding down. A weightless transport past gas grills and lawn furniture, and someone's tipped-over silver Schwinn hurtled with ease, the forward lift and thrust squeezing Marley-Anne and me even tighter together.

There are no sentry lights or fancy stone terraces or in-ground swim-ming pools, though the sheets on the Showalters' clothesline seem an iridescent white glow, and when Marley-Anne says, "Duck," I can feel the breezy cotton blow across my back, that sweet smell of starch and hollyhocks, the only flower my mom could ever grow. Shiny black and blue ones the color of Marley-Anne's windswept hair, and I can smell *it* too when I press my nose against the back of her head.

There's a common-ground lot, a small park with a diamond and back-stop, and we're cantering Pony Express across the outfield grass. The field has no bleachers, though sometimes when I walk here at night I imagine my dad sitting alone in the top row. I'm at the plate, a kid again, a late rally on and my head full of banter and cheers and the tight red seams of the baseball rotating slow-motion toward me, waist-high right into my wheelhouse. It could, it just might be, my life re-imagined with a single swing, the ball launched skyward, a streaking comet complete with a pure white rooster tail.

But if you've been deserted the way my dad deserted us, no such fantasies much matter after a while. And what could he say or brag about anyway? Truth told, I don't even remember his voice. It's my mom's crying I hear whenever I think of them together and apart. He might be dead for all I know, which isn't much except that he sure stayed gone both then and now. Marley-Anne and I have never mentioned separation or divorce, an outcome that would surely break me for good. And the notion of her up and leaving unannounced some night is simply way too much for someone of my constitution to even postulate.

We slow to something between a trot and a walk, and Paint isn't frothing or even breathing hard, his ears up and forward like he wants more, wants to go and go and go, and maybe leap some gorge or ravine or canyon or, like Pegasus, sprout wings and soar above this unremark-able northern town. On Cabot Street, under those huge-domed and barely visible sycamores, Marley-Anne has to rein him in, and now he's all chest and high-stepping like a circus horse, his nostrils flared for dragon fire. He's so gorgeous that for a fleeting second I want someone to see us, a small audience we'd dazzle blind with an updated Wild Bill story for them to tell their kids.

We look left toward the Phillips 66 and right toward the all-night laundromat where nobody's about. We keep to those darker stretches between the streetlights and, where Cass intersects with Columbus, there's the Dairy Queen with its neon sign a blurred crimson. The coast is clear, and we stop in the empty parking lot as if it were a relay station on the old overland route to Sioux Falls or San Francisco.

"So far so good," I say, and when Marley-Anne tips her head back I kiss her wine-smooth lips until she moans.

"Hey," she says, her mouth held open as if a tiny bird might fly out. "Hey," like a throaty chorus in a song. When I smile at her she half smiles back as if to say, We're managing in our way just fine, aren't we, Reilly Jack? You and me, we're going to be okay, aren't we? Isn't that how it all plays out in this latest, unrevised chapter of our lives?

I nod in case this *is* her question, and Paint pirouettes a perfect one-eighty so he's facing out toward East Main. Already one walleyed head-light wavers in the huge double plate-glass window of the Dairy Queen as that first car of the morning passes unaware of us. Otherwise the street is deserted, the yellow blinker by the Holiday Inn not quite done repeating itself. Above, up on 1-75, a north-south route to nowhere, is that intermittent whine and roar of transport trailers zipping past. But there's an underpass being constructed not far from here, no traffic on it at all, and beyond that the sandpit and some woods with a switchback two-track that will bring us out to County Road 667.

Saint Jerome's Cemetery is no more than another half-mile distant from there, and I can almost smell the wild honeysuckle by the care-taker's shack, its galvanized roof painted green, and a spigot and hose and pail to give the horse a drink. The deceased are enclosed by a black wrought-iron fence, and there's a gate where we'll hang the bridle and turn Paint loose to graze between the crosses and headstones, and per-haps some flower wreathes mounding a freshly covered grave. Another somebody dead out of turn, as my mom used to say, no matter their age or circumstance, whenever she read the obituaries. Out of turn, out of sorts, just out and out senseless the way this world imposes no limits on our ruin—she'd say that too. She'd say how it grieved her that noth-ing lasts. "Nothing, Reilly Jack, if you love it, will ever, ever last." Then she'd turn away from me and on her way out glance back to where I was sitting alone in the airless kitchen.

And what are the chances that I'd end up here instead of in another life sleeping off the aftereffects of a late Saturday night at the Iron Stallion, where all the usual suspects were present and accounted for, and the jukebox so stuffed full of quarters that its jaws were about to unhinge and reimburse every drunken, lonely last one of us still hum-ming along. But *here*, at 5:45 AM eastern standard, I kiss Marley-Anne again and our hearts clench and flutter, Marley-Anne shivering and her eyes wide open to meet my gaze. Paint is chomping at the bit to go, and so Marley-Anne gives him his lead, his left front hoof on the sewer cover echoing down East Main like a bell.

Already somebody is peppering his scrambled eggs, somebody sipping her coffee, and what's left of this night is trailing away like a former life. The house we lived in is still there exactly the way we left it, the front door unlocked and the pickup's keys in the ignition. *That* life, before those cloud-swirl white splotches on a certain pinto's neck first quivered under Marley-Anne's touch.

THE WIDOW JOY

fiction by ROSELLEN BROWN

It was hard to decide what was the worst thing about being a widow—missing Stan, worrying about money; there were lots of what her son callously called "downsides"—but Joy thought, sometimes, that the worst was that now she was "a widow." A thing, a category, something that began with an indefinite article. She had been an English teacher before the children were born and still tended to think in terms of parts of speech, which she knew was pedantic but couldn't help. It was one of those traits, she noted bitterly, that was far more pathetic in a widow than in a woman with a man around the house.

"Well, before you were, I don't know, a wife," her daughter Stacy said. "A married woman. That was a 'thing.'"

"Different. Wives can be all sorts of kinds of people. Widows are first and foremost pathetic. I'm not the first person to think so."

"God, Mom, you make it sound like it's your fault Daddy died. I don't know why that makes you pathetic. Do you think people *blame* you that he died?"

Joy waved her hand, which she seemed to be keeping notably well manicured these days, one of the many parts of her person that needed extracareful maintenance because she felt herself under scrutiny. That horrible ugly-syllabled term, just listen to it, like some kind of punishment you got in prison, secretly, in a hidden room under glaring lights: "I'm sorry, but you can't see her right now. She's *under scrutiny.*"

"Nobody blames me for his heart—though come to think of it there might be some food police types who'd like to get me for murder by cholesterol or, you know, not enough antioxidants. No, I mean—" But she stopped. Stacy was twenty-four. She was still dazzling, open to anything and anything had yet to happen. Why even bother trying to explain the hopelessness of it to someone mired in hope? Joy felt shelved, like a book nobody intended to read anymore.

This conversation had not taken place until well after Stan's sudden disappearance. Joy tended to think of it that way, not quite as a death, which was a heavy, frightening word that seemed to demand preparation, but as a mysterious, almost casual withdrawal of himself from her presence, as if he had just, on a whim, stepped out of sight.

He had been, in fact, already out of her sight. He had gone out to the deck above her garden to sit in the mild sun with his newspaper, and since she was used to seeing him slip into a doze—he was a urologist; he worked hard all week, fixing the plumbing, he liked to say—she waited a long time before she called him in for lunch and discovered that he was gone. Just like that, this large, complex, talkative, sweet, skillful man had somehow escaped, or been kidnapped, across the border into the other world while she was rolling out a double pie crust. They were having company that night, and she had found a sale on the perfect pie apples, sweet-sour, tough, easily peeled. She had gone outside to announce lunch and to show him proudly the endless ruddy peel she held between her fingers like a tapeworm, the best she'd ever made.

People said, months later, that she didn't show enough evidence that she'd lost her husband but that—*that*, she said, exactly *that*—was the problem: he only felt lost, mislaid, temporarily missing. Death that comes so casually, so surreptitiously, is hard to take seriously. She begged his forgiveness for not believing he no longer existed.

But the months went by, she turned fifty, and Stan didn't reappear. Aside from the loss of him, poor dear man, she finally feared the loss of herself. She wasn't Joy first anymore; she was a widow. She had been abducted, too.

They had had a comfortable life full of what she was occasionally embarrassed to call middle-class pleasures: the large house with its more-interesting-than-most paintings and dustables; the travel, sometimes to the appealing places where Stan's medical conferences were cannily set—Helsinki, Tokyo, Honolulu. (Nobody had ever adequately explained to her why the American Renal and Urology Association had to meet in distant countries, in the finest hotels, as if its members couldn't concentrate anywhere closer to home and the English language. But since she got to go along, she wasn't asking.) They entertained not lavishly but generously. Stan loved his work, he still got excited about diagnosis and surgery. Joy loved her combination of mothering (though that would soon give out) and community volunteering, which she could do when she felt like it, and not do when she didn't. Her friends purported to love her for her high spirits, her taste, her sense of absurdity that was not so profound as to make her too critical of them.

And this was absurd: it had begun to look as if she would be alone, manwise, for the rest of her life. Why? Why? She liked herself. She was a good companion. She wasn't enough to keep herself company, was all: she needed somebody to ask and answer and agree and disagree. It had nothing to do with not being sufficiently competent, nothing to do with patriarchy or subservience. It was much simpler: she would never get used to so much silence.

So she was heavy. Zaftig, if you liked flesh broad and round as a Renoir. Stan had called thin women stringy chickens and luxuriated in her. She was still funny, still described as "lively," whatever that meant—she could hear her friends repeating the word to their few unattached male friends: "Lively, friendly. Comfortable." Which translated as "heavy." *Comfortable* meant built like a couch, soft as a beanbag chair. The personal ads, if you dared to read them, all asked for "slender." They liked personality, they went for financially independent, but first and foremost these nervy searchers, who could be ugly as the bottom of your boot, and fat and sloppy or scrawny and underbuilt, what they were looking for, to a one, was slender.

The dirty secret was that there were no men out there, not men anybody would be caught wanting. Not exactly a surprise, but when you don't have to notice it, you don't. She felt as if she'd been willfully blind while a disease raged outside her window: the peculiarly bereft loneliness of the once-coupled spinster who dared to ask for good luck another time around.

Spinster? Who spins, who knits, who weaves? The widow.

Stacy said there were no worthwhile men at her age either, but

that was a lie, or at least a friendly exaggeration. And Fort Worth was not—whatever the opposite of Fort Worth was. New York? L.A.?

The first likable man she met, five years after Stan's unanticipated evaporation, was dying. He had started a conversation at the drug store prescription station where she was renewing (it was too funny to be true) her estrogen replacement pills. He had said to her, amiably, "We all end up here, don't we? Remember when you used to meet your friends at the soda fountain and keep your back to the old geezers at the pharmacist's window?"

Later she told him that was the most unpromising opening line she'd ever heard.

Charles, called Chas by those who were fond of him, was dying in a more drawn-out and less sensational way than Stan had, of leukemia, which gave him good periods and after a while subtracted them, leaving him stranded like a fish on the beach of his life, then kindly wet him down again as the tide turned. And then again. And still again.

He was a widower, so, even without discussing it, they shared certain feelings. They knew the faint brush of condescension from the fixer-uppers, who arranged dates with shockingly inappropriate "singles" with whom they had nothing in common but their loneliness. They felt their children's sighs, whether sighed or not, over the difficulty they presented; felt the children's guilt at seeing them unhappy and their helplessness to do anything about it, which at best makes for false cheer and at worst for anger. Impotence was what parents of grown children tended to feel; it was unnatural the other way around.

She and Chas would have surprised anyone who saw them together, though no one did: they had houses, they didn't need to skulk around looking for privacy. They did not exactly have what would have been called sex, but they had everything that usually came before and after it: hugging, kissing, tender speech, ecstatic sound, then a surprised and urgent clinging that was nearly—not quite but not unlike—the actual pleasure of consummation; and then the sweet falling away, the luxuriant side-by-side stretching out or curling up, front to back, her ample breasts pushed against his wasting spine and shoulders. His medications, uncountable—the day they met at Walgreen's she saw his bill and was staggered by it—made him incapable but not, as he put it, unwilling. Willingness, she laughed, was what sex was really about, wasn't it? Wanting each other, which became a kind of having. Remembering, imagining. "It's all right," she told him the first time. "The part of me that's empty isn't the part down *there*."

He had kissed the tops of her ears when she said that, tiny, fluttering, grateful kisses, and she felt the electric connection so deeply her chest flushed red and her heart beat noisily as though she'd gone everywhere with him and back.

The other thing that interested her in her miniromance with Chas was that so much that had mattered to her all her life, and deeply, seemed distant and very nearly irrelevant when she was with him. Old people got like this, she knew: her own mother, after eighty had stopped criticizing Joy's failings, her weight, her hair, her clothes. She had turned all her fading vision in on herself, which, given the encroaching darkness, took so much out of her there wasn't any left for her carping habit. Joy was glad and sorry to be exempt; unexamined, she was lonelier still. Now, was desperation doing to her what weariness had accomplished on her mother?

The things that seemed to be fading in importance: that she was Jewish, volubly, commitedly so, and he was some anonymous form of WASP, the kind that hardly knows which denomination it is, let alone cares. "Whatever church was nearby, that's where we went. Except Catholic, of course. You don't just *stop in* at a Catholic church!"

She liked concerts, museums, grand or subtle things on her walls but something original, something genuine, while Chas's idea of culture tended toward the rodeo ("Actually," he instructed, "it's rightly called the Fat Stock Show") and the kind of music you went to Las Vegas for—he and his wife had done this more than once—or to Branson, Missouri, to hear Wayne Newton and Johnny Cash and Amy Grant, that white gospel girl. Give or take an Amy or two, guys with suits that reflected light, and big big cuffs. This made her put off introducing him to her friends. It was craven, she knew, but there was too much explaining involved.

But in spite of his macho heroes Chas was a gentle man, and he thought Joy was a goddess. His wife, dead only a few years, had been, she surmised, a frail birdlike woman in stature and personality— "delicate" is how Chas delicately put it—and he feasted on Joy's body like a man who'd been pent up in a small place suddenly let free to leap and frolic. He did more than he should have to please her, and her delight was his delight. He gave her touching gifts, too: a small, bubbled-leather book of love poems beginning with Sappho, with a cloth bookmark sewn in, "like in the Bible," he said abashedly. A box of chocolates that said "Eat me" on the front. A glass unicorn. His own house, or rather the house his wife had furnished, heavy with beige drapery and shiny surfaces, tended toward coverings: an extra roll of toilet paper sat on the formica sink cabinet under a frothy plastic cap, like a lady about to step into the shower; the hall rug was protected by a plastic runner— you could not track mud in if you tried. Their bedroom was cluttered with toadstools, porcelain dogs, and other small objects. In another time and culture, Joy thought, these would have gone to decorate his wife's grave.

But the thing that moved her most, of course, was that he was dying and didn't try to turn away from it. He spoke with stunning matter-of-factness about "then" and "after." These lean, honest-eyed Protestant boys, she thought, not brought up to be histrionic, might lack a little pizzazz in certain respects, but there's useful, sharp-sided grit in their souls. He'd been a mining engineer; he'd worked with oil and stone and earth, the whole physical world like a body laid open to prodding and the removal of its parts. And now he talked about himself as though he were only another element to be thrown into the eternal mix—he wanted cremation and an unceremonious fling, by the practical hands of his three grown daughters, into his favorite trout stream.

"The girls" and their husbands had met her once in their father's house, over a tense meal of dry turkey and cranberry sauce still shaped like the can that left all her appetites unsatisfied. They looked at her suspiciously, as though she might be a gold digger or a floozie, searching, searching for their proper father's possible motives for involving himself with a broad-bosomed woman with tinted highlights in her hair, who opened her mouth wide to laugh and somehow did not seem— well . . . she knew a euphemism when she felt one coming up behind her—*Texas*.

But all that was neither here nor there: Chas was beyond the need for his family's approval, not because he might not be hurt by it but because only a week or so after that dinner, without warning, his dying began in earnest. Suddenly a transfusion could no longer pull him back from the brink. Almost overnight he went from man in possible danger to man in dire straits, uncomplaining, wearing an expression of mild surprise but not fear and certainly not the anger he deserved.

Joy found herself studying him as if he were another species, this second love who was about to slip out of her hands. She was there to see him go, standing beside two of the daughters, who ignored her as if she were invisible, which was fine since this wasn't about any of them. He blinked out gradually and silently, like a lightbulb dimming. And like a bulb, he flared once at the very end, another gift to her. Staring straight ahead where she was not, he cried out "Joy!" as if, astonished, he was calling out to show her something. As if Joy were an emotion, not a name. She had always thought her celebratory name silly, but she forgave her parents then and there for their hopefulness and pre-science.

She didn't allow herself to cry for Chas, though it took a terrible effort. But he would have been very uncomfortable with her tears, and if he could be disciplined, so could she in his honor. She wished he had a gravestone instead of an empty urn. If she'd had any say in the matter she'd have written COMPLETED and meant it for both of them. He had taught her a few things. But no, on second thought, she wasn't finished, not yet, though she had no idea what to do next. Why did all of them, finally, go off by themselves and leave her alone?

Years later, Joy spent a month in Umbria in a stone farmhouse she had rented with a girlfriend, Max—they were still and forever girls—whom she had met as a docent at the Metropolitan Museum. She had left Fort Worth behind, left her children with their blessings and yielded to a desire for a fast-moving city that she hadn't known she possessed. When her friends back home asked if New York weren't too full of distractions, she had to ask them, distractions from what? This, she said, is not the appetizer, it's the main course.

The morning she and Max met they were standing, smitten, in a newly assembled roomful of poignant portraits on something like wood that had adorned mummy cases a few millennia ago. The faces were so contemporary, so rich with feeling, both women confided that they suspected a daring fraud. Could these people truly have lived and died when the world was young—that curly-haired young man with the depressive, down-turned mouth of a dozen teenaged sons she had known; a shy-looking girl with ringlets, the shoulder of her pleated gown not entirely modest in its arrangement. Someone, friend, lover, or mischievous artist in possession of gossip, had helped her slip into eternity looking slightly naughty! Joy and Max shook their heads in unison, full of wonder and confusion.

Did all the mummies have tombs to accommodate these gorgeous likenesses, and their papier-mâché sarcophagi? She loved graveyards, which somehow she put in a category unrelated to the cheerless cemeteries—memorial parks, so called—like the kind into which Stan had disappeared beneath a cold pinkish granite slab with his Hebrew name inscribed above *Beloved Husband, Father, Physician.* Chas, in the possession of his daughters, had indeed become food for the fishes he had menaced with those fluttering flies he'd spent a thousand hours of his life creating.

Now, July in Castello Falignano, the two friends made it a habit to stroll like wanderers in a garden through the hill town's *cimitero*, where life—represented by fresh flowers renewed with awesome frequency—trumped death, no contest. Women in housedresses stood wet-eyed, still, before the tombs of parents who had died forty years ago; they wielded brooms and kept blood-red glass-enclosed candles lit. Time was layered in Castello: the Etruscans, the Greeks, the Romans, and only lately the Christians, had surged up its hills and down again, sometimes in pursuit, sometimes in flight. Manhattan, Joy thought, was just a moment's cinder in the eye of eternity. Blink once and it will be covered by some civilization not yet invented.

She and Max, replete with their morning cappuccini and cornetti, made up stories for the stones, using a dictionary when the going got rough—though *caro italiano* was generally so forgiving of their illiteracy it seemed enough to read English, once you got through the intricacies of conjugal code: *ved* = "widow of" and *in* = "married into the family." The women were most often represented first by their maiden names, then by those veds and ins; she liked that. (The Spanish excelled at respect for matriarchal naming too, though from her experience, neither culture was particularly thoughtful, thereafter, of its women's comfort.)

Little oval portraits in porcelain clung to most of the stones, and these were the provocations that set them off on melodramatic scenarios: oh, the baby dead in 1882 in what appeared to be the rage of a "sudden torrent" that tore her from the bosom of her grief-shattered parents! Joy's eyes willed with tears. Except for the creeping lichen at the edges of her photograph, the baby, like those mummy faces, looked unsettlingly contemporary. A few young men posed in full color beside the motorcycles and cars in which they had likely perished.

But what stopped her, time and again, were the pictures of husbands in their youth—wavy hair, dark suits and bow ties, innocence still rounding their cheeks and brightening their eyes—and beside them (ved!) the ancient crones who outlived them by generations. *Coniugi, Mario Gandolfi 1894–1921*, on the left and, as if in their marriage bed, on the right *Maria Zanardi in Gandolfi 1899–1976*. Joy was off and running: he had the looks of a poet and the soul of an arrogant idler, the soft-voiced serpent kind. He must have liked being a dandy; there were no dandies his age around here, so he got a lot of attention. And that beautiful girl, Zanardi's youngest, fell for him so fast she seemed possessed. A glorious couple, blessed, Mario in a state of grateful reform until consumption invaded his chest and took him in a flash, just after the birth of their second son. Why not? Such stories were a better sport than knowing the truth, which was passive. Flat.

Handsome Mario's was a studio portrait. Maria, staring straight ahead, was the *nonna* in a family snapshot by the time everyone owned a brownie, her eyes like the olives in Greek salads, the tiny ones. Wizened, warped, she had the face of one of those stray apples that gets lost in the back of the fridge and rolls out wrinkled, winy as yeast, hollow inside.

Max had been out of sight for a while, inspecting a mausoleum adorned with what looked, at a distance, like statuary worthy of the Uffizi. She came toward Joy with her arms out as if to say, "Can you believe this?!" She was a broad-shouldered, large-boned woman whose flowing denim skirt and jangling bracelets made her the least Italian-looking person on any Umbrian street, yet she seemed perpetually surprised that no one took her for a native. She made Joy feel delightfully small. "And there are mosaics down at the end of the row that you won't believe! Lots of gold leaf. You hock Mary's halo, you could probably buy yourself a Lexus." She turned her head from left to right, to take in the terraces of tombs, and at the top a pure-lined little Roman church. "I wonder if all this is devotion to, you know, the dead, or maybe just competition with the neighbors."

Joy shrugged. "You'd have to know a lot of local sociology to have a clue." Tranced before the grave of Zanardi in Gandolfi, she was reluctant to move on. "Look at this one, Max."

Max bent to read the dates on the stone. "Wow." She frowned. "Why do I find that sort of grotesque? I'm picturing them showing up together at a party, the beautiful boy with his ancient wife on his arm." She shivered. "It isn't really funny, actually."

"No, it isn't," Joy agreed, bemused and a little shaken. Long widowhood seemed, right here, like a cruel jest, an odd-smelling black flower.

But Max was not the one to sympathize. She had been married for a few years right after college but claimed to remember nothing of her marriage except sullen, silent mealtimes and the humiliation of ducking a plate her husband threw at her one evening at a dinner party. Her sentiment for permanent liaisons seemed to have disappeared around the time the dish hit the wall behind her head. "At least it was before dinner, so the plate was still clean. It would have been ghastly if our friends' carpet got a mess of coq au vin to show for inviting us. In addition, of course, to a really fun evening."

Joy hadn't intruded on Max's cynicism to defend marriage; there

211

seemed no point in generalizing from her own case, though her friend so cheerfully—mock cheerfully—did so. But the Zanardi-Gandolfis deserved defending. "Do you think she remembered him—you know—after all that time?"

"She's staring straight at *something*, isn't she? She looks like she hasn't smiled for fifty years."

Joy considered the group portraits of her own family in the old country—everyone had one. "People never used to smile for their pictures. If you're old enough it probably never occurred to you to make yourself look ingratiating."

Maria's was a snapshot, though, taken, perhaps, by one of her children. Her sons would have been older than their boy-father forever! Probably she confused them, all those men, by the time she died. Though she hardly looked confused; she looked formidable.

"Well." Max laughed and started up the path. Her shoes on the pebbles sounded like someone chewing. She looked back over her shoulder. "Did you notice, most of these old gals don't seem to have gotten married again or they'd be buried with the new family, right? We all figured once was enough!"

Her bitterness was delivered, as usual, with a laugh. Joy forced herself to follow, but her mind was back in the cemetery in Fort Worth. On that pinky-gray stone, Stan's face in a black-and-white oval on the left, as he always stood and as he lay in their king-sized bed, looking sound and avid and engaged, not prepared for the ambush that overtook him. And she—a few more decades and her face would be in collapse, as everyone's was, given the luck to outlive tight skin and bright eyes—and there she would be, looking like his grandmother. And? And? What could she summon up besides affronted vanity?

She thought about it as she walked, passing some magnificence and some absurdity—this certainly was a playground for the living, who flexed their power over the dead bodies of their departed. Again, she pictured herself and Stan, what they would look like, their middle-aged and old-aged faces separated by a few inches of cold stone. The space between them would vibrate with all the things she wished she could tell him—all she had learned since his vanishing! All she had seen! The paradox was that they were the result of his not being with her, but he would appreciate them if only she could convey them. She hadn't, like Max, lost faith in—well, there was no permanence, was there? But there was long-term affection. She supposed she had Stan to thank for that. And Chas, with his innocent enthusiasm. She could have been

212

broken along the way, but, however chipped, she was still whole. She pictured the sun striking their stone and heating it up. She was, peculiar as it seemed, envious of no one but herself.

Max was hidden, again, behind a tomb, but Joy followed the sound of her bracelets and found her shaking her head at an A-frame with an altar inside its glass doors. On a marble ledge gold-framed photographs stood at stylish angles, shadowed by fresh orange gladioli. A broom and a watering can leaned, tucked not quite out of sight, in the corner.

Invigorated by this challenge of death by the routines of daily life, they began their ritual negotiation over which trattoria deserved their business for lunch, and then—she did look forward to it as much as she looked forward to eating—*il riposo*, the shutters closed, Joys imagination quelled, unloading the wonders of the morning, readying for what would come next.

THE POISON THAT PURIFIES YOU

fiction by ELIZABETH KADETSKY

> *I dreamed that the beloved entered my body*
> *pulled out a dagger*
> *and went looking for my heart*
> —*Rumi*

Jack is walking through Connought place. The area is laid out in several concentric circles with a park in the middle. He has noticed that the closer to the park you get, the more you are hassled. Near the perimeter a man selling colorful stuffed puppets from Rajasthan attaches himself to Jack. "Pretty doll you buy sir for pretty daughter?"

"Men beti nahin," Jack responds bluntly, keeping his hands in his pockets. This is decent enough Hindi for "I have no daughter." A few words of Hindi are usually enough to discourage a hustler, but this one persists, in his bad English.

"For cousin sir. Little girl like little doll sir." The man tails Jack for several yards, until the duo is intercepted by a young couple from, probably, France. The woman has a maternal way about her that the vendor seems to sense as well. "Madam pretty doll for pretty daughter." She pauses long enough to gaze at the puppet. *Her first misstep,* Jack chuckles to himself as he separates from the vendor. It will take her hours to shake him.

Closer to the center Jack pauses to sip from his water bottle. He's thirsty enough, but he also thinks of the water as an antidote to the air around him, which is black with ash and exhaust. He lowers it from his mouth and keeps walking, holding the cap in one hand, the bottle in the other. In a few paces he will stop to take another sip, only he doesn't get there. A slight man with a close beard and prominent cheekbones, wearing black trousers and loafers, cuts him off. "Excuse me sir," he says. This man's diction is closer to standard English. Still accented, it suggests a better comprehension of words than the doll hawker's. "You know there are ten million microbes per cubic centimeter of air in Delhi," the man begins.

Jack looks at him dumbly.

The man is gesturing to Jack's water bottle.

"Really it is a health hazard, this."

Jack wants to know what *this* is, but he's wary of giving the man the impression he actually wants to have a conversation. Up to now the interaction has been solely a matter of one man assailing another. Until he gives a sign of consent, he is not actively taking part. Jack has not been a willing interlocutor with anyone in Connought Place, ever. He has only been hustled. He's glad that he's never given in, but as of this morning, he's also decided maybe he should give in sometimes, too.

He made the decision at the Ankur Guest House, where he is staying for five dollars a night near Delhi Station. There are no sheets or towels. He sleeps on a mattress in a room with no natural light, right on the mattress cover. This has given him pause. After five months in India, Jack now believes that comfort is a misnomer. Sleeping on a mattress cover is not uncomfortable. It only requires you to imagine your relationship to the people around you differently. It requires you to allow them closer to you, in every way. Raw and unwashed, the uncovered mattress connects you to the person who was here before you. And by association, it allows you closer to all of Delhi.

Sleeping at the Ankur last night, Jack imagined that his body and the mattress were like two continents buffing against each other. Exposing the continent of his body to the continent of the mattress caused them to join slightly, the contours of one shore interlocking with the contours of the other. He wanted the sand of the far shore to make its way into his own skin, to make it darker and tougher, better prepared for danger.

Jack woke up with the realization that only in this skin with its bigger pores could he engage in an honest relationship with India, He wants to become a part of this continent, to experience a true interchange before he gets on a plane back home—whenever that is. This has become the single precondition for his return, in fact; forging an enduring alliance with this place, and its people, will inure him to the sterile California roadways that await him—their clean yellow lines, their

215

sidewalks freshly scrubbed, the bushes at their shoulders so green, so free of grime and soot they seem to have been painted onto the landscape. He will stay in India longer, as long as it takes to erase this painted landscape from his memory. He will let India deep inside him. The squalor of India will become a part of him, so much so that it will have lost the power to make him feel dirty.

The hustler's open face peering at him, his hand gesturing neatly toward his water bottle, reminds Jack that this very man could be one of the Delhi-ites who has slept on his mattress. The impression of this man's very body could be sunk inside of it. If Jack is willing to sleep on canvas cast in the shape of this man's body, or a body *like* his body, he might at least talk to him.

Jack clears his throat. "What's *this*?" He is aware that his tone might seem mildly threatening.

"You should never leave the top off of the water container, you see." The man pauses, as if Jack should follow his logic effortlessly, which he doesn't. "Delhi is the second most polluted city in the world, see, according to the *India Today*. So you see."

"Actually I don't."

"The microbes. They will fall from the air into your container. And when you sip, you will drink the microbes. Foreign bellies are not constructed to drink microbes. A missing enzyme or something like this. Really you must put on the top. Now. Really sir. Now exactly. It is actually quite imperative." The man is making fluttering gestures with his fingers, so they impersonate butterfly-like creatures dropping from the sky. He looks at the bottle with an alarmed expression. It seems to Jack that even if the man is a hustler, his anxiety about the continuing exposure of his water to the air is genuine.

Jack gazes at the mouth of the bottle and lifts it to his lips. "But I'm drinking."

"Please sir, you must only drink inside. If you don't mind. Could I invite you?"

The heat outside is enormous. Peering back at his bottle, Jack realizes he's drunk a third of it in just the time it took to walk here from the Ankur. This means that right now there's about a half-liter of water moving by gesture of peristalsis into his bladder, and he has to pee. A café, with a toilet, is certainly in order.

With the same neat movement of his hand, the man points to a café on the rim of the park. "I buy you coffee. Western man likes Indian coffee nah? Very sweet. Too sweet."

Jack nods, following.

The café is one of those brightly lit chrome and Formica spaces that in the States would look glaring and uninviting. Here, the layers of grit subdue the harsh tones. The toilet is suitably foul. In India Jack has gotten in the habit of washing his hands before rather than after he pees, for salutary reasons. As expected there's no soap. He pulls a miniature bar from his fanny pack and unwraps it; he bought it for five rupees this morning with the water, at the *paniwalla's*. There is no urinal or squat toilet, only a Western toilet, de rigueur at Connought Place, gathering place for foreigners. The toilet seat is speckled with the requisite drops of urine. Jack considers whether he should risk touching the urine to lift the seat with his hand and thus pee straight into the bowl; leave the seat up and probably wind up adding his own pee to the drops; or clean the toilet seat so as to avoid touching the urine when lifting it. He chooses the latter, allowing that it works against his new resolution about the mattress. He pulls a tissue from his fanny pack as he meditates on the many shades of meaning between *sanitary* and *salutary*.

The man's name is Rohit. He tells Jack about his upbringing shuttling between London and Delhi, and what brought him back to this nation of "wretchedness and dross," as he puts it. Jack considers whether Rohit's diction is that of someone who's lived half his life in London; until now he assumed Rohit was overstating the Western side of his story.

He also realizes that Rohit is a very beautiful man. He has slender wrists with a light covering of long and shiny black hairs. The skin on his face is a deep olive and so smooth that it, like the hairs on his arms, seems to shine. This glow makes it hard to guess Rohit's age. He looks like he's in his twenties, but Indian skin lies. His sharp cheekbones, outlined by the few strands of cheek hair growing down to meet his short beard, create dark shadows on his face, suggesting greater seriousness and age. He guesses Rohit is approximately ten to fifteen years younger than he himself. There is a delicate quality to everything about Rohit, not just his skin and the hairs on his cheeks and forearms, but his body, which looks neurasthenic inside, his loose-fitting trousers. Jack imagines that Rohit is someone who was well cared for by his mother at one time, which is what Rohit is telling him now, in so many words.

"My mother's parents loved me very much, but mostly just from the photographs. I met them one time here in India when I was eight and went to visit the ancestral village. This was a dusty old place with quite

217

an illustrious past. My family were Brahmins, see, and they once owned the entire village. The government took the village from them in the 1970s to give it to the poor—they fancied themselves the Robin Hoods of India, of course. This was bad. Very bad. All over India this transpired. The villages became very poor as a result, because the Brahmins had been managing the land. Now the Brahmins had no jobs—they went to work as clerks in the government, working for the very factotums who'd taken their land away."

Factotums? Jack is impressed with Rohit's diction. "Factotum?"

"Yes. You know. Apparatchik."

"Apparatchik?"

"So sorry. You see here in India we have so great a bureaucracy we have several words to describe it. The Eskimos in your country have ten words for snow. We've borrowed a word from every language for *bureaucrat.*"

"Yes. So the factotums? Or would that be *factoti?*"

Rohit's eyes smile at Jack, and Jack lets his make the same.

"The Brahmins were unhappy everywhere working in these offices, but in my mother's ancestral village, the poor people were unhappy too, and they asked my mother's family to come back to take the land. It was really a very benevolent situation. You have to forget, please, this paradigm that India is divided between possessed and dispossessed, ruler and ruled, oppressor and oppressed. Disregard this entirely, if you please."

Jack continues to be impressed with Rohit's speech, even if he pronounced the *g* in *paradigm* hard, so the word sounded like "paradigem." This is actually the first Jack has heard about the politics of land distribution in India. It's all a little fuzzy to him. He read Marx in college, but poetry was his major. He was thinking more about Rohit's particular way of telling the story than class conflict. He just wants the details to fall in place. "So your family took the village back?"

"Spot on. Then it is sad but everyone in my family has died. Mother father grandmother grandfather. My grandfather just now."

"I'm sorry."

"Yes thanks. So they have left the village to me. I own the village."

"What's it called?" Jack isn't sure he believes Rohit. If Rohit stumbles in coming up with the name, he's probably lying.

Rohit has an easy answer. "Saharanpur."

"Never heard of it."

"No, you wouldn't have. You'd like to come maybe? For luncheon.

There is a very kind family there that treats me like their son. I show you a typical Indian family. Not Brahmins. Kshatriya caste actually."

Kshatriyas are the traditional warrior caste. They are the caste that has always intrigued Jack most in India. He doesn't know much about them, but in his imagination they ride bareback on elephants or tigers as they vanquish invaders—Aryans, Muslims. He's read about a seventeenth-century Kshatriya warrior in his *Lonely Planet* travel guide, Shivaji, who fought off the brutal Mughal conquerer Aurangzeb. "Kshatriya is fine," Jack says. He is aware that his tone might have sounded more condescending, more colonialist, than he would have liked. He meant to be ironic, so to show this in retrospect, he adopts his smile face. He's relieved when Rohit returns it. "Like Shivaji," Jack adds to soften the irony.

Rohit pauses before responding, the way someone does when they don't understand but haven't decided yet whether to admit it. At first this confuses Jack, because there's no way an Indian Hindu could not know about Shivaji. From what Jack gathered from the *Lonely Planet*, Shivaji is as revered among Hindus as Gandhi, maybe even more. Gandhi cooperated with Muslims, after all, while Shivaji fought them. And Jack has never, not once, seen a store selling, say, sheets named after Gandhi. But there are plenty of Shivaji Sheets, Shivaji Sinks, Shivaji Sweets. Given these facts, Jack decides he's misread Rohit's reaction. He peers into the Indian's face and feels a small physical thrill at the idea that between Rohit and himself lies a whole potential universe of missed cues, crossed signals, misinterpreted cultural nuances. Rohit is a mystery indeed.

"Like Shivaji," Rohit says, smiling.

In the dream, Rohit is so delicate, Jack is afraid he'll crush him. He embraces him with all his might nonetheless. He wants to consume Rohit. He is smooth and warm, like sweet Indian tea. Jack kisses him hard on the lips, but the lips respond by staying soft and slippery. They taste of almonds and have the same oily quality. He kisses Rohit's torso, first his nipples, which have only a thin down growing at their circumference and in a thin shiny line at the midline of his chest. His abdomen is flat. His member is large, like the god Shiva's. Jack has seen statues at Mahabalipuram depicting Shiva sitting cross-legged with a lingam the size of a small building growing out of his lap. Jack arranges Rohit in this seated position and puts his mouth on his great lingam. It is warm and smooth, and he worries that he will give it abrasions when he rubs his cheek, coarse with stubble, against it.

When Jack wakes up he's sweating profusely, and he's hard. He rocks from side to side on the mattress, pulling at himself until he comes. He tries to keep his come on his abdomen, but a glob drops onto the mattress. Because of the sweat, it proves hard to clean with a towel; he rubs the stain hard with water, but this only creates a solution of come and sweat, its precise chemical composition suiting it perfectly to the act of seeping deep into the stuffing of the mattress.

Rohit is waiting as arranged outside the café on Connought Circle, wearing the nondescript Delhi garb of trousers, a button-down polyester shirt, and sandals. Jack is wearing shorts, Birkenstocks, and a long Indian *kurta* top cinched at the waist by his fanny pack. Rohit embraces Jack's forearms warmly with both hands. The physical closeness embarrasses Jack. His penis stiffens slightly as he returns the gesture. "Come come. My friend has got the vehicle," Rohit is saying as he leads Jack through the late-morning chaos of Connought Place. "This drive it is ninety kilometers, something like this. We shall arrive promptly in time for luncheon. Promise promise."

Jack has never walked this quickly in this kind of heat. It occurs to him that the brisk movement might have a homeopathic effect against the heat, like drinking hot tea to stay cool the way they do in south India. Walking at this speed, on the heels of an Indian, also has a repellent effect on the usual retinue of Indian hustlers. Jack and his companion move swiftly through the obstacle course.

Another young man, whom Rohit introduces as Vikram, is waiting in a Land Rover. Vikram and Rohit talk in fast Hindi as they gesture for him to step into the backseat. The Indians take the two front seats. It all seems to go by too fast for Jack to consider. Inside, he can only pick up a word of Hindi here or there—numbers, the words for *right* and *left, road, distance, kilometers, the American*. Vikram doesn't address Jack directly, probably, figures Jack, because he doesn't speak English. The Land Rover pulls out into the street at a point where traffic funnels straight into a daisy wheel. He finds the way the vehicles move through the circular space mesmerizing; they intercept each other so that if each were trailing a piece of string, the threads would interlock to create a complicated braid of rope.

The car winds through miles of city, one scrappy block after another.

Socialist realist apartment structures with tilted, laundry-clad balconies give way to store-lined blocks that then shift back to apartments. Signs in Devanagari and Roman script dominate a street front broken only intermittently with signs in Urdu, in the Persian script. Jack tries to parse snatches of Hindi writing, but the car moves too quickly for him to read anything but small chunks, syllables or two-syllable combinations that he sounds out in his head. The act reminds him of learning to read as a six-year-old; he has an image of his first grade teacher pronouncing vowel-consonant combinations written on a blackboard. "*Ab, ah, la,*" he mouths in a low voice.

The Roman script is mostly Hindi and Sanskrit words. Gurukula Apartments; Chapatis Vishnu; Laxshmi Banking; Shivaji Housewares. It amuses Jack to imagine that the Urdu signs, so exotic and lovely in their arabesque shapes, advertise items equally charming and camp: Sheikh Iqbal's Internet, perhaps, or Masjid Mosquito Netting.

They pass a sign reading Santosh Kuti. *House of happiness*, Jack translates to himself. He realizes he doesn't even have a picture in his head of this house in the village that he is visiting, and as he scans his memory for an image of a hut—a *kuti*—in an Indian village, he sees himself lying on a mattress on the floor of a dirt lean-to, a paisleyed Indian tapestry covering the entryway. The tapestry parts, and Rohit walks in—wearing only a *lungi* bound around the waist. The *lungi* hangs low, giving Jack a generous view of the line of hair stretching from Rohit's navel to his groin. He wonders if he will sleep with Rohit, if Rohit knows how to read the hidden give-and-takes of Jack's lovers' calls. If Jack were to look deeply into Rohit's eyes, would his meaning be any clearer to Rohit than Rohit's was to Jack when he stumbled over the name Shivaji?

During the five months he's spent in India, Jack has had several encounters with Indian men, but none that was ever consummated. Once, a dark-skinned south Indian Christian named Michael chatted with Jack in a pizza parlor until late. Jack invited him to sleep over. They walked to Jack's hotel together like schoolboys, holding hands, joking, teasing, jabbing each other in the ribs. This continued when they got to Jack's room, until, innocently enough, Michael announced he was tired and proceeded to make a bed for himself on Jack's balcony. Jack was dumbfounded.

Another time, Jack developed a great friendship with an Indian banker. They shared details about their parents, their pasts, their dreams, catching lunch or dinner together every day without fail for two weeks. One night the banker asked Jack to meet him at a disco. The disco was the closest thing to a gay bar Jack had seen in India. In dim light, men danced together, holding hands, whispering into each other's ears while standing close. There were women too, but they mostly sat alone or in dour groups. The man arrived late, showing up with a woman he introduced as his wife. She was large and unhappy looking, rounding out her capacious Punjabi *kameez* and bloomer pants. Like the other women, she kept to the sidelines. Despite the presence of his wife, the man was unrestrained on the dance floor with Jack. They touched hands, hips, whispered. They were touching shoulders, front to front, when the man's wife broke it up. Broke in, like in any proper waltz. Then Jack saw the man and his wife arguing bitterly, and Jack left without ever again seeking contact. That night he paid for an expensive hotel with fine linens, seeking desperately to close the cavern inside of him, to build a bridge connecting home to here, the past to now.

When Jack looks up again, he realizes they've made it out of the city. The landscape is now rough and desertlike, arid except for occasional outposts of shanties with animals and children running in front. On a particularly barren stretch of road, Vikrain slows the vehicle. Jack makes out two men standing by the side of the road. Rohit stretches across the back of his seat to break the silence with Jack. "Just some guys," he says. "Just some guys we're giving a lift." Rohit's voice is languid, his body limber as it curls over the seat back.

Jack watches the guys approach, walking to either side of the rear. It seems strange. One gets in either back door, so they are sitting on either side of Jack. Rohit begins speaking with them in Hindi, but even though Jack can understand only a word here or there in the conversation, he has the sense that the conversation is wrong. It's as if they already know each other. Jack feels prickles on the back of his neck and remembers the way the dark boys in his high school used to slap the white boys on the backs of their necks to give them red necks. The man on his right interjects the word *"Amriki."* It seems like Rohit and this man are arguing. From behind, Jack can see the back of even Rohit's neck flushing.

"What the fuck's going on?" Jack's voice says. It seems to be speaking on its own. He notices that it sounds more American than it did before,

when he made an effort to pronounce each syllable so Rohit could follow, "Who the fuck are these people? Rohit, tell me the fuck what's
going on."

Rohit arches back over the seat and then slides down so he's peering
between the two front seats straight above Jack's lap, which is now positioned in the center of the backseat. Rohit gently takes Jack's forearms
with the same gesture he used to greet him at the park this morning.
"I'm sorry friend." Rohit is looking deep into Jack's eyes. At the precise
moment that Jack feels cold against the skin of his neck, he senses Rohit's eyes latching onto something inside his own. It's this, only this, that
keeps Jack from swinging at the gun like a spastic. He feels strangely
calm.

"I'm sorry friend. American friend," Rohit says. "Keep your hair on
please. You are kidnapped, for the cause of Kashmiri freedom."

The man on Jack's left takes out a large swath of brown embroidered
cloth and slides it over Jack's head. It is the kind of thing Muslim women
wear to cover their heads and bodies, only this one covers Jack's eyes
as well.

He hears Rohit's voice again from the other side of the cloth. "I'm
sorry friend."

Sitting in the safe house, surrounded by the four Indian men and a
small artillery of heavy weapons, Jack tries to make lists of things to
keep himself calm. There were at least three false notes in Rohit's self-
presentation. First, if he is a Kashmiri militant, he is not a Hindu at
all. He is a Muslim, and this explains his ignorance about Shivaji. Second, if he's Muslim, he hasn't been speaking Hindi at all, but Urdu, its
Muslim stepbrother. And third, his name, Rohit, which is a Hindu
name, is not his name at all. The guys are calling him Johnny now, but
it's probably really something like Omar or Mustafa.

The hood is off now, and Jack is sitting on a cheap, uncovered floor
mattress, chained by his wrists to a pole. The four men from the Land
Rover have fed him dal and vegetables. It was certainly not the luncheon feast Jack was expecting but no more simple than the five-rupee
thalis he's been subsisting on through his travels.

Jack watches his captors as if from the other side of a camera lens.
Two new men have arrived; the men from the car are less languid in
their presence. With their wiry bodies they seem jacked up, like schoolboys whose hours of play have been interrupted by a stern mother. The

new men are of a completely unrelated type from the kidnappers. Rohit and his posse are frail in loose-fitting trousers, with watery eyes and new beard hairs on their cheeks. The two new men are portly, with thick, full beards and loafers rather than sandals. Rohit seems to be the go-between, but Jack can't make out Rohit's speech—he swallows his words and says little, looking away when he addresses the new men. The words of the new men, too, blend into each other, like so much street Hindi at Connought Place. There seem to be many accents and languages, with many words that cross over like bridges between the languages. *Amriki, American. Sheikh. Thug. Badmash.* The familiar yet distant quality of the words makes Jack feel like a child learning to attach loose meanings to approximate sounds. His comprehension, likewise, feels no more sophisticated than a child's.

A sudden movement jolts Jack out of his stupor. One of the portly men has backhanded Rohit. Rohit, who has only about 66 percent body mass to the big man's, stumbles backwards. He looks back at the man, blinking, and then says something odd and confusing to Jack. "Bugger! What kind of a berk are you? Have you gone barking mad?"

Barking mad?

It strikes Jack like the answer to an obvious math problem that what made Rohit so hard to understand was the incongruity of the fact that he has been addressing the men in English all along—and not just impeccable English but a slang obscure to even Jack. "It's not quite cricket then, is it?" Rohit is saying now. "We've nabbed your Nancy boy and it wasn't for jam at all you know," Rohit goes on. He's speaking queen's English. Or is it cockney? "This is all hideous."

Hideous?

Rohit has preserved none of his earlier awkward Indianisms, the dropped articles, the dangling modifiers. Jack thinks of the old Harvard joke. He used to toss it around with his ex, a Harvard grad: *You know where the library's at, asshole?*

Jack realizes his knowledge of language now—Hindi, English, anything—is too rudimentary to parse any single one of these men's identities. He wishes he knew more about London, that he could place "Johnny's" accent in a particular neighborhood or social class, but unfortunately his knowledge of the colonial seat is far less extensive than his understanding of India, England's "jewel in the crown."

Rohit/Johnny is a jewel. This Jack still believes. There is a gemlike quality about him. He's shiny—that impression hasn't faded. Is to be a gem to be a subject? Jack can only take the train of thought so far. Then his mind starts to mist up, and he feels confused and emotional and angry.

He falls into a deep sleep. He dreams that he is back at the Ankur, Rohit lying under a thin sheet on the far side of his mattress. While Jack sleeps, Rohit masturbates. In the morning there is a large brown stain on Rohit's part of the sheet. His come is brown, like a dark ruby.

Jack shakes awake. As in the dream Rohit is next to him on a mattress—now the mattress at the safe house. Everyone else is gone. Rohit is stretched out so only his head and shoulders rest against the wall and his spine is in the shape of the top of a ski. Rohit was half asleep himself. He looks at Jack quizzically but not with the incomprehension of the day of their first meeting—the incomprehension of a man less in control of the common language than his interlocutor—but of a man lumbering back to consciousness through gelatinous layers of sleep.

"It's hideous," Rohit says, slicking back his hair.

"Hideous?"

"What we've done to you. It's all gone squiffy. I'm sorry, brother. Truly sorry. These activities have got to seem absolutely extremist to you."

Squiffy?

"You'll be thinking *I've kissed the Blarney stone*, but we had no intention of harming you. We needed one American, a Sherman Tanks the likes of you, to bring the atrocities in Kashmir to the limelight."

Sherman Tanks?

"The sum of my activities in the past was fund-raising," he goes on. "But we must open eyes. Bosnia. Chechnya. The treatment of Muslims everywhere is atrocious. We have resorted to drastic measures. Sorry for the pig's breakfast." Rohit chews on a fingernail, pushes back another stray lock of hair. "I have sacrificed my career. This will not go to waste if the government will address Kashmir." Rohit fixes Jack with a stare. Jack believes this is an honest stare, that this is the real Rohit—or Abdullah or whatever his name is. He feels that somewhere within the treacherous Rohit there is a kernel of integrity, and he himself has found the pathway to get there.

"Your career?" It had never occurred to Jack what Rohit might do for a living. He supposes he imagined him as a truck driver or a hustler. Or better, probably unemployed.

"I went to a private school, a very beautiful place, in East London. Forest School. You know it?"

Jack looks at him dumbly. He's not used to hearing British English, and it's taking him longer than it should to assimilate his captor's phrases. It's no easier than Hindi. The signposts in Rohit's monologue have likewise left Jack feeling lost and unmoored. He's never heard of the school, could find neither Bosnia nor Chechnya on a map, and knows nothing about Kashmir except that it is, indeed, Muslim, and that because of a contested border, it is at the center of a power struggle between India and Pakistan. This he read in *Lonely Planet*. He has also heard it spoken of in the context of a breakaway struggle for independence. There his knowledge ends.

"I remember one hydrangea bush."

Hydrangea?

"So lovely. We are quite educated, my family. My sister is at Oxford. I myself am enrolled at the London School of Economics. Statistics. And what college is it you attended?"

"UCLA. Poetry."

The longest relationship Jack has ever maintained was with his Harvard ex. Talking with Rohit, Jack remembers several instances where his boyfriend's Ivy snobbery offended him. He often had the same feeling he has now, that there was a code he'd never been given that was essential to understanding the dialogue. Inside references acted as rungs by which to hang onto a conversation. There were cocktail parties where a profusion of disconnected details fused with a self-conscious Boston argot to the point where Jack felt his brain turn to so much twisted rope. He could no longer make out words or meaning at all. He feels that way now.

"You've heard of Convoy of Mercy?"

Jack stays quiet.

"Sending supplies to Bosnia. Bosnia. Now that, friend, is where Muslims must unite. We must fight for our brothers."

Rohit's expression suddenly turns feral. No one has hit him this time, but the abrupt shift in his eyes is as dramatic. "In London we will rise. Rise. Men like you," he adds, now fixing Jack with a look not unlike that of a trapped possum, "you're no better than brown bread. Dead. You're in a Barney, friend."

Jack's relationship with the man from Harvard ended unexpectedly. One day the man didn't show up at their usual meeting time and place. He's had no contact with him since. The loss of Rohit's solidarity is the closest thing he can remember to his feeling of heartache during the days after his boyfriend's disappearance. It's as if a mentally imbalanced, cold-blooded, and militant killer has kidnapped Rohit himself.

Rohit has uncurled himself so that instead of a ski, his body is angled into a taut upright sitting position from which he lunges forward to look straight into Jack's face. Now he stands as if to start pacing, but after just one step, he flings his body in a full circle so he is facing Jack again. Then, as if personifying a strange, genderless demon, he strikes a pose—arms up, fingers pointed and gazelle-like so that Jack can imagine them extended by long painted fingernails. *Voguing*, is what Jack thinks—like the drag queens of Santa Monica Boulevard. Then Rohit begins swiveling his hips in a grotesque gesture accentuated by a circular movement of his wrists. Rohit is doing a dance, a lurid and suggestive belly dance. He puts his hands, fingernails pointing downwards, over his abdomen and slowly begins pulling them up so the very tips of his fingers lift his shirt slightly, exposing his belly. The trail of hairs. The low hang of his trousers.

Rohit stops just as instantly, bringing his face close to Jack's again. He has reverted to the fierce militant. How Jack longs for the person two cycles back—the cultured Muslim university student—or three, even—the obsequious Hindu secular.

"We have asked for a prisoner exchange. One hundred and fifty Kashmiri men have been jailed in Indian prisons under the most untoward, the most brutal conditions. We will accept their release in exchange for you and three others. In your poetry education you undoubtedly learned arithmetic. The algebra of the human soul, it is then. You see your value in this equation. One to forty, is it? You have forty times the value of a Kashmiri then, is it? Our Sherman Tanks. *Hamari Amriki*." Rohit marches more furiously, spinning on his heel now like a parodic soldier from a World War II sitcom.

"Your family will scour the streets of Delhi looking in every ditch, behind every railway track. They will find pieces of you scattered about the slums of this city where Muslims toil in their abject lives. Like the droppings of nightingales, your body will decompose in the streets, in the sewers. Your family will mourn your death like the thousands of Kashmiri mothers and sons crying over our lost martyrs. No one can find you here. Friend."

As Jack watches Rohit fly across the room, he feels himself falling back into the dissociated state of watching his surroundings through a lens. Jack is dropping off to sleep against his will, and for all his efforts to dive back through the lens, he is caught in a thick layer of gelatin through which he cannot plunge back. As his eyes mist over, the last image he catches is of Rohit smacking the walls with his fists and then kicking.

When Jack's eyes close there is still an image of Rohit warring with the wall, only now he is climbing it, then standing with his feet on the ceiling, then pummeling the contours of the room with every limb of his body.

Jack dreams he is in a zoo. Rohit is inside a cage, hanging by claws from its chain-link ceiling and making a terrible shattering sound as he shakes its wall with his bare feet. Jack walks up to the metal wiring and grips it with both hands, pushing his face up to the metal to get as close to Rohit as he can. He wants to offer him a way out. Then Jack looks up and sees that there is cage metal above him as well, and when he looks back to Rohit again, his captor is dressed in a sharp, loose-hanging blue suit and tasseled loafers. He is watching Jack from a spectators bench with a cool, detached stare. Jack rattles the walls of the cage and silently makes a pleading gesture with his eyes. *Let me out.* He no longer has language. Rohit returns the stare coldly.

When Jack shakes awake the first thing he sees is the back of Rohit's neck. Rohit has come back to the mattress and has been sleeping alongside Jack. It is an oddly intimate posture for a man who a short time ago was subjugating a wall in a fit of rage.

To the constant disgruntlement of his mother, Jack was exceptionally wild as a child. He has several fond memories, though, of lying in bed deep in the night with his mother seated next to him stroking his hair. "Even the rottenest boy is an angel when he sleeps," she used to say. Looking at the sleek hairs growing on the back of Rohit's neck, Jack has that same wistful feeling now. Jack always wondered how his mother was able to marshal such deep reserves of forgiveness for her raucous son. But Rohit, vulnerable in sleep, inspires that tenderness in Jack; it's a feeling he doesn't recognize.

Rohit stirs awake and turns, so that now the two men are face to face.

The gun is lying next to Rohit, in easy reach for Rohit but not for Jack, who is still shackled to the wall. Rohit sits up, lies against the wall in the ski position again, and fingers the silencer on the gun. "Tell me friend, how are the birds in America? Girls?"

Girls? Jack wonders if, finally, he is beginning to understand. When Jack was young, when he had his first fumbling adolescent sex, it always began with talk of girls: two boys, snuggling together, talking about girls. It was so commonplace an initiation into adolescent homosexuality that, later, Jack came to assume that male talk of women axiomatically stood for gay sex. Fill in the blank: How do you like girls? How do you like *men?* How do you like sex? How do you like *me?*

Jack pauses. "They're, I don't know, girlish."

"In London, brother, they're nutters, you know, tough."

"Do you like poetry?" Jack recovers. Fill in the blank: *Do you like poetry do you like sex do you like me?*

Rohit cites some words of verse in a language that is not Hindi—or even Urdu, Jack thinks he's sure. Then he translates. "'She hides behind screens calling for you, while you search and lose yourself in the wilderness and the desert.'"

Rumi. Rohit has uttered the unmistakable verse of Rumi. Jack wrote his thesis at UCLA about Rumi, worshipper of a delectable and godly object of passion whose name was Shams. A man. Jack's kidnapper is quoting Rumi. He is quoting Rumi in Persian. No one has ever quoted Rumi to Jack in Persian. It comes like a wash of cold, immersing him in the bright, fresh quality of his earliest sensual memories, when words articulated the sparkling internal sensations of his body. "'The flames of my passion devour the wind and the sky,'" Jack recites in response.

Rohit picks up: "'My body is a candle, touched with fire.'"

Jack feels calm. "'Let me feel you enter each limb, bone by bone.'"

" 'There are no edges to my loving now.'"

"Rumi," Jack says.

Rohit's eyes dance.

"I knew a bird once—" Rohit says.

"For Rumi the love of a woman was an incomplete love, a less than perfect completion of the circle of desire," Jack responds, or deflects.

Rohit nods. "For Rumi the love of a woman was certainly platonic. A metaphor, really, for the true heights of passion a man could achieve."

"A woman's body could never contain the full weight of a man's actual desire," Jack volleys back.

Rohit looks at Jack long with his watery eyes. "We truly understand each other, friend. 'The beloved is all, the lover just a veil.'" He lies back onto the mattress with his hands behind his head, and staring at the ceiling, he begins to hum. Rohit's hum escalates slowly to a chant. It is a gorgeous melody sung in a thin and sinewy high-pitched voice, flowing through the room like the trickle of a drought-choked stream. The chant grows louder, seeming to rebound now around the corners of the room, to flood it with its echo. Jack recognizes it as a thread of Qur'anic chanting—not unlike the melodies mosques broadcast from their towers at daybreak. Rohit is suddenly lost to Jack, lost in a prayer, devotional and otherworldly.

Jack leans back, and listening to the sinewy phrases, feels himself dropping back again behind the lens. With his eyes closed he imagines the water of Rohit's choked stream gurgling over his face. "'The water that pollutes you is poison, the poison that purifies you is water,'" he recites to himself. The stream turns into a rush of water, and then Jack feels he is suffocating as it enters into him, through his lungs, coursing through his own body, as if he is part of the room, a receptacle for Rohit's devotion. Grasping for breath, he swings his arm in front of him to find Rohit on top of him. The Indian is lying above him, the full weight of his body crushing Jack's chest, the kidnapper's hands covering his face.

Rohit is whispering something in Jack's ear. "'You sit on top of a treasure,'" his breath says. "'Yet in utter poverty you will die.' Friend. In utter poverty. You will die."

READING IN HIS WAKE

fiction by PAMELA PAINTER

"At last," my husband said, when I had locked up for the night and come to bed.

"You knew I would," I said.

"But I didn't know when." Propped up in the recently rented hospital bed, he peered more closely at my chosen book. A novel by Patrick O'Brian. "Wait, no, no," he said. "You must begin at the beginning."

"But I like the sound of this one," I said, drawing out the swish of *The Mauritius Command*.

"Ah, but you want to be there when Aubrey and Maturin meet."

"I can always go back," I said, only slightly petulant, aware that at another time we'd never see again I would have been reading favorites, Trevor, Atwood, or Munro. Or tapping into the wall of biographies across from our beds, Rowley's Christina Stead, or Ellman's Joyce. Continuing through the poetry at the top of the stairs: Rivard, Roethke, Ruefle, Solomon, Szymborska.

His eyes gleamed. "But Aubrey and Maturin meet at such an unlikely place—especially to begin the series. They meet at a concert. Italians on little gilt chairs are playing Locatelli." He stopped, out of breath. "Never mind."

"So what's the first one?" If I was going to do this, give him this gift, so to speak, I must do it right. He named *Master and Commander*, and, ignoring the irony, I did as commanded and retrieved *Master and Commander* from his study next door. Carefully I settled in beside him, our old queen set flush to his new bed, and embarked. In running commentary over years of hurried breakfasts and long dinners, he'd extolled

231

to me Patrick O'Brian's sheer genius; how in the first novel he delivers to the reader in dramatic scenes of tense negotiation a detailed account of everything that Jack Aubrey must buy to outfit a ship circa 1859.

Four pages and an "introduction" later, I said, "I see what you mean. A most prickly meeting. Maturin delightfully pissy because a rapt Aubrey, from his seat in the scraggly audience, is audibly 'conducting' the quartet a half beat ahead."

"Don't forget their terse exchange of addresses as if for a duel," he said, laughing and coughing. I looked toward the oxygen machine, then at him. He shook his head.

Relieved, I slid the damp shoulder of his nightshirt into place. "Conflict on page one," I said, making us both happy.

Fifty pages later, when I murmured, "Mmmmmm," he said, "What? Tell me." He turned on the pillow with an effort and put aside his own O'Brian, *The Truelove*. So I read for him; "... *the sun popped up from behind St. Philips fort—it did, in fact, pop up, flattened sideways like a lemon in the* morning *haze and drawing its bottom free of the land with a distinct jerk.*"

"... *distinct jerk*," he repeated.

I said again "... *drawing its bottom free of the land with a distinct jerk.*" A shared blanket of satisfaction settled over us, and we went back to our books, companionably together, and companionably apart.

When I stopped reading to bring him a fresh glass of water to chase his myriad pills, he wanted to know where I was now. I slipped back into bed and tented the book on my flannel chest as I described how Mowett, an earnest member of the square-rigged ship's crew, is explaining sails to a queasy Maturin, and here my husband smiled wryly in queasy recognition of feeling queasy. I took his hand, and went on to describe how Maturin affects interest, although he is exceedingly dismayed to be getting this lesson at the appalling height of forty feet above the roiling seas. "Meanwhile, the reader is getting the lesson, too—and drama at the same time. Here," and I read, *"The rail passed slowly under Stephen's downward gaze—to be followed by the sea ... his grip on the ratlines tightened with cataleptic strength."*

"It makes me want to start all over again," my husband said. Then, not to be seen as sentimental, he held up his book to show he'd just finished the most recent O'Brian. It slipped to the rug, and we left it there.

"You could read Dave Barry now," I said, acknowledging the only good thing about our new sleeping arrangement. My husband used to read Barry's essays in bed, laughing so hard the bed would shake, shake me loose from whatever I was reading. Annoyed, I'd mark my page and say, "Okay, read it to me." The ensuing excerpt was a tone change and mood swing one too many times, because I finally banished Dave Barry from the bed after his column titled "There's Nothing like Feeling Flush," which had my husband out of bed and pacing with laughter. In it, Dave Barry refers to an article published in a Scottish medical journal, "The Collapse of Toilets in Glasgow." Barry says, "The article describes the collapsing-toilet incidents in clinical scientific terminology, which contrasts nicely with a close-up, full-face photograph, suitable for framing, of a hairy and hefty victim's naked wounded butt, mooning out of the page at you, causing you to think, for reasons you cannot explain, of Pat Buchanan." We said it again and again. It answered everything: "for reasons you cannot explain."

"Do you want a Barry book?" I asked. He didn't answer. He was either sleeping or wishing I would shut up.

When we were about to leave for radiation, he was still bereft of a new O'Brian. I found him standing in his study, leaning on a walking stick from his collection, now no longer an affectation.

"The W's are too high," he said, stabbing the air with his stick. "It's Wodehouse I'm after."

"Why Wodehouse?" I said. Jeeves, the perfect valet and gentleman's gentleman, would be totally disapproving of how my husband's shirts went un-ironed and how his trousers drooped on his thinning hips. "I'm almost finished with Trevor's *After Rain*, it has that startlingly dark story about—"

"I think I'll read Wodehouse," he said, his jaw set. Out of breath, he slumped into his desk chair and pointed again. "But I can't reach him." On the shelves behind where my husband was pointing ranged the two hundred-plus books he'd edited at a Boston publishing house, and the four he'd written, the last novel, *A Secret History of Time to Come*, included by the New York Museum of Natural History in a time capsule that would outlast us all. "We have too many books," he said.

"That's what you always say," I said. Hitching up my skirt before the wall of English and European Fiction, I mounted the wobbly wooden ladder we swore at on principle every time we retrieved an out-of-reach

233

book. Waugh Winterson Wodehouse. I called down three titles before he nodded at the fourth. *The Code of the Woosters.* "Why Wodehouse?" I asked again on my descent.

"Ah, you haven't read Wodehouse yet. Arch, mannered humor. You'll see." Then, as if anticipating my early mutiny against O'Brian in deference to Wodehouse, his eyes narrowed, and he instructed, "Keep with the O'Brians for now."

We left for the hospital, armed with our respective books. On the way, I mentioned that Raymond Chandler, also English, and Wodehouse had both attended the posh prep school Dulwich College. "Dulich, but spelled Dulwich," my husband said, surprised by Chandler.

Our bookish, competent doctor always wanted to know what we were reading. My husband waved the Wodehouse at him. "It has a blurb by Ogden Nash," he said, and read, *"In my salad days, I thought that P. G. Wodehouse was the funniest writer in the world. Now I have reached the after-dinner coffee stage, and I know that he is."*

"Woadhouse," the doctor said, making a note on his prescription pad.

"W-o-o-d. I hope he's still funny," my husband said, peering at the doctor over his glasses. "I'm way past the after-dinner coffee. I've reached the medicine stage."

A week later, we were again side by side, my husband's bed rising smoothly and electronically to a barely comfortable position I tried to match with pillows, despairing of the difference in height. I'd finished *Master and Commander* and put it in a safe place because the doctor had meticulously written his home phone number inside its cover. *Post Captain* was next. My husband's long fingers, thin and bony, were oddly free of books because he was listening to the tape of O'Brian's latest Aubrey/Maturin, *The Wine-Dark Sea.* His eyes were alertly closed beneath the Walkman's earphones curving over his new, silky growth of hair.

When he stopped listening to take his pills, I asked him to recall what he'd liked best about *Post Captain.* I closed my eyes against a hysterical welling up of water. And when he'd told me, I thought yes, yes, after years of reading and rereading, arguing, damning, and praising, I knew now almost exactly what he would say. Although I didn't tell him this— but tested more. I badgered him about the repetition of one battle scene after another, asked him to name his favorite title in the series, asked him if Maturin ever dies. I moved on to Ford's *The Good Soldier.* Didn't the narrator's equivocation grate on his nerves? Yes and no. Who was Dante's best translator? Yes, yes. And what did he think of the poem in *Pale Fire*?

"Stop it," he said, his voice stronger than it had been in days. "Enough."

The next evening, when he had finished both sides of the first tape, he told me to look in his desk for a second Walkman. Why didn't matter. "Now, listen to this tape," he said.

"You're still seducing me with literature," I accused him.

He took the tape from his Walkman and inserted it into mine.

"No. No. I can't," I said. "I'll get the plots mixed up." Already I was awash in the unfamiliar world of sloops and frigates, admiring of royals, baffled by masts and yards, and dipping in and out of *A Sea of Words: A Lexicon and Companion for Patrick O'Brian's Seafaring Tales*, chastely beside me on the bed. In love again.

"Here," he said. "Listen."

I donned the earphones, and because he was watching, I closed my eyes. Across the tiny gulf between our beds, his hand found my hand as a calming voice began, *"A purple ocean, vast under the sky and devoid of all visible life apart from two minute ships racing across its immensity."*

Until my husband's hand slipped from mine, until his breath failed, until I called 911, until the ambulance arrived to provide our last voyage together, on that last evening I sailed precariously in two different seas, astride two listing vessels, keeping a third in view against a dark horizon, reading in his wake.

NARRATOR

fiction by ELIZABETH TALLENT

Near the end of what the schedule called the welcome get-together two women—summer dresses, charm—stood at the foot of the solemn Arts and Crafts staircase where he was seated higher up, mostly in shadow. That could have been me his silence fell on: I had wanted to approach him, and had held off because all I had for a first thing to say was *I love your work*, and I had no second thing. Brightly, the women took turns talking in the face of his eclipsing wordlessness. *This is you in real life?* I said to him in my head. The women at the foot of the stairs were older than me, in their late thirties—close to his age, then, and whatever was going on with him, they looked like they could handle it, and this was a relief, as if being his adoring reader conferred on me the responsibility to protect us all from any wounding or disillusioning outcome. But they were fine. Unless they let it show that they were hurt, his silence could be construed as distractedness or even, attractively, as brooding, and who gained from letting his rudeness be recognized for what it was? Not him. Not them. They might feel the need to maintain appearances if they were going to be his students in the coming week, as I would not be, having been too broke to enroll before the last minute, and too full of doubt about whether I wanted criticism. I didn't get to watch how the stairwell thing ended. A boy came up to me, and I made my half of small talk: New Mexico, yes as beautiful as that, no never been before—what about you, five hundred pages, that's amazing. Throughout I was troubled by an awareness of semi-fraudulence; his confidence was so cheerfully aggressive that mine flew under his radar. The full moon would be up before long and if I wanted we could ride

236

across the bridge on his motorcycle, an Indian he'd been restoring for years—parts cost a fortune. There was a night ride across the bridge in his novel and it would be good to check the details. *Long day*, I said— *the flight, you know?*

Enough students were out, in couples and noisy gangs, that I didn't worry, crossing campus. True about the moon: sidewalks and store-fronts brightened as I walked back to my hotel, followed, for a couple of bad blocks, by a limping street person who shouted, at intervals, *Hallelujah.*On the phone my husband told me a neighbor's toddler had fallen down an old hand-dug well but apart from a broken leg wasn't hurt, and he had finished those kitchen cabinets and would drive them to the job site tomorrow, and our dog had been looking all over for me, did I want to talk to him? *Goofball sweetheart why did you ever let me get on that plane?* I asked our dog. When my husband came back on the phone he said *Crazy how he loves you* and So *the first day sucked, hunh?* and *They're gonna love the story. Sleep tight baby. Hallelujah.*

Though I hadn't done it before, the homework of annotating other people's stories was the part of workshop that appealed to the diligent student in me. The bed strewn with manuscripts, I sat up embroidering the margins with exegesis and happy alternatives—if someone had pointed out that *You should try X* can seem condescending, I would have been really shocked. At two A.M., when the city noise was down to faraway sirens, I collected the manuscripts and stacked them on the desk. They were not neutral, but charged with their writers' realities the way intimately dirtied belongings are—hairbrushes, used ban-daids—and I couldn't have fallen asleep with them on the bed. Where, in Berkeley, was his house, and was he asleep, and in what kind of bed, and with whom beside him? Before I left the party I had sat for a while on his step in the dark stairwell. All I had to go on were the narrators of his books, rueful first-person failers at romance whose perceptive-ness was the great pleasure of reading him, but I felt betrayed. Savagely I compared the ungenerosity I'd witnessed with the radiance I'd hoped for. How could the voices in his novels abide in the brain of that with-holder? The women had not trespassed in approaching, the party was meant for such encounters. Two prettier incarnations of eager me had been rebuffed, was that it? No. Or only partly. From his work I had pieced together scraps I believed were *really him*. At some point I had forsaken disinterested absorption and begun reading to construct a him I could love. Think of those times I'd said not *His books are wonderful,* but *I'm in love with him.* Now it was tempting to accuse his

237

work of inauthenticity rather than face the error of this magpie compilation of shiny bits into an imaginary whole. He had never meant to tell me who he was. Nothing real was lost, there was no fall from grace, not one page in his books is diminished, not one word, you have the books, and the books are more than enough, the books will never dismay you, I coaxed myself. But the feeling that something was lost survived every attempt to reason it away.

The days passed without my seeing him again, and besides I was distracted by an acceptance entailing thrilling, dangerous phone calls from the editor who had taken the story, whose perfectionism in regard to my prose dwarfed my own. Equally confusingly, my workshop wanted the ending changed. The ending had come in a rush so pure that my role was secretarial, the typewriter chickchickchickchickchick-tsinging along, rattling the kitchen table with its uneven legs; now I couldn't tell if it was good or not, and I needed to get home to regain my hold on intuition. At the farewell party in the twilight of the grand redwood-paneled reception room hundreds of voices promised to stay in touch. At the room's far end, past the caterer's table with its slowly advancing queue, French doors stood ajar, and two butterflies dodged in, teetering over heads that didn't notice. They weren't swallowtails or anything glamorous, but pale small nervous slips dabbling in the party air, and my awareness linked lightly with them, every swerve mirrored, or as it felt enacted, by the consciousness I called mine, which for the moment wasn't. After a while they pattered back out through the doors. Then there he stood, watching them go. And maybe because rationality had absented itself for the duration of their flight, what happened next felt inevitable. I stared. His head turned; when he believed I was going to retreat—when I, too, was aware of the socially destined instant for looking away—and I didn't, then the nature of whatever it was that was going on between us changed, and was, unmistakably, an assertion. Gladness showered through me. I could take this chance, could mean, nakedly—rejoicing in being at risk—*I want you*. Before now I'd had no idea what I was capable of—part of me stepped aside, in order to feel fascination with this development. But did he want this? Because who was I? He broke the connection with a dubious glance down and away, consulting the proprieties, because non-crazy strangers did not lock each other in a transparently sexual gaze heedless of everybody around them, and he wasn't, of course he wasn't, sure what he was getting into. If I hadn't been so happy to have discovered this crazy recklessness, no doubt I would have been ashamed. As it was I was alone until he looked up to see whether he was still being stared at, as he was, greenly, oh shamelessly, by me, and he wondered whether something was wrong with me, but he could see mine was a sane face and that I, too, recognized the exposedness and hazard of not breaking off the stare and this information flaring back and forth between us meant we were no longer strangers.

We spent the night over coffee in a café on Telegraph Avenue, breaking pieces off from our lives, making them into stories. At the next table two sixtyish gents in identical black berets slaughtered each other's pawns. Look, I told him, how when one leans over the board, the other leans back the exact, compensatory distance. When I recognized what I was up to, proffering little details to amuse him and to accomplish what my old anthropology professor would have called *establishing kinship—We're alike, details matter to us, and there will be no end of details—*I understood that delight, which had always seemed to belong among the harmless emotions, could in fact cut deep. It could cut you away from your old life, once you'd really felt it. The most fantastic determination arose, to stay in his presence. At the same time I understood full well I would be getting on an airplane in—I looked at my watch—five hours. He, too, looked at his watch. Our plan was simple: *not* to sleep together, because that would make parting terrible. We would stay talking until the last minute, and then he would drive me to the airport, stopping by my hotel first for my things. I didn't have money for another ticket and couldn't miss my early-morning flight.

He left it till late in the conversation to ask, "You're, what—?"

"Twenty-four." I stirred my coffee like there was a way of stirring coffee right.

"What's in New Mexico?"

"Beauty." I didn't look up from my coffee to gauge if that was too romantic. "The first morning I woke up there—in the desert; we'd driven to our campsite in the dark—I thought, *This is it, I'm in the right place.*"

Another thing he said across the table, in the tone of putting two and two together: "The story that got taken from the slush pile, that was yours."

A workshop instructor who was a friend of the editor's had spread the word. "Someone"—the moonlight motorcycle-ride guy—"told me, 'It's lightning striking, the only magazine that can transform an unknown into a known.' Not that I'm not grateful, I'm completely grateful but what if I'm not good at the *known* part."

"Why wouldn't you be good?"

"Too awkward for it."

"You're the girl wonder."

That shut me up: I took it to mean that instead of complaining, I should adapt. I was going to go on to hear a correction encoded in other remarks; this was only the first instance. "You're chipper this morning, kid"—that was a warning whose franker, ruder form would have been *Tone it down.* "You look like something from the court of Louis Quatorze" meant I should have blow-dried my long hair straight, as usual, instead of letting its manic curliness emerge. When he would announce, of his morning's work, "Two pages" or "Only one paragraph, but a crucial one," I heard, "And what have you gotten done? Since your famous story. What?" I understood that I could be getting it all wrong, but I couldn't not interpret.

Those first charmed early-summer days he put on his record of Glenn Gould's Goldberg Variations, which I had never heard before, and taught me to listen for the snatches of Gould's ecstatic counter-humming. When I was moved to tears by Pachelbel's Canon in D he didn't say *Where have you been?* He played Joni Mitchell's "A Case of You." He sang it barelegged, in his bathrobe, while making coffee to bring to me in the downstairs bedroom. One morning, sitting up to take the cup, I asked, "Do you remember at the welcoming party, you were sitting in the stairwell and two women came up to you? And you wouldn't say anything?"

He needed to think. "Esmé and Joanie, you mean. They just found out Joanie's pregnant. Try getting a word in edgewise."

My stricken expression amused him; he said, "You have lesbians in New Mexico, right?"

It seemed easier to make a secret of that first, accusatory misreading of him than to try to explain.

I hadn't caught my flight. Instead we made love in the hotel room I hadn't wanted him to see, since I had left it a mess. "Was this all you?" he asked, of the clothes strewn everywhere, and it was partly from shame that I lifted his t-shirt and slid a hand inside. When we woke it was early afternoon and my having not gone home became real to me. My husband had a daylong meeting that prevented his picking me up at the airport—at least he was spared that.

240

Where he lived was a comradely neighborhood of mostly neglected Victorians, none very fanciful, shaded by trees as old as they were. His place was the guest cottage—"So it's small," he cautioned, on the drive there—belonging to a Victorian that had tilted past any hope of renovation. In its place some previous owner put up a one-story studio-apartment building, rentals that, since he disliked teaching, provided the only reliable part of his income. His minding about precariousness (if it was) was embarrassing. It was proof that he was *older*. Even if they could have, no one I knew in New Mexico would have wanted to use the phrase *reliable income* in a sentence about themselves: jobs were quit nonchalantly, security was to be scorned. With the help of an architect friend—a former lover, he clarified as if pressed; and never do that, never renovate a house with someone you're sleeping with—all that was stodgy and cramped had been replaced with clarity and openness, as much, at least, as the basically modest structure permitted. This preface sounded like something recited fairly often. The attic had been torn out to allow for the loft bedroom, its pitched ceiling set with a large skylight, its wide-planked floor bare, the bed done in white linen. The white bed was like his saying *reliable income*—it was the opposite of daring. No man I had ever known, if it had even occurred to him to buy pillowcases and sheets instead of sleeping on a bare mattress, would ever have chosen all white—my husband, for some reason I was imagining what my carpenter husband would say about that bed. Sleeplessness and guilt were catching up with me, and there was the slight feeling any tour of a house gives, of coercing praise. I was irritated that in these circumstances, to me costly and extraordinary, the usual compliments were expected. "Beautiful light," I said. The narrow stairs to the loft were flanked by cleverly fitted bookshelves, and more bookshelves ran around the large downstairs living room, off which the galley kitchen and bathroom opened, and, on another wall, doors leading to his study and the guest bedroom that would be mine, because, he said apologetically, he couldn't sleep through the night with anyone in bed with him—it wasn't me; he hadn't ever been able to. Was that going to be all right? Of course it was, I said. I sat down on the edge of the twin bed. *I can get the money somehow, I can fly home tomorrow.* Even as I thought that he sat down beside me. "When I think you could have gotten on that plane. I would be alone, wondering what just hit me. Instead we get this chance." In that room there was a telephone, and he left me alone with it.

241

He had his coffee shop, and when he was done working, that's where he liked to go—at least, before me he had gone there. Time spent with me, in bed or talking, interfered with the coffee shop, and with research in the university library and his circuit of bookstores and Saturday games of pick-up basketball, but for several weeks I was unaware that he, who liked everything just so, had altered his routines for my sake. From the congratulatory hostility of his friends I gathered that women came and went—"Your free throw's gone to shit," said Billy, owner of the shabby, stately Victorian next door whose honeysuckle-overrun backyard was a storehouse of costly toys—motorcycles, a sailboat. "How I know you have a girlfriend." I would have liked to talk to someone who knew him—even Billy, flagrantly indiscreet—about whether my anxious adaptation to his preferences was intuitive enough, or I was getting some things wrong. Other women had lived with him: what had they done in the mornings, how had they kept quiet enough? One was a cellist—how had *that* worked? His writing hours, eight to noon, were non-negotiable. If he missed a day his black mood saturated our world. But this was rare.

The check came, for the story. Forwarded by my husband, who I called sometimes when I was alone in the house. "You can always come home, you know," my husband said. "People get into trouble. They get in over their heads."

The house was close enough to the university that, days when he was teaching, he could ride his bicycle. Secretly I held it against him that he was honoring his responsibilities, meeting his classes, having conversations about weather and politics. My syllogism ran: what love does is shatter life as you've known it; his life isn't shattered; therefore he is not in love. Of the two of us I was the *real* lover. This self-declared greater authenticity, this was consoling—but, really, why was it? The question of who was more naked emotionally would have struck him as crazy, my guess is. But either my willingness to tear my life apart had this secret virtuousness, or the damage I was doing was deeply—callously—irresponsible.

By now I knew something about the women before me, including the Chinese lover whose loss he still wasn't reconciled to, though it had been years. I stole her picture and tucked it into *Middlemarch*, the only book in this house full of his books that belonged to me, and when he admitted to not liking Eliot much I was relieved to have a book which by not mattering to him could talk privately and confidentially to what was left of me as a writer, the little that was left after I was, as I believed I wanted to be, stripped down to bare life, to skin and heartbeat and sex, never enough sex, impatient sex, adoring sex, fear of boredom sex. The immense sanity of *Middlemarch* made it a safe haven for the little insanity of the stolen photograph. Whenever I went back to *Middlemarch*, I imagined the magnanimous moral acuity with which the narrator would have illumined a theft like mine, bringing it into the embrace of the humanly forgivable while at the same time—and how did Eliot get away with this?—indicting its betrayal of the more honorable self I would, in *Middlemarch*'s narrator's eyes, possess. But I didn't go back often; sex and aimless daydreaming absorbed the hours I would usually have spent reading, and when I went up to the loft, I left the book behind—I didn't want him noticing it. He had a habit of picking up my things and studying them quizzically, as if wondering how they had come to be in his house, and if he picked up *Middlemarch* there was a chance the photo would fall out. If I fell asleep in his bed after sex he would wake me after an hour or two, saying *Kid, you need to go downstairs*. On the way down I ran my fingers over the spines of the books lining the stairwell. If you opened one it would appear untouched; he recorded observations and memorable passages in a series of reading notebooks.

My scribbled-in *Middlemarch* stayed on the nightstand by the twin bed, and I had hung my clothes in the closet, but that didn't mean I felt at home in the room, with its dresser whose bottom drawer was jammed with photos. What did it mean that this drawer, alone in all the house, had not been systematically sorted? Near the bottom of the slag heap was an envelope of tintypes: from a background of stippled tarnish gazed a poetic boy, doleful eyes and stiff upright collar, and I wanted to take it to him and say *Look, you in 1843*, but that would prove I'd been rifling through the drawer, and even if he hadn't said not to, I wasn't sure it was all right. His childhood was there, his youth, the face of the first author's photo. Houses and cities before this one. His women, too, and I dealt them out across the floor, a solitaire of faces, wildly unalike: I wanted to know their stories. No doubt I did know pieces, from his work, but here they were, real, and I would have listened to them all if I could, I would have asked each one *How did it end?* When he was writing he would sometimes knock and come in and rummage through the pictures, whose haphazardness replicated memory's chanciness. As with memory there was the sense that everything was there, in the drawer—just not readily findable. Disorder is friendly to serendipity, was that the point? When he found what he wanted he didn't take it back to his desk but stayed and studied it, and when he was done dropped it casually back into the hodge podge. If I opened tile drawer after he'd gone there was no way to guess which photo he'd been holding.

There were things that happened in sex that felt like they could never be forgotten. Recognitions, flights of soul-baring mutual exposure, a kind of raw ravishment that seemed bound to transform our lives. But, sharing the setting of so many hours of tumult—the bed—and tumult's instruments—our two bodies—these passages lacked the distinctness of *event* and turned out to be, as far as memory was concerned, elusive. And there was sadness in that, in coming back to our same selves. By midsummer, something—maybe the infuriating inescapability of those selves, maybe an intimation of the monotonousness sex could devolve into, if we kept this up—caused us to start turning sex into stories. Sex with me as a boy, the one and only boy who ever caught his eye, a lovely apparition of a boy he wanted to keep from all harm, but who one day was simply gone, sex as if he was a pornographer and I was a schoolgirl who began, more and more, to conjure long-absent emotions, tenderness, possessiveness, even as the schoolgirl became more and more corrupt, telling sly little lies, the sex we would have if after ten years' separation we saw each other across a crowded room, sex as if I had just learned he'd been unfaithful to me with one of his exes, sex as if I was unfaithful, the sex we would have if we broke up and after ten years ended up in the same Paris hotel for some kind of writers' event, a book-signing maybe, and sometimes it was his book and sometimes it was mine, sex with me in the stockings and heels of a prostitute, with him as a cop, me as a runaway desperate for shelter, with him as a woman, with the two of us as strangers seated near each other on a nightlong flight.

These games always began the same way. Ceremonious, the invitation, somber and respectful in inverse proportion to the derangement solicited. *What if you are. What if I am.* We never talked about this, and though either could have said *Let's not go there*, neither of us ever declined a game described by the other. The inventing of parts to play was spontaneous, their unforeseeableness part of the game's attraction, but a special mood, an upswell of lurid remorse, alerted me whenever I was about to say *And then after forever we see each other again.* In

244

these scenarios where we had spent years apart, the lovely stroke was our immediate, inevitable recognition of each other—not, like other emotions we played at, a shock, not a wounding excitement, but an entrancing correction to loss. All wrongs set right. *And we look at each other. And it's like—*

While he wouldn't drink any coffee that wasn't made from freshly ground Italian dark roast (which I had never tried before) and he had a taste for expensive chocolate, he seemed mostly indifferent to food, and never cooked. What had he done when he was alone? Was it just like this, cereal, soup from cans, microwaved enchiladas? Should I try to make something—would that feel, to him, to me, ominously wife-y? He liked bicycling to the farmer's market and would come back with the ripest, freshest tomatoes. He taught me to slather mayonnaise across sliced bakery bread, grinding black pepper into the bleeding exposed slices before covering them with the top slice, taking fast bites before the bread turned sodden, licking juice from wrists and finger-tips, the tomatoes still warm from basking in their crates at the farmer's market, their taste leaking acid-bright through the oily mayonnaise blandness, the bread rough in texture, sweet in fragrance. There was at least a chance he'd never told any other lover about tomato sandwiches. After weeks of not caring what I ate, I had found something I couldn't get enough of, and as soon as I finished one sandwich I would make another, waiting until he was out to indulge, and it didn't matter how carefully I cleared away all traces of my feast, he could tell, he was quick with numbers and probably counted the tomatoes.

Really the little house was saturated with his vigilance; there was no corner I could narrate from. When I went elsewhere, tried working in a café (not his) for example, it was as if the house was still with me, its atmosphere extending to the little table where I sat with my books and my legal pad and my cup of coffee with cream and two teaspoons of brown sugar stirred in, and even the music in the coffee shop, which should have had nothing to do with him, caused me to wonder whether he was thinking of me and wanted me to come home or whether he was relieved to have an afternoon to himself, and whether the onset of irritation was inevitable in love, and if it was how people could stand their lives, but look, everyone at the tables around me was standing their life, and I had more than most, I was in love. With *him*, and that was extraordinary, it was surreal—naturally it required adaptation, but

245

I ought to rejoice, day by day, in the revision asked of me, I ought to get a handle on my moods. Two hours had passed; I gave up trying. He was sitting with Billy on Billy's front steps and greeted me by saying, "Everest redux." Billy said, "Can I have a kiss for luck? Leaving for Kathmandu early in the A.M. Oh and forgot to tell you"—turning to him—"Delia's going to housesit. I don't want to be distracted on the Icefall by visions of Fats"—his skinny, hyper Border Collie—"wasting away in some kennel. Only good vibes. Last year when I got up into the Death Zone I hallucinated my grandmother." Deepening his Texas drawl: "'Time you *git* back home.' Actually one of the sherpas looked a whole lot like her. Brightest black eyes. See right through bullshit, which you want in a sherpa or grandma. I lied a lot when I was little, like practice for being in the closet. So, Delia. Fats loves her. So, she'll be staying here." He said, "Always smart not to leave a house empty," but I knew Billy was curious if I would show that I minded, because Delia was his most recent ex, the lover before me, and thinking *only good vibes, right,* I said, "Fats will be happy" and kissed Billy on his sunburned forehead.

I gave up on the coffee shop but when I tried writing in the afternoons in the guest bedroom, sitting up in the twin bed with a legal pad on my knees, he would wander in and start picking up various objects, my traveling alarm clock, my hairbrush, and I would drop the legal pad and hold out my arms. Maybe because he was becoming restless, or was troubled by what looked, in me, like the immobilizing onset of depression, he talked me into going running and that was how we spent our evenings now, on an oval track whose cinders were the real old-school kind, sooty black, gritting under running shoes. If there had been a meet that weekend the chalk lines marking the lanes were still visible, and the infield was grass, evenly mown, where he liked, after running, to throw a football, liked it even more than he ordinarily would have because football figured in the novel he was writing about two brothers whose only way of connecting with each other was throwing a football back and forth, and he needed the sense impressions of long shadows across summer grass and the Braille of white x's stitched into leather to prompt the next morning's writing. When he held a football his tall, brainy self came together, justified. Pleasantly dangerous with the love of competition, though all there was to compete with at the moment was me. When he cocked his arm back and took a step, tiny grasshoppers showered up. The spiral floated higher, as if the air was tenderly prolonging its suspension, and took its time descending. The thump of flight dead-ending against my chest as I ran pleased me. He had trouble accepting that I could throw a spiral, though he might have known my body learned fast. I couldn't throw as far, and he walked backwards, taunting for more distance. Taunting I took as a guy-guy thing; my prowess, modest as it was, made me an honorary boy, and was sexy. One bright evening as I cocked my arm back he cried *Throw it, piggy!* Shocked into grace I sent a real beauty his way, and with long-legged strides he covered the grass and leaped, a show-offy catch tendered as apology before I could call down the field *What?*, but I was standing there understanding: *piggy* was a thing he called me to himself, that had slipped out. In my need and aimlessness and insatiability I was a pale sow. How deluded I had been, believing I was a genius lover no excess could turn repellent. The next morning I woke up sick, ashamed that wherever he was in the house he could hear me vomiting, and when I said I wanted a hotel room he told me a tenant had moved out from one of his units and I could have the key.

These studio units, five of them, occupied the shabby one-story stucco box that stood between his house and the street. Flat-roofed cinder-block painted a sullen ochre, this building was a problem factory. Termites, leaks, cavalier electrical wiring. With his tenants he was on amiable terms, an unexpectedly easy-going landlord. The little box I let myself into had a floor of sky-blue linoleum—sick as I was, that blue made me glad. The space was bare except for a bed frame and mattress where I dropped the sheets and towels he'd given me. The hours I spent in the tiny bathroom were both wretched and luxurious in their privacy; whenever there was a lull in the vomiting I would lock and unlock the door just to do so. Now he is locked the fuck out. Now I let him back in. Now out forever. After dark I leaned over the toy kitchen sink and drank from the faucet. It was miraculous to be alone. There was a telephone on the kitchen's cinder-block wall, and as I looked at it, it rang. Thirteen, fourteen, fifteen. I slept in the bare bed and woke scared that my fever sweat had stained the mattress; it was light; that day lasted forever, the thing sickness does to time. His knocking woke me; he came in all tall and fresh from his shower. Having already worked his habitual four hours. First he made the bed; with the heel of his hand he pushed sweaty hair from my face; I was unashamed, I could

247

have killed him if he didn't make love to me. "I'll check in on you to-morrow," he said. I barely kept myself from saying *Do you love me. Do you love me.* Nausea helped keep me from blurting that out; the stren-uousness of repressing nausea carried over into this other, useful re-pression. "I'm so hungry," I said instead. "Can you bring me a bowl of rice?" In saying it I discovered that the one thing I could bear to think of eating was the bowl of rice he would carry over from his house. I needed something he made for me. When I woke it was night. Cool air and traffic sounds came through the picture window, and seemed to mean I was going to be able to live without him. Now and then the phone began to ring and I let it ring on and on. Sometime during that night I went through the cupboards. I sat cross-legged on the floor with a cup of tea and ate stale arrowroot biscuits from the pack the tenant had forgotten, feeling sick again as I ate. It didn't matter that I knew that very well, and even understood it; the bowl of rice was now an obsession. It seemed like the only thing I had ever wanted from him, though in another sense all I had done since staring at him that first time was want things from him. In the morning while it was still dark he let himself in—of course there was a master key—with nothing in his hands, and when we were through making love he said, "You're going to bathe, right?" Then I was alone without a bowl of rice, cross-legged on the kitchen floor with the cup of tea I'd made and the last five arrowroot biscuits, locked deep in hunger, realizing that because the hunger felt clear and exhilarating, with no undertow of nausea, that I was either well or about to be. I called and made a reservation on a flight to New Mexico that had one seat left.

When the taxi pulled up before dawn he was sitting on the curb, his back to me, a tall man in a child's closed-off pose, ignoring the head-lights that shone on him. Against black asphalt the hopping gold-gashed dot dot dot was the last flare-up of his tossed cigarette. I thought, and came close to saying, *You don't smoke.* He stood up and said, "I won't try to stop you," and it was another blow, not to be stopped.

In the novel he wrote about that time I wasn't his only lover. House-sitting next door, the narrator's sensible, affectionate ex affords him sexual refuge from the neediness of the younger woman he'd believed he was in love with, whose obsession with him has begun to alarm him.

Impulsively, after the first time they slept together, she left her husband for him. How responsible did that make him, for her? He understands, as she doesn't seem to, that there's nothing unerring about desire. At its most compelling, it can lead to a dead end, as has happened in their case. This younger, dark-haired lover keeps *Middlemarch* on her night-stand, and rifling through the book one night while she's sleeping the narrator finds the naked photograph of the Chinese woman whose de-votion he had foolishly walked away from and he thinks, I could get her back. She lives not very far away, and I would have heard if she got married—people can't wait to tell you that kind of thing, about an ex. Here the novel takes a comic turn, because now he needs to break up with two women, his house-sitting ex, likely to go okay, and, a more troubling prospect, this girl inexplicably damaged by their affair, turned from a promising actress whose raffishly seductive Ophelia had gotten raves into a real-life depressive who hasn't gone on a single audition. He needs to rouse her from her depression, to talk to her frankly, encouragingly. A tone he can manage, now, because of what he hopes for. Tricky to carry off, the passage where, tilting the picture to catch what little light there is, he falls in love—the novel's greatest feat, also the one thing I was sure had never happened. I don't mean the novel was true, only that the things in it had happened. The likelier explana-tion was, he'd gone into the guest bedroom while I was out. Farfetched, his coming into the room while I slept—why would he?—though I could see why he wanted, thematically, the juxtaposition of sleep and epiphany, and how the little scene was tighter for suspense about whether the dark-haired lover would wake up.

Twelve years later, on our way home from the funeral of a well-loved colleague who had lived in Berkeley, two friends and I stopped in a bookstore. Between the memorial service and the trip out to the cem-etery the funeral had taken most of the day. Afterward we had gone to dinner, and except for the driver we were all a little drunk and, in the wake of grieving funeral stiltedness and the tears we had shed, trying to cheer each other up. Death seemed like another of Howard's con-tradictions: his rumbling, comedic fatness concealed an exquisite sen-sibility, gracious, capable of conveying the most delicate illuminations to his students or soft-shoeing around the lectern, reciting *In Brueghel's great picture The Kermess.* If Howard's massiveness was bearish, that of his famous feminist-scholar wife was majestic, accoutered with scarves, shawls, trifocals on beaded chains, a cane she was rumored to have aimed at an unprepared grad student in her Dickinson seminar— *My soul had stood, a loaded gun*, David said; Josh corrected, *My life*, with the affable condescension that, David's grin said, he'd been hoping for, since it made Josh look not so Zen after all. Josh was lanky, mild, exceedingly tall, with an air of baffled inquiry and goodwill I attributed to endless zazen, David sturdy, impatient, his scorn exuberant, the professional vendettas he waged merciless. It was David I told my love affairs to, and when I had the flu it was David who came over, fed Leo his supper, and read aloud. Through the wall I could hear David's merry *showed their terrible claws till Max said "BE STILL!"* followed by Leo's doubtful *Be still!*

That evening of the funeral one of us suggested waiting out rush hour in the bookstore and we wandered through in our black clothes, David to philosophy, Josh to poetry, me to a long table of tumbled sale books on whose other side—I stared—*he* stood with an open book in his hand, looking up before I could turn away, the brilliant dark eyes that had held mine as I came over and over meeting mine now without recognition, just as neutrally looking away, the book in his hand the real object of desire, something falsely assertive and theatrical in the steadiness of his downward gaze that convinced me he had been attracted to me not as a familiar person but as a new one, red-haired now, in high heels, in head-to-toe black, a writer with three books to my name, teaching at a university a couple of hours away, single mother to a solemn, intuitive toddler who spoke in complete sentences, light of my life though he wasn't going to get to hear about my son, wasn't going to get a word of my story, and in the inward silence and disbelief conferred by his not knowing who I was there was time for a decision, which was: before he can figure out who he's just seen, before, as some fractional lift of his jaw told me he was about to, he can look up and meet your eyes again and know who you are, before before before before before before before before he can say your name followed by *I don't believe it*, followed by *I always thought I'd see you again*, look away. Get out. Go. And I did, and though behind me where I stood on the street corner the bookstore door opened now and then and let people out none of them was him. Person after person failed to be him. He hadn't known me. I had known him—did that mean I had been, all along, the real lover? What we had should have still burned both of us. If it had been real, if we had gone as deep as I believed we had, he could never have failed to recognize me. After a while my friends came out carrying their bags, and David told me, "This is the first time I've ever seen you leave a bookstore empty-handed, ever," and we pulled our gloves on, telling each other taking a little time had been a good idea, and our heads were clear now, and we could make the drive home. Of course, that was when he came out the door—long-legged, striding fast. Pausing, fingers touched to his lips, then the upright palm flashed at me—a gesture I didn't recognize, for a second, as a blown kiss—before he turned the corner.

"Wasn't that—?" David said.

"Yes."

"Did he just—"

"When we're in the car, you two," Josh said. "I've got to be at the Zen Center at five in the morning."

"The day before, he told me his biggest fear wasn't that they wouldn't get all the cancer. His biggest fear wasn't of dying, even, though he said that was how his father died when Howard was only nine, under the anesthetic for an operation supposed to be simple, with nobody believing they needed to say goodbye beforehand, and now that he was facing *a simple operation* himself, one nobody dies of, he couldn't help thinking of his father. No. His biggest fear was that he'd be left impotent. Of all the things that can conceivably go wrong with prostate cancer surgery, that was the most terrifying."

"What did you say?" Josh asked, from the backseat.

"'Most terrifying?' I'm wondering why it's me, the gay boy, Howard chooses to confide in about impotence. Because my whole life revolves around penises? I'm a little unnerved, because, you know Howard, his usual decorum, where's that gone? But I want to be staunch for him, I love this man. And he says, 'Not for me. If it came down to living without it, I would grieve, but it wouldn't be the end of the world. For me. Whereas for Martha.'"

"'Most terrifying,'" Josh said. "I'm very sorry he had to make those calculations."

"'Martha can't live without it.'"

"You were right there," Josh said. "You reassured him."

"Of course I reassured him." David checked Josh's expression in the rear-view mirror. "But it's not something I imagined, that the two of them ever—or still—"

"Or, hmmm, that she could be said—"

"You idiots, he adored her," I said. "That's what he was telling David. Not, 'My god, this woman, it's unimaginable that I'll never make love to her again.' But 'How can she bear the loss.'"

Josh took off his tie, rolled it up, tucked it in his jacket pocket, and then handed his glasses forward to me, saying, "Can you take custody?" I cradled them as cautiously as if they were his eyes. Once he was asleep, David said, "That was him, wasn't it?"

I told him what happened. "After I'd gone he must have stood there thinking, But I know her, I know her from somewhere. Then he gets it—who I am, and that I'd walked away without a word. Which has to have hurt."

"It's generally that way when you save your own skin—somebody gets hurt."

"Even hurt, he blows me a kiss. That makes him seem—"

"Kind of great," David said.

"Wasn't I right? Walking away?"

"Don't misunderstand me," David said. "There's no problem with a little mystery, in the context of a larger, immensely hard-won clarity." He yawned. "I'm not the idiot." He tipped his curly head to indicate the back seat. "He's the idiot. Did I reassure him. Fuck. I'm the most reassuring person alive."

Oncoming traffic made an irregular stream of white light, its brilliance intensifying, fusing, then sliding by. I held up Josh's glasses and the lights dilated gorgeously. I said, "You know why we'll never give up cars—because riding in cars at night is so beautiful, it's telling stories in a cave with the darkness kept out, the dash lights for the embers of the fire."

"You don't have to tell me any stories," David said. "I'm absolutely wide awake."

I didn't sleep long, but when I woke he was in a different mood.

"You know, his novel," David said, "—the one about you—is that a good book?"

"If you like his voice it's good."

"On its own, though, is it?"

"Mine wasn't exactly a disinterested reading," I said. "The style is his style, and like all his work it moved right along, but the novel overall felt tilted in the narrator's favor, and it would have been more compelling if he had made the dark-haired lover—"

"You," David said.

"—okay, me, but I really am talking about the character now, who is all shattered vulnerability and clinging, the embodiment of squishy need. If he had granted her some independent perceptions, even at points conflicting with his, made her more real, more likable, then her realness would test the narrator's possession of the story, and cast some doubt on the narrator's growing contempt. If it's less justified, more ambiguous, then his contempt isn't just about her and how she deserves it, it's also about him and how ready he is to feel it. If it's not so clear that he's right to feel what he feels, then everything between them gets more interesting, right?"

"That's a sadder ending," David said. "The way that you tell it."

"I wasn't thinking it was sad," I said. "I was thinking it was—better."

A SINGLE DELIBERATE THING

fiction by ZEBBIE WATSON

It had been a long, rainless July and before that, a dry June. The pastures were brown, the grass chewed to stubs and coated in dust. The horses stayed in all day and if I tried to turn them out before dark, they stood by the gate and sweated and stamped. Most farms got the corn planted early enough that it grew shoulder-high and deep rooted, but the second cutting of hay would be late and small and the soy beans were doing poorly, their leaves chewed by the deer and withering on the stem. I was counting swallows and waiting for the letter from Kentucky that might let me know if you still loved me.

There were more swallows that summer than I can ever remember seeing. In spring there had been the usual number of mud-daubed nests—one under the eaves in the front of the barn, one in Otter's stall, and one on the side of the garage—but somehow, come July, the fields positively crackled with the glint of the sun off their blue-black backs. Most days I counted more than thirty of them. They would perch in a row on the telephone wire that ran up the drive, and when I passed under them, they'd peel off one by one in all directions, sleek and made of angles, to swoop across the fields and turn their wingtips vertical. Dad said it was because there was no mud for a second nest; there was nothing else for them to do.

When you told me you were enlisting, you said we should just break up then because you would probably be sent some place out of state. That made sense, but then the night before you left, when you came over to say goodbye, you hugged me on the front porch and pressed a folded paper into my palm with your address at boot camp and left without coming inside. I wasn't sure if that meant you wanted me to write or not, and if that was your way of letting me choose, I didn't get it at the time.

I wrote you mid-June. I think now that I shouldn't have, but what can I say, it was habit to want to tell you things. When I saw fox kits playing in the field, when I counted thirty-seven swallows on the wire, when Grace jumped her first full course without refusing a fence, I wanted to tell you. I also wanted to apologize for saying you looked dumb with your head shaved, you know it would have grown on me. And then I added that I didn't care if you were giving up college or if we would have to be apart a lot because I didn't need that much from you anyway. And I didn't get why you thought staying together would be hard when it had always been easy before. And finally I told you that I wouldn't mind waiting most of the time, which, I realize now, is funny, because after a couple weeks the waiting started to drive me crazy. I knew the mail would be slow but the relentless heat made the days longer and they eventually began adding up and summer dragged on indefinitely.

I should have kept busy riding but Mom and I were only riding in the late evening when the flies were more bearable. You know how grumpy the mares get in the heat, some days I didn't even bother. One night I was riding Grace behind the house and she was already so annoyed to be out that when a horsefly landed on her rump she bucked once and launched me right over her head. She was good for the most part, but that night not so much. Maybe I'd have ridden more if you were home to come out with me, my mom never wanted to. She's even less tolerant than the mares. I never told her I had written you but sometimes I swear she knew by the way she'd say *why don't you do something different with your hair*, or *you'll meet so many cute boys in college*. Other times it seemed like she'd forgotten, she didn't ask, as if hearing from you was never on the table to begin with. Family dinners were spent mostly just complaining about the lack of rain and worrying about Notes.

We took Notes in March from a friend of a friend. They told us he couldn't be ridden due to his age and his heaves, but as soon as the summer humidity set in, it was obvious that his breathing was so bad he should have just been euthanized. We saw that and acknowledged that but still he was already so dear and familiar and Otter, who in seventeen years had never bonded closely with the other horses, loved Notes instantly and fiercely. The two of them grazed nose to nose although Notes barely came up to Otter's chest, and Otter would chase the two mares if they came close to his pony. He lost weight quickly when summer came; he wasn't too thin when you saw him last, but by the end his ribs showed with every breath and his hollow neck tied into bony withers. My parents would talk about it every time the temperatures rose, watching in the late evening as Otter's tall dark shape moved in protective circles around Notes' small white one, and we were all guilty of too much hope. It became a pattern of *maybe this summer won't be too bad*, and then *we got him through the last heat wave, we can't give up now the humidity's broken a bit*. But July dragged on and I was still waiting for your letter and drenching Notes with cold water every afternoon to keep him cool.

I wish now that I could have just made a decision for him. That's a lot of afternoons in the barn with sweat between my shoulder blades and nothing to do but listen to Notes' wheezing and think about when your letter might come. I imagine that summer in Kentucky must have been even hotter than Virginia so I thought of you every time sweat soaked through the back of my shirt, knowing you were wearing combat boots and fatigues. I thought of how easily your nose and ears sunburned, and how dark your freckles would be. I thought that maybe it had taken a long time for you to get my letter, and that maybe you were too tired each night to write back. At some point I realized that I hadn't even told you to write back, I was just leaving it up to you to decide, I was only ever asking you to decide. My parents must not have known or else they would have kept saying things like *teenage love will die naturally anyway* or *you two would have eventually grown apart at college*. They assumed my worry was about Notes, which makes sense because he was the one I sat next to as I waited.

The day before he died, looking back, I think we knew. It was an unbearably heavy week, the air was so thick and the temperature barely dipped into the eighties at night. When Mom brought the horses in that morning, Notes ate his small handful of grain and lay down, already tired and heaving. I confess we were so used to his flaring nostrils that it didn't seem much worse than usual, but I could tell she was worried when she left for work. She asked me to check on him in the afternoon, reminding me about his medication, as if I didn't do it every day.

I checked on him every day but that day I avoided it, waiting until after lunch when it would be time for his medicine. I remember that I went out on the porch to water the plants and saw a dozen or so of the swallows gathered in a low dip in the driveway that would become a puddle were there any rain. They moved so unnaturally, their bodies stooped and narrow, it was striking. I watched them, amazed that some deep instinct drove them to this low place—that they knew if there were mud to be found it would be there—and yet somehow ashamed to see them that way. I loved the tiny sharpness of their hunched shapes when they perched, but on the ground they groveled, moved like bats in daylight, it made me feel so helpless. I took the watering can to soak the dust they were pecking and they scattered before me. It was a relief to watch them skim away across the pasture.

I went out to the barn after lunch. The place where I'd poured water for the swallows was dry; I hadn't seen them come back. The barn was dark and still, no air moving despite the open doors and windows. Notes was standing up eating his soaked hay, but I could hear the rapid pace of his breathing. Otter was napping with his head in the corner and a hind-leg cocked, bits of straw in his tail from having lain down earlier. Grace and Sassy were sleeping too. Their flanks were already dark with sweat despite the box fans in every stall that were always on those days. I refilled the water buckets then crushed Notes' Albuterol pills and mixed them with his Ventipulmin in a syringe. Otter woke up at the sound of the feed room door so I grabbed mints from the bag and gave him one. Notes came to the front of his stall and nickered. His nicker was an unbearable choking noise. His eyes looked bright though, glinting out from his thick forelock, his small, sculpted ears alert. I fed him a mint and his lips were damp and green from the hay, leaving slime on my palms.

He was used to the routine and allowed me to hold his head with an arm over his neck and squeeze the medicine into his mouth. I could feel the strain of his breathing through his whole body and he was drenched in sweat underneath his heavy mane. We'd clipped his coat twice already that summer, Mom did it in the spring and then I clipped him again in June since his hair was so thick, but he sweated and labored anyway. In that moment I felt suddenly desperate, as if all summer I'd been telling myself he was dying but didn't see it until then. It wasn't a decision, not really, I just grabbed scissors from the shelf and began to cut his mane off in chunks, twisting bunches of it in my fists and letting them fall to the ground. Otter watched us over his stall door and chewed his hay in tense, intermittent bites. Notes didn't move, just stood with his head low, looking out from behind that long white forelock. I cut that too.

257

I fetched the electric clippers from the cabinet, unwound the cord, and knelt down next to him, feeling the cool of the concrete spread up through my knees. I started between his ears and ran the clippers down the crest of his neck in one long stroke, watching the jagged tufts of hair pour off. I clipped more slowly down each side, evening out the edges, meticulously, my free hand over his neck and pulling him closer to me as I shore off the remains of his forelock, carefully moving between his ears and following the swirl of a cowlick. When I was finished, Notes' skin showed black and dusty through the stubble.

I sat back on my heels. Notes turned and nosed my hand for a treat and I gave him another mint. The roached mane did not flatter his thin neck. You know, he was actually only about twenty, but he looked so old and sick. I don't know what could have happened to make him that way. His grey coat was dingy and yellow from sweat and dust. I took him outside to the water pump, Otter watching us suspiciously, and washed him, spending a long time with my fingertips working suds into his coat and tail until he was clean. The swallows swooped and chattered in the sunlight as I worked. The medication had kicked in and Notes was breathing a little more freely when I put him back inside. I swept up the hair and threw it away.

I didn't even bother checking the mailbox that afternoon. I think my parents were used to me doing it because they asked me where the mail was but I just answered *Notes is bad today* and they forgot about the mail. I wish I'd added *we should do it tomorrow*, but I knew they'd realize that themselves. I heard them in the kitchen after dinner talking about him and they both came out to the barn that evening to help me feed and turn the horses out. They commented on how clean he was but didn't mention the haircut. He was clean; he glowed in the dim, late-evening light walking across the pasture with Otter shadowing his steps. As I washed my own hair that night, I thought that Otter should be with him when we put him down, and that you weren't going to write back.

Notes died sometime that night. We found him not far from the barn, in the spot where he and Otter always stood. His body looked very small. Otter was still next to him and wouldn't come to the gate, but when I took him in on a lead he didn't protest. Dad called a friend with a backhoe and they buried him on the edge of the field behind the house, by the woods, with two of Dad's old foxhunters and my first pony. I stayed in the barn while they did, watching Otter chew hay and feeding him mints. I didn't cry until Dad came back with a banded lock of Notes' tail he'd saved, and I thought about the feel of his mane in my fists as I cut it. Otter was quiet all day but when he went back out at night, he whinnied once and looked back toward the barn as if waiting.

The next day, it finally rained, one of those wicked summer storms that can only come after weeks of relentless heat. The worse the weather, the bigger the snap, and this one broke with a rare violence. We could feel it coming, all morning the air crackled and the swallows were nowhere to be found. It finally came early afternoon, like something out of an ancient mythology. It was then that I realized I'd done nothing all summer but wait for rain, that I hadn't done a single deliberate thing. The electricity went out and we watched from the house as waves of rain swept through like fists, wind bowed the trees, and the sky flared a sick, tornado green in the distance. When it was over, I turned the horses out and they went like new colts, all high-kneed and quivering. Grace dropped right to her knees to roll, then ran off bucking and nipping at Sassy's flank. Otter sniffed the ground where Notes had lain, then trotted off after the mares.

The storm brought down trees all over the place. Dad and I were at the end of the driveway clearing branches a few days later when the mailman brought your letter. I took the bundle from the mailbox and rifled through it and when I saw my name in your handwriting, I didn't know what to do anymore. You'd decided to have your say after all, but I'd stopped waiting. Dad asked if there was any interesting mail and I answered *Nothing*. The swallows flitted from the wire one by one as I walked back up the drive to the house, my back sticky with sweat and your letter tucked between other envelopes in my hand. I wondered when you had sent it and why it took too long to arrive.

Briefly, I held the envelope over the trashcan, but that felt too impulsive. Instead, I put it in the bottom drawer of my desk, under some old school papers. Notes' tail was still on my dresser and I didn't know what to do with that either, so I put it in the drawer as well.

I just wanted you to know, that's what I did.

MADAME BOVARY'S GREYHOUND

fiction by KAREN RUSSELL

I. FIRST LOVE

They took walks to the beech grove at Banneville, near the abandoned pavilion. Foxglove and gillyflowers, beige lichen growing in one thick, crawling curtain around the socketed windows. Moths blinked wings at them, crescents of blue and red and tiger-yellow, like eyes caught in a net.

Emma sat and poked at the grass with the skeletal end of her parasol, as if she were trying to blind each blade.

"Oh, *why* did I ever get married?" she moaned aloud, again and again.

The greyhound whined with her, distressed by her distress. Sometimes, in a traitorous fugue, the dog forgot to be unhappy and ran off to chase purple butterflies or murder shrew mice, or to piss a joyful stream onto the topiaries. But generally, if her mistress was crying, so was the puppy. Her name was Djali, and she had been a gift from the young woman's husband, Dr. Charles Bovary.

Emma wept harder as the year grew older and the temperature dropped, folding herself into the white monotony of trees, leaning further and further into the bare trunks. The dog would stand on her hind legs and lick at the snow that fused Emma's shoulders to the coarse wood, as if trying to loosen a hardening glue, and the whole forest would quiver and groan together in sympathy with the woman, and her phantom lovers, and Djali.

At Banneville the wind came directly from the sea, and covered the

260

couple in a blue-salt caul. The greyhound loved most when she and Emma were outside like this, bound by the membrane of a gale. Yet as sunset fell Djali became infected again by her woman's nameless terrors. Orange and red, they seemed to sweat out of the wood. The dog smelled nothing alarming, but love stripped her immunity to the internal weathers of Emma Bovary.

The blood-red haze switched to a silvery blue light, and Emma shuddered all at once, as if in response to some thicketed danger. They returned to Tostes along the highway.

The greyhound was ignorant of many things. She had no idea, for example, that she was a greyhound. She didn't know that her breed had originated in southern Italy, an ancient pet in Pompeii, a favorite of the thin-nosed English lords and ladies, or that she was perceived to be affectionate, intelligent, and loyal. What she did know, with a whole-body thrill, was the music of her woman coming up the walk, the dizzying explosion of perfume as the door swung wide. She knew when her mistress was pleased with her, and that approval was the fulcrum of her happiness.

"Viscount! Viscount!" Emma whimpered in her sleep. (Rodolphe would come onto the scene later, after the greyhound's flight, and poor Charlie B. never once featured in his wife's unconscious theater.) Then Djali would stand and pace stiff-legged through the cracked bowl of the cold room into which her mistress's dreams were leaking, peering with pricked ears into shadows. It was a strange accordion that linked the woman and the dog: Vaporous drafts caused their pink and gray bellies to clutch inward at the same instant. Moods blew from one mind to the other, delight and melancholy. In the blue atmosphere of the bedroom, the two were very nearly (but never quite) one creature.

Even asleep, the little greyhound trailed after her madame, through a weave of green stars and gas lamps, along the boulevards of Paris. It was a conjured city that no native would recognize—Emma Bovary's head on the pillow, its architect. Her Paris was assembled from a guidebook with an out-of-date map, and from the novels of Balzac and Sand, and from her vividly disordered recollections of the viscount's ball at La Vaubyessard, with its odor of dying flowers, burning flambeaux, and truffles. (Many neighborhoods within the city's quivering boundaries, curiously enough, smelled identical to the viscount's dining room.) A rose and gold glow obscured the storefront windows, and cathedral bells tolled continuously as they strolled past the same four landmarks: a tremulous bridge over the roaring Seine, a vanilla-white dress shop, the vague facade of the opera house—overlaid in more gold light—and the crude stencil of a theater. All night they walked like that, companions in Emma's phantasmal labyrinth, suspended by her hopeful mists, and each dawn the dog would wake to the second Madame Bovary, the lightly snoring woman on the mattress, her eyes still hidden beneath a peacock sleep mask. Lumped in the coverlet, Charles's blocky legs tangled around her in an apprehensive pretzel, a doomed attempt to hold her in their marriage bed.

II. A CHANGE OF HEART

Is there any love as tireless as a dog's in search of its master? Whenever Emma was off shopping for nougat in the market, or visiting God in the churchyard, Djali was stricken by the madness of her absence. The dog's futile hunt through the house turned her maniacal, cannibalistic: She scratched her fur until it became wet and dark. She paced the halls, pausing only to gnaw at her front paws. Félicité, the Bovarys' frightened housekeeper, was forced to imprison her in a closet with a water dish.

The dog's change of heart began in September, some weeks after Madame Bovary's return from La Vaubyessard, where she'd dervished around in another man's arms and given up forever on the project of loving Charles. It is tempting to conclude that Emma somehow transmitted her wanderlust to Djali; but perhaps this is a sentimental impulse, a storyteller's desire to sync two flickering hearts.

One day Emma's scents began to stabilize. Her fragrance became musty, ordinary, melting into the house's stale atmosphere until the woman was nearly invisible to the animal. Djali licked almond talc from Emma's finger-webbing. She bucked her head under the madame's hand a dozen times, waiting for the old passion to seize her, yet her brain was uninflamed. The hand had become generic pressure, damp heat. No joy snowed out of it as Emma mechanically stroked between Djali's ears, her gold wedding band rubbing a raw spot into the fur, branding the dog with her distraction. There in the bedroom, together and alone, they watched the rain fall.

By late February, at the same time Charles Bovary was dosing his young wife with valerian, the dog began refusing her mutton chops. Emma stopped checking her gaunt face in mirrors, let dead flies swim in the blue glass vases. The dog neglected to bark at her red-winged nemesis, the rooster. Emma quit playing the piano. The dog lost her zest for woodland homicide. Under glassy bathwater, Emma's bare body as still and bright as quartz in a quarry, she let the hours fill her nostrils with the terrible serenity of a drowned woman. Her gossamer fingers circled her navel, seeking an escape. Fleas held wild circuses on Djali's ass as she lay motionless before the fire for the duration of two enormous logs, unable to summon the energy to spin a hind leg in protest. Her ears collapsed against her skull.

Charles rubbed his hand greedily between Emma's legs and she swatted him off; Emma stroked the dog's neck and Djali went stiff, slid out of reach. Both woman and animal, according to the baffled Dr. Bovary, seemed bewitched by sadness.

This strain of virulent misery, this falling out of love, caused different symptoms, unique disruptions, in dogs and humans.

The greyhound, for example, shat everywhere.

Whereas Emma shopped for fabrics in the town.

On the fifth week of the dog's fall, Charles lifted the bed skirt and discovered the greyhound panting up at him with a dead-eyed calm. He'd been expecting to find his favorite tall socks, blue wool ineptly darned for him by Emma. He screamed.

"Emma! What do you call your little bitch again? There is something the matter with it!"

"Djali," Emma murmured from the mattress. And the dog, helplessly bound to her owner's voice—if not still in love with Madame Bovary, at least indentured to the ghost of her love—rose and licked the lady's bare feet.

"Good girl," sighed Emma.

The animal's dry tongue lolled out of her mouth. Inside her body, a foreboding was hardening into a fact. There was no halting the transformation of her devotion into a nothing.

III. WHAT IF?

"If you do not stop making poop in the salon," Félicité growled at the puppy, "I will no longer feed you."

In the sixth month of her life in Tostes, the dog lay glumly on the floor, her pink belly tippled orange by the grated flames, fatally bored. Emma entered the bedroom, and the animal lifted her head from between her tiny polished claws, let it drop again.

"If only I could be you," Emma lamented. "There's no trouble or sorrow in *your* life!" And she soothed the dog in a gurgling monotone, as if she were addressing herself.

Dr. Charles Bovary returned home, whistling after another successful day of leeches and bloodletting in the countryside, to a house of malcontent females:

Emma was stacking a pyramid of greengage plums.

The little greyhound was licking her genitals.

Soon the coarse, unchanging weave of the rug in Emma's bedroom became unbearable. The dog's mind filled with smells that had no origin, sounds that arose from no friction. Unreal expanses. She closed her eyes and stepped cautiously through tall purple grass she'd never seen before in her life.

She wondered if there might not have been some other way, through a different set of circumstances, of meeting another woman; and she tried to imagine those events that had not happened, that shadow life. Her owner might have been a bloody-smocked man, a baritone, a butcher with bags of bones always hidden in his pockets. Or perhaps a child, the butcher's daughter, say, a pork chop–scented girl who loved to throw sticks. Djali had observed a flatulent Malamute trailing his old man in the park, each animal besotted with the other. Blue poodles, inbred and fat, smugly certain of their women's adoration. She'd seen a balding Pomeranian riding high in a toy wagon, doted on by the son of a king. Not all humans were like Emma Bovary.

Out of habit, she howled her old courtship song at Emma's feet, and Emma reached down distractedly, gave the dog's ears a stiff brushing. She was seated before her bedroom vanity, cross-examining a pimple, very preoccupied, for at four o'clock Monsieur Roualt was coming for biscuits and judgment and jelly.

A dog's love is forever. We expect infidelity from one another; we marvel at this one's ability to hold that one's interest for fifty, sixty years; perhaps some of us feel a secret contempt for monogamy even as we extol it, wishing parole for its weary participants. But dogs do not receive our sympathy or our suspicion—from dogs we presume an eternal adoration.

In the strange case of Madame Bovary's greyhound, however, "forever" was a tensed muscle that began to shake. During the Christmas holidays, she had daily seizures before the fireplace, chattering in the red light like a loose tooth. Loyalty was a posture she could no longer hold.

Meanwhile, Emma had become pregnant.

The Bovarys were preparing to move.

On one of the last of her afternoons in Tostes, the dog ceased trembling and looked around. Beyond the cabbage rows, the green grasses waved endlessly away from her, beckoning her. She stretched her hind legs. A terrible itching spread through every molecule of her body, and the last threads of love slipped like a noose from her neck. Nothing owned her anymore. Rolling, moaning, belly to the red sun, she dug her spine into the hill.

"Oh, dear," mumbled the coachman, Monsieur Hivert, watching the dog from the yard. "Something seems to be attacking your greyhound, madame. Bees, I'd wager."

"Djali!" chided Emma, embarrassed that a pet of hers should behave so poorly before the gentlemen. "My goodness! You look possessed!"

IV. FREEDOM

On the way to Yonville, the greyhound wandered fifty yards from the Bovarys' stagecoach. Then she broke into a run.

"Djaliiiii!" Emma shrieked, uncorking a spray of champagne-yellow birds from the nearby poplars. "*Stay!*"

Weightlessly the dog entered the forest.

"Stay! Stay! Stay!" the humans called after her, their directives like bullets missing their target. Her former mistress, the screaming woman, was a stranger. And the greyhound lunged forward, riding the shoals of her own green-flecked shadow.

In the late afternoon she paused to drink water from large cups in the mossy roots of unfamiliar trees. She was miles from her old life. Herons sailed over her head, their broad wings flat as palms, stroking her from scalp to tail at an immense distance—a remote benediction— and the dog's mind became empty and smooth. Skies rolled through her chest; her small rib cage and her iron-gray pelt enclosed a blue without limit. She was free.

From a hilltop near a riverbank, through an azure mist, she spotted two creatures with sizzling faces clawing into the water. Cats larger than any she'd ever seen, spear-shouldered and casually savage. Lynxes, a mated pair. Far north for this season. They were three times the size of the Bovarys' barn cat yet bore the same taunting anatomy. Analogous golden eyes. They feasted on some prey that looked of another world— flat, thrashing lives they swallowed whole.

Gazehound, huntress—the dog began to remember what she'd been before she was born.

Winter was still raking its white talons across the forest; spring was delayed that year. Fleshless fingers for tree branches. Not a blade or bud of green yet. The dog sought shelter, but shelter was only physical this far out, always inhuman. Nothing like the soft-bodied sanctuary she'd left behind.

One night the greyhound was caught out in unknown territory, a cold valley many miles from the river. Stars appeared, and she felt a light sprinkling of panic. Now the owls were awake. Pale hunger came shining out of their beaks, looping above their flaming heads like ropes. In Tostes their hooting had sounded like laughter in the trees. But here, with no bedroom rafters to protect her, she watched the boughs blow apart to reveal nocturnal eyes bulging from their recesses like lemons; she heard hollow mouths emitting strange songs. Death's rattle, old wind without home or origin, rode the frequencies above her.

A concentrated darkness screeched and dove near her head, and then another, and then the dog began to run. Dawn was six hours away.

She pushed from the valley floor toward higher ground, eventually finding a narrow fissure in the limestone cliffs. She trotted into the blackness like a small key entering a tall lock. Once inside she was struck by a familiar smell, which confused and upset her. Backlit by the moon, her flat, pointed skull and tucked abdomen cast a hieroglyphic silhouette against the wavy wall.

The greyhound spent the next few days exploring her new home. The soil here was like a great cold nose—wet, breathing, yielding. To eat, she had to hunt the vast network of hollows for red squirrels, voles. A spiderweb of bone and fur soon wove itself in the cave's shadows, where she dragged her kills. When she'd lived with the Bovarys, in the early days of their courtship, Emma would let the puppy lick yellow yolks and golden sugar from the flat of a soft palm.

Undeliberate, absolved of rue and intent, the dog continued to forget Madame Bovary.

Gnawing on a femur near the river one afternoon, she bristled and turned. A deer's head was watching her thoughtfully from the silver rushes—separated, by some incommunicable misfortune, from its body. Its neck terminated in a chaos of crawling blackflies, a spill of jeweled rot like boiling cranberries. Its tongue hung limp like a flag of surrender. Insects were eating an osseous cap between the buck's yellow ears, a white knob the diameter of a sand dollar. A low, bad feeling drove the dog away.

V. REGRET

Regret, as experienced by the dog, was physical, kinetic—she turned in circles and doubled back, trying to uncover the scent of her home. She felt feverish. Some organ had never stopped its useless secretions, even without an Emma to provoke them. Hearth and leash, harsh voice, mutton chop, affectionate thump—she wanted all this again.

There was a day when she passed near the town of Airaines, a mere nine miles from the Bovarys' new residence in Yonville; and had the winds changed at that particular moment and carried a certain woman's lilac-scented sweat to her, this story might have had a very different ending.

One midnight, just after the late April thaw, the dog woke to the sight of a large wolf standing in the cave mouth, nakedly weighing her as prey. And even under that crushing stare she did not cower; rather, she felt elevated, vibrating with some primitive species of admiration for this more pure being, solitary and wholly itself. The wolf swelled with appetites that were ancient, straightforward—a stellar hunger that was satisfied nightly. An old wound sparkled under a brittle scabbard on its left shoulder, and a young boar's blood ran in torrents from its magnificent jaws. The greyhound's tail began to wag as if cabled to some current; a growl rose midway up her throat. The predator then turned away from her. Panting—*ha-ha-ha*—it licked green slime from the cave wall, crunching the spires of tiny amber snails. The wolf glanced once more around the chasm before springing eastward. Dawn lumbered after, through the pointed firs, unholstering the sun, unable to shoot; and the wind began to howl, as if in lamentation, calling the beast back.

Caught between two equally invalid ways of life, the greyhound whimpered herself toward sleep, unaware that in Yonville Emma Bovary was drinking vinegar in black stockings and sobbing at the exact same pitch. Each had forgotten entirely about the other, yet they retained the same peculiar vacancies within their bodies and suffered the same dread-filled dreams. Love had returned, and it went spoiling through them with no outlet.

In summer the dog crossed a final frontier, eating the greasy liver of a murdered bear in the wide open. The big female had been gut-shot

for sport by teenage brothers from Rouen, who'd then been too terrified by the creature's drunken, hauntingly prolonged death throes to
wait and watch her ebb out. In a last pitch she'd crashed down a column
of saplings, her muzzle frothing with red foam. The greyhound was no
scavenger by nature, until nature made her one that afternoon. The
three cubs squatted on a log like a felled totem and watched with grave
maroon eyes, their orphan hearts pounding in unison.

Still, it would be incorrect to claim that the greyhound was now feral,
or fully ingrained in these woods. As a fugitive the dog was a passable
success, but as a dog she was a blown spore, drifting everywhere and
nowhere, unable to cure her need for a human, or her terror at the
insufficiency of her single body.

"Our destinies are united now, aren't they?" whispered Rodolphe
near the evaporating blue lake, in a forest outside of Yonville that might
as well have been centuries distant. Crows deluged the sky. Emma sat
on a rock, flushed red from the long ride, pushing damp woodchips
around with her boot toe. The horses munched leaves in a chorus as
Rodolphe lifted her skirts, the whole world rustling with hungers.

In the cave, the dog had a strange dream.

A long, lingering, indistinct cry came from one of the hills far beyond
the forest; it mingled with Emma's silence like music.

VI. A BREAK

The dog shivered. She'd been shivering ceaselessly for how many days
and nights now? All the magic of those early weeks had vanished, replaced by a dreary and devoted pain. Winter rose out of her own cavi-
ties. It shivered her.

Troubled by the soreness that had entered her muscles, she trotted
out of the cave and toward the muddy escarpment where she'd buried
a cache of weasel bones. Rain had eroded the path, and in her eagerness
to escape her own failing frame, the mute ruminations of her throbbing
skeleton, the dog began to run at full bore. Then she was sliding on the
mud, her claws scrabbling uselessly at the smooth surface; unable to
recover her balance, the greyhound tumbled into a ravine.

An irony:

She had broken her leg.

All at once Emma Bovary's final command came echoing through
her: *Stay.*

Sunset jumped above her, so very far above her twisted body, like a heart skipping beats. Blood ran in her eyes. The trees all around swam. She sank further into a soggy pile of dead leaves as the squealing voices of the blackflies rose in clouds.

Elsewhere in the world, Rodolphe Boulanger sat at his writing desk under the impressive head of a trophy stag. Two fat candles were guttering down. He let their dying light flatter him into melancholy—a feeling quite literary. The note before him would end his love affair with Emma.

How shall I sign it? "Devotedly"? No . . . "Your friend"?

The moon, dark red and perfectly round, rose over the horizon.

Deep in the trench, nostalgias swamped the greyhound in the form of olfactory hallucinations: snowflakes, rising yeast, scooped pumpkin flesh, shoe polish, horse-lathered leather, roasting venison, the explosion of a woman's perfume.

She was dying.

She buried her nose in the litterfall, stifling these visions until they ebbed and faded.

It just so happened that a game warden was wandering in that part of the woods, hours later or maybe days. Something in the ravine caught his eye—low to the ground, a flash of unexpected silver. He dropped to his knees for a closer look.

"Oh!" he gasped, calloused hands parting the dead leaves.

VII. THE TWO HUBERTS

The greyhound lived with the game warden, in a cottage at the edge of a town. He was not a particularly creative man, and he gave the dog his same name: Hubert. He treated her wounds as those of a human child, with poultices and bandages. She slept curled at the foot of his bed and woke each morning to the new green of a million spring buds erupting out of logs, sky-blue birdsong, minced chlorophyll.

"Bonjour, Hubert!" Hubert would call, sending himself into hysterics, and Hubert the dog would bound into his arms—and their love was like this, a joke that never grew old. And like this they passed five years.

Early one December evening Hubert accompanied Hubert to Yonville, to say a prayer over the grave of his mother. The snow hid the tombstones, and only the most stalwart mourners came out for such a grim treasure hunt. Among them was Emma Bovary. From within

269

her hooded crimson cloak she noticed a shape darting between the snowflakes—a gray ghost trotting with its lips peeled back from black gums.

"Oh!" she cried. "How precious you are! Come here—"

Her whistle crashed through the dog's chest, splintering into antipodal desires:

Run.

Stay.

And it was here, at the margin of instinct and rebellion, that the dog encountered herself, felt a shimmering precursor to consciousness— the same stirring that lifted the iron hairs on her neck whenever she peered into mirrors, or discovered a small, odorless dog inside a lake. Suddenly, impossibly, she *did* remember: Midnight in Tostes. The walks through the ruined pavilion. Crows at dusk. The tug of a leather leash. Piano music. Egg yolk in a perfumed hand. Sad, impatient fingers scratching her ears.

Something bubbled and broke inside the creature's heart.

Emma was walking through the thick snow, toward the oblivious game warden, one golden strand of hair loose and blowing in the twilight.

"Oh, monsieur! I, too, once had a greyhound!" She shut her eyes and sighed longingly, as if straining to call back not only the memory but the dog herself.

And she very nearly succeeded.

The greyhound's tail began helplessly to wag.

"Her name was Deeeaaaa . . . Dahhh . . ."

And then the dog remembered, too, calloused hands brushing dead leaves from her fur, clearing the seams of blackflies from her eyelids and nostrils, lifting her from the trench. Their fine, sturdy bones clasped firmly around her belly as she flew through evening air. The rank, tuberlike scent enveloping her, the firelight in the eyes of her rescuer. Over his shoulder she'd glimpsed the shallow imprint of a dog's body in the mud.

With a lovely, amnesiac smile, Emma Bovary continued to fail to remember the name of her greyhound. And each soft sound she mouthed tugged the dog deeper into the past.

It was an impossible moment, and the pain the animal experienced— staring from old, rumpled Hubert to the absorbing, evanescing Emma— did feel very much like an ax falling through her snow-wet fur, splitting down the rail of her tingling spine, fatally dividing her.

"My dog's name is Hubert," Hubert said to Madame Bovary, with his stupid frankness. He glanced fondly at little Hubert, attributing the greyhound's spasms in the cemetery drifts to the usual culprits: giddiness or fleas.

Writhing in an agony, the dog rose to her feet. She closed the small, incredibly cold gulf of snow between herself and her master.

"Sit," she then commanded herself, and she obeyed.

THE EPICUREAN

fiction by LOUIS B. JONES

Whenever Candace Roan called me during the day (I was a construction laborer in that year while I planned to go back to school; and I
existed in a state of constant romantic expectation, waiting for the ringing of a phone inside a foreman's trailer out on a job site somewhere,
and for the foreman to emerge holding the cordless phone saying *It's
for you*, begrudgingly), we would meet in her condominium above
Highway 101, to eat one of her artfully cooked dinners, as prelude,
while the steady river of freeway traffic below provided a kind of moral
white-noise curtain I associate with that decade, when all the world
seemed newcomers to California, all our souls bathed in a million head-
lights' combined glamour. She always sent me home before I might
possibly fall asleep in her bed—she had a long drive herself, back to
the Sunnyvale house where she lived—but for a while we would lie
together and talk and—on this particular occasion—eat pears and
grapes from a bedside bowl. I was ten years younger than she was. She
worked during the day as a lawyer at a multinational accounting firm,
wearing suits that repelled touch, but inwardly she was nagged by a
talent for pleasure, captivating to herself. That was how I constructed
her in my own mind. The truth is, I never did understand her, and still
don't today: what put that light in her eye; what motivated her to shop
for the ingredients and the fresh flowers and drive all the way up from
Sunnyvale alone, and light the candles; or what she saw in me at all.
Now I'm past her age at that time, and at least I know enough to see
now how mysterious it all was, our appearances for each other, or for
ourselves, every so often in that condominium borrowed from her cor-

poration, white-carpeted, with window shades of hanging vertical plastic slats, a dining room table of glass. Beginning at dusk above the rivers of rush hour, with the choice of wine or the revelation of sherbet, concluding with talk against the bedstead among shifting dunes of our embraces in repose, the whole evening would elapse in wonderments—for example, I had never eaten an artichoke—until the end when I lay in bed beside her listening to her stories of daily events around her office. I felt large and happy and useful, eating grapes. She used to say this debauchery (as she called it) was a temporary stage her pilgrim soul was going through while she was newly divorced and still young enough, and she used a theological adjective for it, "Kierkegaardian." I'd known her when she was Candy Pfleger in our youth in Illinois; our families were members of the same church; she sang in the choir while I was a Sunday-school student, far beneath her notice then; Candy Pfleger was just as far above my notice; she made almost no impression in my memory. Then her family moved away to Cedar Rapids, Iowa.

Now out here in California, reincarnated for a time in a version of an inconsequential paradise, the most fantastic scandal, to me, about Candace Roan was that she had studied seriously to be a nun. A real Dominican nun. She had actually been in a convent. One night while we took bites of fruit and sipped sweet dessert wine in a shared snifter, she told me a story of something that happened during the year when she was on the brink of taking her vows. I had been teasing her about what a wonderful cliché it was, that a nun should disguise a sexpot, who, as on a night of full moon, at last scaled the high wall and got out on the streets and never looked back, devoting herself to sin. It provoked this response: she drew a breath and held it, thinking about whether or not to speak, and then she told me that she had once done something . . . evil. That pause was there. Evil is a simplistic or melodramatic idea, probably seldom useful in application, and she arrived at the word with some self-amazement, and some confusion, reluctant to settle such a stole around her own shoulders, her at-that-moment naked shoulders.

It was during her time in a San Francisco convent. To narrate, she took back her leg and her arms and sat up against the bedstead, and bowed her head to focus on the past, holding in both hands our misty glass snifter of wine. I saw I wouldn't get another sip. She was taking possession of it as storyteller rather formally. She said, first of all, nuns are not necessarily innocent in any special sense of the word: a convent is just another human institution, and those high walls of dirty yellow brick (on Geary Boulevard, beyond the big red Gap Superstore) enclose a society like any other, just as liable to meanness or injustice, politics or subterfuge, wit or pleasure or irony. Indeed, some of those women are very sharp and couldn't possibly dedicate themselves to "innocence," in any simple understanding. Innocence—she tagged the tip of my nose with a green grape, making me blink—is *mysteriously* distributed, both low and high in Creation. She certainly didn't think of herself as naïve, when she first arrived at the Convent of the Blessed Virgin Mary—an Iowa girl in San Francisco, doing three years of service in the world before her novitiate. Twenty-two was an age she considered replete. She had lived a full, happy, hedonistic life as a modern girl on a modern college campus. In Cedar Rapids all the usual versions of sin can be found: smoking marijuana in a dorm room, envying her friends' beauty or money, letting herself be taken to burlesque clubs on the Coralville strip, drinking Singapore Slings and sniffing lines of cocaine in a condominium swimming pool complex with a lonely older man, a man too old for such folly, a man who feels he has nothing at stake in his life; and among her girlfriends the pleasures of the dark heart, like malicious gossip or frankly revealing clothes or, for a while, systematically hurting the feelings of a rich handsome selfish Chicago boy. Everything. The whole world is right there in Iowa, the same satisfactions of vanity. And of course, as everywhere, the several possible sexual contortions. She'd been, during a time of early discovery, the sensualist that commercial culture urges girls to be—or at least she'd tried her best to be—though she couldn't help feeling secretly that, honestly, for women sex wasn't the great mind-emptying solution it seemed to be for men. In taking the chastity vow, she'd felt the most difficult trial would be, not to deprive herself of pleasure, but to deprive herself of children. She had come from a good family. She had had a warm, confiding relationship with her father, cut off by his too-early death. Also, she loved men, men in general, she loved being around maleness, which a number of nuns did not: a surprising number of nuns had had terrible early experiences. Perhaps her own men tended to be outside the norm, a bit thoughtful or impractical, or sad, or sensitive, rather than the louder, simpler, more aggressive type of male norm, whose nature seems imbued with a mysterious essential wrath, and whom she found herself steering clear of. They were fine. They were for other women.

I loved this aspect of Candace Roan's present day epicureanism, that she'd been dedicated to austerity once. What I wanted to know was, why did she enter the convent in the first place? What was it about her personality? She thought maybe what was different about her (if any-thing was "different" about her!) was that she had an irrepressible tendency to consider the long-term consequences of deeds, the conse-quences of people's lives. Even in the midst of pleasure's physical drama—as a girl in a Coralville, Iowa, motel room, or in the backseat of her traveling textbook salesman's car—she would find herself watch-ing from above, as an out-of-body experience, and she pitied the strug-gle itself. Even at the supreme sexual moment, that fish-out-of-water moment, she saw the clinging soul as pounded away into an abyss. It amounted to a betrayal, *her* betrayal, of that already unhappy man, the traveling college-textbook salesman with the Springsteen tickets and the cocaine, who by his joviality always kept her at a distance. Having once pictured the sex-act that way, she couldn't shake it, the picture of his spiritual death at her lips. The word "sin" is too clumsy; the reality it tries to capture is subtle and fluid. To use the word was to handle one of the mysterious old chalices. (She looked up from the half-full snifter directly into my eyes and she said, "You won't understand this; but even to practice law is a perfect, masterful kind of sin. I mean, strictly in pure New Testament terms. As a lawyer I'm," she lifted her elbows beslimed, "deep in terrible sin and iniquity in the world. Sin is just the most . . . fantastic thing!") Her family hadn't been Catholic. On all sides for gen-erations they were liberal Congregationalists who had no metaphysical interests. This religion was to her such an old museum, enshrining so many barbaric dioramas, so many traditional errors and lurid lights— to navigate its dark corridors required, of a modern girl, an openness to unprejudiced thought, as well as a personal, private, interpretive creativity, plenty of constant self-interrogation. She believed at twenty-two, when she came to the San Francisco convent, that she would be able to reconcile, within herself, all the paradoxes and fond hypocrisies, such as, for example, the glowing arrogance that furnished the spine of "humility"; the crazy *vengefulness* in good works, visible in some of the nuns; the men's politics in the Vatican, even the whole religion's his-torical origin in a sensationalized Galilean rumor as hysterical and du-bious as Elvis sightings. She had always seen all those problems, with perfect clarity. They were a part of *the world*. That is, they would be a part of any possible world.

But preserving a kind of "innocence" was exactly a Sister's main job too, preserving a kind of original integrity. There really is such a thing as "sin" moving in the world, beginning only as a shadowy whorl in the heart, but these little whorls result in real actions and events, the great weather-systems of envy and gluttony and sexiness we live in the midst of, and feel so unhappy inside of. When she first arrived in San Francisco she often found herself driving past the great bath houses and pleasure clubs—one on Market Street in a building whose glass door had torn-off corners of old posters Scotch-taped to its surface (a detail that always struck her as emotionally moving); another on Folsom in an ornate brick warehouse with arches like an ancient stadium, looking prosperous and Byzantine even in these latter days of the great venereal plague—and she could imagine in general what took place inside. Men in a state of loneliness—in a state of spiritual solitude in the midst of the crowd—inhaled or swallowed enough chemicals to numb themselves against knowledge or remembrance, and then, by rubbing, erased the soul. The moment of erasure, itself, was ecstasy, the ultimate. All else—at their jobs, or in their schools, or at home—they experienced as boredom, boredom their wives, boredom their children, boredom the newborn day, boredom the starry sky, boredom.

And it wasn't only the fun-seekers. They were the mere victims. She could also drive past the palaces of the rich, on San Francisco's hills, where lived the people she worked for today, guarding their money at the office of Gartner Sachs Boldon. But when she was twenty-two, she had located sin outside her own soul. And then one night, as she put it, God frightened her. In her bed at the convent one midnight, she had a dream, in which she was personally present at the Crucifixion—she was there in Jerusalem in the crush of the crowd—it was a cloudy, sweaty day on a muddy hill, and she was aware of perspiration inside her dress—and immediately she could see, first-hand, what had always been obvious but was never discussed: that it was exciting. That she wanted this. Our Lord, pinned back, had thrown aside his head to bare his throat, and he lengthened his belly and pushed his hip forward beneath the ragged cloth and the leverage-motion of a man's hips was something one recognizes in an instant. It was always so obvious. It hung above every altar. It was pleasure, this pain, and she herself, in the crowd on that stormy hill where black clouds swelled in the sky, was so excited her throat closed on itself, in the wish for the legionnaire's spear to tap again at the breast and make the hips lift harder.

Well, this was disturbing. It wasn't a nightmare at all, it was a dream of temptation. When she awoke, it was still there. It wouldn't go away. She set forth to spend a day inside the convent dwelling on the possibility that she was unworthy of any vocation—moving through her prayers and offices and classes, trying to be invisible along the convent's walls.

Cleaning was what they did a lot of at the San Francisco BVM, a Dominican sister-convent to the Dubuque convent, cleaning for its own sake, in fourteen bathrooms with thirty-three toilet bowls distributed among three buildings. The work did bring a satisfaction to the worker on her knees after, say, a theology class in which her own brilliancy was exalted even above the quaint doctrines of the Church Fathers. The polishing of an old white hexagonal-tile floor made, on earth, a luster for a background, the better for God to observe the see-through soul, the soul of one asking to serve, the soul of one asking for simplicity. The chapel she felt unworthy to enter now, with this dream. But there were regular prayers and offices and meditations during the day; they were all unavoidable; she went in with downcast eyes, so dishonest her faith had always been. On the crucifixes of the altars, out here always more Hispanically lurid than Iowa crucifixes, the abdominal muscles were defined like rope-braids and the nipples explicitly pointed. She was in a kind of hell, in Augustinian terms: her natural sin, vanity, fixed her real distance from God.

But as the day went on, Freud had already saved her soul. Her undergraduate major had been pre-law, a choice made in remembrance of her father, who had had a law practice in Cedar Rapids before he died. But even for a pre-law student, it's hard to get through a modern liberal education without some exposure to psychoanalytic theory. It's modern knowledge: every possible perversion swims and evolves in the dark undersea we all contain. She was being warned. She'd seen herself as a simple thing. In driving past the late-night clubs of San Francisco, she'd believed she was giving little thought to what went on among the lost souls. But clearly her subconscious mind had considered it, in artistic detail. "The abyss" is in the convent, too. It's everywhere. It's in her bed where she lies down. Obedience and poverty are easy; chastity is a vow most mysteriously complicated. In the Dubuque BVM, everyone knew who the lesbians were, a discernible group, almost enviable, for their shared secret, and for some sophistication they affected to have, or really did have; yet Candace had thought herself—quite charitably!—*better* than some of her sisters. She had thought she knew better than they, from examination of her own soul, that lust was the sister of pride, the embrace of a mirror-image. Vanity was the effigy there worshipped. The most austere command at the summit of the Gospel was the prayer always to disregard oneself, and empty oneself, to keep winning back one's usefulness as a vessel. God must use this vessel as it is, as He created it. At last she was able to tell that other

277

human being in the confession booth behind the wooden grate, tell him that she had recognized depravity in herself, and that she had dreamed of depravity in the Savior.

Her sin was treated (by sleepy old Father Bernard, his bucktoothed lisp, his excess saliva) with a bored insouciance that was absurdly out-of-proportion—miraculously out-of-proportion—to her sense of her own monstrosity. He assigned her only the most routine penances. So that during the rest of that day, she caught herself being visited again by miscellaneous gladness, a common bird that alights everywhere. She didn't have to be told by Father Bernard, she knew for herself, that this was the beginning of a new responsibility. Her weakness would be a gift: it would make her stronger in service in the world. She applied in the office for social work, and the next day was summoned to discuss an assignment. Her undergraduate background in law would make her especially suitable for the work Sister Thomas had found for her. The convent worked with county and state agencies in providing aid for the families of inmates in prisons.

So it happened that, in the world, she met the actual man who went along with the dream. Mike happened to come along at a time when he could be a specimen of earthly love for her, as if the phenomenal world presents itself as a readily evolving hallucination whose purpose is to edify us. Candace took a sip of her dessert wine and paused in her story: once that name Mike had been spoken, her story faltered and developed a different pace, so that I myself, lying in her bed, became jealous of that name, though of course I knew I was not entitled to jealousy, a latecomer to her passion, a mere effigy (she'd used that word) in her wine-dimmed eyes, safe here in the future. His name was Mike O'Callan, and he was twenty-six—four years older than she—but to her, he would always seem younger somehow, maybe because of his wiriness and his energy-level. He and his girlfriend lived in Marin County in a bad neighborhood. People in San Francisco didn't think Marin County *had* bad neighborhoods. But there it was: a few blocks of apartment buildings of brown stucco, with lived-in-looking parking lots, where lived-in-looking cars put down roots, beyond a section of body-and-fender shops, stereo-installation places, storefront offices for wiring money to Mexico. Mike was older than Candace but blessedly immature, Irish of complexion, pale and freckled. She portrayed him as having a thatch of black hair, so black it was blue, and dark navy-blue irises and wet-looking black eyelashes, and a repressed grin of hope. He was not tall, actually a little bit shorter than Candace, but he radiated bravery. He had the springy, coiled energy of a rock-and-roll drummer. Because that's what he was. Before his prison term, he'd been a drummer for several different bands concurrently. On his release he intended to go straight back to music. He seemed shy but he wasn't; and sometimes his glance upon her lasted too long. His prison term was for manslaughter. When she first saw him, it was through the glass barrier at the Marin County Jail, while he stood listening, impatiently, to his parole officer before his release. Mike's girlfriend Rosarita, standing beside her in the waiting area, gasped softly against Candace's ear in rapture, "Muy guapo, no? Muy listo."

"Sí," said Candace, agreeing, but falling. Immediately she recognized the possibility of weakness, but she didn't censor it, she cherished it as a gift from God. Something exalted and detached in her highest soul—a faculty of infinite discrimination, almost spiritually gourmet—saw this boy's body as a test. The simple word of Rosarita's—*listo*—was obscene in Candace's ear. In Spanish it meant *ready* as a particular type of intrepid male handsomeness; and he was, definitely, all that. Yet there was suddenly, in Candace's mind, an unavoidable channel leading straight from his "readiness" to the idea of her own vulnerability.

But she was an adult, an adult of some spiritual attainments, or at least pretensions to spiritual attainment. And her bones were formed in Cedar Rapids, not this place of unwise decisions. Though she wore no habit, she knew that on this scene she faded to the background colors of the general bureaucracy. Her intention was to be useful. She picked up Blame (that was the unfortunate name of the seven-year-old girl Mike and Rosarita had adopted as a foster-child), and she pointed through the bullet-proof glass barrier and said, "Look, Blame, there's your dad!"—shifting the unexpectedly heavy girl to her hip.

Blame, who had learned skepticism too early, complained, "I don't see any space rocks."

A gift of genuine moonrocks had been promised her. Mike had claimed that the penitentiary was a very interesting place full of illustrious people, and that one of his fellow inmates during his Vacaville transfer was a former NASA engineer who owned moonrocks. He'd bring Blame a genuine moonrock from jail.

Blame was the reason Candace was here at all. The father had been Mike's brother. So Mike was an uncle to her during a period when both of Blame's parents were irresponsible. In the venereal plague that had fallen on San Francisco, both of the parents had died—having first christened her with that unhappy syllable, chosen for its mellifluousness and without regard to its meaning—so Blame was an orphan. Mike was the only one in the world she had. And he had already come to be responsible for her during the period of her parents' doomed hilarity. They expired within weeks of each other, and she became an orphan while her Uncle Mike was in prison.

Mike and Rosarita tried legally to adopt her but were denied, because Mike's murder conviction worked against him. Then they tried applying to be her foster-parents, which involves an entirely different and more lenient bureaucracy, and even though they weren't married, this effort succeeded. Rosarita was the foster-parent of record, and Mike's felony was ruled irrelevant. Candace, therefore, had come into their complicated lives as a representative of Catholic Relief, the agency that worked with the government to visit Blame regularly in her new home. Her job was to prevent the girl from reverting to the status "ward of the state." She was supposed to provide guidance and support and, minimally, interview Blame's foster-parents once a month to fill out a routine form. But frequently during the last few months, she had chosen to exceed her duty by coming over to babysit Blame and free up Rosarita, a single mother during these last months of "Michael's" prison term. (Rosarita insisted on calling him Michael, though he was utterly a Mike, from his jet-black tousled short haircut down to his canvas basketball sneakers.)

On their babysitting outings, Candace took Blame to the public library and the Discovery Museum and the Exploratorium. The child would allow herself to be led listlessly to each exhibit and stand before it with stubbornly averted eyes. Then they would visit—the one thing Blame liked—Baskin-Robbins 31 Flavors ice cream parlor, where she ate fast and hard in silence. She was a very dim-eyed little girl, but she would be beautiful, with blonde hair and dark coffee-colored skin, and high cheekbones like a Cherokee. Unfortunately, Candace had begun to notice a pattern: when she came to pick up Blame, Rosarita would be ready to leave the apartment, all dressed up in a blue brassiere, a red leather jacket, and a skirt of some elasticized material whose side-slit, when stretched against her thigh, looked like a bite ripped out. Now that Mike was getting out of prison, trouble was obviously coming. In which Candace found she felt strangely *complicitous*. And she was aware of the deep psychological question, how intentional are our accidental complicities?

When the armored door's lock was buzzed, a disgusted-looking po-
liceman held it open and Mike flew out to Rosarita and they began
kissing each other in that munching manner people learn from watching movie actors. Little Blame, standing alone, hung her head. Candace
pulled the girl over, against her own hip. Rosarita actually started lifting
her knee around him. Candace, in the audience along with Blame,
began to feel as annoyed by the performance as the little girl obviously
was. But she was better able to hide her opinion, and managed to beam
maternally upon the porn.

They stopped kissing and Rosarita said, "This is the lady from Catho-
lic Relief," speaking with prim resentment. Mike wasn't paying attention.
He got down on his knees to hug Blame. He said sing-songily, *"Hiya,
Daddy, d'ja bring me any thing from jail?"*

Blame went limper in his hug, averting her face.

Mike stood up and presented himself to Candace, saying, "You're the
Sister." His eyes met hers with suspicion, and vulnerability—and an
overly long personal interest—quickly severed. O'Callan. He probably
would have run into *Irish* Catholicism; there was something of that
prepared disappointment in his eyes; and Candace made a nice smile
for him, through the lacy mist of that particular set of prejudices. Together within that Catholic mist, Mike and Candace were joined by an
understanding actually prior to, and deeper than, his relationship with
Rosarita.

"Pleased to meet you," he said, and he told his little family, "So let's
get out of here." His mouth was small and tender and mobile. Against
observing him too closely, Candace hooded herself, as they filed toward
the elevator, she last of all, their shepherdess.

It was like a freight elevator, old and scuffed, oversized, its walls
burnished by violence. The four of them stood in there, all sharing
Mike's new freedom. On his forearm he carried a paper bag containing
whatever they release you with. "Let's get a martini," he said. "Oh,
before I forget"—he stood on tiptoe to reach into his jeans pocket, and
he pulled out a little vial—"here's your rocks from space." He handed
it to Blame.

Blame looked at the thing as if it smelled bad. It was a glass vial with
a metal cap. The cap had a tiny rubber diaphragm, of the land you can
poke a syringe through. Inside were two pebbles. A strip of paper had
been taped on the side reading, in ball-point pen, *"Lunar Basalt, U.S.
Space and Aeronautics."*

If they were fake—of course, they had to be fake!—they were an artful fake. Candace considered Mike O'Callan from a longer perspective. His crime had been killing an acquaintance at a party. The whole story was something Candace had pieced together from Rosarita's not-very-objective narrative. One summer night there was a party in an apartment building on Conn Street, across from the 7-Eleven where the *campesinos* loiter each morning hoping for work. The party was in a ground-floor apartment, and Mike O'Callan had first impressed Rosarita Gustan by his manner of entrance; he pulled his motorcycle directly up onto the rear patio outside the sliding glass doors, and dismounted there. Rosarita's boyfriend of the time was David James, whom Rosarita referred to as if he were famous. *Oh, he thinks he's very hot because he has hair like Rod Stewart and he owns a drapery cleaning business. You don't know Rod Stewart. Rod Stewart sings 'If you want my body, come on baby, let me know,' and his hair is like all fwissh. But David James is a big shit. I'm sorry, Sister, but he is. His hair is exactly like Rod Stewart, with the bleach-blond and the teasing and the ratting, with the comb and mousse. Exactly the same. Forgive my language, Sister, but he was a shit truly.* In her work with Catholic Relief, Candace had been coming to see that the commonest factor in these tragedies was this self-absorption which manifested itself in the world as stupidity. There was no other word for it, for all these bad decisions, this deafness to reason. All originating in self-absorption. That and, of course, drug-abuse. Those are the two offices by which Satan, so to speak, works in the world, and which the justice system is beset by, and baffled by: drugs and selfishness. At this party on Conn Street, both of those elements seem to have been present. In David James's case it was alcohol and cocaine together in combination. In Mike's case it was a powder, common in California at the time, with the silly name of angel dust. Angel dust was compounded of PCP, which was a horse tranquilizer. It mostly had the effect of making humans supernaturally excited. Fights developed. Both medications numbed combatants to pain, while also blessing them with transcendent radiant strength.

At the Conn Street party, David James had been insulting Rosarita, in some fashion which Rosarita was too pious to describe in the ear of a nun. The trouble came when Mike O'Callan defended Rosarita's honor. Within the two boys' shared numbness, an angelic brawl ensued. David James went through the sliding glass door onto the rear patio, and then went on fighting while he bled. That was the cause of his death, hemorrhaging.

A large man who had been sitting in the corner all night—a man Rosarita said she had mistrusted as too mature for this crowd, too tall and big-around and humorless, too middle-aged and sober—stood up and waded in to separate the fighters. This was a remarkable detail in Rosarita's story. The man had kept quiet all night. He'd contributed nothing to the general celebration, and didn't seem to know anybody. He hadn't once moved from his corner chair. At this point he got up, crossed the floor to step out on the patio, and ended the fight, with a simple gesture of parting curtains. Which Rosarita demonstrated. He stood there in a traffic-cop posture for a minute, then turned away and sat back down and picked up his drink again. David James lay himself gently down upon the leafy, low hedges bordering the patio. Mike hopped on his motorcycle and stepped down on the starter and sped away, after having first given a long look at David James lying there. David James wasn't going to get up. Then in the lull while people were waiting for the police to arrive—when most of the guests had gone out to stand out front on the sidewalk with their drinks, and those holding drugs had vanished into the night, and somebody had cut the stereo, and one girl sat quietly crying on the shag-carpeted stair—in that quiet space, the big peacemaker sitting in the corner said the only thing he said all night: "It's always either a woman or a hat."

That was how Rosarita told the story. What Candace imagined most personally was Mike's escape by motorcycle, alone in the long dark alley behind Conn Street. It would have been two or three in the morning. All the windows at the backsides of the apartment buildings would have been dark, and his single trembling headlamp would have whitened trashcans and garage doors in his immediate future. The walls of the alley would have reflected back the roar, so that Mike was traveling in a tunnel of noise, a tunnel of his own making. *Everywhere I'm not, it's peaceful and people are sleeping, far and wide over the land.* That's what she pictured him thinking as he thundered up the alley. *Only where I am, only where I pass, is this roar and turmoil, this unfolding tunnel.* He was too young to have entered that tunnel. The death was an accident. But Mike was smart. When the police did come for him, he cooperated. He knew that, in the long run, he would outlive this mistake and make something better of his life. He was very smart indeed. You could see it in his eyes, their shy flicker, their obstinacy. He was so vibrant and tender and somehow humorous, in his nifty jeans and sneakers and T-shirt, it made her stomach all watery.

At last Mike did present himself as a test of Candace's faith. There came a day when she had to go on a long car trip with him, to Santa Rosa, to take his little girl to the Department of Health and Human Services. The trip was necessary to qualify Blame for social security payments. Because her biological parents had died of their immune deficiencies, she had to undergo a medical exam to qualify for state assistance. Blame herself didn't have an immune deficiency, but a complete physical was a requirement of the Child Welfare Board. The only state facility for such an exam was a half-day's drive away in Santa Rosa; and she was required to stay overnight in the hospital for a blood metabolism test; Candace had to be present as a case officer; Rosarita, on account of a girlfriend's bridal shower, was unable to come.

So it was just Mike and Candace, with Blame; and after they'd arrived in Santa Rosa, Candace's nun-like Ford Fairlane (property of the convent) broke down. In the medical clinic's parking lot, it wouldn't start. A tow-truck mechanic told them it needed a part that wouldn't be available until the following day, so Mike and Candace would have to stay in a motel. If this was a test of her worthiness for a vocation, then pure prayer would be the only guide, to pondering what is imponderable. The motel was a Best Western called "The Easter Bunny's Hole." It was thematically united by the image, everywhere on placemats and menus and on the tall highway sign, of a rabbit with a golf club, a kilt, and a tam o'shanter. It was built around a paved courtyard where cars could be parked, surrounding a small central garden. The garden wasn't really a "garden" but an oval of blinding-white ornamental gravel, where two empty benches faced each other and topiary shrubs, which were once supposed to be animals, stood in disintegration.

Mike and Candace got there on foot, from the garage the car was towed to. He carried her briefcase for her, and she walked with her arms folded over the front of her sweater. It was like being in high school. Even the sound of the big dangerous freeway beside them made them children again. They ate dinner at a chain restaurant with orange upholstery, and then, as night fell, she and Mike went back to the motel to reserve two rooms. He telephoned Blame, who was happy in the hospital with TV and ice cream. After that, with a whole evening to kill, they went next door to a bar, where one of the two necessary conditions for a stupid mistake could be procured: an intoxicating substance. She felt safe with Mike. Rather, he seemed afraid of *her*—afraid of her holiness or impatient with cloistered innocence, what's the difference?

Oh, but she was afraid of him. His sense of humor was the dangerous part, it was so insolent. On the long drive north he'd done a lot of clowning around, mostly in trying to cheer up the stony, unforgiving Blame. He asked if Candace was "a novitiate or a novice or something," gesturing toward the absent habit, her bright hair. Candace, who was doing the driving (through what she discovered to be rather amazingly pretty, Iowa-like land north of San Francisco), explained that the novitiate comes later, after formal vows. This period of working for Catholic Relief in San Francisco was supposed to be her time of postulancy. Mike gave a little groan of recognition, "You're a postulant." Then he grumbled to Blame, "I'm a postulant, don't touch me—oh yuck!—I'm covered with little postules." He elbowed the girl sitting between them (who was not amused but grew all the more hollow-eyed, as if she were being personally mocked, as part of a long ongoing campaign of humiliation), and he started lifting his arms stickily, speaking in an English accent. "Whoops, uh-oh, I think I'm postulating. Sorry. I may have postulated on your upholstery. Just a little bit. Not much. I'm a postulant, you know." Blame shrugged in a show of irritation. Efforts at comedy were making the girl weakly *angry*, which perhaps meant her defenses were softening. How sweet was her rock-and-roll foster-dad, how courageous and delicate both. Candace drove along at the wheel just like a wife. Later at the motel desk, when she and Mike were reserving their (separate) rooms, he said, "Don't worry, you're safe with me. I wouldn't touch a postulant with a ten-foot pole. Really. No offense. It's true. I'd be afraid to wake up tomorrow morning and find I was postulating." It made the front-desk girl in her Best Western smock, typing in the reservation form, pause suspiciously.

When they got to the bar next to the motel, he ordered a double martini dirty. "Which is like plenty of olive juice." His looking nineteen was irrelevant. It arrived, and he took a sip. And though he couldn't have suddenly been drunk, it licensed him to mischief and he leaned back saying, "But you don't really *believe* all that."

He was referring to her vocation as a nun. In the car driving up through Sonoma County, he'd begun his campaign by saying she could be just as good a servant of God without joining an order and buying into all the Christianity. "There's that good ol' rule about always telling the truth," he said, "because of the tangled web we weave when first we practice to deceive."

"Deceive?"

"Deceiving the little people. Letting them think there's a god who pays attention. Or deceiving yourself. Calling it faith." This was a kind of mask he liked to wear: the defiant, the miscreant. The Lucifer mask. It seemed a way of asking for help or at least for serious engagement. She thought about his remarks while she was driving, and said after watching the road for a while, "Christianity binds me to a mystery. One *recognizes* that much of it is arbitrary, or simply invented by humans, or absurd. Tertullian said he believed *because* it's absurd. But it's a discipline. We're all living within a mystery, Mike. Even if you're not religious. Don't you agree?"

What she said had made Mike's eyes glow in slits, which might have been mistrust, or might have been admiration. He'd had no reply and only watched the scenery of Sonoma County go past. But now behind his silver martini in the bar's dimness, he wanted her to know he'd been thinking about it. He went on, "You're too intelligent. You're too intelligent to believe a rotten corpse will suck itself back together and start flying around. Everybody's too intelligent to believe that. The priests are too intelligent. The theologians are too intelligent. The Pope, and even every little believer, *everybody is* too smart to believe that. Not in their heart of hearts."

Before her cylinder of iced orange juice on the table, she folded her hands. "Okay, let me see if I can answer you," she said. "The tradition is *historical*." By historical she meant contaminated-by-the-world, in a sense she couldn't explain in five minutes over a drink. "The Church *grew*, in the hands of historical human beings just as fallible as you and I. Nevertheless, it's not for me to sit here in judgment and sort out the 'true' from the 'false,' according to my little categories. The human being is, like"—she flexed her shoulders within a straitjacket—"the human being lives inside this very limited set of perceptions. It's limiting. But if I know I'm limited, I can understand some things and *relax* in that assumption. And also I can do worldly work *within* that assumption. What's really amazing about all the . . . bullshit" (she made a pause, to indicate it really was an inappropriate word but also that she took some pleasure in saying it and wasn't incapable of mischief, wasn't one of the nuns who'd been called to the convent only because the world was an empty place for her), "what's really interesting, Mike, is that some of the bullshit may be true! Even all the miracle nonsense! Maybe, just to just go along with *life*, you have to be a little bit of an idiot." She presented herself: idiot—smile, shoulders, lips, breasts— and then, amending herself, grabbed the chilly pole of orange juice in front of her and pushed herself back on her side of the booth. Whenever other people were taking liquor she always got sympathetically more informal.

Mike said, "Right. So you preserve the lie to keep the little people faithful." He hadn't been listening at all. "You and the Pope, you all take the responsibility of being the liars, so the common people will have something to believe in. Like me with Blame's 'Outer-Space Rocks.'"

"Well *that*. Come on, Mike, that's different." She had chastised him the week before, for picking up ordinary pebbles from the prison-yard and calling them extraterrestrial. "That truly is a lie. In the long run, that's a disservice to the child. But religious myths—religious myths are different."

"Ah! Oh! Now they're 'myths.'"

"Religious *stuff* is different from bare-faced lies. It's a *fact* that those pebbles are not from outer space."

"They're definitely from outer space." His gaze was a little prolonged. He had a disturbing way of holding his attention upon her, as if they were talking about not pebbles but the inevitability of sleeping together. Surely it was only habitual with him and he had no notion of its effects in the world.

She thrust both her wrists between her knees and clamped her shoulders high, looking off to one side. "Mike, they're not from outer space."

He dove under the table. From the dirty floor he pinched up a bit of nothingness between his thumb and forefinger. He then held it up to her examination: "Look! Dust from outer space!" His arms floated up, to stir the outer space they were suspended in, even on this planet. "We are *in* the Void."

It was sweet, his little joke, it helped her to remember, he was like a child, like a little brother to her, there was no danger of sex here, she might be the younger one, but she was infinitely older in terms of spiritual responsibility. He had a marriage-like relationship with Rosarita. A very challenging relationship! They were trying to be parents to this girl. Yet, as things stood now, Rosarita and Mike could hardly even be worthy friends to each other. Candace's job was to help them, two of her fellow-creatures in danger, and she had been provided with a few tools, being from Cedar Rapids and working within the Church.

She resolved that she would pray for guidance tonight in earnest, in the mildew-smelling motel room.

She inhaled the wintry air at the surface of her orange-juice glass, all a-click with ice cubes, Iowa-February air at the rim.

Then Mike read her mind: "It won't last with Rosarita, you know," he said. "She's—you might say she's one of God's children who has many turns to take on a dark road before she'll come to the light."

Candace wasn't sure she herself wasn't being ridiculed.

He went on, "She means well. But she's pretty materialistic. No, I take it back. She *doesn't* mean well. Rosarita is one person who could use a little religion. Me and her are not simpatico. You know why we're together? Really? 'Cause I'm the hero who slayed the evil boyfriend. So we had to get together. It was so romantic. It was inevitable. The only problem is, she likes to party. And I'm a musician. Which is bad for her, 'cause musicians don't bring home enough money for the kind of partying she likes. See, I want to ask you something." He pushed his martini aside. "I want to ask you to let me still be Blame's dad. Rosarita and I are going to separate. That's inevitable. I'm moving out. But I want custody of Blame. I'll get an income soon. And Blame shouldn't live with Rosarita. That's a bad situation. You have the power. I know you do." He nodded toward the seat beside her, where her briefcase lay, her real date tonight. "You can just *tell* the county I'll be a responsible dad."

He leaned back and, in a single draught, took the rest of his double martini. He was too young to be drinking like that. It was all a part of his being so *listo* and foolish. Candace was weak from looking at him— at his sapphire-blue eyes in this amber bar—so that she had to look away, to let her vision drink of the lonely spaces of the earth, the emptiness of the world, that people daily thrust themselves through, the jukebox halo, the corridor to the bathrooms, the empty bandstand, the unforgiving white light of a "PHONE" sign.

She'd been foolish. There were spaces on the government forms and she should have long ago reported how the State of California's monthly three hundred dollars was being spent. It was mostly spent on Rosarita's clothes and drugs, while Candace's own money bought school supplies and shoes for Blame. She should have said all that specifically in the monthly expenditures form. But it would have caused Blame to be removed from the home, and all the visits would be over. So she was already compromised. And had been for months. She had been foolish and irresponsible, and Mike knew exactly why: there was that look in his eye, of confidence and sure traction. He said, "Hey. Why don't you have a real drink. I'll have a drunken nun on my hands. You're far from the monastery. I'll get you drunk so you'll promise to—well, basically *lie* to Child Welfare for me."

She almost could have ordered a drink. But that was identifiably the advisement of the devil because she'd never liked alcohol. She disliked even the taste unless it was buried under sugar and fruit juice. Therefore, she might have ordered a drink only as an active choice to blind herself. In her endangerment, as a kind of self protection, she insulted him: "Charm will always be your impediment in life, Mike." She was still looking away from the table.

The insult worked. He didn't answer, but looked surprised, and then tried to drink from a martini glass where there was nothing left. She hated that, his being afraid of her. He cleared his throat and said, "I may not be perfect." The implication was that perfection was what *she* generally consorted with, up in her "monastery" on Geary Street, as he'd referred to it.

He said, "I'm just trying to be practical: practical about what's going to happen to Blame. She's not that adoptable. Face it. She doesn't make herself too attractive. She doesn't go out of her way. And besides, people only want little babies. People don't want a grown kid. And there's HIV. Nobody adopts a child whose parents were HIV-positive. By law they'd have to be told."

She could see what was happening: poor Mike loved that unpromising child. In his innocence he was entering that worldly ambush, love, actual love, its betrayals and inconstancies—for in fact, that little Blame was not going to return any gift of love. Candace despised her own failure of mercy, but it was the realistic truth. And it was her job here to be realistic, not sentimental.

"Why don't you and Rosarita try to get to know each other?" she said, with the sweetly flowing voice of hypocrisy. She didn't *want* those two to get to know each other and learn to stay together. In Rosarita, Candace had seen a certain something reptilian in the mouth and lips, beneath her cosmetics and hairstyle, something maimed and greedy that no spiritual counsel would ever repair. She disliked Rosarita—her slashes of make-up, her tits-and-ass, her little five-foot-one body grabbable like a phone receiver—and she wanted Mike to get away from her.

Yet she carried on with her speech. "You know what the Church's position is, on relationships that aren't working? First of all, get married. That would be fundamental. There's no progress until you're married. There isn't even any authentic *conversation* until you're married. Until you're married, you're not even really talking, honestly.

"Then when you marry, in God's eyes, you'd both enter into a sacra-mental state where all this deception and self-deception would have to stop. You'd be living within a promise. You'd be living within a mystery. You'd have to start working with her, and she with you. And learning about yourselves. And you'd be asking the divine will to work through you both . . ." Candace was a flute through which these meaningless formulae were passing, which might have the incantatory effect of mak-ing her believe too, because they *were*, if remotely, the truth.

"Neither of you is spiritually ready for a relationship. Really, *none* of us is ready. We're all still learning. We all need God's help. You and Rosarita together would ask for God's help, and the *three* of you then would make spiritual progress. Right now, unmarried, you're going to be in a state of sin and can't ask for blessings. You're living in untruth. The sacrament would show your commitment in God's sight." Her lips were saying this, but her arms and body wanted to move to comfort him, while he visibly shrank harder before her, his eyes dull upon his empty glass.

Somehow he must have signaled the woman behind the bar, who nurselike brought him another double martini, which he gathered into the armful of tabletop he was poring over.

Then, just at the moment Candace could feel her whole body want-ing to hold him, and be held by him, he said angrily, "Why do *assholes* and fucking bitches have any say over my life?"

Her only prayer, her only desire, had been to serve. She walked with her briefcase across the parking lot to the motel, to her room to pray, leaving Mike alone at the table after his outburst. On her knees, at the bedspread of green corduroy, with the flow of old smooth pebbles over her wrist and through her fingers, she let her lips carve the same an-cient scarabs as ever, *now and at the hour of our death,* and *trespass against us,* the English translation of the Vulgate's extinct language. The more you repress doubt, the more it goes away in the wilderness to gather strength and return as an army with power and glory. So she needed to hold her doubt always openly before her, as her form of prayer. The motel ceiling plaster was textured, impregnated with little snowdrift-sparkles, yellowed over the years. A philosopher they'd been studying in an anthology this month—maybe A. J. Ayer or Martin Marty, one of the liberals—said something memorable on the topic of the Ontological Proof: It doesn't matter whether God "exists," because by faith a believer—an ardent woman on her knees in a motel room holding a plastic rosary—can *imagine* a God sufficient to "organize the psyche." Organizing the psyche was supposed to be enough. But an organized psyche, she felt now, amounted to faithlessness and lostness. An organized psyche is isolation. An organized psyche is hell. It was the cause of all her lonely doom, that she had an organized psyche. She stood up. She thought she would read the Bible. In the bathroom before the mirror, she put on pajamas and washed her face, and so by scrubbing went back to girlhood, bringing back a dullness in the skin to let the soul shine. She got under the covers, to read by lamplight. Her back was against the wall that divided her room from Mike's. She couldn't hear him in there. He was still in the bar drinking. The Pauline letters seemed quibbling and political, Ecclesiastes fatuous and terribly innocent, complacent. The Book of Job offered the usual familiar lines. She closed her old, creased, no-longer-lustrous Revised Standard Version and lay it down, its page edges dyed peppermint-red. In the bedside drawer was the common ugly green Bible, "Placed by THE GIDEONS," which turned out to be a King James version. She found herself reading in the middle of Genesis and came across a terrible sentence she'd never noticed before. So deep is that page, it keeps sending up beams from darkness and sunken facets as the light outside shifts. Or, maybe she was only a worried superstitious woman looking for signs in texts. After Abraham was told by God to take his only son Isaac up on the mountain to kill him as a sacrifice, the old man rose early in the morning. He laid the wood for the burnt offering upon his son to carry; and he took in his hand the fire and the knife. So they went, both of them together. And Isaac said to his father Abraham, "My father!" And he said, "Here am I, my son!"

The boy then asked, "Behold, the fire and the wood; but where is the lamb for a burnt offering?" The boy was asking that question in all innocent belief and trust.

The father's maniacal answer to his son—that God will provide the lamb—must have been spoken in an abyss of sadness, continuous with the abyss of the night sky over Moriah. His was no organized psyche. *God will provide the lamb.* That abyss was religion. It was obedience. She didn't *want* an organized psyche. The "self" is all we have here on earth, but it's what we're asked to give up, amounting to the most joyful obligation. As she lay there, she heard noises from Mike's room next door. A woman's giggles. Then the slam of the door.

Then somebody went past her window, a silhouette, past the drawn drapes. It was a female. Candace turned off the bedside light, and she slipped out of bed to look through the parting of the drapes.

The woman crouched at the ice machine scooping the cold treasure into a wooden night-table drawer. It was the bartender, from across the parking lot, the maker of double martinis. How quickly Mike had attracted her. And how subtly! They must have made their bargain by the surest of glances. Bringing him a second double martini would have been part of that secret communication. It must be this way always, with Mike. Females scheme to put themselves in his path. And so a man like him finds it hard to grow spiritually, his mind too readily emptied by the grab for the obvious handle. The woman ran back to Mike's room, the door slammed, and the bedsprings next door clanged. The walls were so thin, now Candace would have to listen to the sounds of love, inches from her own bed. Her first thought—which was forgivable by the Lord, as all things are forgiven by the Lord—was that she could crouch upon the bed and listen at the wall, in the kneeling position she preferred, and let her practiced finger in its piano-lesson posture keep striking the same middle C she'd discovered long ago in her childhood, because this was a lost moment, in a lost place. But she didn't do that—for in truth, no moment or place is ever lost. Nothing is lost. No one is lost. She put on her trenchcoat, over her pajamas, and she went outside.

On her feet, she wore her old flats. California summer nights were cold, not hot like Iowa's. She could spend an hour out here if she liked, sitting on one of the benches in the sad topiary garden in the middle of the parking lot. There are times for simply being still and waiting. This was surely one of them. Life is long. And the capacity for contemplation is the peculiarly human attribute, "an activity of soul in accordance with virtue," as the *Summa* declares, at a simplistic but surprisingly inevitable mountaintop of Christian ethics. She sat on the bench. The stars were few. Somewhere out there on the street, a car stereo was playing menacing hip-hop music—it was coming closer—then the boom of its bass (while she sat very still) passed by, like the plague that passed over in Egypt. It must be deafening inside that Japanese pick-up truck; she got a glimpse of the scrawny white boy inside alone, within his storm of revengeful music. The world is deep.

Maybe this was the guidance that was coming to her in the world: she would no longer be tempted by Mike. Mike was manifestly weak. There were probably drugs in the room. At least alcohol.

Consequently—and this was painful—she would have to make sure Mike was denied custody of the little girl who, at that moment, was sleeping hard alone in a hospital bed. She filled her lungs with air, because it would strengthen and refresh her, to have made that decision, though it would be sad for all concerned. Particularly for Blame. The long corridors of the state welfare system would take all hope from Blame but perhaps give her faith. In those corridors, she would be disappointed in human nature. And she would be disappointed in herself. That was a cost. It was Mike's loss that seemed the most terrible. He was so bright. It was such a waste. He was throwing so much away, in throwing himself away. Herself, she wasn't worried about. She knew she would be fine. She had recovered her humility. Her serenity of spirit.

She tucked herself deeper into her trenchcoat against the night air. That air, too, was God. Every atom of herself was God. As a way of saying goodbye to the whole situation, she leaned over and picked up a chunk of the ornamental white gravel from the ground and spilled it around on her palm, tilting her hand around, rolling it on its facets, thinking of maybe pocketing it as a souvenir, because now, thanks to Mike O'Callan, she could see it as a rock that actually does exist in outer space. As does everything. That was a gift. Nobody but Mike could have seen it that way. It's wasteful the way some people decide to level off and stop growing. He had had a unique sweet insight: that the commonest pebble underfoot is suspended in original outer space at all times, fresh right out of the Big Bang.

"What did happen to Blame?" I said. Candace's story seemed to be over because she sat against the bedstead without adding anything more, cradling that little philosophical remark of her friend Mike. That little joke seemed to be, for her, the high point of the story. However, Blame was still a loose end.

"Yes, I know" was her response, self-accusatory. She was looking into her empty snifter.

Then she went into explanations. "The rationale at the time would be: God has His own ways of bringing everybody closer to Him, closer to God. Blame too. Me too. And Mike and Rosarita. Everybody's struggle in life is their own process of coming closer. I guess if I imagine the worst for her, she would have gone into the foster-care system. A series of situations, then." She smiled into her snifter but blearily, seeing those situations. "Of course, in the end we all get *absolutely* close. Guess nobody escapes that. Some just start sooner."

"So. That was the night you lost your faith," I gloated, wanting to tickle her, to cheer her. Telling this story had made her too serious and thoughtful. The night wasn't exactly young anymore, and the sound of the freeway seemed to counsel an eagerness: there was still time for more love, and love is scarce. It's like an economic good, in that way: scarce.

She said, "No, you never lose 'faith,' exactly. It's something that stays with you and just gets complicated. But I did realize that night, what saved me was my particular gift: that I didn't care about passion and the whole thing. Some women do have that as a determinant, passion, which in their lives they have to deal with. Even way back in Cedar Rapids. When I was pretending to be promiscuous. *Not* having that, it's really a blessing."

About this particular blessing, she looked permanently sad.

"You?" I leered, clowning, always clowning; my finger crept on her ankle. "Don't like passion?" Just look around: the sheets were tossed all over, the dining room table was still uncleared, my own body lay alongside hers. My happiest usefulness in the world was in my readiness to expand and fill any void, a readiness on a job site or on graduate-school applications, pure expansion. She turned and looked at me and my little joke, with a softening: I was like a nice beach she could sail close to but would never set foot on. I wasn't sure I liked that rather simplified view of myself. I added, "Maybe that was then," while my fingers went on walking, making a miniature threat to stalk up her knee. Candace always was fond of my sense of humor and she tapped me on the nose once more with a green grape, making me blink again within the mask of innocence she liked to keep me in during our time to-gether.

MIDTERM

fiction by LESLIE JOHNSON

Midmorning in mid-October, in the middle of the campus, Chandra stopped in the center of the crisscrossing sidewalks. She pulled the phone from her handbag and pretended to be texting someone; she smiled down at the screen as if someone had texted her back. She felt other students brushing past her on the walkway, but didn't look up at their faces.

She had left her dorm room fully intending to go to class, even though she wasn't prepared. Today in Gender Perspectives they were supposed to be discussing sex slaves in third world nations, a series of articles based on the real-life stories of young women who were prisoners in brothels forced to do disgusting things or be brutally punished. Chandra hadn't gotten the reading done, but she could still go to class, and when it was her turn to speak, she could say it was horrible, she couldn't believe that such things were happening to young, helpless girls in this day and age, and how could she be wrong? It *was* horrible. She *couldn't* believe it. If she read the articles, Chandra figured she would probably feel exactly the same way as she felt now anyway. She wasn't afraid to go to class. The professor was nice. If she could tell that Chandra hadn't done the reading, she wouldn't embarrass Chandra in front of everyone. She might ask in a concerned voice to speak to Chandra after class, though, and Chandra could tell her that she was a little behind because she'd had the flu.

Chandra had spent the last two days in her dorm room, pretending to have it. Not that she really needed to put on a show. Her roommate,

Jillian, didn't care. They were not enemies, but they were not friends. Between her boyfriend and her sorority, Jillian rarely slept in the room and used it mostly for the closet space. When Chandra had heard the key in the door on Monday morning, she pulled the sheet up to her neck and mumbled that she wasn't feeling well. Jillian wrinkled her nose and opened the window between their beds to let the germs out. Chandra had spent the day watching YouTube videos on her laptop. She had an open bag of animal crackers in her desk drawer, with seventeen crackers left inside, and she ate four at a time, every three hours, and threw the leftover one, a walrus, out of the window into the night sky.

On Tuesday, she had the same bad feeling that made her stay in her dorm room. Not sick, but not regular—a feeling like something bad was happening and she just didn't know exactly what it was yet.

This morning, Wednesday, Chandra had awoken with fresh resolve. Enough already. *Up and at* 'em, as her mother used to screech through her bedroom door. She made her way to the dorm bathroom down the hallway. After seven weeks at college, it still felt funny to Chandra to wear shower shoes, which were highly recommended to avoid fungus. She always carried an extra towel with her and hung one on the hook outside the showers and kept one wrapped around her body until she was inside the stall. When she let the towel drop and she was standing there in only her shower shoes, she thought sometimes of those porn girls, naked but still wearing high heels.

This morning she had taken her time, even though she knew there were people waiting for their turn. She closed her eyes and turned her face up to the showerhead and let her hands rest on the sharp knobs of her hip bones, which were her favorite part of her body. She would go to class today, and tomorrow, and then all she had on Friday was math lab. Hump day. That's what her dad had always called Wednesday. And the torture chamber was what he always used to call his job. *Oh, boo hoo hoo!* Chandra could remember how her mother used to mock him when they'd fight at night before the divorce. *You have to talk on the phone and write claims and report to a boss! Poor you! Too bad you can't get work at a plastics factory and breathe toxic chemicals all day and die in your fifties!* Because that was how Chandra's grandfather whom she never met—her mom's dad—had died. From lung cancer, even though he never smoked; they all knew it was the plastic fumes. And she'd started to cry a little, not about her grandfather she never met, but at the memory of her dad's voice saying, *It's over-the-hump day, Sweetie Peetie. Can we do it? Can we make it over?*

Now the walkways were clearing, everyone delivering themselves to their 9:50 classes, and Chandra should have been inside Auerbach Hall, but she remained in the middle of the intersecting sidewalks. She was wearing her hair tied back with paisley scarf and her brown boots and black leggings and a long corduroy shirt over a purple knit turtleneck. She looked fine. She should go to class. She looked fine.

The campus was still. The red brick buildings, the bright yellow tree-tops shimmering in a crisp breeze. Maybe, she thought, she should get a coffee at the student union. And a banana, maybe. She hadn't eaten yesterday except for some peanuts from the vending machine. She could have a banana, and maybe a Pop-Tart with the crusts cut off.

She hated to go to the cafeteria, but she could do it. She could go in there and get a coffee and a Pop-Tart. She was looking toward the union at the end of the walkway, and suddenly someone was standing under the big maple tree next to the building. A guy. A tall guy wearing a peacoat. Where did he come from? He seemed to be standing very straight on purpose. Was he looking at her? It seemed like he was look-ing at her! Chandra held her phone to her ear and tossed back her head and tapped the toe of her boot on the walkway and laughed, and even though she knew the guy was too far away to hear, she said out loud, "Seriously? Listen, I gotta call you later." Then she dropped the phone into her handbag and walked with purpose on the walkway to the left, toward the union, keeping her eyes on the building, not allowing her-self a glance at the tree or the guy standing under it, but then she did glance, and he was gone. Disappeared. She stopped and looked around, but didn't see him walking away in any direction—not toward the li-brary, not toward Dana Hall. She turned in a slow circle.

"Hello."

She jerked her shoulders, taking a breath—more of a stupid-sounding hiccup, actually. With three more steps toward the union, she could see his body lying flat on the ground like a corpse beneath the tree. He propped himself up, one elbow at a time. His reddish-brown hair stuck up on one side; crumbled pieces of brown leaves clung to his coat sleeves. Was he smiling at her? His lips were curled up a little, anyway. Chandra's stomach twisted. "Sorry, like, were you," she mumbled, pushing a piece of hair into her scarf, *"were you saying something?"*

"I said hi."

He had a patch of acne on one side of his jaw, and his Adam's apple looked weird, like a big walnut inserted for no good reason under the skin of his neck. His eyebrows were bristly, but his eyes underneath them were okay. Greenish-brownish. Looking up at her. She said, "Hi."

"You want to see something?"

Chandra didn't answer, but she didn't keep walking either.

He said, "You have to come closer to the tree to see what I'm talking about." He pointed up at something in the branches of the maple. "From underneath."

Three students came out of the union. One of them was saying *Shit! Shit!* in a gleeful voice. Chandra looked over her shoulder at them, long enough to see them huddle together as one of the girls cupped her hands to help the boy get his cigarette lit in the breeze. Chandra looked back at the guy under the tree. He was sitting up normally now, cross-legged, and so she sat down next to him, with a couple of feet or so between them. "What?" She looked up into the branches, where he'd been pointing. "What were you looking at?"

"I'm looking at a particular leaf, the one on the smaller branch that's attached to the largest branch, right *there*—" He pointed above their heads. "The one that's completely red, the deepest red compared to the ones around it. Do you see the one I'm talking about?"

Chandra craned her neck. The maple leaves were mostly lemon yellow, some tinged orange, their tips transitioning to scarlet. A few mostly red. She tried to spot the guy's perfect red leaf among the foliage. "I see it," she lied.

"I'm watching it until it falls."

"Why?"

"Because. I believe it will be worthy of seeing."

"Hmmm." Chandra saw the three students walking away, their laughter fading. The guy stretched out on the ground again, his hands behind his head, and Chandra extended her legs and leaned back on her elbows. Above her, sunlight illuminated the bright leaves; they trembled like chandelier crystals. She said, "I'm supposed to be in class."

"We're all *supposed* to be somewhere. But I can *choose* to see one red maple leaf come to the end of its life. To see the moment it releases from its branch."

"I guess."

"We see only what we look at. To look is an act of choice."

Chandra let her arms splay, relaxed her head on the ground, gazing up at the canopy of golden-plum. "I guess."

"Have you read Berger? *Ways of Seeing?*"

"I take it you have."

He made a noise, a sort of grunting sound. "I sound like an asshole?"

Without moving her head, Chandra shifted her eyes. His face was a couple of feet away from hers on the ground. "Maybe." She pretended to laugh a little, so he would know she was kidding. He smiled, and Chandra felt suddenly aware of her knees. Why was she wearing leggings? What had made her think this morning that she looked good in leggings? Her knees were too knobby for leggings. They stuck out like knots in the middle of her thighs and calves, like that big bulge on the tree branch over her head where another branch must have broken off in a storm or something.

"Ahhh!" The guy's mouth gaped, his eyes suddenly widening. His face flushed so the acne on his jaw didn't look so noticeable. He quickly rolled and lifted from the ground into a crouching position on his knees. "Did you see it? Did you?"

"I did," Chandra lied again. "I saw it."

He smiled, a big smile showing his teeth, which were large and straight, and Chandra wanted to ask him if he had a retainer from his orthodontist that he still wore to bed at night like she did. She said, "I was going to get a coffee."

He pulled up the sleeve of his leafy jacket. There was a watch on his wrist, the kind with hands and Roman numbers, which made Chandra wonder. Who wore a watch? He said, "Let's wait ten minutes. At eleven we can get early lunch."

We. She felt the veins in her neck start to pulse, the way they did when she got nervous. She took out her phone and scrolled Facebook. She clicked on a video link of someone feeding a doll-sized baby bottle to a squirrel in a blanket. She said, "Wanna see something?"

He held up his arms in an X, shaking his head. "I gave it up." "What?"

"Technology. Personal technology, that is. I understand that the cafeteria we're waiting to eat in is powered by technology. But you know— my cell phone. My laptop. Even my iPod. That was the hardest, actually. Because I love my music. So much."

"What do you *mean?*"

"I'm unplugged. I disconnected myself from cyberspace and all the gadgets. It's an experiment, right? To see what I discover about myself, living, you know. Without the texts, tweets, sound bites, Instagrams, everything constantly separating us from the life that's happening for real right in front of us. Around us. I'm going to write about it."

Chandra nodded. "Steinmetz gave us that same extra credit, but his was just for cell phones. We were supposed to not use them for a weekend and keep a journal about it. Some people were going to do it, but then he said you actually had to give him your phone for the weekend. He was going to lock them in his desk. So nobody did it."

The guy's mouth twisted to one side. "This isn't *extra credit.*"

He looked at his watch again. "You should come with me. After our lunch. Did you know that you're allowed to listen to the rehearsals in Jaffrey Hall? The music students are practicing for the parent weekend concerts, and we can just walk into the auditorium today at 1:10 and listen. I went yesterday for classical. Chamber groups playing Bach concertos. Amazing. When was the last time you actually *felt* the vibration of a cello's strings?"

He stood up, and so did Chandra. He was at least a foot taller than she was. Between the flaps of his coat she could see his gray sweater underneath. He was thin, but not too thin. She could see some extra flesh at his stomach, which she liked. Chandra liked to be much thinner than any guy she was standing near. It made her feel larger somehow, or stronger or something, rather than smaller. Which made no sense, but, she thought, maybe was kind of interesting. Maybe she could put that in the paper she was supposed to be writing for Professor Steinmetz.

He'd begged her not to write about anorexia when they turned in their issue proposals. He was on the young side for an English professor. He wore jeans and sneakers and denim shirts. He was popular with students for the way he'd get all worked up in class. Once he dropped to his knees and begged them to care about a short story by someone named Junot. His forehead would get red where his hair was receding, and Chandra had heard other girls laughing about it after class, but in the way you laugh at someone you think is cute. *Not another eating disorder paper!* He pleaded with her, pretending to be desperate, clutching his hands by his chest. *And not the effect of the media on self-esteem!* She asked Steinmetz why that was a bad topic, and he said it wasn't a *bad* topic, but he'd read so many student essays about it in the last three years that if he got one more, he might break down and start weeping in his office.

The guy was pointing at the iPhone in Chandra's hand. "Try giving it up for just one day—not even a whole day, just till later this afternoon. Just try it."

"I could turn it off for a while, I guess." She didn't turn it off, but she slipped it away, into its spot in the interior pocket of her bag.

He shook his head. "No. It's not the same. You have to be actually separated from it or it doesn't work. Trust me." He looked past her shoulder to the entrance of the union, took a few running steps to it, and returned with a flier he'd ripped off the notice board. "Come on! Give me your phone!"

"So you don't have Steinmetz for comp, right?"

"I had him last year for freshman lit." He rolled his eyes. "What a self call."

When Chandra couldn't think of another topic, Steinmetz had told her that if she *had* to write about anorexia, she'd better make it unique to her own life and relevant to her own generation, or she'd be responsible for making an aneurysm burst inside his skull. But maybe she could write about giving up her cell phone instead, like this guy. Even though she already missed the extra credit, she could probably still write her paper about it. She was supposed to have a rough draft done already and she hadn't even started. As she reached into her bag and handed over her iPhone and watched the guy fold the orange flier around it, she was already forming sentences in her head. *I wrapped my phone in a flier for an Alpha Phi Halloween costume contest and placed it in a hole in a big tree, like that character in* To Kill a Mockingbird.

The guy covered her phone in the tree's hollow with fallen leaves. She said, "What if someone steals it?"

"Look! It's perfectly camouflaged. No one would ever, ever notice it there." He grinned at her. She felt her heart race, like she was being talked into something dangerous.

If she came back to the tree later and her phone was gone, she'd have to email her mom and get a replacement on their Verizon insurance. They'd had to do that once before, when Chandra left her phone at her dad's apartment, but he said it wasn't there. Chandra's mother had wanted to go over and help her look, but her dad's girlfriend, Melanie, wouldn't allow it. It was Melanie's apartment, technically, so she had the right.

"What's your name, anyway?"

"Eli."

"I'm Chandra."

She followed Eli into the cafeteria. There were a few students at the long tables in the dining room, but the food stations were mostly empty. A cafeteria worker in a paper hat was clearing out the pastry case, and another was stocking the salad bar, getting ready for the lunch wave. Eli moved in long strides to the Grill. Chandra stood a few feet behind him as he ordered a double cheeseburger.

"The grill's gotta heat up," said the bleary-eyed student worker in a stained chef hat. He was separating a stack of frozen patties with a metal spatula. He wore those clear plastic gloves, but Chandra saw him wipe his nose with his gloves on and then start poking at the raw hamburger with the same fingers. She held her empty plastic tray in front of her chest like a shield.

Eli told the grill guy that he'd be back for the burger and pushed his tray along the metal counter to the Chicken Basket, where he ordered nuggets and fries, and to Pizza & Pasta, where he heated up two slices of pepperoni in the serve-yourself microwave. Chandra got a cup of black coffee at the Starbucks counter and a packet of blueberry Pop-Tarts at Toast & Bagels. She peeled apart the foil wrapper and placed one of the Pop-Tarts in a toaster and waited, glancing over at Eli, who'd returned to the grill for his double burger. He waved at her, and she felt herself smile. She hoped her smile didn't look stupid—too big, maybe, or too small.

They met up at the long counter that led to the cash registers. There was no line at all yet. Chandra wondered why she hadn't figured this out on her own, instead of always fighting the lunch crowd after classes let out at 12:10.

"This is like Disney World," she told Eli. "You have to know all the off times."

"Disney World." Eli repeated the word flatly.

"My mom had a book, like a guide book thing, that told you when to go to the rides and restaurants and stuff at the times when most other people *wouldn't*. So you didn't have to wait so long . . ."

She let her voice trail off and turned her face away, began pushing her tray toward the register. Why was she talking about Disney World? God. Why did she have to be so weird? Her neck was red, she knew it, she could feel it getting hotter, and even though she was wearing a turtleneck the redness probably showed on that part of her skin between her throat and her jaw.

"Hey." Eli bumped the edge of his tray against hers, then hooked his finger around its edge. "That's all you're getting?"

"I told you. I was just going for coffee in the first place."

"Well, put your stuff on my tray, then. That's not enough to waste a swipe on."

She watched as he balanced his pizza on top of his fries and cookies on top of the burger's bun, making room for Chandra's coffee and Pop-Tart. He slid her empty tray out of the way, and she walked beside him to the register, where he discussed with the cashier whether it should be two swipes or three swipes on his meal card; Eli said the pizza was a side dish, but the cashier said it counted as a meal.

Eli shrugged. "Whatever."

Chandra walked with him to the condiment counter. "It's barely mid-term. You're going to run out of swipes."

"I'm not worried about it."

He squirted ribbons of ketchup over his chicken and fries; Chandra stirred Equal in her coffee. They sat across from each other at a table by the window with a view of the quad. If she craned her neck, she could see the tree where her phone was hidden, under the leaves in the hollow space of the trunk. What was she *doing*? She should go out there and get her phone while the quad was still quiet, before classes switched again. Put it back in her bag where it belonged.

Her mom had bought her this bag at Urban Outfitters before college, the same day they shopped for bedding and dorm supplies at Target and Bed, Bath, and Beyond. What if her mom was texting her right now? What if, Chandra wondered, something suddenly happened, like what if her dad had a heart attack out of the blue and her mom didn't want to go to the hospital and sit beside Melanie in the waiting room and wanted Chandra to go in her place?

She knew the chance of something happening the moment you randomly think of it happening was probably like zero. Thinking of it probably made it even less than zero, because when things happened it was never when you thought of them. Someone could be texting her about something right now, though, that she would never ever think of in a million years just sitting here thinking about *different* things.

If she had her phone she would know for sure that nothing was happening. She should go get her phone out of that tree.

"So you have the kind of family," Eli said, "that goes to Disney World together. One of those families?" Beneath his curly hair she could see his forehead wrinkle.

"Not really." She stabbed at her Pop-Tart with the cafeteria fork. "We only went once. When I was eleven."

Eli hunched over his tray, feeding himself with both hands, pizza rolled in one fist, his burger in the other.

"We're not rich," Chandra said, "if that's what you mean."

Eli hurried to chew and swallow, wiped at his mouth. "That's not what I meant. It's not the money thing. It's more about these premade experiences society wants you to have, you know? It's like, *Oh boy, the Magic Kingdom!* Prepackaged family fun."

"It's easy, I guess, for the parents. If you can pay for it."

"Exactly! That's exactly it!" Eli's spine straightened and he tilted forward across the table, like a drawbridge lowering. His swampy green eyes blinked slowly and reopened, focusing in on her face, a sudden zoom lens. Chandra tried to remain still, instead of looking away. She'd read that advice in *Seventeen* a long time ago and still remembered it. Eye contact, the article had said—don't underestimate it! No one had looked at her like this, Chandra realized, since she'd arrived at college. Looked closely at her face. Except maybe a couple of her professors, like Steinmetz. Chandra's mother used to stare at her now and then, sizing her up, making her lift up her shirt sometimes to check her rib cage, or inspecting her front teeth to make sure they weren't shifting in their gums after how much they'd paid the orthodontist.

Steinmetz. Chandra tried writing a sentence in her head again: *Without my phone I took the time to really look into the eyes of my friends while I was talking to them instead of constantly checking my screen.* She hoped she could remember it later when she got to the writing lab. What time was it? She reached by instinct for her bag, then drew her hand back. There was still time, probably, to knock out a couple pages of a draft before her 2:05 comp class. Even if they were terrible, at least Steinmetz would give her points for making an effort.

"People," said Eli, "want to buy premade experiences because it's easier. Safer, maybe. I think my parents sent me to camp for every vacation of my whole life. Computer camp, rock-climbing camp, video game-design camp, et cetera, and that's the same thing, right? You pay for it, and somebody has figured out every step of the way for you in advance, and you just follow along and you're expected to love it. And if you don't love it, then what's wrong with you, right?"

Without thinking Chandra picked up a piece of Pop-Tart, and now it was in her mouth, the dry crumbs mixing with a bit of moist filling on her tongue, and she wanted to spit it out on her napkin, but Eli was still looking right at her. She chewed, and her stomach talked to her the way it did, yelling at her, and she took another piece from her plate. "You're supposed to *appreciate* everything," she said.

"So true! Even if you didn't choose any of it. And college is the same exact thing, right? Pay your money and they give you a program and tell you what to think and what classes to take and you join a fraternity and they tell you what parties to go to. You can get all the way through your *college experience,* as they call it, without having one actually authentic experience of your own."

Suddenly, the quad's walkways began to fill from four directions, like faucets turning on, students streaming from the buildings. Classes were changing.

"My mom would kill me," Chandra said, "if she knew I skipped class this morning. She told me that skipping just one college class is like flushing $500 down the toilet, when you figure how much you're paying for tuition each semester."

"Can you put a price, though, on an hour of time? Time from your actual *life?*"

"My mom can. She totally guilts me about it. Just last week she texted me: *Better not be wasting grandpa's money.*"

"That's way aggressive."

"That's what's paying my tuition. A lot of people got cancer from the factory where he worked. My grandfather. This was a long time ago, like twenty years or something. Some lawyers started a big lawsuit with all of them, a class action thing. It took a really long time. My grandpa died, and it still was going on, and then finally they ended up winning. My mom was his only family, so she got the money—my grandpa's lawsuit money—and she saved it. And that's what's paying my tuition. Which she likes to remind me."

She felt a pain blossom inside, deep between her stomach and lungs, thinking about what she would say to her mom when the college mailed home her midterm grades next week. Her mom had made Chandra sign the FERPA agreement that let the school disclose her student information. She had a right to know Chandra's grades, her mom had pointed out, if she was the one paying for them.

Eli was still watching her. Listening to her. She felt herself starting to blush and couldn't stop herself from looking away, out the window. She noticed a girl walking by, someone decent looking, who had the same bag as she did from Urban Outfitters, which made Chandra feel sort of good for a moment. Like she knew how to choose things in an okay way. If someone saw her through the window sitting here at the table with Eli, she thought, that would be okay. She imagined for a minute that her roommate might walk by and notice her and ask her about it later and Chandra would have something to say. *Oh, that guy? He keeps asking me out on weird dates, like to jazz concerts and stuff. But he's kind of interesting. I have coffee and stuff with him sometimes.*

Eli pushed his tray toward her side of the table. "Have a nugget. I ordered too many." There were four ovals of chicken left on the tray, dried ketchup spotted on their greasy tan coating. "Go on. You look like you need to eat."

This guy, Chandra thought—Eli—he was attracted to her. Wasn't he? She picked up one of the greasy chicken pieces and brought it to her lips and waited for a few moments before wrapping it in one of her crumpled napkins.

He pushed back his chair, lifting his arms, palms upturned toward the window. "The day is ours!"

She followed him outside, where a spiral of colored leaves swirled in a sudden wind.

"Do you miss it?"

For a minute she thought he was reading her mind because she was thinking about her old house on Riley Road, where she lived when she was little. Autumn was her dad's favorite season. He liked the leaves. He hated shoveling the driveway in the winter, couldn't stand mowing the lawn in the heat of summer, but for some reason he always liked raking in the fall. He'd build these huge piles, orange and red, right under her swing set and give her pushes while she pumped herself high enough to let go and jump. He'd cover her under the dry crackling leaves, making her disappear. Pretend to start walking away. *Hey, do I hear a squirrel?* And she'd wait, wiggling just a little, waiting for him to reach in and grab her and pull her out.

"Leave it. You can live without it." Eli tugged on the sleeve of her shirt, and she realized they were standing by the tree where her phone was hidden. "*Live* being the key word."

Chandra looped a strand of her hair around her finger, twirled it for a minute before tucking it behind her ear. That was another sign that Chandra had read about that was supposed to hold a guy's attention without words—touching your own hair.

"Let's go over to Jaffrey. The jazz groups are probably starting now."
She shrugged.

"You don't like jazz? Maybe you should try it. You might be surprised."

"I didn't say I didn't like it." Her voice came out with an edge, and she saw the way he noticed it. His head drew back a little, his eyebrows lifting.

"I'm tired of sitting," Chandra said, and realized that this was actually true. "That's all college is, mostly. Sitting around and listening to things."

Eli's lips parted. She'd surprised him; she could tell.

"If I'm skipping class again," she said, her voice still louder than usual, "I want to *do* something. I don't want to sit around."

He looked at the watch under his coat sleeve, then grinned. "I know something we can do. Come on!"

He reached out his hand behind him, and Chandra took it, felt the momentum of his larger body pulling hers along. How long had it been since she'd held a guy's hand? She remembered for the second time today that trip to Disney World with her parents when she was eleven, how they'd walked through Fantasyland with the three of them holding hands, Chandra in the middle, her parents lifting her feet off the ground to a sing-song rhythm on every third step—one two *three*!—and Chandra knew she was too old for it but she didn't care.

Eli was leading them forward, past the library and the computer lab, all the way to the sports complex. They practically jogged past the recreation center, and through the glare on the wide front windows Chandra could see students on the treadmills. She tossed her head back and mimed an uproarious laugh, a silent one so Eli wouldn't notice, to let them know, if any of them recognized her dashing by, that she was on her way to doing something unpredictable and hilarious.

When they turned the corner of the building, Eli slowed up and they walked together to a large red door. "This is where the athletes work out," Eli said, pushing it open. She followed him inside to a gray-carpeted lobby with framed team pictures hung in neat lines on the tan brick walls. Smiling faces, bodies in matching red and white uniforms, posed in gymnasiums or fields or courts. The air smelled like a sweet medicine; fluorescent lights hummed overhead. Something she couldn't see was making a steady ticking noise. "Are we supposed to be in here?"

He grinned at her. "This'll be good. I haven't done this for a long time." She followed him down a short hallway to another door, also painted red.

"What? What are we doing?" She whispered, because Eli's voice was hushed too, like they were in the library.

"I was friends last year with this kid on the lacrosse team. He got put on probation, so they moved him out of the athlete dorm into Warner on my floor. We used to do this sometimes."

Eli pressed a series of numbers on the keypad above the doorknob;

the small circle on the pad flickered green. *"Yes."* Eli opened the door, stepped forward, and gestured like a magician. "Voila!"

She entered a small, darkened room with tiled walls and two small swimming pools, side by side. Eli shut the door behind her. There was a long bench against one wall; on the opposite wall, a freezer and a shelf with stacked towels and a large rolling hamper on wheels. Directly across from Chandra and Eli was a double door made of glass, which led to an adjacent room, also dark, with shadowed shapes of exercise machines.

"Where is everyone?" she whispered. The room felt warm, the air heavy with moisture. "What are we doing here?"

"Welcome to our private spa!" Eli tossed his jacket on the bench. "It's all ours till 2:00. Or 1:45, to be on the safe side. That's when the teams start afternoon practice and the injured guys, or the guys with physical therapy routines, come in here to work with the trainers. But from 10:45 to 1:45, this room is always locked. Unused. Shame to let it go to waste, right?"

He sat down and kicked off his Sperrys, peeled off his socks. He said, "All the athletes have their classes scheduled between 9:25 and 1:30. Then they have afternoon practice, and then dinner and study hall, and then night practice. Like clockwork. My lacrosse friend had to write down everything he did every day and every night while he was banned from the team to prove himself, and then have it signed every week by the team manager."

"Didn't he just make stuff up?"

"Of course he did. And then he would feel guilty and cry sometimes. Actually cry. He told me he felt like a piece of shit for being dishonest and breaking the honor code, like he was in the fucking Navy SEALS or something. And I was like, *Dude, you play lacrosse. For a second-rate conference. Get over yourself.*" He pulled off his long-sleeved shirt. He got up from the bench and padded in his bare feet around the pool. With just his T-shirt on, his biceps looked weaker than she'd imagined.

"People," said Chandra, "are so full of themselves."

"That's right." He pointed at her across the water. "You get it. You know that, Chandra? You so get it."

She was still standing there with her Urban Outfitters bag over her shoulder, sweating in her corduroy shirt. Suddenly, he reached toward the wall, and Chandra covered her eyes, expecting sudden brightness from a light switch, but instead a churning noise started, like a big engine. It was the water in one of the pools, violently bubbling. The smell of chlorine lifted, making her eyes water. Eli pulled off his T-shirt and unzipped his jeans.

"Stop!" Chandra covered her stinging eyes.

"Oh, come on. Your underwear is just like a swimsuit. It's just the same as swimming in our swimsuits."

"What if someone comes in?"

"If someone starts to press the combination on the locked door, we'll hear it and run out the glass door. And if someone comes in the trainers' room from the other side, we'll see them before they see us and run out the other way."

He was wearing boxers. Chandra watched as he sat down by the edge of the pool and lowered both feet in the water. "Aahhh!" He pushed himself off the edge with a splash, standing now in the pool up to his waist, his arms lifted like chicken wings. "And besides," he said, "what if someone did come in and find us? I mean, what's the worst thing that would happen? They'd tell us to leave? We'd get a warning?"

It was dark, Chandra thought. But not so dark that he wouldn't see her body. Could she actually do this? She placed her bag on the bench and took off her shirt. Even though she was wearing a turtleneck underneath it, she felt her heart start to race. She could feel his eyes on her back.

"You said you wanted to *do* something. Get in. Come on."

She balanced on one leg and pulled off her right boot and then the left. She took off her socks. The mats under her feet felt rough and prickly. She curled her arches and moved around the pool toward the shelf of towels with slow, quick steps, like one of those old-time Chinese girls with foot binding that her professor in Gender Perspectives had told them about. She wrapped a towel around her body and tried to figure out if she could take off her turtleneck and leggings and make it to the whirlpool without dropping the towel until she was completely submerged in the dark water.

"Come on. You're wasting time."

The silliness had disappeared from Eli's voice. He sounded annoyed. Pinching the towel at her breastbone with one hand, Chandra pushed at the elastic band of her leggings with the other, trying to wriggle them off her hips.

She heard him suck in a breath of air and then splash underwater, saw the dark shape of him coiling into a mass on the bottom. Quickly she pulled off her turtleneck and covered up again with the towel. He rose up from the bubbling water with a grunt, shaking his head, flinging

309

drops that hit her bare forearms. She pulled her feet free from her leggings and walked to the metal ladder on the far side of the pool, holding on to it with one hand, keeping her towel secure with the other; she felt with her feet for the textured steps leading down the pool's wall, and then the slippery bottom as she lowered in. Hot water from a jet spray pelted her back. The towel swirled up and she held it like a cape at her neck; it floated behind her shoulders as she folded her arms over her stomach, squatting in the pool up to her neck.

Eli's head bobbed above the surface a few feet away. The darkness of the room made his face look older, Chandra thought—handsome, kind of, with his hair slicked back. His eyes looked deeper in the steamy air, which she hoped was making her own face look better, too, more mysterious maybe, and if her mascara was running, hopefully it wouldn't show. The churning water swirled around Chandra like a force field, protecting her body from scrutiny. Eli was moving toward her now. This was happening. If he kissed her, Chandra decided, she would kiss him back. She was doing it. Finally, she was having a college experience.

"I'm so bad, letting you talk me into this," she said, hoping her voice sounded flirty and mocking in a fun way. "This is the *third day* I'm missing classes. I'm so behind."

"That's nothing." Eli laughed, low and abrupt.

She felt his toe slide against her toe underwater. He said, "This is my fifth week."

"What do you mean?"

He grinned, his teeth glinting in the dark. "I haven't been to classes for five weeks."

She felt the space between their bodies in the water get smaller as he moved closer, the pressure of the waves against her stomach building. "But . . ."

"I had it figured out by the second week. That I was going to live by my own rules for a change, you know? Relinquish the façade."

"Can you do that? Just not go to your classes for that long? Haven't they *said* anything to you?"

"Oh, I'm sure my student email account is full of dire warnings from my professors, at least the ones who bother to take attendance. But, as you know, I'm not reading them. Or anything else online. Because I'm choosing to spend my time actually living my life."

"I didn't know you could *do* that. Just never go to your classes."

"*I'm* doing it." His white teeth flashed.

"But for how long?" Chandra felt a twist of anxiety in her chest.

Eli grunted. "A couple more weeks, probably. The midterm grades will all be submitted by next week, and then the week after that they'll probably come get me out of the dorm. And that'll be it."

"They'll make you leave?"

"I'm already on academic probation from last year. So yeah. They'll undoubtedly request my departure." This time his laugh was louder and seemed to echo off the slippery walls.

"Then you'll go home?"

She saw his shoulders shrug, above and below the water's surface.

"Where do your parents live?" she asked.

His body was so close to hers in the whirlpool. If she lifted her hand, her fingers would touch his chest. "I'm not going there," he whispered, and it sounded to Chandra like he was about to cry.

"Eli," she said, "I'll help you. You can stay in my dorm. They won't know where to look for you."

"I'll disappear." He sucked in a breath. "Poof!"

With a sudden *whoosh* he dunked himself under the water, and then his long legs and one of his knees, or maybe both of them, were pressing against her legs and his hands were on her waist, his thumbs on either side of her belly button and his fingertips on her back, and where was her towel? Her towel was gone, she realized, both frightened and glad, and Eli's head was above hers now, he was gulping at the air, and she leaned back in his hands, arching her neck, the crown of her head touching the water. She let her hands reach up to his shoulders and looked into his eyes.

"*Chandra,*" he said.

His hands loosened their grip on her waist; she felt the support slip away and had to plant the balls of her feet on the bottom of the pool to keep herself from falling backwards into the water.

"Chandra, your *bones.* Jesus."

She pushed off with her feet and flailed with her arms, moving in slow motion through the water away from him. Her towel, where was her towel? She spotted it swirling in a jet stream near the metal ladder and lunged for it.

"God, Chandra, chill *out.* I just, you know . . . It's kind of shocking—"

"Shut up!" She managed to pull herself out of the pool; the rushing of the whirlpool engine seemed to be right inside her head now.

She grabbed at her boots and bag and her big corduroy shirt by the bench, but then as she ran around to the other side of the pool and tried to pick up her turtleneck and leggings, she lost her grip on the towel again and it dropped to the floor. She started to cry, and she could picture herself standing there like a hunchback, cradling her load. She couldn't bear to turn around to look at Eli, watching her from the pool. She could feel her bare back and her soaking panties clinging to her ass in the horrible invisible air.

"It's sad," Eli said. "What this fucked-up society does to people."

"Don't *say* anything!" She pushed against the glass door and ran to one of the treadmills in the physical therapy room, crouched on the other side of it, and waited for a couple minutes, afraid that he would follow her. But he didn't.

She struggled to pull her leggings on over her wet skin, then her two shirts and her boots. She raked her fingers through her tangled hair. She found her way to a different doorway on the other side of the room, back to the lobby, past the rows of team pictures, all those smiling athletes posing with the Hawk mascot, its cartoonish beak and red wings. Who was the person hidden in that bird costume? Chandra wondered.

As she stepped outside into the October air, the wind wrapped itself around her wet scalp like an icy tourniquet. She held her Urban Outfitters bag against the side of her body and began marching across the campus, headed toward the student union. Had she muted her phone before she let Eli hide it in that hole in the big tree? She couldn't remember! What if someone had texted her, what if her mother had called, and someone walking by heard her Rihanna ringtone—*yellow diamonds*—and found it there. By now maybe Professor Steinmetz had sent her an email about missing class again. To voice his concern. That's how he would say it, or something like that.

Maybe she could write her paper for him about money. She didn't want to write anymore about giving up her cell phone; she had nothing to say about *that* topic. She wished she were smart enough to write an essay about money, about how money could make you hate someone, like the way she guessed Eli hated his parents, like the way her father hated her mother for not giving him her lawsuit money to buy a Sonic burger franchise, which would have been the whole solution to his whole life, or at least that was what he believed. He would have screwed it up, her mother had told her, *guaranteed*, and then where would that have left Chandra, and her college education, and her future wedding, God willing? But Chandra didn't know. She didn't know where that would have left her, or where she was left now.

She started walking faster. The union was still far away, and she wanted to be there. She wanted to start running, but that would look so weird, wouldn't it? She was wearing her boots, the ones with high heels. People didn't run in high-heeled boots. But still, she could feel herself picking up her feet between each quickening step.

She used to run all the time. She missed running. Maybe she could write her paper for Professor Steinmetz about running. It was during that horrible summer when she'd started running, the summer when she was fourteen, after her parents had sold the house and moved into their separate apartments in different towns. She would start at her mother's apartment in Vernon and walk all the way to their old house in Woodlen, on Riley Mountain Road. It was a yellow Cape Cod with a slate-blue door and matching shutters. It took her two hours and twenty minutes. When she got there, she would stand by the mailbox for a few minutes. Sometimes, if no one was around, she would walk onto the front yard and stand there. She didn't know who had bought the house. Her parents never told her, and it seemed somehow too embarrassing to ask them. Shameful, for some reason. When she stood on the front lawn, a trespasser, sometimes she would feel her heart start thumping. She would count to ten, or twenty, or sometimes fifty, and then step back to the street.

And then she would run home. She could slow way down on the upward hills, but she had to keep lifting her feet. If she didn't run home, she told herself, then she couldn't go back. It would be the last time.

That's how it started, Chandra thought. At some point during the summer, Melanie commented on how good Chandra was looking. Chandra remembered the day that Melanie seemed to notice her in a new way, surveying her with a lifted eyebrow. Lean, Melanie had said. Lean and fit, not sloppy like so many teenage girls with their belly shirts and pudgy thighs and boobs bouncing around. When school started at the end of August, Chandra had to stop her journeys to the old house, but she found other ways to test herself. She kept going and going.

Right now, all she wanted was her phone back. As she made it past the computer lab, the union came into view, and there was the tree in the distance, its golden leaves glowing in afternoon sunlight. She could feel her fingers twitching in anticipation. She wanted it back so badly. She would text someone, anyone, just to hear it buzz, just to feel it trembling there in the palm of her hand.

THE TOWER

fiction by FREDERIC TUTEN

Sometimes his urine was cloudy. Sometimes gritty with what he called "gravel." Sometimes his piss flowed bloody and frightening. No matter how disturbing, Montaigne recorded his condition in his travel journal as coolly he did the daily weather. He was always in various degrees of pain, and he noted that too, but dispassionately, like a scientist in a white lab coat.

Even before he suffered from kidney stones and the burning pain that came with them, Montaigne had long thought about death, and not only his own. He had thought about how to meet it and if doing so gracefully would change the encounter. His closest friend, the man he had loved more than anyone in the world, was to love more than anyone in the world, had died with calm dignity. In his last minutes, in his last words, his dear friend did not begrudge life or beg for more time or express regrets over what was left undone or make apologies to those he might have or had offended or injured. Montaigne thought that when death approached, he would neither wave him away nor welcome him, but say to death's shadow on the wall, "Finally, no more pain."

I put my book aside when she walked in.

"I'm leaving you," she said. She had a red handbag on her arm.

"For how long?"

"For always."

"And what about Pascal, will you take him?"

"He's always favored you." I was very glad. I could see Pascal sitting in the dining-room doorway, pretending not to listen.

"Yes, that's true."

314

"Don't you care to know why I'm leaving?" she asked, petulantly, I thought.

"I suppose you'll tell me."

"I will, but maybe another time." She stared at me as if wondering who I was. Then she started to speak but was interrupted by a car-horn blast. I looked out the window and saw a taxi with a man behind the wheel.

"May I help you with your bags?" I asked.

"I'll send for them later, if you don't mind."

"Who will you send?"

"The person who comes." She stared at me another moment and then left.

I heard a motor start up, then the swerve of the car leaving the curb. Pascal took his time walking over to me and then, with a faint cry he jumped into my lap, curling himself on my open book. I stroked his head until he made that little motor purr that all cats make when they pretend to love you.

One day Montaigne went all the way from his home in Bordeaux to Italy for its famous physicians and for a change in diet, for that country's warm climate and healing sky. He went to soak himself in the mineral baths, which sometimes gave him relief—also noted in his journal. He recorded but never whined about the biting stones in his kidneys or the bedbugs in the mattress in a Florence hostel or complained about that city's summer heat, so great that he slept on a table pressed against an open window.

He traveled alone. Once, in Rome, Montaigne hired a translator, a fellow Frenchman, who, without notice or reason, left him without a good-bye. So, armed with maps and charts and curiosity, he went about the city with himself for company and guide. In that ancient city he witnessed horrific public executions of criminals, men drawn and quartered while still alive. He visited the libraries of cardinals and nobles, returning to his hostel to note in the same disinterested voice the books and the tortures he had seen and the hard stone that had that day passed through his urine.

I knew there was no hope in lifting Pascal up and dropping him on the carpet so that he would leave me alone to read. I knew he would just bound up again and sit on my book again and that he would do the same one hundred and one times before I gave up and left the room or left the house or left the city. So I took the string with a little ball attached to it that I kept tucked under the pillow and let it drop on the floor. He leapt off my lap and began pawing the rubber ball. I pulled it away and he followed with a one-two punch. Montaigne had once asked himself: Is it I who plays with the cat or is it he who plays with me?

The house seemed full now that she had gone, the rooms packed with me. I wandered about savoring the quiet, the solitude, the way my books, sleeping on their shelves, seemed to glow as I passed by—old friends who no longer need share me with another. I thought I would spend the rest of the day without a plan and do as I wished. Maybe I would sit all day and read. Maybe I would go out with my gun and empty the streets of all the noise. I would then at last have a silent, empty house surrounded by a tranquil, soundless zone. That was just a thought. I have no gun.

After his beloved friend died, Montaigne went into seclusion, keeping himself in a turreted stone tower at the edge of his estate. It was cold in winter and hot in summer and not well lit, the windows being small. He had had a very full life up to the point of his withdrawal, if fullness means social activity and a role in governing. He was a courtier in the royal court and the mayor of Bordeaux and was always out day and night doing things. But now in that tower Montaigne was determined to write, which he did, essays, which some think were addressed to his dead friend. His mind traveled everywhere, his prose keeping apace with all the distances and places his mind traveled. He wrote about cannibals. He wrote about friendship. What is friendship, he asked, and answered: When it is true, it is greater than any bond of blood. Brothers have in common the same port from whence they were issued but may be separated forever by jealousy and rivalry in matters of inheritance and property. Brothers may hate each other, kill each other, as the Old Testament so vividly illustrates. But friends choose each other and their intercourse deepens in trust, esteem, and affection; their intellectual exchange strikes flames.

He stayed in his tower for ten years, his world winnowed down to a stone room of books and a wooden table. Crows sat on his window ledge and studied him, imperturbable in their presence. His wife visited and in his place saw a triangle. Sometimes he would look at his friend's portrait on the table, a miniature in a plain silver frame, and say, "We've worked enough for now, let's go to lunch. What do you think?" Sometimes he just stayed in place until the evening, when he dined on cold mutton and lentils and read in the wintry candlelight. Once, as he climbed the stair to his bedchamber, he noticed his bent shadow trailing him on the wall. Just some years ago his shadow had bounded ahead of him, waiting for him to catch up. Now he grew tired easily; writing a page took hours and he was always in pain. He pissed rich blood. He howled. But he sat and wrote until he finished his book. Then he went on his extensive travels.

I went into the kitchen and made a dish of pears and Stilton and broke out the water biscuits; I opened the best wine I had ever bought, one so expensive that I had hid it from her, waiting for the right occasion to spring it. I sat at the kitchen table. Pascal leaped up to join me. I opened a can of boneless sardines, drained the oil, slid the fish onto a large, white plate, and set it beside me so that Pascal and I could lunch together. He was suspicious, sniffed, then retreated, and then returned to the same olfactory investigation until he finally decided to leave the novelty to rest. The bouquet rose from the wine bottle like a genie and filled the room with sparkling sunshine and the aromatic, medieval soil of Bordeaux. It pleased me to think that Montaigne might have drunk wine from the same vineyard, from the same offspring of grapes.

I went up to her bedroom and opened the closets. So many clothes, dresses, shoes, scarves, belts, hats. The drawers were stuffed with garter belts and black bikini panties that I had never been privy to seeing her wear. Soon the closet would be empty and I would leave it that way. Or leave it that way until I decided what to do with the house, too small for two, too large for one and a cat. She had left the bed unmade, the blankets and sheets twisted and tangled, as if they had been wrestling until they had given up, exhausted. I sniffed her pillow, which was heavy with perfume and dreams. Pascal came in and danced on the bed, where he had never been allowed. I left him there stretched out on her pillow and went down to my study.

It welcomed me as never before. My desk with its teetering piles of books and loose sheets of notes and a printer and computer and a Chinese lamp, little pots full of outdated stamps and rubber bands, an instant-coffee jar crammed with red pencils, green paper clips heaped in a chipped, blue teacup, a stapler, an old rotary phone, framed prints of Goya's *Puppet* and Poussin's *Echo and Narcissus*, Cézanne's *Bathers*, and Van Gogh's *Wheat Field in Rain* greeted and accepted me without any conditions. I could sit at my desk all day and night and never again be presented with the obligation to clear or clean an inch of the disorder. Now, if I wished, I could even sweep away every single thing on the desk and leave it bare and hungry. Or I could chop up and burn the desk in the fireplace. I would wait for a cold night. There was plenty of time now to make decisions.

317

I went back to the living room and turned on the TV and madly switched channels, finding I liked everything that flashed across the screen, especially the Military Channel, where I watched a history of tank battles and decided I would rather have been in the Navy if it had come to that. Montaigne, surprisingly, detested the sea, from where much contemplation springs. All the same, perhaps the swell of a wave and a splash of the brine might have made him a more dreamy man of the sky than the solid man of the earth, where he was so perfectly at home. Later, watching another channel, I bought four Roman coins, authentic reproductions of Emperor Hadrian's young lover, Antinous, whose death he grieved until his last imperial breath. On another channel, I ordered a device that sucked wax from the ears. It was guaranteed that my hearing would improve within days. But then, after it was too late to change my mind, I realized I did not need or want to improve my hearing. Except for the music I love, I thought I don't care to hear well at all. Most of what is said is better left unsaid and left unheard. It is the voices from the silent world of the self that matter, like the ones that Montaigne heard and wrote down in his tower room. I thought I might demolish the house now and build that tower in its place and live in the comfort of its invisible voices, and sit there and transcribe the voices as they came.

I grew bored with TV and realized that I missed reading my book of Montaigne's travels, that I missed him. Montaigne was someone I was sure that I could travel with, because he was someone whom I could leave or accompany whenever I chose. And there would be no recriminations, no arguments, no pulling this way and that about where to eat and how much to cool down or heat up the hotel room—or any room anywhere. I went back to my chair and opened Montaigne's book, sure that Pascal would soon arrive and jump up. But a half hour passed and he still had not come. I missed him and the game we played. So, after several more minutes, I went to find him. He was nowhere to be found. But the window to my wife's bedroom was open and I surmised he had left through it and to a world of his own making.

I was about to settle back to my reading when there was a strong knock at the door. I opened it to a man in a blue suit.

"Is she here?"

"Not presently," I said.

"Will she return presently?"

"Who knows?" I said.

"Well, I looked for her everywhere and thought she might have returned here," he said, peering in the doorway.

"Not here," I said, slowly closing the door.

"Do you mind if I come in a minute? Just to rest my feet."

"Have you been searching for her on foot?"

"Not at all," he said, nodding over to the cab standing before the house. "But I'm exhausted from looking for her."

"Come in," I said, not too graciously.

He went immediately to my favorite chair but before he could plunk himself down, I said, "That one's broken."

He sat down on the couch and gave me a sheepish grin. "Thanks buddy."

I pretended to be reading my book but I was sizing him up, slyly, I thought. I did not find him remarkable in any way.

"Is she a reliable woman?" he asked.

"Absolutely. And punctual too."

He looked about the room and folded his hands the way boys are told to do in a classroom. "Does she read all these books?"

"Some, but not all at once."

"That's very funny," he said, with a little sarcastic smile. Then, changing to a more agreeable one, he asked, "Got something to drink? Worked up a thirst running around town looking for her."

"I just opened a bottle of wine you may like."

"Is it from California?"

"No."

"From France?"

"No, from New Zealand."

"I'll pass then. How about a glass of water, no ice." I didn't answer. He stared at me a long time but I waited him out. I noticed he wore burgundy moccasins with tassels and was without socks. That he had an orange suntan that glowed.

"She has me drop her off at the mall and says to come back and get her in a an hour or two. But she never shows up."

"Was your meter running?"

"My Jag's in the shop. The cab's from my fleet."

"By the way, have you seen a cat out there in the street?"

"A salt-and-pepper one with a drooping ear?"

"Yes."

"No, I haven't." Then, in a shot, he added, "Is she your wife?"

"We're married," I said.

"She told me you were roommates."

"We do share rooms, though not all of them."

He stood up, pulled down his jacket, which seemed on the tight side, and came up close to me. "You're better off without her, pal. With all due respect, she's a flake but the kind that fits me,"

He went to the door and I followed, my book in hand, like a pistol. Would you still like that water?" I asked, in a most agreeable way.

"Don't tell her you saw me," he said.

"Cross my heart and hope to die," I said.

He gave me a long look, half friendly, half bewildered, half menacing. "You're not so bad for a dope."

He sped off in his cab—Apex. Twenty-four Hours a Day. We Go Everywhere. The street was empty. The sidewalk was empty. The houses and their lawns across the road were empty. The sky was empty. The clouds too. I shut the door and returned to my favorite chair and went back to my book.

Montaigne wrote brief notes to his wife describing his adventures with bedbugs and the summer heat, never referring to his urinary condition or to his pains, which worsened with each day. He noted that the Italians painted their bedpans with scenes from classical mythology, favoring those of Leda and her admiring swan. They were comforting, those bedpans, so unlike the severe white porcelain ones in France that never thought to combine art with excrement.

I was near the end of the book and that left me in a vacuum for the remainder of the day. I thought that now that I was at large, I would need to plan for the evening and the night ahead. I would leave tomorrow to itself for now. But then the door swung wide open and she appeared, fancy shopping bags in hand.

"Well, aren't you going to help me?" I relieved her of two of the larger bags and settled them on the sofa. "There's another one on the porch," she said, as if I had been malingering. I retrieved it and another one at the doorstep, a large, round, pink box.

She sat on the sofa and kicked off her shoes. She looked about as if in an unfamiliar place. "What have you done?"

"To what?" I asked.

"To the room! It looks different. Did you change anything?"

"Nothing."

She looked at me suspiciously then said, "Something's different."

"It knows you've left. Rooms always know when someone has left."

She pretended to yawn. "Sure."

"And they shift themselves to the new situation," I added. "Like when a person dies in a bedroom and the walls go gray and cold. Or when a child is born and the room goes rosy and roomier."

"Has anyone been here since I left? I can smell that someone has."

"Now that you mention it, yes."

"Was he wearing a blue suit?"

"I didn't notice."

"Let me show you something," she said, removing her dress. She fussed about the shopping bags and pulled out a red skirt and red jacket with large buttons. "Whataya think?" she asked, fastening her last fat button.

"You look like a ripe tomato."

"It matches my handbag," she said, waving it before me. "I realized after I left this morning that my bag needs something to go with it."

"Everything matches and matches your hair too."

"You've always had a good eye," she said.

"For you," I said, in a kind of flirty way that I wasn't sure I meant.

"If you don't mind, I'm going upstairs to pack some things."

"Let me know if you see Pascal up there, please."

"That's another thing. I cringed every time you explained to a guest that Pascal was named after some French philosopher," she said, turning from me.

"If you had ever seen Pascal stare up at the night sky and give a little shiver, you'd understand," I said.

She was already hallway up the stairs and I wasn't sure she had heard me. But then she shouted down, "Did he say when he'll come back?"

I pretended not to have heard her. She came down the stairs again and said, "Well?"

"He didn't say. But his Jag is in the shop."

"I don't care about the books. You can keep them all," she said. "They prefer you anyway, like the cat."

"I named him Pascal, after his namesake, who asked for the patience to sit. I named him Pascal because he sits quietly in the window box and I can see in his eyes that he is training himself against his nature to learn to sit."

She gathered up the red dress suit and the handbag and, without a word, went back up the stairs. I returned to my book but my heart was not in it. Montaigne was on his way back to Bordeaux to his wife and his old life of solitude and voices. To his old known comforts. For all its vaunted claims, travel is a deterioration, taking minutes off one's life with every passing mile. So, for all his bravery, his condition worsened with each jolt of the carriage, with each bug bite and bad meal. By the time he finally arrived home, the blood in his urine had grown darker, the pain stronger, the loneliness greater.

I returned to the kitchen and to the remains of my lunch, still scattered on the table like the flotsam of a minor wreck. I sipped a glass of wine. It tasted of damp nails forgotten in a dank cellar. I sat there as the dusk filtered through the kitchen window, softening the edges of the table and the chairs and the hulk of the fridge. My hand looked like a mitten. Montaigne should never have left his tower, I thought, and gave voice to it in the shadows, "'You should have stayed home," I said, advice given too late to an old friend.

Then I went to the door, thinking that Pascal might be there sitting on the step, waiting for me to let him in after his adventures in the wide world. Or maybe he would be just sitting and waiting for the night and the chill of its distant stars.

—*For Edmund White*

COUNSELOR OF MY HEART

fiction by LYDIA CONKLIN

After crossing Memorial Drive onto the bank of the Charles, Molly let her quasi girlfriend's dog off leash. Chowder bounded next to her, limbs flapping against the snow—so puppyish she wanted to push him over. But nothing could annoy her now, not even the stupid dog. She had a day off from the hot dog stand. The air smelled like fire.

She was just wishing the dog away when she became half-aware of the squirrel skittering over the frozen river, making the sound of a rake dragged over plastic. Later she'd wonder why she didn't turn and face the squirrel, seriously question his purpose on the ice. Did he think he'd buried a nut out there? *Had* he, actually? Was it floating, swollen, an inch above the river bottom?

Chowder took his time noticing. He was a foolish dog, though German shepherds are supposed to be bright. Perhaps the white ones, rabbity and smiling, had the smarts bleached out. Beth, whom Molly was dating, had owned Chowder for ten years. Ten frustrating years, Molly imagined, though she'd only met Beth last year. She could picture the rodent-like puppy the dog must have made, the cakes he must have flattened, the urine he must have sprinkled on carpets like holy water.

When Chowder saw the squirrel, he didn't stop to point or stare, judge distance or his probability of success. He tore off across the frosty grass and rinds of stale snow and slipped onto the river. He turned wild for a second, properly vicious. His hackles went up and his tail flagged, his teeth golden against his white coat. Even when his paws slipped, they slipped together, all four at once, so he sailed farther and faster across the ice.

Just as Chowder was about to seize the squirrel, she heard thunder and the ice gave way.

For a heartbeat his tail stuck out, the bottlebrush whiter than the ice or the overcast sky. Molly wondered if anyone was watching from the Weeks Footbridge or the Leverett Towers or the mysterious factory across the river. But then Chowder was gone and the squirrel was gone and Molly was still standing on the bank. She hadn't even taken a step.

There was a hole in the river now. A gray-blue shadow that didn't look big enough to swallow a Chihuahua, much less a shepherd and a squirrel. Molly watched the hole for longer than any mammal could hold its breath, then realized she should've run to the edge, at least tried the ice, before letting the dog go.

Walking back through Harvard Square, dusk hazing the air, Molly felt the weight of the leather leash around her neck. She was balling it up to stick in her bag when a kid in a "Veritas = Beer" shirt said, "All you need is a dog!"

A shot of acid hit Molly's throat. She wanted to spank the kid but instead she asked, "Are you volunteering?"

She returned to Hurlbut Hall, more commonly known as Pukeass Hall, to the first floor suite where Beth was a tutor. Molly was staying with Chowder while Beth presented a paper in Delaware. Harvard tutors were allowed to have pets on the first floor. Beth said that was because the dogs could exit quickly without sloughing dandruff on the stairs and halls. Some of the students on the upper floors had sensitivities.

"You mean allergies?" Molly asked. That was reasonable. Molly was surprised they let a dog in the dorms at all.

"No," said Beth. "If there were allergies I wouldn't be in Hurlbut. But some of the students are sensitive."

That was an understatement. The Harvard kids were at Beth's door from dawn until dawn again. There was never a moment you could crawl between the sheets without some wiener tapping that tight knock that said, *While I acknowledge in theory that I'm being a pain, I nevertheless require your immediate response.*

The freshmen wanted advice about applying to medical school or to report G-Chat alerts that were turned up too loud and poop residue on the toilet seat and gum plastered over showerhead holes. The gum was intended to increase water pressure but just ended up steaming people in mint. Beth indulged the students like precious, dear children, nodding deeply at their monologues, sometimes even tapping their shoulders and rolling her eyes at their pain.

Molly entered the suite. There were armchairs in the front room, everything layered with overlapping rugs and Southwestern blankets. There were too many patterns but that was what you needed to make a dorm cozy when you were in your late twenties and no longer willing to surrender to bluish industrial white.

When she sat down she felt, for an instant, the smiling muzzle of Chowder in her lap. This was the first time she'd sat on the chair without him burrowing in, as though out of sweetness, and then taking a drag of her crotch. Beth wasn't coming back until later tonight, but Molly should call and tell her what had happened. Beth loved Chowder more than she loved Molly, or her family, or herself. Only God knew why.

Molly listened to the ocean on the receiver for a while before dialing out of the Harvard system. Beth was in session or in the hotel revising. Her presentation was in an hour, and her phone would be off. Molly would leave a message using her ghastliest voice. Delivering the news would be easier when Beth called back expecting something dire.

But then, suddenly, Beth was on the line.

"I have to get dressed in two minutes," she said, as if they were already midconversation. "Judith Butler is here. I can't believe no one told me. I have to raise the barn. I have to."

Beth always mixed up aphorisms, which Molly found endearing, considering Beth was in her fourth year of a comp lit PhD program. She'd finished her course work but couldn't begin her dissertation until she accumulated three first-author publications. She was presenting a paper today at a conference called "Bodies that Matter."

"Then raise the barn," Molly said. Usually she hated talking about Beth's stress, which washed over Molly like secondhand smoke, reminding her of all the careers she wasn't pursuing, all the progress she wasn't making. But right now she'd take any topic over Chowder.

"How am I supposed to raise the barn if I've been writing this paper for three months and I've already raised the goddamn barn a thousand times, like practically out of the atmosphere, and now I can't raise it any higher or everything's going to topple like some kind of, I don't know, tower of napkins? Whatever that's called?"

Molly pictured a soft, wobbling skyscraper. Beth's versions were always better.

"My talk's in an hour, Molly. You never call. Why now?"

325

The leash was coiled on the floor, spring-loaded like it might strike. If Molly dumped the news on Beth now, her presentation would be ruined. "I guess I'll talk to you when you get home."

"OK. Kiss the beast."

Molly tried to hang up before that last part. A pang ripped her shoulder. She should've told Beth. But she shouldn't have let Chowder off the leash in the first place. As long as she was wishing.

She leaned back in the armchair. She'd wait until the panel started, and then she'd leave a message. She tried to relax into the stiff upholstery, taking in these last few hours of calm, but she couldn't hold still. She kept noticing Chowder's accessories and thinking about how they would never be squeezed or squished, thrown or caught, eaten or slurped up again. So she gathered everything dog-related and stuffed the whole mess under the sink. She stacked his bag of kibble on the last inch of drooly water in his bowl. She piled the squeaky T-bone steak on the pack of Snausages and added a clump of fur that had floated around the room for weeks, like a fuzzy flying saucer. It felt good to snatch the soft disk out of the air and confine it.

But she still couldn't rest; she needed something to get the relaxing started. Ever since she was fifteen, she'd leaned on substances at times like this. Just thinking about her adventures was enough to make her grin. She'd mixed NyQuil with root beer, huffed computer keyboard cleaner, and never said no to cocaine, even if it had that grainy yellow look and was mostly lactose or baking soda. Even now that she was living the domestic life, she needed a boost sometimes, though she tried to hide the worst from Beth. A couple glasses of wine usually did the trick, but alcohol wasn't allowed in freshman dorms. Fortunately, Molly had a sandwich bag of pot for emergencies.

Sometimes Beth let her smoke in the bathroom, the last room in the railroad suite, with her head out the window, at night, when no one was on Prescott. This seemed more incriminating than smoking inside and lighting a cranberry-scented candle afterward, but Beth was more afraid of the little Harvard shits than the campus police or even the real police. Right now, though, it didn't matter. Molly had killed Beth's dog. She smoked right there in the armchair.

Molly's own apartment was in Allston, across the river, where there were no rules or snotty students. But life in Allston wasn't paradise. She had cockroaches and rats. Not mice, but rats. She'd had mice at first, had wished away the one-ounce fluffs only to meet bulge-backed, two-pound goblins that dragged themselves across the floor without bothering to scamper. If you yelled or stomped they just planted their hips and stared, as though saying, *You're sixty times my body weight and that's the best you can do?* Even so, she preferred her place to this womb of eighteen-year-olds. She felt caught with Beth, too domestic. She was afraid of how much she liked just hanging out and having sex, watching TV, reading for the first time in years. Wasn't she too young to be this boring?

Ever since Molly graduated from Northeastern four years ago, she'd been working at the vegan hot dog stand and playing as many shows as she could get at T.T.'s and the Lizard Lounge and sometimes, if she was lucky, Club Passim. She had a couple good songs, one about a boy riding the Hi-Line through Montana, one about coming out in fourth grade. She had some bad songs, too—she knew they were bad—but she had to play them for filler.

She first saw Beth at a gig, from her perch atop her rickety industrial stool. She noticed Beth because she was older, heavier, and more fastidiously dressed than her normal fan base. Large-bosomed and prim, Beth was a virgin at twenty-seven. She reminded Molly of a counselor at a summer camp she'd never attended, who was critical of the children but stood naked before them. Who taught them how to pull the udder of a cow with slipping, lubricated fingers and didn't realize how sexual it was. Molly referred to Beth among her coworkers as Counselor of My Heart. After five friend dates she cornered Beth before a screening of *Happy Together* at the Brattle and kissed her. To Molly's surprise, the involvement actually went forward from there. Beth had come close to saying she loved Molly the other day, at least Molly thought she did. Her eyes were glassy with nervousness, and she said she had to tell Molly something. Molly changed the subject fast. Maybe she didn't believe Beth could love her, being so much smarter, so much more put together. Not dependent on substances. Not a failed musician.

Molly got viciously high. But no matter how high she got she couldn't stop thinking about Chowder. She saw that pale wolf's tail sticking out of the ice, pictured paws pedaling in water thick with cold. She needed a distraction, so she found her travel guitar, three-quarters size and a gift from Beth, which frankly was higher quality than her official guitar. She warmed up on scales and picked out a new tune. Just A-D-A-D-A-D-G, plain as can be. She tried to make it funny. Tried to cheer herself up so she could forget for a minute. "Counselor of my heart," she sang. "Counselor of my heart, don't come home too soon. Counselor of my heart, I hope your flight's delayed."

Just as she wound down the first verse, there was a tight rap at the door. Molly put out the joint and kept playing. "Will you forgive me, counselor of my heart? Will you still sleep with me like you do so well?"

The rapping continued. The Harvard kids were so urgent. They even brushed their teeth urgently, specks of blood flinging onto the mirrors. They washed their faces until they shone like peeled beets. On their eyelids were fierce marks where they bore down too hard with eyeliner pencils.

Molly composed one more verse, "Counselor of my heart, will you survive today? Will you get a new dog, a smart dog, a graceful dog? Golden dogs, gorgeous dogs, sexy dogs, Harvard dogs?" before she had to admit the kid wasn't leaving. She flicked the smoke away and pulled the door open an inch.

A boy stood in the fluorescent-lit hall. He had unfashionable glasses and sandy hair and wore flannel pants and a T-shirt that read "Give Bone Marrow" above a rubbery, grinning femur.

"Excuse me, ma'am," he said with odd formality, considering his outfit. "Has Beth Barrett yet returned?"

"No." Molly tried to limit her interactions with the students. If anyone said "Hi" to her in the hall, it was always that hi-I-have-a-question voice. *Hi, I have ulterior motives. Hi, I want to take advantage of you really fast.* Molly started to close the door.

"Wait," the boy said. "Who's on duty? The third-floor guy? There's a problem."

"There's no problem," Molly said. "Why don't you run along?"

"But it smells like marijuana. I think it's from six-A."

"That's no concern of yours."

Molly couldn't read the boy's expression because the lenses of his glasses were so dense and uneven. As he shifted, his eyes broke up.

"Where's the dog?" he asked. "Beth said someone was staying with the dog."

Molly didn't like that "someone." It sounded too much like "anyone," even though she didn't call Beth her girlfriend yet, wasn't ready to have a real girlfriend. Just like she wasn't ready to have a real job or a real musical career, as if she had the option for either.

"I don't hear him. Chowder. Chowder."

Molly cracked the door wider. The kids pushed and pushed but they didn't know themselves what for. "Come in." She didn't want him shouting about drugs and the dog so the RA on the third floor could hear. That kid was only a junior himself and not much more mature than the freshmen. Even he sometimes whined to Beth, bleating his dull troubles.

The kid entered the room. "Beth said I could walk Chowder anytime. I want to walk him."

Molly slouched against the wall, as if claiming her territory by osmosing into it. There was a quality in this kid that made her want to thoroughly disappoint him. "This isn't a good time."

Molly had come over to find students weeping in the armchair, the shepherd huffing their crotches. From the intensity of their wails you'd have guessed they were failing or brokenhearted, but they were usually upset about a cavity or a B-. Beth left the door open to guard against lawsuits, but Molly closed it now.

"Sit down." The boy was skinny, a slice shaved off some other boy. He picked up the leash, held it distastefully, like a snakeskin.

Molly remembered him now. She'd seen him with Beth in the hall, cuddling the shepherd's big head, his fleece matted with fur. He was probably one of those kids with a dog back home who couldn't stand a life free of gamy smells and feces handling.

"Sit down, please." Molly took the leash. "And stop grabbing things that don't belong to you." The Harvard kids, for all their intensity, just wanted to be treated like children. They relaxed when following orders.

Molly closed the door to Beth's bedroom, creating the possibility that Chowder was somewhere in the suite, even though the softest rap sent him rocketing to the door, woofing with his tongue out, ecstatic to meet whomever might emerge from beyond the wooden frame. Rapists and serial killers, he welcomed them all.

The boy sat down.

"Who are you?" he asked. "I've seen you."

"I'm Beth's, you know, person." Saying that out loud felt weird. Molly didn't know if she'd ever before admitted to an official relationship with Beth, or anyone for that matter. The fumbling sentence was out before she considered that perhaps Beth did not want students knowing she was gay. Perhaps that was why "someone" was watching the dog. Of course, Molly was wearing a man's flannel and had shaggy, short hair. She was always around, and there was only one bed.

The boy's eyes inflated. "Beth's, like, a gay lesbian?"

"Yup." In fact, Beth's sexuality wasn't official. She hadn't come out to her family or friends. She didn't even know the term "come out," but said "come forth," as in, "Do you think Larry Summers will ever come forth from the closet?" (Her gaydar was also abysmal.) But she sure acted gay enough. Molly had long thought the information should be public. And she'd always known she'd have to follow through while high. She relit the joint, watching the fleshy machine of the boy's brain kick into gear.

"You're smoking marijuana."

Molly wagged her eyebrows. "Sure about that, kid?"

"James," he said. Then, defiantly, he reached out his knobby hand for the joint. She let him have it because, why not? Everything was going to shit today, and she was too high to care. James took a drag, his eyes filling with water.

"You don't have to hold it in for an hour."

He let the smoke leak out his nostrils, trying not to snort at the burn. It was nice to share with someone for once in her life, even a rookie. Beth never caved to a drag, even on her most anxious nights. "Pot makes me paranoid," she said. Or, "Pot makes me stupid." It wasn't until she said, "Pot makes me gassy" that Molly realized pot didn't make Beth anything because she'd never tried it.

After they'd been smoking for a while, James's eyes went pink and he slumped into the armchair, painting his pajamas with a full coat of dead dog hair. Why was he in pajamas at six o'clock in the evening? Because the Harvard students wore their pajamas all day, all over town: their genitals bouncing in sweat pants, their stomachs expanding against the forgiving pressure of elastic waists.

"So," James said. "Tell me. Where's the dog?"

At first Molly thought she wouldn't say. Why would she, when he could use it against her later? Plus he was just an entitled kid; he wouldn't understand her position. But one of the symptoms of Molly's high was babbling. And once she started talking she couldn't help telling the whole story.

She described Chowder going down the bank, how she could've grabbed his brush of tail while he was still on land, if she'd only reacted quickly enough. She told him each nuance of how she felt during the entire episode: How at first she wanted to laugh at the tail disappearing, how funny it was, like a cartoon where the world could break open. How her next thought was relief. She actually considered that Chowder hadn't pooped yet, and now she wouldn't have to touch it. But then she thought of Beth, and a fist squeezed her heart.

"I didn't even go on the ice," Molly said.

"That would've been stupid," James said. "If he fell through, you obviously would have."

He said it like he was answering an exam question, without consideration for the feelings involved. "I should've tested the edge. At least so I had."

James fingered his eyes so hard that Molly couldn't tell if the resultant tears were from grief or physical pain. "Chowder, Jesus. What a dog."

"I know," said Molly, and now that he was dead, she sort of meant it. There was something of value in all that dumb affection, probably.

"You must really love her," James said.

Molly didn't want to walk into a trap, but she was curious. "Why do you say that?"

"You're crying over a dog."

"You're crying, too." He was, though his tears didn't dilute his rational tone of voice.

"They're just dogs. He was sort of old, right? Dogs die. They just die. You know, at our farm? Dogs were always dying. We threw the extra litters into Canada."

"I thought you were from Greenwich." Everyone here was from either New York City or Greenwich, Connecticut, or other less popular rich towns.

"What? No. Minnesota." James struggled up in the chair, trying to achieve a more dignified posture. He threw out a hand in a loose gesture. "The point is, they're animals. They do the best they can. Like people come here more for Chowder than Beth. He did his job, and now he's gone."

"Not naturally, though." Molly squeezed her eyes shut, trying not to picture Chowder's claws scraping the river bottom, his eyes popping blood vessels.

"Still."

Molly was beyond high, out of her mind. She was deep in the sky above Prescott Street, watching the plain square roof of Hurlbut Hall. She was seeing how Beth loved her with a consuming energy. Beth was the smartest person Molly had ever known, the most patient with Molly's flimsy musical career, her fake job. Who cared about her prudishness, her stress? Those features hardly mattered when you looked at their life together. "Yes, I do. Very much."

"Do what?" asked James.

Molly shook the hot idea from her head. "Never mind."

Molly and James rallied to make a cake. They stirred together quantities of flour, sugar, Swiss Miss, maple syrup, minimarshmallows, frozen blueberries, and rice milk. They left the mixture lumpy because James insisted it would be tenderer that way.

They put the cake in the oven with the heat all the way up so it would be ready faster. They smoked again. Then they fell asleep in the armchairs.

When Molly woke, the door was open and the smoke alarm was screeching high, even wails. She could've slept through all that if it weren't for Beth crying, "Are you OK? Molly?" Hearing her name spoken by Beth, even loudly and sharply, always got to her. Molly sat up, stood up, stumbled, and fought for the kitchen through the smoke. Somehow she managed to turn off the oven and remove the battery in the alarm and open all the windows in the front room and hallway before she even realized she was moving. Smoke alarms were not uncommon rivals for her.

The air thinned, and Molly squinted. James was still asleep in his chair, and Beth was standing in the doorway in a dress shirt with her breasts pushing gaps between the buttons. She held a leather duffel.

"Molly?" she said. "What's going on?" She didn't seem sure which way her voice should tip.

"We forgot the cake," Molly said. "I'm sorry."

"Why is James Masterson here?" Beth looked at James as if he was a ferret who'd crawled in out of nowhere. She was cold, furious. A smell came off her, the wrong kind of hormone.

"I'll get rid of him."

Molly couldn't believe how badly she'd messed up. Why was it always her instinct to bury a mess with another mess? Once at a party she'd hid a wine stain with a turned-over plate of deviled eggs.

As soon as she could make her feet move again she shook James awake, his mouth spilling drool down his bone marrow shirt.

"Hi, girls," he said.

Beth stared at Molly like she didn't know who Molly was. Molly hoped it wasn't a relationship-ending stare. She suspected it was.

"Come on, James," Molly said. "Let's go to bed." She grabbed his arm, but it was limp.

"Oh, my murderer," he said. The words were hollow and chilling. Molly flinched. She had to get him out of here.

"He's high," Molly said. "I'm going to walk him home." She got James to stand, but he couldn't stabilize. She had to pass Beth with the boy held out in front of her like a floppy shield. Beth peered into James's fogged-up eyes and said, "James?"

"Thank you for all you do. On behalf of all students. Sincerely." He saluted her and relaxed against Molly's support, deflating.

In the hall, Molly propped him against the wall.

"Are you really that high?" Usually White Kush didn't have a late-onset effect, but you never knew, especially with kids. He could have "sensitivities."

"Didn't I do a good job?" He looked like a puppy now, his sandy hair flipped up. "I thought if I acted that bad I could pretend tomorrow I don't remember. That would be good, right? That would get you out of trouble?"

She guessed that made sense. If James had been coherent there would have been a whole different scene. Beth would've insisted on questioning him, and no one could stand up to Beth's questions, not even Molly. "Why'd you call me a murderer, though?"

"Come on," he said. "You killed her dog. We can't hide that from her."

Molly wanted to hit him. He was an entitled brat just like she'd always suspected, meddling in her affairs without a blip of remorse. But she made herself breathe. And then she realized he was right. She did have to tell Beth about Chowder. Of course she did. That would be the first question when she reentered the suite. And now there was an opening. *Why did James Masterson call you a murderer? Oh, that? Because I am one.* She could've slapped herself for forgetting to leave a voice mail while Beth was on her panel. At least James didn't tell Beth that Molly had outed her. And she was glad to have talked to James about her relationship, actually. She knew now, for certain, that she loved Beth. But she might be too late.

When she entered the suite, the cake was on the burners and Beth was fanning smoke out of the window with a rag. "What are you doing? Why was James here? Why is a cake burning in the oven? Why is the dog food under the sink? And where is Chowder?"

The questions rushed at Molly, pricking her skin. Beth would find out any second what had happened. There were only a few more moments left in her life where Beth wouldn't know. Molly covered her face against the assault. "I'm high."

"Great. I'll add that to the list of delightful events that occur when I leave for two days. You corrupt my students; you give them drugs. Jesus. I could lose my job." She held her hand to her mouth.

"I'm sorry." Saying the words felt like eating an insubstantial snack, just reminding you how hungry you were.

"Oh, great. That makes it all OK. Everything's solved now, because you're sorry."

That was it. Beth had unplugged something deep in Molly's core. She thought of poor, idiotic Chowder at the bottom of the river. She thought of James Masterson's innocence, gone. She thought of her relationship with Beth, ending tonight, just when Molly had decided it was what she wanted. And there was nothing she could do to change any of these things. She leaned against the cold tiles and cried. She cried so hard she had to run to the bedroom and lie on the quilt and just keep crying, the bed a mossy landscape beneath her, pulling her in.

Beth loomed in the doorway. "Are you for real?"

Molly nodded into the quilt. Then she shook her head. She wanted to stop crying, but holding it in just made the sobs bounce out more erratically.

"Relax," Beth said. "They're not that innocent."

"But your job," Molly said. "And the dog."

Beth paused. Molly could tell she knew something was seriously wrong and wasn't sure if she was ready to find out what. Maybe Beth was thinking of what James had said, wondering who the murderer was. There were only so many people it could be. Maybe, hopefully, Beth thought something worse had happened than actually had. But nothing could be worse, not for Beth.

"Where's the dog?"

It wasn't fair to tell her this way, really, courting her pity first. Even though she didn't like the dog taking up half the bed, didn't like that Beth hugged and fondled him when she could've hugged and fondled Molly, didn't like the white hair on her mostly black wardrobe or cupping shit—a thin skin of plastic the only protection against that sick warmth—she was thinking now about Beth alone. What if Beth ended up not really being gay, or what if the relationship got too serious for Molly and she left? She didn't like thinking about Beth stuck in Hurlbut with all these kids, no Molly, not even Chowder.

"He's dead," Molly said. She'd blown her load earlier, describing the incident to James with nuance and remorse. Now the plain truth was out, ugly and unwieldy. She sponged her tears with the corner of her flannel. Then she described what had happened. Beth shook her head. She put her fingers on her forehead and closed her eyes. When Molly was done, they went minutes without talking, Beth raising a finger whenever Molly tried to start saying something. After a long time, Beth said, "Show me."

"What do you mean?" Molly flashed on pulling the soggy body out of the river.

Beth put on her boots, and Molly had no choice but to do so, too. Free of the cake smoke, Prescott was like the top of a mountain, the air so thin you had to breathe fast to get enough. They took Bow Street to Memorial Drive and crossed to the river.

There were just a couple of pinpricks of light in the sky. They were probably airplanes and satellites but maybe they were planets, and for now, at least, Beth wouldn't leave her side. Even though it was dark, the ice on the river was lit white as though illuminated from below.

Beth tried to walk down onto the ice but Molly stopped her. "It's dangerous."

That's all Beth needed to hear, logical Beth. When her cheeks caught the glow of the river, Molly saw they were wet. Molly tried to hold her but Beth shoved her away. Beth didn't have to say anything—Molly could see the hate in her face, her lip tangled under her teeth, her eyes hooded and fierce.

They looked at the river for a long time. Molly switched her weight from one foot to the other. She was dying to know what would become of the two of them, but she had to wait. Now that things were on the edge of over, Molly couldn't stand it. She couldn't give up the intellectual discussions with Beth as they walked along the Charles, going to old movies on big screens, traveling to the city to try new teas. So it was a boring life, who cared? No one could be wild forever. Would she really rather snort cut cocaine in the bathroom of a naked party in Jamaica Plain?

The hole was gray in the white ice and didn't look like it went all the way through to the water. Maybe a shell had formed since that afternoon, so now Chowder had a roof over his head, a warped view of the winter sky.

Beth walked back to Hurlbut. Molly didn't know if she should follow or take the footbridge to Allston. But there was the cake and the mess in the suite. At least she could clean up. Then, if Beth wanted, she'd leave.

Beth got ready for bed as though Molly weren't there. Molly's hands shook as she pushed the disintegrating sponge over the burners. She was about to wash the cake out of the pan when she found it was white inside, that only the edges were black. The middle was fluffy and wet

335

with blue explosions where the berries broke under heat. The high temperature must have flash cooked the interior; it made an uncommon, silky texture. Molly dug cake out of the black pocket and heaped it on a plate. The cake looked like rice or porridge, but was soft and, when Molly tried it, sweet. She was so hungry that she wanted to eat all of it. But instead, she brought it to Beth. Maybe if there were another element in the room, Beth would forget how angry she was.

"What is this?" Beth asked when Molly held out the plate with arms stretched long and trembling, trying to keep herself as distant as possible.

"Blueberry vanilla hot chocolate cake." That sounded better than it was.

Beth took a bite. She made a face but kept eating. Molly watched her chew, waiting to be told to leave. Beth hated sweets, and made slow progress. Molly hoped she was eating as a grudging sign of forgiveness. Or maybe, at least, she was delaying.

Beth turned off the light and put the plate on the floor. For a moment, Molly stood there in the dark. But then, since she hadn't been told not to, she got undressed. She laid herself down stiffly, facing the ceiling. She felt like if she moved at all it would be over.

"I know he's just a dog," Beth said, her voice shaky, her breath smelling like stress and travel.

Molly couldn't believe Beth was saying that. Beth, whose dog had been her main concern for years, her golden boy, her heir. Molly didn't know what to say. So she said, "Animals have a purpose. Then they leave." James's words sounded lame in her strained voice.

"You shouldn't have let him off the leash. You don't have enough control." Beth shifted onto her back, a quarter roll toward Molly. "I'll have to pay off James Masterson. Jesus."

"I'm sorry." Molly felt like she was getting used to saying this. Like she could go on apologizing forever, knocking chips off the block of what she'd done.

She reached through the sheets and found Beth's wrist. She squeezed it, like they used to do in Girl Scouts, in a circle while singing. The gesture was stupid, but it was all she had. Beth turned in the blue light and looked at Molly as if she was from a different world.

"I fucked up. But I have to tell you something."

"What?" Beth sounded skeptical, as if maybe Molly had killed another of her animals, or corrupted poor James Masterson in even more twisted ways.

Molly took a breath. She thought of that dead dog, once full of joy. "I'm in love with you." It came out like bad acting. She wanted to stuff the words back down her throat.

Beth's eyes worked over each piece of Molly's face. "That's crazy." She shook her head. "That's rat-shit crazy."

Beth would yell at Molly for an hour in the morning. She'd cry every night before bed for days, sleep with the leash tight around her forearm like tefillin. The leather would go soft from how hard she gripped it, would lose its ability to harness a cat. She wouldn't say she loved Molly for months. Sometimes she'd barely even look at her. Molly would suffer. Maybe more than she deserved.

But for now, Molly tried not to think about the future. She rolled on top of Beth, their bodies gluing with thick warmth. She focused on the love that was between them now, however hard it could be to find.

Pushcart Press thanks the following presses for originally publishing these stories and memoirs:

Poetry, Gettysburg Review, Willow Springs, Oxford American, Antioch Review, Tin House, TriQuarterly, The Pinch, Iowa Review, Zoetrope: All Story, Ploughshares, Missouri Review, Bellevue Literary Review, The Sun, Georgia Review, Speakeasy, Threepenny Review, Colorado Review, Conjunctions, Southern Review